CHR   CLE

EMILY FORBES

SAFE IN THE
SURGEON'S ARMS

BY
MOLLY EVANS

MILLS
BOON

Emily Forbes is an award-winning author of Harlequin Mills & Boon® Medical Romance™. She has written over 20 books and has twice been a finalist in the Australian Romantic Book of the Year Award, which she won in 2013 for her novel *Sydney Harbour Hospital: Bella's Wishlist*. You can get in touch with Emily at emilyforbes@internode.on.net, or visit her website at emily-forbesauthor.com.

Molly Evans has taken her experiences as a travel nurse across the USA and turned them into wondrous settings for her books. Now, living at six thousand feet in New Mexico is home. When she's not writing, or attending her son's hockey games, she's learning to knit socks or settling in front of the kiva fireplace with a glass of wine and a good book.

Visit Molly at mollyevansromance.wordpress.com for more info.

HIS LITTLE CHRISTMAS MIRACLE

BY

EMILY FORBES

Published in Great Britain 2015
by Mills & Boon, an imprint of Harlequin (UK) Limited,
Eton House, 18-24 Paradise Road, Richmond, Surrey, TW9 1SR

© 2015 Emily Forbes

ISBN: 978-0-263-24739-8

Harlequin (UK) Limited's policy is to use papers that are natural,
renewable and recyclable products and made from wood grown in
sustainable forests. The logging and manufacturing processes conform
to the legal environmental regulations of the country of origin.

Printed and bound in Spain
by CPI, Barcelona

Dear Reader,

I can't believe that after twenty-one books this is my first story with a Christmas theme—and not just any Christmas but a white one!

White Christmases are a foreign concept to most Australians—for us it is the subject matter of fairytales and dreams. Although I'm sure most of us would say it is something we'd love to experience. Many years ago I was lucky enough to spend a winter in Canada. While minus seventeen degrees Celsius wasn't quite what I had imagined, it was a novelty to listen to Christmas carols about reindeers, snow and sleigh bells while I was surrounded by ice and snow instead of at a hot, sandy beach.

I love Christmas, and I love summer, but there's no denying that a wintry Christmas, complete with sleigh rides, open fires and fir trees decorated with lights and a dusting of snow, is very romantic—and I did enjoy setting the scene for Jess and Lucas's own fairytale Christmas.

I hope you enjoy their story and, wherever you may be in the world, I wish you a very Merry Christmas!

Emily

**Visit the author profile page at
millsandboon.co.uk for more titles**

PROLOGUE

'AND SO IT BEGINS,' Kristie said as she stuck her head into her cousin's bedroom.

'So what begins?' Jess asked as she tied off her plaits and pulled a red knitted hat over her white-blonde hair. She picked up her sunglasses and ski gloves and followed her cousin out of their family's five-star apartment.

'Operation Find Jess a Boyfriend,' Kristie replied.

'What! Why?'

'Because you're almost eighteen and you have no idea what you've been missing. It's time to find you a gorgeous boy. One you won't be able to resist, someone who can kiss their way into that ivory tower of yours and sweep you off your feet. We've talked about this.'

They had but Kristie was always talking about boys in one way or another and Jess mostly ignored her. Kristie was boy crazy—she fell in love every couple of weeks— but Jess was different. Most boys Jess met seemed immature and silly. She didn't see what all the fuss was about. Seventeen- and eighteen-year-old boys were just that. Boys. And Jess wanted Prince Charming. And Prince Charming would arrive in his own time. She didn't think Kristie was going to be able to conjure him up.

'I think you're forgetting something,' Jess said as they dropped their skis onto the snow and clicked their boots into the bindings, ready to tackle their first day on the slopes of the Moose River Alpine Resort.

'What's that?'

'I'd never be allowed to find my own boyfriend. Everyone I've ever dated has been a friend of the family.'

'*You're* not going to find him, I'm going to find him for you,' Kristie explained. 'And let's be honest, you'll never get laid if you only date guys your dad picks out. For one they'd be too terrified of what he'd do to them if he found out and, two, I'm sure your dad deliberately picks guys who are potentially gay.'

'That's not true,' Jess retorted even as she wondered whether maybe it was.

But surely not? Some of those boys had kissed her and while the experiences certainly hadn't been anything to rave about she'd always thought that was her fault. The boys had been cute enough, polite and polished in a typical trust-fund, private-school, country-club way, but not one of them had ever set her heart racing or made her feel breathless or excited or any of the things she'd expected to feel or wanted to feel, and she'd decided she was prepared to wait for the right one.

'Maybe I don't want a boyfriend,' she added.

'Maybe not, but you definitely need to get laid.'

'Kristie!' Jess was horrified.

'You don't know what you're missing. That's going to be my eighteenth birthday present to you. I'm going to find you a gorgeous boy and you're going to get laid.'

Kristie laughed but Jess suspected she wasn't joking. Kristie didn't see anything wrong with advertising the fact that she wanted to hook up with a boy but Jess could think of nothing more embarrassing. Despite the fact that they spent so much time together their personalities were poles apart. Less than three months separated them in age but Kristie was far savvier than Jess, not to mention more forthright and confident.

'This is your chance,' Kristie continued. 'We have one week before your parents arrive. One week with just my parents, who are nowhere near as strict. That's seven days to check out all the hot guys who'll just be hanging around the resort. You'll never get a better opportunity to hook up with someone.'

'Maybe I don't want to hook up with anyone. Promise me you won't set me up,' Jess begged. Kristie's seven-day deadline coincided with Jess's eighteenth birthday. Her parents were coming up to the resort to celebrate it with her and once they arrived Jess knew she wouldn't have a chance to be alone with a boy. Surely not even Kristie could make this happen in such a short time even if Jess *was* a willing participant. And while she wasn't averse to the *idea* of the experience, she wanted it her way. She wanted the romance. She wanted to fall in love. She wanted to be seduced and made love to. *Getting laid* did not have the same ring. Getting laid was not the experience she was after.

But then she relaxed. She might get a chance to kiss a boy but even though Kristie's parents were far more lenient than her own she still doubted that she would get an opportunity to lose her virginity.

'We won't be allowed out at night,' she said when Kristie didn't answer.

Kristie laughed again. 'Do you think you're only allowed to have sex after midnight?' she called back over her shoulder as she skied over to join the lift line for the village quad chair. 'No one is keeping tabs on us during the day. We could sneak off whenever we wanted.'

Sex during the day! Jess hadn't considered that possibility. But it still wasn't going to happen. As much as Kristie wanted her project to get off the ground, Jess couldn't imagine getting naked in the middle of the day. In her fantasy she imagined soft lighting, perfumed candles, the right music and a comfortable bed. Preferably her own bed. With clean sheets and a man who adored her. A quick fumble in the middle of the day with some random guy from the resort, no matter how cute, just wasn't the same thing.

'Today is the beginning of the rest of your life. It's time you had some fun,' Kristie told her as she joined the line. 'This place will be crawling with good-looking boys. We'll be able to take our pick.'

Getting a boy's attention was never a problem. Jess knew she was pretty enough. She was petite, only one hundred and sixty centimetres tall, and cheerleader pretty with a heart-shaped face, a chin she thought was maybe a bit too pointy, platinum-blonde hair, green eyes and porcelain skin. Finding a boy who ticked all her boxes was the tricky part. And if one did measure up then getting a chance to be alone was another challenge entirely.

Kristie's joke about Jess's ivory tower wasn't completely inaccurate. Jess did have dreams of being swept off her feet, falling madly in love and being rescued from her privileged but restricted life. It seemed to be her best chance of escaping the rules and boundaries her parents imposed on her. She couldn't imagine gaining her freedom any other way. She wasn't rebellious enough to go against their wishes without very good reason.

But she couldn't imagine falling in love at the age of seventeen and she wasn't about to leap into bed with the first cute guy who presented her with the opportunity. That didn't fit with her romantic notions at all. But although Jess could protest vigorously, it didn't mean Kristie would give up. And she proved it with her next comment.

'What about him?' she asked as they waited for the quad chair.

Jess looked at the other skiers around them. It was just after nine in the morning. The girls had risen early, keen to enjoy their first morning on the slopes, but everyone else in the line was ten years younger or twenty years older than them. They were surrounded by families with young children. All the other teenagers were still in bed, and Jess couldn't work out who Kristie was talking about.

Her cousin nudged her in the side. 'There.' She used her ski pole to point to the front of the line and Jess realised she meant the towies.

Two young men, who she guessed to be a year or two older than she was, worked the lift together. They both wore the uniform of the mountain resort, bright blue ski jackets with a band of fluorescent yellow around the upper arm and matching blue pants with another yellow band around the bottom of the legs. A row of white, snow-covered mountain peaks was stitched across the left chest of the jacket with 'Moose River Alpine Resort' emblazoned beneath. Their heads were uncovered and Jess could see one tall, fair-headed boy and another slightly shorter one with dark hair.

They had music pumping out of the stereo system at the base of the lift. It blasted the mountain, drowning out all other noise, including the engine of the chairlift. Jess watched as the boys danced to the beat as they lifted the little kids onto the chair and chatted and flirted with the mothers.

The fair one drew her attention. He moved easily, in time with the music, relaxed, unselfconscious and comfortable in his skin. Jess couldn't ever imagine dancing in front of strangers in broad daylight. She wasn't comfortable in a crowd. But there was something erotic about watching someone dance from a distance. She wouldn't normally stare but she was emboldened by her anonymity. He didn't know her and from behind the security of her dark sunglasses she could watch unobserved. Like a voyeur.

Kristie shuffled forward in the line and Jess followed but she couldn't tear her eyes away from the dancing towie. Watching the way his hips moved, she felt a stirring in her belly that she recognised as attraction, lust, desire. Watching him move, she could imagine how it would feel to dance with him, how it would feel to be held against him as his hips moved in time with hers. She found her hips swaying to the beat of the music, swaying in response to this stranger.

The song changed, snapping her out of her reverie, and she watched as he mimicked some rap moves that had the kids in front of her in stitches. The dark-haired one was chatting to a mother while the fair one lifted the woman's child onto the seat before giving him a high five. He lifted his head as he laughed at something the child had said and suddenly he was looking straight at Jess.

Jess's pulse throbbed and her stomach ached with a primal, lustful reaction as his eyes connected with hers. They were the most brilliant blue. A current tore through her body, sending a shock deep inside her all the way to her bones. She was aware of Kristie moving into position for the lift but she was riveted to the spot, her skis frozen to the snow. She was transfixed by eyes the colour of forget-me-nots.

'Careful. Keep moving unless you want to get collected by the chair.' It took Jess a second or two to realise he was talking to her. He had an Australian accent and in her bewildered and confused state it took her a moment to decipher it and make sense of his words. While she was translating his speech in her head he reached out and put one hand on her backside and pushed her forward until she was standing on the mat, ready to be swept up by the chairlift. Jess could swear she could feel the heat of his hand through the padding of her ski suit. She was still standing in place, staring at him, as the chair swung behind her and scooped her up, knocking into the back of her knees and forcing her to sit down with a thump.

'Have a good one.' He winked at her as she plopped into the seat and Jess felt herself blush but she kept eye contact. She couldn't seem to look away. *Let me off*, she wanted to shout but when she opened her mouth nothing came out. Her eyesight worked but she appeared to have lost control of all her other senses. Including movement. She was enchanted, spellbound by a boy with eyes of blue.

'They were cute,' Kristie said as the lift carried them up the mountain and Jess forced herself to turn her head and look away. Maybe that would break the spell.

'I guess,' she said. She felt like she had a mouthful of marbles as she tried to feign indifference. Kristie would have a field day if she knew what Jess had really been thinking.

'What do you think?' Kristie asked. 'Worth a second look?'

The girls had the quad chair to themselves but that didn't mean Jess wanted to have this discussion. She knew if she agreed it would only serve to encourage Kristie's foolish plan.

'You're not serious!' she cried. 'I don't think they're my type.' She suspected she'd have nothing in common with them. She knew she wouldn't be cool enough.

'Why not?'

'You know the reputation those guys have.' The towies—usually an assortment of college students taking a gap year, locals and backpackers—had a reputation as ski-hard-and-party-harder people.

But Kristie was not about to be deterred. 'So...' she shrugged '...that all adds to the excitement and the challenge.'

'I'm not going to hook up with a total stranger,' Jess said. Obviously the lessons of her upbringing were more deeply ingrained in her than she'd realised. Her movements were carefully orchestrated, her whereabouts were always mapped out, and she'd never really had the opportunity to mingle with strangers. Prince Charming was going to have his work cut out for him.

'I know your parents want to know where you are every minute of the day but they're not here,' Kristie replied, 'and despite what they tell you, not every spontaneous situation is dangerous and not every stranger is a psychopath. I'm not saying you have to marry the guy, just have some fun.'

'He looked too old for me,' Jess protested.

'You're always complaining about how immature boys our age are. Maybe someone a bit older would suit you better. Shall we head back down? Take another look?'

The quad chair took them to the basin where all the other lifts operated from. No one skied straight back down to the bottom of this lift unless they'd forgotten something and needed to return to the village. Jess didn't want to be that overtly interested. She needed time to think. 'No. I want to ski,' she said as they were deposited in the basin.

The slopes were quiet at this hour of the day and it wasn't long before Kristie decided she was overheating from all the exercise and needed to discard some layers. Jess suspected it was all an act designed to invent a reason to return to their apartment and hence to the quad chair, but she was prepared to give in. She knew she didn't have much choice. She could have elected to stay up on the mountain but they had a rule that no one skied alone and she had to admit she was just a tiny bit curious to have another look at the boy with the forget-me-not-blue eyes. After all, there was no harm in looking.

But by the time they had changed their outfits and returned to the quad chair there were two different towies on duty. Disappointment surged through Jess. It was silly to feel that way about a random stranger but there had been something hypnotic about him. Something captivating.

They rode the lift back to the basin where they waited in line for another quad chair to take them to the top of the ski run. As they neared the front the two original towies appeared, each with a snowboard strapped to one foot as they slipped into the singles row and skated to the front of the line.

'G'day. Mind if we join you?'

Jess and Kristie had no time to reply before the boys had slotted in beside them and Jess found herself sandwiched between her cousin and the boy with the tousled, blond hair and amazing blue eyes. He shifted slightly on the seat, turning a little to face her, and the movement pushed his thigh firmly against hers.

'Have you had a good morning?' he asked her. 'You were up at sparrow's.'

'Pardon?' Jess frowned. His voice was deep and his accent was super-sexy but the combination of his stunning eyes and his Aussie drawl made it difficult to decipher his words. Or maybe it was just the fact that she was sitting thigh to thigh with a cute boy who was messing with her head. Either way, she couldn't think straight and she could make no sense of what he was saying.

'Sparrow's fart,' he said with a grin before he elaborated. 'It means you were up really early.'

His blue eyes sparkled as he smiled at her but this time it was the twin dimples in his cheeks that set Jess's heart racing. His smile was infectious and she couldn't help but return it as she said, 'You remember us?' She was surprised and flattered. The boys would have seen hundreds of people already today.

'Of course. Don't tell me you don't remember me?' He put both hands over his heart and looked so dramatically wounded that Jess laughed. She'd have to watch out—he was cute and charming with more than a hint of mischief about him.

And, of course, she remembered him. She doubted she'd forget him, but she knew his type and she wasn't about to stroke his ego by telling him that his eyes were the perfect colour—unforgettable, just like him. She knew all the towies were cut from the same cloth, young men who would spend the winter working in the resort and then spend their time off skiing and drinking and chasing girls. They would flirt with dozens of girls in one day, trying their luck, until eventually their persistence would pay off and they'd have a date for the night and, no matter how cute he was, she didn't want to be just another girl in the long line that would fall at his feet.

'Well, just so you don't forget us again, I'm Lucas and that's Sam,' he said, nodding towards his mate, who was sitting on the other side of Kristie.

'I didn't say I'd forgotten you,' Jess admitted. 'I remember your accent.' But she wasn't prepared to admit she remembered his dancing or had been unable to forget his cornflower-blue eyes. 'You're Australian?'

'Yes, and, before you ask, I don't have a pet kangaroo.'

'I wasn't going to ask that.'

'Really?'

'I might not have been to Australia but I know a bit about it. I'm not completely ignorant.'

'Sorry, I didn't mean to imply that,' Lucas backtracked.

'It's okay.' She'd stopped getting offended every time people treated her like a cheerleader but while she was one she was also a science major. 'I know most of you don't have pet kangaroos and I know you eat that horrible black spread on your toast and live alongside loads of poisonous snakes, spiders and man-eating sharks. Actually…' she smiled '…I'm not surprised you left.'

Lucas laughed. 'I'm not here permanently. I'm only here for the winter. It's summer back home. I'll stay until the end of February when uni starts again.'

'So where is the best place to party in the village?' Kristie interrupted. 'What's popular this season?'

Kristie knew the village as well as anyone—she didn't need advice—but Jess knew it was just her cousin's way of flirting. To Kristie that came as naturally as breathing.

'How old are you?' Sam replied.

'Nineteen,' she fibbed. She was only three months older than Jess and had only recently turned eighteen but nineteen was the legal drinking age.

'The T-Bar is always good,' Sam told them, mentioning one of the après-ski bars that had been around for ever but was always popular.

'But tonight we're having a few mates around,' Lucas added. 'We're sharing digs with a couple of Kiwis and Friday nights are party nights. You're welcome to join us.'

'Thanks, that sounds like fun,' Kristie replied, making it sound as though they'd be there when Jess knew they wouldn't. Which was a pity. It did sound like it might be fun but there was no way they'd be allowed out with strangers, with boys who hadn't been vetted and approved. Although Kristie's parents weren't as strict as hers, Jess's aunt and uncle knew the rules Jess had to live by and she didn't think they'd bend them that far.

'We're in the Moose River staff apartments. You know the ones? On Slalom Street. Apartment fifteen.'

'We know where they are.'

They were almost at the top of the ski run now and Jess felt a surge of disappointment that the ride was coming to an end. The boys were going snowboarding and Jess assumed they'd be heading to the half-pipe or the more rugged terrain on the other side of the resort.

They wouldn't be skiing the same part of the mountain as she and Kristie.

She pretended to look out at the ski runs when she was actually looking at Lucas from behind the safety of her sunglasses. She wanted to commit his face to memory. He was cute and friendly but she doubted she'd ever see him again. He wasn't her Prince Charming.

CHAPTER ONE

JESS ZIPPED UP her ski jacket as she stood in the twilight. She was back.

Back in the place where her life had changed for ever.

Back in Moose River.

She remembered standing not far from this exact spot while Kristie had told her that day marked the beginning of the rest of her life, but she hadn't expected her cousin's words to be quite so prophetic. That had been the day she'd met Lucas and her life had very definitely changed. All because of a boy.

Jess shoved her hands into her pockets and stood still as she took in her surroundings. The mountain village was still very familiar but it was like an echo of a memory from a lifetime ago. A very different lifetime from the one she was living now. She took a deep breath as she tried to quell her nerves.

When she had seen the advertisement for the position of clinic nurse at the Moose River Medical Centre it had seemed like a sign and she'd wondered why she hadn't thought of it sooner. It had seemed like the perfect opportunity to start living the life she wanted but that didn't stop the butterflies in her stomach.

It'll be fine, she told herself as she tried to get the butterflies to settle, *once we adjust.*

In the dark of the evening the mountain resort looked exactly like it always had. Like a fairy-tale village. The streets had been cleared of the early season snow and it lay piled in small drifts by the footpaths. Light dotted the hillside, glowing yellow as it spilled from the windows of the hotels and lodges. She could smell wood smoke and pine needles. The fragrance of winter. Of Christmas. Of Lucas.

She'd have to get over that. She couldn't afford to remember him every few minutes now that she was back here. That wasn't what this move was about.

In a childhood marked by tragedy and, at times, fear and loneliness, Moose River had been one of the two places where she'd been truly happy, the only place in the end, and the only place where she'd been free. She had returned now, hoping to rediscover that feeling again. And while she couldn't deny that Moose River was also full of bittersweet memories, she hoped it could still weave its magic for her.

She could hear the bus wheezing and shuddering behind her, complaining as the warmth from its air-conditioning escaped into the cold mountain air. It was chilly but at least it wasn't raining. She was so sick of rain. While Vancouver winters were generally milder than in other Canadian cities there was a trade-off and that was rain. While she was glad she didn't have to shovel snow out of her driveway every morning, she was tired of the wet.

Jess could hear laughter and music. The sound floated across to the car park from the buildings around her, filling the still night air. She could hear the drone of the snow-making machines on the mountain and she could see the lights of the graders as they went about their night-time business, grooming the trails. She glanced around her, looking to see what had changed and what had stayed the same in the seven years since she had last been here. The iconic five-star Moose River Hotel still had pride of place on the hill overlooking the village but there were several new buildings as well, including a stunning new hotel that stood at the opposite end of Main Street from the bus depot.

The new hotel was perched on the eastern edge of the plaza where Main Street came to an end at the ice-skating rink. There had been a building there before, smaller and older. Jess couldn't recall exactly what it had been but this modern replacement looked perfect. The hotel was too far away for her to be able to read the sign, although she could see the tiny figures of skaters gliding around the rink, twirling under the lights as snow began to fall.

She lifted her face to the sky. Snowflakes fell on her cheeks and eyelashes, melting as soon as they touched the warmth of her skin. She stuck out her tongue, just like she'd done as a child, and caught the flakes, feeling them immediately turn to water.

But she wasn't a child any more. She was twenty-four years old, almost twenty-five. Old enough to have learned that life was not a fairy tale. She didn't want a fairy-tale ending; she didn't believe in those any more but surely it wasn't too late to find happiness? She refused to believe that wasn't possible.

Seven years ago she'd had the world at her feet. She'd been young and full of expectation, anticipation and excitement. Anything had seemed possible in that winter.

In the winter that she'd met Lucas. In the winter that she'd fallen in love.

Sometimes it seemed like yesterday. At other times a lifetime ago. On occasions it even seemed like it was someone else's story but she knew it was hers. She was reminded of that every day. But as hard as it had been she wasn't sure that she would do anything differently if she had her time again.

She could still remember the first moment she had laid eyes on him. It was less than two hundred metres from where she now stood. She'd been seventeen years old, young and pretty, shy but with the self-assurance that a privileged lifestyle gave to teenagers. In her mind her future had already been mapped out—surely it would be one of happiness, wealth, prosperity and pleasure. That was what she and her friends, all of whom came from wealthy families, had been used to and they'd had no reason to think things would change. She'd been so naive.

At seventeen she'd had no clue about real life. She'd been happy with her dreams. Her biggest problem had been having parents who'd loved her and wanted to protect her from the world, and her biggest dream had been to experience the world she hadn't been allowed to taste.

To her, Lucas had represented freedom. He'd been her chance to experience the world but the freedom she'd tasted had been short-lived. And the real world was a lot tougher than she'd anticipated. Reality had slapped her in the face big time and once she'd been out in that world she'd found there had been no turning back.

Reality was a bitch and it had certainly killed her

naivety. She'd grown up awfully quickly and her clue-less teenage years were a long way behind her now.

She was still standing in the car park, mentally rem-iniscing about that winter, when an SUV pulled up in front of her at a right angle to the bus. The driver put down his window. 'Jess? Jess Johnson?' he said.

Jess shook her head, clearing the cobwebs from her mind. 'Sorry,' the driver said, misinterpreting the shake of her head. 'I'm looking for a Jess Johnson.'

'That's me.'

The driver climbed out of the car. 'I'm Cameron Baker,' he introduced himself as he shook Jess's hand. Cameron and his wife, Ellen, owned the Moose River Medical Centre. He was Jess's new boss. 'Let's get your gear loaded up. Is this everything?'

Jess looked down at her feet. The bus driver had unloaded her belongings. Three suitcases and half a dozen boxes were piled beside her. All the necessities for two lives.

'That's it,' she replied. 'I'll just get Lily.'

She climbed back into the bus to rouse her sleep-ing daughter.

She scooped Lily up and carried her from the bus. She was keen to introduce her to Moose River but that would have to wait until tomorrow.

This was Lily's first visit to the mountain resort. Jess had avoided bringing Lily here before now. She'd made countless excuses, telling herself Lily was too young to appreciate it, but she knew that was a lie. Jess had been skiing since she was four and Lily was now six and there were plenty of other activities here to keep young children entertained for days. Lack of money had been another excuse and even though Jess hadn't been able to afford to bring her that was still only part of the truth. The reality was that Jess hadn't wanted to return. She hadn't wanted to face the past. She'd thought the memories might be too painful. But it was time to give Lily a sense of where she had come from. It was time to come back.

Cameron loaded their bags and Jess climbed into the back of the vehicle, cradling a sleepy Lily in her arms as he drove them the short distance to their accommodation. The job came with a furnished apartment, which had been one of a number of things that had attracted Jess to the position, but she hadn't thought to enquire about any specifics, she'd just been relieved to know it had been organised for her and she was stunned when Cameron pulled to a stop in front of the Moose River staff apartments.

She picked Lily up again—fortunately Lily was small for her age and Jess could still manage to carry her—and followed Cameron inside the building, counting off the apartment numbers as they walked down the corridor. Thirteen, fourteen, fifteen. Cameron's steps started to slow and Jess held her breath. It couldn't be. Not the same apartment.

'This is you. Number sixteen.'

She let out her breath as Cameron parked the luggage trolley, loaded with boxes and bags, and unlocked the door. There'd been a brief moment when she'd thought she might be staying in apartment fifteen but she might just be able to handle being one apartment away from her past.

She carried Lily inside and put her on the bed.

'I'm sorry, they were supposed to split the bed and

make up two singles,' Cameron apologised when he saw the bedding configuration.

'It doesn't matter,' Jess replied. 'I'll fix it tomorrow.' She couldn't be bothered now. She had enough to think about without fussing about the bed. She and Lily could manage for the night.

'Ellen has left some basic supplies for you in the fridge. She promised me it would be enough to get you through breakfast in the morning,' Cameron said, as he brought in the rest of Jess's luggage.

'That's great, thank you.'

'I'll let you get settled, then, and we'll see you at the clinic at eleven tomorrow to introduce you to everyone and give you an orientation.'

Jess nodded but she was having trouble focusing. She was restless. There were so many memories. Too many. More than she'd expected. Thank goodness Lily was dozing as that gave her a chance to shuffle through the thoughts that were crowding her brain. She paced around the apartment once Cameron had gone but it was tiny and in no more than a few steps she'd covered the kitchen and the dining area and the lounge. All that was left was the bedroom and a combined bathroom-laundry. There wasn't much to see and even less to do as she didn't want to disturb Lily by beginning to unpack.

She crossed the living room, opened the balcony doors and stepped outside. Night had fallen but a full moon hung low in the sky and moonlight reflected off the snow and lit up the village as if it was broad daylight. To her left was the balcony of unit fifteen, the two-bedroom apartment that Lucas had stayed in seven years ago. The apartment where she and Kristie had gone on the night of the party was only metres away.

She could see the exact spot where she'd been standing when Lucas had first kissed her.

He had been her first love. He had been her Prince Charming. She'd fallen hard and fast but when he'd kissed her that first time and she'd given him her heart she hadn't known there would be no turning back.

Now, at twenty-four, she didn't believe in Prince Charming any more.

CHAPTER TWO

'MUMMY?'

The sound of Lily's voice startled her. Jess was still on the balcony, standing with her fingers pressed against her lips as she recalled the first kiss she and Lucas had shared. She shivered as she realised she was freezing. She had no idea how long she'd been standing out there in the cold.

She didn't have time for reminiscing. She had responsibilities.

Lily had wandered out of the bedroom and Jess could see her standing in the living room, looking around at the unfamiliar surroundings. She was sucking on her thumb and had her favourite toy, a soft, grey koala, tucked under one arm. With white-blonde hair and a heart-shaped face she was the spitting image of Jess, just as Jess was the image of her own mother.

'I'm hungry,' Lily said, as Jess came in from the balcony and closed the doors and curtains behind her.

'You are?' She was surprised. Lily wasn't often hungry. She was a fussy eater and didn't have a good appetite and Jess often struggled to find food that appealed to her daughter, although fortunately she would eat her vegetables.

'Let's see what we've got.' Jess opened the fridge, hoping Cameron had been right when he'd said that his wife had left some basics for them. She could see bread, milk, eggs, cheese and jam.

'How about toasted cheese sandwiches for dinner?' she said. 'Or eggs and soldier toast?'

'Eggs and soldier toast.'

Jess put the eggs on to boil and then found Lily's pyjamas. By the time she was changed the eggs were done. Lily managed to finish the eggs and one soldier. Jess slathered the remaining soldier toasts with jam and polished them off herself.

Lily was fast asleep within minutes of climbing back into bed, but even though Jess was exhausted she found she couldn't get comfortable. Lily, who was a restless sleeper at the best of times, was tossing and turning in the bed beside her and disturbing her even further. She would have to split the bed apart tomorrow; she couldn't stand another night like this.

She got up and put the kettle on, hoping for the hundredth time that she'd made the right decision in moving to Moose River.

It seemed surreal to think that returning to the place where things had started to go wrong had been the best solution, but she'd felt she hadn't had much choice. She'd needed a job with regular hours and this one had the added bonus of accommodation, which meant she could be home with Lily before and after school and she wouldn't need to leave Lily with a childminder or take extra shifts to cover the rent or babysitting expenses. She also hoped that living in Moose River would give Lily the opportunity to have the childhood she herself had missed out on. A childhood free from worry, a childhood of fun and experiences.

She carried her decaf coffee over to the balcony doors. She drew back the curtains and rested her head on the glass as she gazed out at the moonlit night and let the memories flood back. Of course they were all about Lucas. She couldn't seem to keep thoughts of him out of her head. She hadn't expected Moose River to stir her memory quite so much.

What would he be looking at right now? Where would he be?

Probably living at Bondi Beach, running a chain of organic cafés with his gorgeous bikini-model wife, she thought. They would have three blue-eyed children and together his family would look like an advertisement for the wonders of fresh air and exercise and healthy living.

But maybe life hadn't been so kind to him. Why should it have been? Why should he be glowing with health and happiness?

Perhaps he was working in a hotel restaurant in the Swiss Alps and had grown fat from over-indulging in cheese and chocolate. He could be overweight with a receding hairline. Would that make her feel better?

What was it she wanted to feel better about? she wondered. It didn't matter where Lucas was or what he was doing. That was history. She'd woken up to herself in the intervening years. Woken up to real life. And he wasn't part of that life. He was fantasy, not reality. Not her reality anyway.

Jess shook herself. She needed to get a grip. Her situation was entirely of her own choosing and she wouldn't change it for anything, not if it meant losing Lily.

She sighed as she finished her coffee. Her father had

been right. Lucas hadn't been her Prince Charming and he wasn't ever coming to rescue her. Wherever he had ended up, she imagined it was far from here.

Their first fortnight in Moose River went smoothly. Lily settled in well at her new school. She was thriving and Jess was thrilled. She loved the after-school ski lessons and Jess was looking forward to getting out on the slopes with her this weekend and seeing how much she'd improved in just ten days. It was amazing how quickly children picked up the basics.

She wondered about Lily's fearless attitude. If Lily wanted something she went after it, so different from Jess's reticence. Was that nature or nurture?

Jess had vowed to give Lily freedom—freedom to make her own friends and experience a childhood where she was free to test the boundaries without constant supervision or rules. A childhood without the constant underlying sense that things could, would and did go wrong and where everything had to be micromanaged.

Moose River was, so far, proving to be the perfect place for Lily to have a relaxed childhood and Jess was beginning to feel like she'd made a good decision. Lily had made friends quickly and her new best friend was Annabel, whose parents owned the patisserie next to their apartment building. By the second week the girls had a routine where Lily would go home with Annabel after ski school and have a hot chocolate at the bakery while they waited for Jess to finish work. Jess had been nervous about this at first but she'd reminded herself that this was a benefit of moving to a small community. She'd wanted that sense of belonging. That sense that people would look out for each other. She wanted somewhere where she and Lily would fit in.

Initially she'd felt like they were taking advantage of Annabel's mother but Fleur was adamant that it was no bother. Annabel had two older siblings and Fleur insisted that having Lily around was making life easier for everyone as Annabel was too busy to annoy the others. Jess hated asking for favours, she preferred to feel she could manage by herself even if she knew that wasn't always the case, but she was grateful for Fleur's assistance.

Her new job as a clinic nurse was going just as smoothly as Lily's transition. Her role was easy. She helped with splints, dressings, immunisations and did general health checks—cholesterol, blood pressure and the like. It was routine nursing, nothing challenging, but that suited her. It was low stress and by the end of the two weeks she was feeling confident that coming here had been the right decision for her and Lily.

Not having to work weekends or take extra shifts to cover rent or child-care costs was paying dividends. She could be home with Lily in time for dinner and spend full, uninterrupted days with her over the weekends. It was heaven. Jess adored her daughter and she'd dreamt of being able to spend quality time with her. Just the two of them. It was something she hadn't experienced much in her own childhood and she was determined that Lily would have that quality time with her. After all, they only had each other.

She checked her watch as she tidied her clinic room and got ready to go home. Kristie was coming up for the weekend—in fact, she should already be here. She was changing the sheet on the examination bed when Donna, the practice manager, burst into the room.

'Jess, do you think you could possibly work a little later today? We've had a call from the new hotel, one of their guests is almost thirty-six weeks pregnant and she's having contractions. It might just be Braxton-Hicks but they'd like someone to take a look and all the doctors are busy. Do you think you could go?'

'Let me make some arrangements for Lily and then I'll get over there,' Jess said when Donna finally paused for breath. Jess was happy to go, provided she could sort Lily out. She rang Kristie as she swapped her shoes for boots and explained the situation as she grabbed her coat and the medical bag that Donna had given to her.

Thank God Kristie was in town, she thought as she rang Fleur to tell her of the change in plans. Of course, Fleur then offered to help too but Jess didn't want to push the friendship at this early stage. She explained that Kristie would collect Lily and take her home. She could concentrate on the emergency now. It was always a balancing act, juggling parenting responsibilities with her work, but it seemed she might have the support network here that she'd lacked anywhere else.

Jess hurried the few blocks to Main Street. The five-star, boutique Moose River Crystal Lodge, where her patient was a guest, was the new hotel on the Plaza, the one she'd noticed on the night they'd arrived. She and Lily had walked past it several times since. It was hard to miss. It wasn't huge or ostentatious but it was in a fabulous position, and she'd heard it was beautifully appointed inside.

In the late-afternoon light, the setting sun cast a glow onto the facade of the lodge, making its marble facade shine a pale silver. On the southern side of the main entrance was an elevated outdoor seating area, which would be the perfect spot for an afternoon drink on a sunny day; you could watch the activities in the plaza from the perfect vantage point.

A wide footpath connected the lodge to the plaza and in front of the hotel stood a very placid horse who was hitched to a smart red wooden sleigh. Lily had begged to go for a ride when they had walked past earlier in the week but Jess had fibbed and told her it was for hotel guests only because she doubted she could afford the treat. She had meant to find out how much it cost, thinking maybe it could be a Christmas surprise for Lily, but she had forgotten all about it until now.

She walked past the horse and sleigh and tried to ignore the feeling of guilt that was so familiar to her as a single, working mother, struggling to make ends meet, but walking into the lobby just reinforced how much her life had changed from one of privilege to one much harder but she reminded herself it was of her own choosing.

The lobby was beautifully decorated in dark wood. Soft, caramel-hued leather couches were grouped around rich Persian rugs and enormous crystal chandeliers hung from the timber ceiling. It looked expensive and luxurious but welcoming. Although it was still four weeks until Christmas, festive red, green and silver decorations adorned the room and a wood fire warmed the restaurant where wide glass doors could open out onto the outside terrace. Jess tried not to gawk as she crossed the parquet floor. She'd seen plenty of fancy hotels but this one had a warmth and a charm about it that was rare. Maybe because it was small, but it felt more like an exclusive private ski lodge than a hotel.

She shrugged out of her coat as she approached the reception desk.

'I'm Jess Johnson, from the Moose River Medical Centre. Someone called about a woman in labour?'

The young girl behind the desk nodded. 'Yes, Mrs Bertillon. She's in room three zero five on the third floor. I'll just call the hotel manager to take you up.'

'It's okay, I'll find it.' Jess could see the elevators tucked into a short hallway alongside the desk. The hotel was small so she'd have no trouble finding the room. She didn't want to waste time waiting.

She stabbed at the button for the elevator. The doors slid open and she stepped inside.

Jess found room 305 and knocked on the door. It swung open under her hand. There was a bathroom to her left with a wardrobe on the right, forming a short passage. Jess could see a small sofa positioned in front of a large picture window but that was it.

She called out a greeting. 'Mrs Bertillon?'

'Come in.' The faceless voice sounded strong and Jess relaxed. That didn't sound like a woman in labour.

A woman appeared at the end of the passage. She was a hotel employee judging by her uniform. 'She's through here.' The same voice. This wasn't Mrs. Bertillon. 'I'm Margaret. I was keeping an eye on Aimee until you got here,' she explained, and Jess could see the relief on her face. She'd obviously been waiting nervously for reinforcements. 'I'll wait outside now but you can call for me if there's anything you need,' she said, hurriedly abdicating responsibility.

Jess introduced herself to Aimee and got her medical

history as she washed her hands and then wrapped the blood-pressure cuff around her patient's left arm. This was her first pregnancy, Aimee told her, and she'd had no complications. Her blood pressure had been fine, no gestational diabetes, no heart problems. 'I've had some back pain today and now these contractions but otherwise I've been fine.'

'Sharp pain?' asked Jess.

'No. Dull,' Aimee explained, 'more like backache, I suppose. Ow...'

'Is that a contraction now?'

Aimee nodded and Jess looked at her watch, timing the contraction. She could see the contraction ripple across the woman's abdomen as the muscles tightened. This wasn't Braxton-Hicks.

'Your waters haven't broken?' she asked, and Aimee shook her head in reply.

Once the contraction had passed she checked the baby's size and position, pleased to note the baby wasn't breech. But she wasn't so pleased when she discovered that Aimee's cervix was already seven centimetres dilated. Aimee was in labour and there was nothing she could do to stop it.

'Where is your husband?' Jess asked. She'd noticed a wedding ring on Aimee's finger but wondered where Mr Bertillon was.

'He's out skiing,' Aimee replied. 'Why?'

Jess smiled. 'I thought he might like to be here to meet your baby.'

'It's coming now?'

'Mmm-hmm.' Jess nodded. 'You're about to become parents.'

'Oh, my God.'

'Does your husband have a mobile phone with him? Would you like me to call him for you?' Jess asked.

'No. I can do it. I think.' Aimee put a hand on her distended belly as another contraction subsided. 'If I hurry. Jean-Paul will be surprised. This was supposed to be our last holiday before the baby arrived and it wasn't supposed to end like this.' She gave a wry smile. 'Maybe we've been having too much sex. Is it true that can bring on labour?'

Jess couldn't remember the last time she'd had too much sex. She could barely remember the last time she'd had *any* sex. She nodded. 'But not usually at this stage. I think your baby has just decided to join the party.' She concentrated on Aimee. Thinking about sex always made her think about Lucas, especially since she was in Moose River, but now wasn't the time for daydreaming. Aimee needed all her attention.

Aimee's cell phone was beside the bed. Jess passed it to her and then picked up the hotel phone and asked for an ambulance to be sent. Aimee needed to go to the nearest hospital that had premature birthing facilities, which meant leaving Moose River.

Another contraction gripped Aimee and Jess waited as she panted and puffed her way through it. Jess checked her watch. The contractions were two minutes apart. How long would the ambulance take? She had no idea.

Once that contraction had passed and Jess saw Aimee press the buttons on her phone to call her husband she went to gather towels from the bathroom. She stuck her head out into the corridor and asked Margaret to fetch more towels from Housekeeping.

'How did it go? Did you reach Jean-Paul?' Jess asked when she returned to Aimee's side.

'No. It goes straight to his message service.' Aimee gasped and grabbed her belly as another contraction ripped through her. 'He's gone skiing with a snowcat group so I can only assume he's out in the wilderness and out of range.'

Margaret came into the room with an armful of towels and Jess asked if there was any way of getting a message to Jean-Paul.

'Yes, of course,' Margaret replied. 'Will you be all right on your own with Aimee while I organise that?'

Jess nodded. Margaret wasn't going to be of any further use. It was the ambos Jess wanted to see. Jess tucked several of the towels underneath Aimee. She knew it was probably a futile exercise but if Aimee's waters broke she was hoping to limit the damage to the hotel bedding. Another contraction gripped Aimee and this one was accompanied by a gush of fluid. Fortunately it wasn't a big flood and Jess suspected that meant the baby's head was well down into Aimee's pelvis.

Jess used the time between contractions to check Aimee's cervix. Eight centimetres dilated. This was really happening. If the ambos didn't hurry she would have to deliver the baby. What would she need?

She'd need to keep the baby warm. She put a couple of the clean towels back on the heated towel rail in the bathroom.

Aimee's cries were getting louder and she had a sheen of perspiration across her forehead. 'I want to push,' she called out.

'Hang on,' Jess cautioned, and she checked progress again.

Oh no. The baby's head was crowning already.

Jess felt for the cord. It felt loose and she just hoped it wasn't around the baby's neck.

'Okay, Aimee. This is it. You can push with the next contraction.'

Jess saw the contraction ripple across Aimee's skin. 'Okay, bend your knees and push!'

The baby's head appeared and Jess was able to turn the baby to deliver one shoulder with the next contraction and the baby slid into her hands. 'It's a girl,' she told Aimee. Jess rubbed the baby's back, checking to make sure her little chest rose and fell with a breath and listening for her first cry before she placed her on Aimee's chest and fetched a warm towel. She took one-minute Apgar readings and clamped the cord just as the ambos arrived. Relief flooded through her. She'd done the easy bit, now they could finish off.

'Congratulations, Aimee.'

'Thank you.' Aimee's smile was gentle but she barely lifted her eyes from her baby. She was oblivious to the work the ambos were doing. Nothing could distract her from the miracle of new life.

Jess could remember that feeling, that vague, blissful state of euphoria. She tidied her things, packing them into her bag as she thought about Lily's birth. Like Aimee, she'd done it without the baby's father there.

She hadn't wanted to do it alone but she hadn't had a lot of choice. She hadn't expected their relationship to end so suddenly. She hadn't expected a lot of things.

By the time she'd discovered she was pregnant the ski fields had closed for the season and Lily's father had been long gone, and despite her best efforts she hadn't been able to find him. So she'd done it alone and she'd done her best.

She snapped her medical bag closed with shaky hands. Now that the drama was over her body shook with the adrenalin that coursed through her system. She stripped the bed as the ambos transferred Aimee and her baby onto a stretcher and wheeled them out the door.

She could hear voices in the hallway and assumed that Jean-Paul had been located. That was quick. She could hear an Australian accent too. That was odd. Jean-Paul didn't sound like an Australian name. She listened more carefully.

A male voice, an Australian accent. It sounded a lot like Lucas.

Her stomach flipped and her heart began to race. She was being ridiculous. It had been seven years since she'd heard his voice, as if she'd remember exactly how he sounded. She only imagined it was him because he'd been in her thoughts.

It wouldn't be him. It couldn't be him.

But she couldn't resist taking a look.

She picked up the medical bag and stepped out into the hallway. The ambos had halted the stretcher and a man stood with his back to her, talking to Aimee.

'We've got a message to your husband,' he was saying. 'We'll get him back as quickly as possible and I'll make sure he gets brought to the hospital.'

The man was tall with broad shoulders and tousled blond hair. Jess could see narrow hips and long, lean legs. His voice was deep with a sexy Aussie drawl. Her heart beat quickened, pumping the blood around her body, leaving her feeling light-headed and faint.

It was him. It was most definitely him.

She steadied herself with one hand against the wall as she prayed that her knees wouldn't buckle.

It was Lucas.

She didn't need to see his face. She knew it and her body knew it. Every one of her cells was straining towards him. Seven years may have passed but her body hadn't forgotten him and neither had she. She recognised the length of his legs, the shape of his backside, the sound of his voice.

The ambos were pushing the stretcher towards the elevator by the time she found her voice.

'Lucas?'

CHAPTER THREE

JESS FELT AS if the ground was tipping beneath her feet. She felt as if at any moment she might slide to the floor. She could see the scene playing out in front of her, almost as though she was a spectator watching from the sidelines. She could see herself wobbling in the foreground and she could see Lucas standing close enough to touch. If she could just reach out a hand she could feel him. See if he really was real. But she couldn't move. Life seemed to be going on around her as she watched, too overcome to react.

He turned towards her at the sound of his name.

'JJ?'

She hadn't been called JJ in years. It had been his nickname for her and no one else had ever used it.

She couldn't believe he was standing in front of her. Lucas, undeniably Lucas. He still had the same brilliant, forget-me-not-blue eyes and the same infectious, dimpled smile and he was smiling now as he stepped forward and wrapped her in a hug. She fitted perfectly into his embrace and it felt like it was only yesterday that she'd last been in his arms. Memories flooded back to her and her stomach did a peculiar little flip as her body responded in a way it hadn't for years. She tensed, taken by surprise by both his spontaneous gesture and her reaction.

He must have felt her stiffen because he let her go and stepped away.

Her eyes took in the sight of him. He looked fabulous. The years had been kind to him. Better than they'd been to her, she feared. His hair was cut shorter but was still sandy blond and thick, and his oval face was tanned, making his blue eyes even more striking. He had the shadow of a beard on his jaw, more brown than blond. That was new. He wouldn't have had that seven years ago, but he hadn't got fat. Or bald.

Her heart raced as she looked him over. He was wearing dark trousers and a pale blue business shirt. It was unbuttoned at the collar, no tie, and he had his sleeves rolled up to expose his forearms. He looked just as good, maybe even better, than she remembered.

Her initial surprise was immediately followed by pleasure but that was then, just as quickly, cancelled out by panic. What was he doing here? He wasn't supposed to be here. He was supposed to be in Europe or Australia. Eating cheese in Switzerland or surfing at Bondi Beach. He wasn't supposed to be in Canada and especially not in Moose River. *She* was the one who belonged here. *She* was the Canadian.

'What are you doing here?' she asked him.

'I'm the hotel manager.'

'In Moose River?'

'It would seem so.' He grinned at her and her stomach did another flip as heat seared through her, scorching her insides. He didn't seem nearly as unsettled as she was about their unexpected encounter. But, then, he'd always adapted quickly to new situations. He seemed to thrive on change, whereas she would rather avoid it.

The ambos and Aimee and her baby had disappeared and a second elevator pinged as it reached their floor.

'Are you finished up here?' he asked.

Jess nodded. It seemed she'd lost the power of speech. It seemed as though Lucas had the same effect on her now as he'd had seven years ago.

'I'll ride down with you,' he said.

He waited for her to enter the elevator. She tucked herself into the corner by the door, feeling confused. Conflicted. She wasn't sure what to think. She wasn't sure how she felt. One part of her wanted to throw herself into his arms and never let him go. Another wanted to run and hide. Another wanted desperately to know what he was thinking.

Lucas stepped in and reached across in front of her to press the button to take them down to the lobby. She hadn't remembered to push the button, so distracted by him she wasn't thinking clearly.

He was standing close. She'd expected him to lean against the opposite wall but he didn't move away as the elevator descended. If she reached out a hand she could touch him without even straightening her elbow.

He was watching her with his forget-me-not-blue eyes and she couldn't take her eyes off him. His familiar scent washed over her—he smelt like winter in the mountains, cool and crisp with the clean, fresh tang of pine needles.

The air was humming, drowning out the silence that fell between them. She clenched her fists at her sides to stop herself from reaching out. She could feel herself being pulled towards him. Even after all this time her body longed for his touch. She craved him.

They stood, for what seemed like ages, just looking at each other.

'It's good to see you, JJ.' His voice was a whisper, barely breaking the silence that surrounded them.

He stretched out one hand and Jess held her breath. His fingers caught the ends of her hair and his thumb brushed across her cheek. The contact set her nerves on fire, every inch of her responding to his touch. It felt like every one of her cells had a memory and every memory was Lucas.

'You've cut your hair,' he said.

'Many times,' she replied.

Lucas laughed and the sound was loud enough to burst the bubble of awareness and desire and longing that had enveloped her.

She didn't know how she'd managed to make a joke. Nothing about this was funny. She was so ill prepared to run into him.

Last time he'd seen her she'd had long hair that had fallen past her shoulders. She'd cut it short when Lily had been born and now it was softly feathered and the ends brushed her shoulders. She'd changed many things about herself since he'd last seen her, not just her hair. It was almost a surprise that he'd recognised her. She felt seventy years older. Not seven. Like a completely different person.

She *was* a different person.

She was a mother. A mother with a secret.

The lift doors slid open but Jess didn't move. Lucas was in her way but even so she didn't think she was capable of movement. She needed the wall to support her.

Her legs were shaking. Her hands were shaking. She knew her reaction was a result of the adrenalin that was coursing through her system. Adrenalin that was produced from a combination of attraction and fear. Why had he come back? And what would his presence mean to her? And to Lily?

'Mr White.' A hotel staff member approached them. Lucas had his back to the doors but he turned at the sound of his name and stepped out of the elevator. 'Mr Bertillon is nearly back at the lodge. He's only a minute or two away. What would you like me to do?'

'I'll meet him here. Can you organise a car to be waiting out the front? We need to get him down the mountain to the hospital asap.'

Jess pushed off the wall and forced her legs to move. One step at a time, she could do this. Lucas turned back to face her as she stepped into the lobby. 'Have you got time for a coffee? Can you wait while I sort this out?'

Jess shook her head. 'I have to get back to the medical centre,' she lied. She had no idea how to deal with the situation. With Lucas. She had to get away. She needed time to process what had just happened. To process the fact that Lucas was here.

'Of course. Another time, then.' He put a hand on her arm and it felt as though her skin might burst into flames at his touch. Her pulse throbbed. Her throat was dry. 'We'll catch up later,' he said.

Jess dropped the medical bag off at the clinic before trudging through the snow back to her apartment. Seeing Lucas had left her shaky and confused and she used the few minutes she had to herself to try to sort out her feelings.

He said they'd catch up later. What would he want?

She definitely wasn't the naive teenager from seven years ago. She wasn't the person he would remember.

What would she do? She needed to work out what to tell him. How to tell him.

She shook her head. This was all too much.

She'd have to try to avoid him. Just for a while, just until she worked out what having all three of them in the same place would mean for her and Lily. Just until she solved this dilemma.

Seven years ago she'd fallen in love. Or she'd thought she had. Seven years on she had convinced herself that maybe it had just been a bad case of teenage hormones. Lust. A holiday romance. But seeing him today had re-inforced that she'd never got over him. How could she when she was reminded of him every day?

She knew she wouldn't be able to avoid him for ever. Moose River wasn't big enough for that. They were bound to bump into each other. But even if avoidance was a possibility she suspected she wouldn't be able to resist him completely. Curiosity would get the better of her. She'd been thinking about him for seven years. She would have to fill in the gaps. But as to exactly what she would tell him, that decision could wait.

She opened her apartment door and was almost knocked over by an excited Lily.

'Mum, where have you been? Kristie is here. We've been waiting for you for ages.'

'Yes, darling, I know. I'm sorry I'm late,' she said as she kissed her daughter.

Normally, seeing Lily's little face light up when she arrived home after a long day at work was enough to lift her spirits. Normally, it was enough to remind her of why she worked so hard and why she'd made the choices she had, but today all she could think of was all the secrets she had kept and wonder how much longer she had until the secrets came out.

She felt ill. The living room was warm but she was shivering. Trembling, Kristie got up and hugged her and Jess could feel herself shaking against her cousin's shoulder.

Kristie stepped back and looked at Jess while she spoke to Lily. 'Lily, why don't you go and try on that new skisuit I got for you? I think your mum would like to see it.' She waited for Lily to leave the room and then said to Jess. 'What's going on? Did it go badly with the patient?'

'No, that was all fine,' Jess replied. She'd been going to stop there but she knew Kristie would get the news out of her eventually. She'd always known when something was bothering her and she'd always been able to wheedle it out of her. She decided she may as well come clean now. 'It's Lucas.'

'What do you mean, "It's Lucas"? What's he got to do with anything?'

Jess collapsed onto the couch. 'He's not in Switzerland or on Bondi Beach. He's here.'

'Here? In Moose River?'

'Yes.'

'What's he doing here?' Kristie sat down opposite Jess.

'He's managing the Crystal Lodge.'

'The new hotel? How did you find that out?' she asked, when Jess nodded.

'I saw him there.'

'You've seen him?'

She nodded again.

'Oh, my God! What did he say? How did he look? What did *you* say?'

'Not much. Good. Nothing.' She couldn't remember what she'd said. All she could remember was how he'd looked and how she'd felt. How those eyes had made her catch her breath, how her knees had turned to jelly when he'd smiled, how her heart had raced when he'd said her name, and how he'd wrapped her in his arms and she'd never wanted to leave. How, after all these years, she still fitted perfectly in his embrace.

'Look, Mum, it's pink.' Jess jumped as her reverie was interrupted by Lily modelling her new skisuit. 'Isn't it pretty?'

'It's very nice, darling,' she replied, without really looking at her mini-fashionista. She was finding it hard to focus on anything other than Lucas. 'Now, why don't you get ready for a bath while I do something about dinner.'

Lily stamped her foot. 'I want to stay in my suit and I don't want dinner.'

'You need to eat something and you don't want to get your new suit dirty, do you?'

Lily folded her arms across her chest and scowled at her mother. 'I don't want dinner.'

'I bought Lily a burger and fries after school. She won't be going to bed hungry,' Kristie said.

'She ate it?'

'She ate the fries and about half the burger.'

Jess was pleased. Maybe the fresh mountain air was stimulating her appetite. Maybe a compromise could be reached.

'Okay, you don't need to eat but you do need to have a bath and put your pyjamas on. Then you can hop into bed, put the headphones on and watch a movie on the laptop.'

That was a bribe and a compromise but it worked. Lily thought she was getting a treat and she stopped complaining. It worked for Jess too as it meant she and Kristie could talk without fear of being overheard. She knew Kristie would continue to pump her for information and she didn't want to discuss Lucas in front of Lily.

By the time Jess had bathed Lily and got her settled with her movie Kristie had ordered a pizza and poured them both a glass of wine. The moment Jess emerged from the bedroom she could tell she was in for a grilling.

'What are you going to do?' Kristie asked, as Jess drew the curtains on the balcony doors and shut out the night.

'Nothing.'

'You can't do nothing! He deserves to know.'

'Why? My father was right. Obviously the week we spent together didn't mean as much to him as it did to me. If Lucas wanted to be a part of my life he's had plenty of time to look for me before now.'

'You know you don't believe that,' Kristie said. 'You didn't believe your father seven years ago and you don't believe that now. If we could have found Lucas all those years ago he'd be part of your life already.'

'But we couldn't find him and my life is fine as it is,' she argued.

'But what about Lily? Doesn't she deserve to know?'

Jess greeted Kristie's question with stony silence.

'You can't put off the inevitable,' Kristie added. 'It's not fair to Lucas and it's not fair to Lily.'

'But I have no idea what type of man he is now,' Jess countered. He might not be the person she remembered. *Did* she even remember him? Maybe everything she remembered had been a product of her imagination but she knew one thing for certain—she wasn't the person he would remember.

She'd dreamt of Lucas coming back into her life but now that he was here she was nervous. His return brought complications she hadn't considered and consequences she wasn't ready for. She wasn't ready to deal with having him back in her life. She rolled her eyes at herself. Who said he would even want to be part of her life? Or Lily's? This wasn't a fairy tale. This was reality.

She sighed. One thing at a time. That was how she would deal with this. She would gather the facts and then work out her approach, and until then she would stay as far away from him as possible.

'I need some answers before I tell him anything,' she said.

'You can't avoid him for ever.'

'I just need some time to process this,' she said. No matter how much she'd wished for one more chance, now that the moment was here she wasn't ready. 'Whatever we had was over a long time ago. It was a teenage romance—it's water under the bridge now.'

'It might be,' Kristie argued, 'except for the fact that the bridge is sleeping in the other room. There's always going to be something connecting you to him.'

And Jess knew that was the crux of the matter.

Lily.

'You can't keep her a secret any more, Jess.'

CHAPTER FOUR

IT TOOK A lot to frustrate Lucas. He was normally a calm person, level-headed and patient, all good attributes when working in hospitality, but right now he was frustrated. Seeing Jess again had hit him for six. It was a cricketing term but one that perfectly matched how he was feeling. He could cope with the day-to-day issues that arose with the hotel, he'd even coped with the delays and revisions while it had been redeveloped, but he couldn't cope with Jess's disappearance. Not again.

By the time he'd waited for Aimee Bertillon's husband and seen the ambulance off, all the while itching to return to Jess but doing his best to hide his impatience, she had vanished. She had said she couldn't wait and it seemed she'd meant it.

He knew he wouldn't be able to settle, he wouldn't be able to concentrate on work, not while thoughts of Jess were running rampant through his head. He told his PA that he was going out. No excuses, no reasons. He needed to think and he always thought better if he was outside in the fresh air. If she wasn't going to wait for him, he'd go and find her. He changed his shoes and grabbed his coat and walked to the medical centre.

'Can I help you?' The lady behind the desk had a name badge that read 'Donna'.

'I hope so. I'm looking for one of your doctors, Jess Johnson.'

'She's not a doctor,' Donna told him.

Now he was confused as well as frustrated. 'I've just seen her. I'm Lucas White from the Crystal Lodge. I called for a doctor and she came.'

'Jess is a nurse. All our doctors were busy so she agreed to go and make an assessment. Was there a problem? She's gone for the day but is there something I can help you with?'

A nurse.

Lucas shook his head. 'No. Nothing. Thank you.' The only thing he wanted was to know where she was and he didn't imagine that Donna would give him that information. He'd have to come back.

Jess was a nurse. He wondered what had happened. She'd been planning on becoming a doctor—why hadn't she followed her dream?

Night had fallen when he stepped back outside and the temperature had dropped. He pulled his scarf and gloves out of his coat pocket—he'd learnt years ago to keep them handy—and wandered the streets, still hoping to find her.

If he'd known on the day she'd been yanked from his life that he wasn't ever going to see her again he would have tried harder to keep hold of her. When she'd disappeared he'd been left with nothing. Nothing but a sense that he needed to prove himself.

He had left Moose River to return home, vowing he would make it back one day. Vowing to make something of himself. For her. It had been an impulsive, young man's promise, one that seven years later he might have thought would be long forgotten, but even though there had been plenty of other women over the years he'd never got Jess out of his system. She'd been an irresistible combination of beauty, brains, innocence and passion. She had worn her heart on her sleeve and she'd shared herself with him without reservation.

At times it was almost impossible to believe they'd only had seven days together. That one week had influenced him profoundly. It had made him the man he was today, determined to succeed. Determined to find Jess again and prove himself worthy.

It had taken longer than he would have dreamed. If someone had told him at the age of twenty that it would take him almost seven years, he would have thought that was a whole lifetime. But he had done it and he was back.

When the opportunity had presented itself in Moose River he'd jumped at it. At the time it had seemed as though all the planets had aligned. The timing had been right, he'd been ready to spread his wings, and the opportunity to be back in Moose River had been too good a chance to pass up. He'd wanted to prove himself and what better place to do it than in the very place where his dreams had all begun.

He'd returned as a successful, self-made man but things hadn't gone quite as he'd expected. The hotel hadn't been the problem. It had been Jess. He'd been back in Moose River for nine months and hadn't caught sight of her until today. He hadn't imagined that he'd find her, only to have her disappear again. Maybe she didn't feel the same desire to catch up. Maybe she hadn't kept hold of the memories, as he had. Maybe she barely remembered him.

Although he'd seen in her face that she hadn't forgotten him. He'd held her in his arms and it had felt like yesterday and he knew she'd felt it too.

But things had not gone according to his plan. The reunion he'd always pictured had gone quite differently.

But he wasn't a quitter, he never had been, and he wasn't about to start now. He'd found her and he wasn't going to let her disappear again.

He walked past the building where Jess's family had had their apartment all those years ago. He'd called in there before but this time he knew she was in town. She had to be staying somewhere. He pushed open the lobby door and pressed the buzzer for the penthouse.

No answer. That would have been far too easy.

He continued walking and eventually stopped and leant on a lamppost. He looked across the street and recognised the building. He was in front of the Moose River staff apartments. He counted the windows and stopped at unit fifteen. It was in darkness but he could see lights in the gap between the curtains in apartment sixteen. His gaze drifted back to the dark windows of fifteen as his memory wandered.

Jess had given him her heart but he hadn't really appreciated it at the time. He'd been young and hungry for adventure. He hadn't realised what he'd had with her. Not until she'd been long gone. And by then it had been too late.

No one else had ever measured up to her. Or not to his idealisation of her anyway. Perhaps he was looking back on the past with rose-tinted glasses but there had been something special about her and he'd never met anyone else like her. And he'd travelled to almost every corner of the globe. He'd been constantly on the go since he'd left Moose River. He'd immersed himself in the hospitality trade before he'd even finished studying, learning the lessons that enabled him to take the next step, getting the knowledge and experience to embark on a solo project. Getting ready to prove himself to Jess and her father.

But he wasn't to know his efforts were to be in vain.

Apartment fifteen remained dark. He wasn't going to solve the puzzle that was life or even the problem that was Jess and her whereabouts while standing out here in the cold. There were plenty of issues waiting for his attention back at the lodge. He could make better use of his time. He pushed off the lamppost and trudged back through the snow. He'd continue to search for her tomorrow.

Lucas had been up since five. He'd been unable to sleep and he'd done half a day's work already. It was Thanksgiving weekend in the United States and the official start of the ski season in Moose River, Canada. Crowds were building and the Crystal Lodge was fully booked. This was what he'd wanted. What he'd been working towards. No vacancies. He wanted Crystal Lodge to become one of the premier hotels in the resort. But now he feared that wasn't enough. Jess was back and he wanted her too.

He loved his job, he loved his life and he'd thought that he was happy with his success, but seeing Jess yesterday had shown him that all his success was nothing if he had no one to share it with. Seeing her yesterday reinforced that he'd spent seven years making something of himself, of his life, and he'd done it for her. But had she moved on? What would be the point of making himself worthy of Jess if she didn't want to have anything to do with him?

He stood by the window of his office and watched the snow fall. It had started early this morning and the forecast was for heavy falls over the weekend. It was perfect for the start of the season.

Next week all the Christmas decorations would be up around the village. They were already multiplying at a rapid rate and Lucas knew his tradesmen were at work this morning, building a frame for the thirty-foot tree that would be on display in front of the hotel on the plaza. He planned to switch on the lights on the tree next weekend to coincide with the opening of the Christmas market that was to be held in the plaza. There were plenty of things needing his attention, he had plenty to keep him occupied, but all he could think about was Jess.

He needed a break from the indoors. He muttered something to his PA about inspecting the progress on the framework for the tree and then wandered through the village, retracing his steps to all the places he and Jess had spent time seven years ago. Not that he expected to find her in the same places but he was happy to let his feet lead the way as it left his mind free to reminisce.

He headed up the hill, past the popular après-ski venue, the T-bar, and skirted the iconic Moose River Hotel, which set the standard for accommodation and was the hotel that Lucas measured the performance of Crystal Lodge against. The village was blanketed in snow. It was as pretty as a picture but everyone was bundled up against the weather and he knew he could walk right past Jess and never know it. He may as well return to the lodge and do something more productive.

He was halfway down the hill, passing the tube park, when he spotted her. She was leaning on the railing at the bottom of the slope and he could see her profile as she watched people sliding down the hill in the inflatable rubber tubes. She was wearing a red knitted cap and he had a flashback to the day he'd first met her. How the hell did he remember that? The sound of laughter floated up to him as people raced down the lanes and Lucas felt like laughing along with them. He'd found her.

'JJ!'

Jess turned around at the sound of her nickname. Her heart was racing even before she saw him. Just hearing his voice was enough to make her feel like she was seventeen once more and falling in love all over again. He was smiling at her and she couldn't help but smile back, even as she cursed her heart for betraying her brain.

'I was hoping to bump into you.'

That was ironic. She'd been hoping to avoid him.

'You were? What for?'

'Old times' sake. I wanted to invite you for coffee. Or dinner?'

'I don't think so,' Jess replied. She was nowhere near ready to spend one-on-one time with Lucas. She knew she owed it to him to catch up but she wasn't ready yet. She needed time to prepare. She needed time to plan a defence. And she definitely needed more than twenty-four hours.

'Jess!'

Kristie was flying down the slope towards them in a double tube. The snow had been falling too heavily to make for pleasant skiing with a beginner so she and Kristie had opted to bring Lily to the tube park instead. But she hadn't anticipated that they'd bump into Lucas. Not here.

She used the interruption to her advantage, choosing to wave madly at her cousin and hoping to divert Lucas's attention.

'Is that Kristie?'

'Yes.' Kristie had Lily tucked between her knees and she was screaming at the top of her lungs as they raced alongside the person in the adjacent lane. Kristie always took things to the extreme and Lily was yelling right along with her, looking like she was having the time of her life.

Jess could remember coming to the tube park with Lucas. She could remember sitting in the tube between his thighs with his arms wrapped around her and yelling with delight, just like Lily was now. Life had been so much simpler then but she hadn't appreciated it at the time.

'Who's that with her?' Lucas asked, as he spotted Lily.

Jess had successfully diverted Lucas's attention away from herself, only to focus it on Lily. The one thing she didn't want.

She was tempted to tell him that Lily was Kristie's but she knew she'd be caught out far too easily in that lie. 'That's my daughter,' she said.

'You have a daughter?'

Kristie and Lily hopped out of the tube and Kristie started dragging it back to the conveyor belt that would take them back to the start of the lanes at the top of the hill. Lily waved to Jess but followed Kristie. Luckily, she wasn't ready for the fun to end yet so didn't come over to her mother. Jess was relieved. She didn't want to have to introduce Lily to Lucas. Not yet. She definitely wasn't prepared for that.

'She's the image of you,' Lucas said, as Lily stepped onto the conveyor belt. 'How old is she?'

'Five.' Jess's heart was beating at a million miles an hour as she avoided one lie only to tell another.

Lily was, in fact, six, but luckily she was small for her age. While Jess didn't want to give Lucas a chance to put two and two together, she wasn't completely certain why she'd lied. She didn't expect him to remember that it had been seven years ago that they had spent one week together. It was obvious he hadn't forgotten her but to think he would remember exactly how many years had passed might be stretching things. Just because that time had become so significant to Jess, it didn't mean it would be as important to him. Why should it be? It had been just one week for him. For her it had been the rest of her life.

'Is that the reason you don't want to catch up? You're married?'

Jess shook her head. 'No.'

'Divorced?'

'No, but I still can't go to dinner with you. Life is more complicated now.' She had to think of Lily. But she knew she was also thinking of herself. She wasn't ready for this.

'I guess it is.' He nodded his head slowly as he absorbed her words. 'But, if you do find yourself free at any time, or if your complications become less complicated, you know where to contact me.'

He didn't push her. He didn't suggest she bring Lily

along to dinner and Jess knew he wanted to see only her. Alone.

Was it possible that her father had been right? If she'd been able to find Lucas all those years ago would he have wanted to know about Lily or would he have chosen to have nothing to do with her? She didn't think that was the sort of person he was. But what would she know? It wasn't like they'd had time to really get to know each other.

She wondered if he'd ever thought about being a father. Maybe he already was one. The question was on the tip of her tongue but she bit it back. Did she want to know more about him? Did she want to know what his life was like now? What if he had children of his own? Other children? Would that be too painful?

Surely it was better, safer, easier if she kept her distance.

He smiled. His forget-me-not-blue eyes were shining and his dimples flashed briefly, tempting her to say, *Wait, yes, of course I'd love to have dinner with you.* But she nodded and let him go.

She watched him walk down the hill and thought about how different her life could have been.

Jess stood at the balcony doors as the last rays of the sun dipped behind the mountain. She had thought that spending the morning at the tube park would have exhausted Lily but she seemed full of beans and Jess didn't have the energy to cope with her at the moment. Thank goodness for Kristie. She had taken Lily off to the shops, leaving Jess alone to think.

She looked to her left, down to the village. In the foreground she could see the balcony of apartment fifteen,

Lucas's old apartment. She tried to look past it as she didn't want to think about him but she knew she couldn't help it. Her mind had been filled with memories of him all day and right there, on that balcony, was where they had shared their first kiss.

When Lucas and Sam had invited them to their party Jess had never imagined actually going. But Kristie had managed to come up with a semi-believable story about a school friend's birthday and before she'd known it Jess had been at Lucas's door.

He and Sam had been sharing the apartment with two other boys and it had already been crowded when they'd arrived. People had spilled out of the living room into the corridor between the flats, overflowing into the bedrooms and out onto the balcony. But somehow Lucas had met her and Kristie at his front door.

He'd smiled at her and his blue eyes had lit up. His grin had been infectious and full of cheek and Jess had known right then that he would love creating mischief and mayhem. 'You look great,' he told her.

She and Kristie had spent ages getting ready, all the while ensuring that it had looked effortless. Kristie had straightened Jess's hair so that it hung in a shiny, platinum cascade down her back. She had coated her eyelashes with mascara to highlight her green eyes and swiped pink gloss over her lips.

She'd been nervous about coming to the party, worried about being in a room full of strangers, but one smile from Lucas and all her nervousness had disappeared. He hadn't felt like a stranger. She'd felt safe with him. She'd trusted him. All those years of listening to her parents telling her to be wary of strangers, of forbidding her to go out alone, and what had she done

EMILY FORBES   63

at the first opportunity—she'd disappeared to a party with a stranger just because he'd been cute and he'd flirted with her. He'd been so gorgeous and she'd been pretty sure she was already in trouble but she'd been unable to resist.

Even Kristie couldn't have predicted this turnaround in such a short time. Jess, who'd never gone against her parents' wishes, had been rebelling big time because a cute boy had smiled at her and made her laugh. She hadn't known him but she hadn't cared. She would get to know him. She'd felt like she'd been where she was supposed to be. Here. With him.

He took the drinks they carried, opened one for each of them and handed them back before stashing the rest into a tub that had been filled with snow. Kristie had used a fake ID to buy the pre-mixed cans of vodka and soda and they'd shared one as they'd walked to the party. Jess had needed it for courage; she hadn't really planned on having another one but she supposed she could nurse one drink for the evening. It's not like anyone would pay attention to what she was doing.

'I'm glad you could make it,' he said to her, as Kristie spotted Sam and made a beeline for him.

'We almost didn't.'

'How come?'

'We're not normally allowed to go to random parties.'

'Who would stop you?'

'Our parents.'

'So you're not nineteen, then?'

Jess frowned. What did her age have to do with anything? 'What?'

'If you were nineteen you'd be making your own decisions.'

They'd fibbed to her aunt and uncle about where they were going but she'd forgotten that Kristie had also lied to the boys about their age.

'I'll be eighteen next week.' She hoped that wouldn't matter. She wasn't sure what she wanted to happen but she wanted a chance to find out. She didn't want Lucas to decide she was too young but he didn't mention her age again.

'So you've sneaked out and no one knows where you are. Are you sure that's wise?'

'You seemed trustworthy.' Jess smiled. 'And as long as we're home before midnight, everything should be fine,' she added, aware that she was babbling. Normally if she was nervous she'd be tongue-tied but she had forgotten to be nervous. Was it the half a drink she'd had or was there something about Lucas that made her feel comfortable?

'What trouble can you get into after midnight that you can't get into before?' he asked.

'You sound like Kristie.'

'You have to admit I have a point.' Lucas was standing very close to her. When had he closed the distance? She was leaning with her back against a wall and he was standing at a right angle to her, his left shoulder pressed against the same wall, inches away from her. His voice was quiet and he had a mischievous look in his blue eyes.

'I don't know the answer,' she said. 'I just know we need to be home before our curfew. I don't want anyone looking for us and finding out we're not where we said we'd be. I don't tend to get into trouble.'

'Not ever?' He grinned at her and suddenly Jess could imagine all sorts of trouble she could get into.

Trouble, mischief and mayhem. All sorts of things she'd never exposed herself to before.

She shook her head. 'I've never had the opportunity.'

Her parents knew where she was every minute of the day and Jess knew how stressed they would be if she ever sneaked off and went against their wishes. She had never wanted to test the boundaries before, aware of how upset they would be. But neither they nor her aunt and uncle had any idea where she was tonight. If she was careful she could have some fun and they would be none the wiser.

'Maybe you just haven't recognised opportunity when she's come knocking,' Lucas said. 'Or maybe you need to create it.'

His last sentence was barely a whisper. His head was bent close to hers and she held her breath as he dipped his head a little lower. He was going to kiss her! She closed her eyes and leant towards him.

'Hey, Lucas,' someone interrupted. 'Your shout.'

'You've gotta be kidding me.' He lifted his head and turned to face the room. Over his shoulder Jess could see a couple of his mates holding empty beer bottles up in the air and laughing, and she knew they'd deliberately interrupted the moment. Jess could have screamed with frustration. She'd never forgive them if she'd missed an opportunity that she couldn't get back. What if the moment was gone for ever?

'Come on.' He took her by the hand and her skin burned where his fingers wrapped around hers. He pushed through the crowd until they came to a pair of doors that opened onto a balcony. He led her outside to where there were more tubs filled with snow and beers.

He let her go as he grabbed a couple of beers in each hand and asked, 'Will you wait here?'

She wasn't sure what she was waiting for but she nodded anyway. She seemed destined to follow his lead. Something about him made her finally understand what got Kristie all hot and bothered when it came to boys. Her hormones were going into overdrive and she was certain she could still feel the imprint of his fingers on hers. She couldn't think about anything except what it would be like to be kissed by Lucas. He was cute and confident, his accent was completely sexy and the way he looked at her with those brilliant blue eyes made her want to leap in, even though she didn't have the faintest idea about how to do that. But she suspected he knew what to do and she would happily let him teach her.

He took the beers inside and when he came back to her he was holding two coats and another drink for her that she didn't really want. He handed her the can, not realising she hadn't finished her first drink.

'You're not having anything?' she asked.

'I don't feel like drinking tonight.'

He was looking at her so intensely that even with her limited experience Jess knew exactly what he did feel like doing and the idea took her breath away.

'I don't want this either,' she said.

Lucas reached out and closed his hand around hers. It was warm, really warm in contrast to the cold drink. He took the can from her and stuck it into a tub with the beers.

Lucas was making Jess feel light-headed and giddy and she didn't want alcohol to interfere with her senses. She wanted to remember this moment, how it made her feel. She finally felt as if the world made sense.

She had always believed in love at first sight. She didn't know why, but she liked the idea that people could recognise their soul mate the very first time they saw them and she imagined that this was how it would feel. Like you couldn't breathe but you didn't need to. She felt as if she could exist just by looking into Lucas's eyes. She felt as though she didn't need anything more than that. Ever.

'I thought we could stay out here,' he said. 'There'll be fewer interruptions and, you never know, we might find the only thing that interrupts us is opportunity.' He was standing only inches from her. She could see his breath coming from between his lips as little puffs of condensation that accompanied his words and it was only then she noticed the cold. He opened one of the coats and held it for her as she slipped her arms into the sleeves. It smelt like him, fresh and clean with a hint of pine needles, but it swamped her tiny frame.

'How long are you staying at the resort?' he asked, as he rolled the sleeves up for her. He had closed the balcony doors and while they could still see the party through the glass the music was muted and they had the balcony to themselves.

'A little over two weeks. Until the New Year.'

'Do you come here often?'

'We spend most Christmas vacations here.' That was true of the past nine years. Prior to that, when her brother had been alive, they'd spent every second Christmas in California with her mother's family. But that had all changed after Stephen had died. But she didn't think Lucas needed to hear that story. Tonight wasn't about her family. It wasn't about her past. Tonight was about her. Tonight was her chance to experience all the things that Stephen's early death had robbed her of.

'Christmas in the snow,' he said. 'I'm looking forward to seeing what all the fuss is about. This will be my first white Christmas.'

'Really?'

He nodded.

'I'll have to make sure you get the full festive season experience, then,' Jess said with a smile. She'd worry about how to actually achieve that later.

'Don't worry, I intend to.'

He was watching her closely and she started to wonder if she had food caught between her teeth. Why else would he be staring at her like that? 'What is it?' she asked.

'I want to know what you're thinking,' he told her.

'About what?'

'About me.'

She hesitated before answering. She could hardly tell him she thought he was gorgeous or that he might well be her soul mate. He might appreciate her honesty but then again he might think she was completely crazy. She played it safe. 'I don't know anything about you.'

'What would you like to know?'

'I have no idea.' She wasn't very good at social conversations. She'd never really had to talk to a stranger before. She usually only got to talk to people with whom she already had some sort of connection—family, school friends or family friends. There was never anything new to learn about any of them. Every one of them was the same. Rich, well educated and well spoken, they all lived in Vancouver's exclusive suburbs, had private school educations, holiday homes, overseas vacations and were gifted new cars on their sixteenth birthdays. She was surrounded by trust-fund children. Lucas was a clean slate and she didn't know where to begin.

'Well, why don't I start?' he said.

'All right.'

'Do you have a boyfriend?'

She shook her head. 'No. Why?'

'I want to kiss you and I want to know if that's okay.'

Jess's green eyes opened wide. He was offering her a chance to experience freedom. To do something spontaneous, something that hadn't been sanctioned by her parents.

She'd broken so many rules tonight, what was one more? And, besides, there wasn't actually a rule forbidding her to kiss boys. It was more that she was rarely given the opportunity. And that was what it was all about, wasn't it? Opportunity.

Her freedom in Moose River was on borrowed time and if she didn't grab the opportunity with both hands now she knew she'd miss it altogether. She didn't have time to stop and think. She didn't have time to weigh up the options and the pros and cons. Her time was finite. It was now or never.

She didn't do anything she would regret. Not that night at least. Lucas was cute and he was interested in her and there was no one in the background, keeping tabs on her. For the first time ever she could do as she pleased. And she wanted to kiss Lucas.

'Have you made up your mind yet?' he asked.

He bent his head. His lips were millimetres from hers.

She'd wanted a chance to make a decision for herself. But some decisions, once made, couldn't be reversed. Right then, though, she wasn't to know that this kiss would mark the moment when she stood at the crossroads of her life. She wasn't to know that this would be the moment when she decided on a path that would change her life for ever.

She nodded, ever so slightly, and closed her eyes in a silent invitation.

His lips were soft. The pressure of his mouth on hers was gentle at first until his tongue darted between her lips, forcing her mouth open. She let him taste her as she explored him too. She felt as though he'd taken over her body. She felt as if they had become one already, joined at the lips. Her nipples hardened and a line of fire travelled from her chest to her groin, igniting her internally until she thought she might go up in flames. Her body was on fire as she pushed against him, begging him to go deeper, to taste more of her.

She could feel herself falling in love with each second.

He could kiss her as much as he liked for the rest of for ever if he kissed like that.

CHAPTER FIVE

'JESS? JESS!'

Jess turned around from the window as the sound of Kristie's voice dragged her back to the present. She needed to focus. Judging by Kristie's tone, it seemed she might have been calling her for a while. 'What?'

'Lily was talking to you.'

'What are we doing tonight, Mummy?' Lily asked, but Jess couldn't think. Her mind was still filled with thoughts of Lucas and it took her a moment to come back to the present. She was distracted but that wasn't Lily's fault and it wasn't a good enough reason to ignore her daughter.

Kristie rescued her. 'How would you like to do something special with me, Lily?' she offered.

'Like what?'

'It'll be a surprise. I know you love surprises. Go and pack a bag with your pyjamas and a toothbrush while I think of something.'

Kristie waited for Lily to leave the room. 'You should ring Lucas and see if he's free for dinner.'

'What? Why?' How was it possible that Kristie could read her mind?

'I know you haven't stopped thinking about him

since this morning, probably since yesterday. I know you said you were going to avoid him but you can't pretend you don't want to see him. You've been miles away all afternoon. So the way I figure it is you might as well go and see him while I'm here to look after Lily. I'll take her on a sleigh ride, she's desperate to do that—she won't even care what you're doing.'

'She told you she wants to go on a sleigh ride?' That was enough to stop Jess from thinking about Lucas. 'Would you mind doing something else? I really want to do that with her. I'm saving up to take her as a Christmas surprise.' Her heart ached. She knew Lily wanted to take a sleigh ride from Crystal Lodge more than anything and even now that she knew Lucas's involvement with the lodge she wasn't going to let it derail her plans. Logistics weren't the issue but money was. She didn't have the cash to spare so, until she got her first pay cheque, the sleigh ride would have to wait.

Jess could see Kristie biting her tongue and knew she wanted to offer to pay for it but she'd learnt the hard way that Jess was determined to make it on her own.

Kristie looked at her but didn't argue the point. 'Sure. Can I take her to our apartment?' she asked. 'I won't tell her it belongs to our family—we can drink hot chocolate and toast marshmallows in front of the fire and watch the replay of the Thanksgiving parade. She can have a sleepover and then you can have the night free to do as you please.'

Jess wasn't convinced this was a good idea. 'You know what happened last time we hatched a plan like that,' she said. 'I ended up pregnant.'

Kristie just shrugged and smiled. 'Lily would like a sibling. She'd probably like a father too. I think this is fate intervening. Leading you to decisions that I know you don't want to make. Perhaps you should let fate dictate to you. I think you owe it to Lucas to meet up. Don't you?'

'No,' Jess replied.

She'd refused to wear a dress. As if that meant she had some control over the situation. She didn't want to feel like she was going on a date. They were just two old acquaintances catching up. She tucked her jeans into her boots and tugged a black turtleneck sweater over her head. Jess did put on make-up—she was too vain not to—but kept it simple. Foundation, mascara, some blush and lip gloss. She still wanted to look pretty but not desperate. Adding a red scarf for some colour, she headed out the door.

She'd insisted on meeting him at the hotel. This wasn't a date so he didn't need to collect her, she was quite capable of walking a few streets. She stepped from the plaza into the lodge. Tonight she had more time to take in her surroundings and she stopped briefly, gathering her thoughts as she admired the room. There were two beautifully decorated Christmas trees in the lobby, one at each end, and the lobby itself was festooned with lights, pine branches, red bows and mistletoe.

The lodge was celebrating Christmas in style and decorations were multiplying in the village too. The Christmas spirit was alive and flourishing in Moose River and Jess smiled to herself. As a child she had loved Christmas. She had looked forward to it all year, partly because the festive season also included her birthday, but it had been her favourite time of year for so many reasons. Until her brother had died.

After Stephen's death Christmas had lost its sparkle. She knew he was always in her parents' thoughts, particularly her mother's, especially at certain times of the year, including Christmas, and that had taken the shine off the festivities. Even though he wasn't spoken of for fear of further upsetting her mother there was always the underlying sense that someone was missing and Christmas had never been the same. Until Lily was born. And now Jess was desperate to have the perfect Christmas. She wanted to create that for Lily and she had hoped that being in Moose River would give her that chance. This was her opportunity to put the sparkle back.

She felt someone watching her and she knew it was Lucas. Jess turned her head. He had been waiting for her by the bar and now he was walking towards her, coming to meet her in the lobby.

Seeing him coming for her made her feel as if she was coming home but she resisted the feeling. She belonged here in Moose River so she should already feel at home, she shouldn't need Lucas to make her feel that way.

He was wearing a navy suit with a crisp white shirt and a tie the colour of forget-me-nots. She'd never seen him in a suit before. His hair had been brushed, it wasn't as tousled as she was used to, and she fought the urge to run her fingers through it and mess it up a bit. He looked handsome but she preferred him more casually styled. But perhaps the old Lucas wouldn't have fitted into this fancy hotel. She wondered how much he'd changed. Probably not as much as she had. The thought made her smile again.

He smiled in response. A dimple appeared in his

cheek, a sparkle in his eye. Now he looked like the Lucas she'd fallen in love with.

He reached out and took both her hands in his then leaned down and kissed her cheek, enveloping her in his clean, fresh scent. The caress of his lips sent tingles through her as her body responded to his touch. She could feel every beat of her heart and every whisper of air that brushed past her face as his lips left their imprint on her skin. Despite what she thought, her body didn't seem to remember that this wasn't a date or that seven years had passed. Her body reacted as if it had been yesterday that Lucas had been in her bed.

She'd been on a few dates over the past few years but she'd eventually given up because no one else had ever had the same effect on her as Lucas had. The attraction she'd felt for Lucas had been immediate, powerful and irresistible, and she'd never felt the same connection with anyone else. Not one other man had ever made her feel like she might melt with desire. Not one of them had made her feel like she was the centre of the universe, a universe that might explode at any moment. What was the point in dating? she'd asked herself. Why waste time and energy on someone who wasn't Lucas? If she couldn't have Lucas she'd rather have nothing.

And it seemed he hadn't lost the ability to make her feel truly alive. Just a touch, a glance, a kiss could set her off. She'd need to be careful. She'd need to keep her wits about her and remember what was at stake.

'JJ,' he said, and his voice washed over her, soft and deep and intimate. How could she feel so much when so little was said? 'Thank you for coming.'

As if she'd had a choice.

Despite her show of determination to Kristie earlier

in the day, she'd known her resolve wasn't strong enough to withstand the temptation of knowing that Lucas was only a few streets away. She'd known she'd pick up the phone and call him.

'I hope you don't mind if we stay in the hotel to eat?' he asked.

'I'm not dressed to eat here,' she said, as she took her hands out of his hold and shrugged out of her coat. Jeans and an old sweater were not five-star dining attire, even if the jeans hugged her curves and the black top made her blonde hair shine like white gold.

He ran his eyes over her and Jess could feel her temperature rise by a degree for every second she spent under his gaze. She could see the appreciation in his eyes and the attention felt good.

'You look lovely,' he said as he took her coat. It had been a long time since she'd wanted to capture a man's interest and despite telling herself this wasn't a date it was nice to know that Lucas liked what he could see. 'And you're safe with me. I can put in a good word for you if need be.' He was laughing at her and she relaxed. His words reminded her of their first night together all those years ago. She'd felt safe then and she felt safe now.

'Are you sure? I don't want to drag down the standards.'

'Believe me, you're not lowering our standards.' He ran his gaze over her again and Jess's breath caught in her throat as she saw his forget-me-not-blue eyes darken. 'We're fully booked for the weekend and I'd like to be close to hand in case there are any issues.'

She was worried that eating in the hotel would give him the upper hand. He would be in familiar surroundings and she felt underdressed and out of place. But, then again, she consoled herself, this wasn't a competition, it was a friendly dinner.

'Are you expecting problems?' she asked, as she walked beside him into the restaurant. He had his hand resting lightly in the small of her back, guiding her forward. His touch was so light she should hardly have felt it but she could swear she could feel each individual fingertip and her skin was on fire under the thin wool of her sweater.

'There are always teething problems with a new project—the only unknown is the scale of the disaster,' he said, as he checked in her coat and greeted the maître d'.

She followed him to a table positioned beside the large picture windows looking out over the outdoor terrace and onto the plaza. Lucas pulled out her chair for her and reached for a bottle of champagne that was chilling in a bucket next to her. He popped the cork and poured them each a glass.

'To old friends,' she said, as they touched glasses.

'And new memories,' he added. 'It's good to see you, JJ.'

She took a nervous sip of her champagne as the waiter approached their table.

'We're not ready to order yet,' Lucas told him.

'It's fine, Lucas,' Jess told him. 'You must know what's good—why don't you choose for us both?' She sounded breathless. She was nervous, on edge from conflicting emotions—guilt, lust, fear and desire—and she doubted she'd be able to eat anything anyway. The sooner he ordered the sooner she'd be able to escape before she said or did something she might regret. She'd been desperate to see him but now she was worried that she'd made a mistake.

She looked out the window as Lucas gave the waiter their order. Christmas lights were strung up around the terrace and stretched across to the plaza. They surrounded the ice-skating rink and looped through the bare branches of the trees. The ice and snow sparkled under the glow of the lights as skaters glided around the rink. It was the perfect image of a winter wonderland.

'It's a beautiful view,' she said, as the waiter departed, leaving them alone again. She got her breathing under control and returned her gaze to Lucas. 'It's a beautiful hotel.'

'You like it?'

'It's perfect. Just looking at it makes me happy. Someone has done a very good job.' The entire lodge—the furnishings in the rooms, the decorations in the lobby and the views from the restaurant—all conspired to make her feel as though the hotel was giving her a warm hug. Or maybe that was Lucas.

'Thank you,' he said.

'You?'

Lucas nodded. 'This is my vision.'

'Really? I thought you were the hotel manager.'

'That's my official title but this is my hotel.'

'Yours? You own it?'

'Yes. This is my baby.'

'You dream big, don't you?' she said.

'What do you mean?'

'You told me you wanted to work in the hospitality industry when you finished university. You never said you actually wanted to own a hotel.'

'You remember that?'

I remember everything about you, she thought, but she said nothing. She just nodded as the waiter placed their first course on their table.

'I have you to thank for that,' he told her.

'Me?'

'I started planning this the day you vanished from my life.'

'I didn't vanish,' she objected. 'My father dragged me away. I didn't have a choice.'

'In my mind you vanished. I never saw you again. I looked for you, every day, until the end of the season, until the day I left, but you had disappeared.'

'You looked for me?' She'd never dared to imagine that he would have thought about her.

'Of course. Did you think I would just let you go? Especially after what happened that day. I went back to your apartment the next day but there was no answer. Eventually I found the caretaker and he told me you'd all left. I was sure you would get in touch with me and I kept looking, thinking maybe you'd be back before the season ended. When that didn't happen I started writing to you, long letters that I was going to post to your family's apartment, but I never finished them.'

'Why not?' How much simpler might things have been if he'd done that. Then she might have been able to find him when she'd needed to.

'I was never good with words. I decided that words were empty promises and that I was better off showing you what I wanted you to know. It's taken longer than I thought. But now we have a chance to fill in all the gaps. To catch up on what happened that day and in the past seven years.'

Jess could remember every second of that day. Every

moment was imprinted on her brain, each glorious moment, along with every humiliating one. It had certainly been a birthday to remember.

She had wanted to sleep with him from the moment he'd kissed her. After that first night at his party she would have gladly given him anything he'd asked for but for as long as she could remember she'd fantasised about her first sexual experience and it had involved a big bed, clean sheets, flowers, music and candles. Not a single bed in a shared flat. Getting naked in Lucas's flat in a bedroom he'd shared with Sam had not been an option and so she'd had to wait and hope for a different opportunity. And then, on the morning of her birthday, her aunt and uncle had announced they were going cat skiing, leaving the girls on their own, leaving Jess free to spend the afternoon with Lucas.

They had spent any spare moments they'd had together since meeting seven days earlier. With Kristie's help Jess had sneaked off at every chance she'd had. She'd never done anything like that before but being with Lucas was more important than being the perfect daughter. Lucas had unleashed another side to her personality and she hadn't been able to resist him.

On her eighteenth birthday her aunt and uncle's plans had given her the ideal opportunity to create the perfect setting in which to let Lucas seduce her. It had to be that way. Lucas would have to seduce her as she didn't know where to start. She would create the opportunity for seduction and Lucas would have to do the rest.

And, just as Kristie had predicted several days earlier, Jess found herself planning sneaky afternoon sex. Only it had been more than that. She had gifted her virginity to Lucas. She had offered herself to him. She had offered him her body and her heart and he had taken them both. She had given herself to Lucas and in return he had given her Lily. It had been the perfect birthday. Up to a point.

'That day didn't end quite how I'd expected,' she said.

'No. Me neither. But I have to know what happened to you. Where did you go?'

'We left Moose River that night.'

'All of you?'

Jess nodded.

'Because of me?' Lucas asked.

'Because of both of us,' Jess said. 'But mostly because of my father. I still don't know how I'd forgotten they were arriving that night. I can't believe I lost track of time so badly.' She'd been swept away by Lucas and once she'd had a taste of him she hadn't been able to get enough. He had brought her to life. Her body had blossomed under the touch of his fingers and the caress of his lips. He had introduced her to a whole new world. A world of pleasure, fulfilment and ecstasy. He had consumed her body, her mind and her heart, and she had forgotten about everything else, including the imminent arrival of her parents.

Everyone had got more than they'd bargained for that day.

Jess could still remember the moment she'd heard them arrive. The moment her ecstasy had turned to dread. The moment her fantasy had become a nightmare.

Lucas's head had been buried between her thighs and he had just given her another orgasm, her second of the day, when she'd heard the front door of the apartment slam. And then she'd heard Kristie's loud, pan-

icked voice welcoming them. Jess had known Kristie
had been trying to warn her. Thank God she'd been
there and had been able to stall them just long enough
for Lucas to scramble to the bathroom. Jess could still
recall how his round white buttocks, pale in contrast
to his Aussie tan, had flexed as he'd darted to the bathroom. She'd just had time to throw his clothes in after
him and then pull on her sweatpants and a T-shirt before her father had come into her room to wish her a
happy birthday.

Their hurried dressing hadn't been enough to fool
him. He'd taken one look at their semi-dressed state
and the rumpled bed and had gone completely berserk.
Being caught out by her parents hadn't been anywhere
near how she'd imagined that afternoon would end.

Her father had been furious with her, upset and disappointed, and disparaging of Lucas. He'd thrown him
out without ceremony after a few well-chosen remarks
before making Jess pack her bags. Her aunt and uncle
had arrived home from their day of cat skiing in the
middle of the circus and both girls had then been bundled into the car and returned to Vancouver, where Jess
had been subjected to endless lectures about abuse of
trust and lack of respect for her aunt and uncle as well
as for her parents' rules.

'I was so worried about you.' Lucas's words broke into
her reverie. 'I thought your father was going to have a fit.'

'He was always over-protective but his reaction was
extreme, even by his standards. I was so embarrassed
by the way he spoke to you. I still haven't forgiven him
for that.'

Lucas smiled as the waiter delivered their appetis-
ers. 'I feel I should thank him.'

'*Thank* him?'

Lucas nodded. 'His diatribe started me on this mission. He accused me of being a good-for-nothing bum and I wanted to prove him wrong.'

Jess looked around her at the opulent hotel. 'You did all this to get back at my father?'

'I wanted to prove to him that I was worthy of his daughter. He was my inspiration but I did this for you.'

'For me?'

He picked up her hand and Jess felt his pulse shoot through her. His thumb traced lazy circles in her palm and her body lit up in response to his touch. It gave life to her cells and awakened her dormant senses. She felt seventeen again, full of newly awakened hormones.

'Your father suggested I would never measure up to his expectations. But it was your expectations I was worried about. I wanted to be someone who was important to you. I wanted to be someone who could fight for you. Who could protect you. I didn't stand up for you that night and I want you to know that won't happen again.'

'I'm not the same person I was then, Lucas.'

She remembered that awful day as if it were yesterday. The shame. The heartbreak. She had felt as though things could never be worse. Until she'd found out that, really, they could. In fact, they could be a *lot* worse.

Everything had changed after that, including her. The only thing that hadn't changed, apparently, over the past seven years was how Lucas affected her. As his eyes locked onto hers she knew she would jump right back into bed with him tonight if he asked. She could feel every cell in her body yearning for him. She felt as though if she didn't keep tight control of her emotions her body would dissolve. The heat between them was enough to melt her core and she could feel herself burning.

She could get lost in him so easily and she couldn't let that happen. She needed to resist him, needed to keep her distance, but when he looked at her like he was doing now, like she was the only person in the world, she didn't think she had the willpower to stay away. Sitting there, looking in to his blue eyes, she could pretend that her life was still simple and easy and privileged.

But that wasn't the truth.

She fought the urge to give in to him. To do so would mean telling him all her secrets. She knew that it was inevitable but she was terrified of what he would think when he found out. Would he forgive her? Would he reject her? Would he reject them both?

What a complicated situation. Coming back was supposed to be the answer. It was supposed to help her get her life on track, to give her and Lily the freedom she craved, but all she'd got were complications and confusion. All she'd got were more questions and fewer answers.

She suspected it would be impossible to get out of this with her heart intact and she wasn't sure if she could stand to lose him a second time. But that wasn't going to be her choice to make.

She picked up her glass as it gave her a chance to remove her hand from his, which was the only thing to do if she wanted to think straight. There were things she needed to tell him.

Jess sipped her champagne, steadying the glass on her lip to disguise the shake in her hand. All the times she'd wished he'd been with her and now here he was.

It was time for the truth. She couldn't keep her secret any longer. She took a deep breath and put her glass down on the table. Starting the tale would be difficult but she feared it wouldn't be the worst part.

'Lucas, there's something I need to tell you.'

CHAPTER SIX

'I'M SORRY TO INTERRUPT, Mr White, but there's an emergency.'

Before Jess could begin to explain, before she could begin to divulge the secrets she'd been keeping, she was interrupted by a tall, thin, young woman dressed impeccably in a tailored black skirt suit, who appeared beside their table. The gold name tag on her lapel read 'Sofia' and her dark hair, cut in a shiny blunt bob, brushed her shoulders as she leant over to speak to Lucas.

'What is it?'

'A child is missing.'

Lucas was out of his seat before Sofia had finished her sentence. 'Are they hotel guests?' he asked.

'No.' Sofia named one of the smaller lodges and Jess recognised the name. It was an old lodge on the edge of the village. 'The search and rescue team has been mobilised but because of the heavy snowfalls they are having trouble finding tracks and have requested all hands on deck.'

'Of course.' Lucas turned to Jess. 'I'm sorry, I'll have to go. I'm part of the volunteer S&R team. We assist the professionals when we're needed.'

'Is there anything I can do?' Jess asked.

'What did you have in mind?'

'I don't know. I could help to look or at least make cups of tea. Someone always does that job.' There had to be something she could do.

'Sofia, can you see if you can rustle up some warmer clothes for Jess and some snow boots while I get changed?'

Jess took that to mean he had given permission for her to accompany him and she followed Sofia and got changed as quickly as possible. She didn't want to hold Lucas up.

Outside the snow was still falling. The Christmas lights around the plaza were doing their best to shine through the weather as Jess wondered what sort of Christmas the family of the little boy would get. She hoped he'd be found.

She could see pinpricks of light throughout the village and up and down the mountain. The lights bobbed in the darkness as the searchers panned their flashlights across the snow. There had to be hundreds of them.

The snow muffled all sound but Jess could hear the occasional voice calling out a name. Otherwise, the village was eerily quiet and Jess guessed that the S&R team didn't want any unnecessary noise that might mask something important. Like the cry of a young child.

Lucas strode out, heading for the lodge where the little boy had gone missing and where the S&R was now being co-ordinated. Jess hurried along beside him. When she slipped on the snow he reached for her hand to steady her. He kept hold of her as they approached the lodge from the rear but he wasn't talking. Jess assumed he was focusing on what lay ahead and she kept quiet too. She didn't want to disturb him or any of the other people who were out searching.

They reached the lodge and Lucas held the door open for her and followed her inside. He made his way directly to a table that had been set up in a lounge area to the right of the entrance and introduced himself to the man who was sitting there. He had a two-way radio in one hand and a large map spread out in front of him.

'The boy's name is Michael. He is seven years old and he was reported missing twenty minutes ago.' The search co-ordinator gave them the little information he had.

'Where was he last seen?'

'He and his brothers were playing in the snow behind the lodge. His brothers came inside thinking he was behind them but he wasn't.'

'Where is the search area?' Lucas peppered the man with questions.

'The lodge is at the epicentre of the search and we've spread out from here. There are people searching at one-hundred-metre intervals from here.' The co-ordinator pointed to concentric circles that had been marked on the map with red pen. 'This is the area we're covering so far.'

'Can someone show me exactly where he was last seen?'

'If you go around the back of the lodge you'll see the snowman the boys were making. That was the last confirmed sighting.'

'I'd like to start from there,' Lucas said, 'unless there's anywhere more specific you want me to begin?'

'There was no sign of him there.'

'I'd like to check again.' Something about Lucas's tone suggested he wasn't really asking for permission. He was a man with a plan.

The co-ordinator nodded. 'Okay. Take these with you,' he said, as he handed him a whistle and a torch.

Lucas turned to Jess. 'JJ, come with me.'

Jess followed him back outside with no real idea about what he expected of her or how much help she could be. She'd have to trust him to direct her.

She hurried to keep up with him as he stomped through the snow around to the back of the lodge. Jess's borrowed boots sank into the snowdrifts that had formed against the walls of the lodge and she was out of breath by the time she rounded the back corner. A lonely, misshapen snowman stared at her as she gulped in the cold air.

Lucas was standing beside the snowman, looking left and right. The snow around the snowman had been flattened and trampled by dozens of feet, the searchers' feet, Jess assumed, although most traces were already being covered by the fresh snow that continued to fall. Jess knew the footsteps of Michael and his brothers would have been obliterated long ago, making the search even more difficult.

Lucas lifted his head and Jess could see him looking up at the roof of the lodge.

'What are you looking for?' she asked.

He took three steps towards the lodge and stopped beside a large mound of fresh snow, which looked as though it had been pushed into a heavy drift by a snow-plough. 'This pile of snow has fallen from the roof.' He pointed up to the roof. 'See how that section of roof is clear of snow?' Above their heads a large section of the lodge roof was bare. The weight of the fresh snowfall had caused the snow beneath to slide off the roof and land in a heap on the ground, a heap that was five or six feet high. 'I've seen this once before. We need to check this drift. Michael could be buried under here.'

Lucas knelt in the snow and started digging with his gloved hands while Jess stared at the huge mound. She felt her chest tighten with anxiety and she struggled to breathe. She felt as though she was the one trapped and suffocating.

How long had Michael been missing? It must be close to half an hour by now. *How long can someone survive without air?* Not long.

She knew that. She'd lived that. Her own brother had suffocated.

Jess was frozen to the spot, paralysed by the memories. She couldn't go through this again.

'JJ, give me a hand.' Lucas was looking at her over his shoulder. His busyness was in stark contrast to her immobility but she didn't think she could move.

'JJ, get down here.'

Lucas raised his voice and his words bounced off the walls of the lodge and echoed across the snow, jolting Jess out of her motionless state.

She knelt down beside him and started digging. If she didn't want to go through this again she only had one option and that was to do everything in her power to save this child. Digging like a mad woman now, she could feel the sweat running between her breasts and her arms ached with the effort of shifting the snow, but she wasn't going to let this be another tragedy. She hadn't been able to save her brother but she'd been eight years old then. She wasn't going to let another little boy die.

'Michael, are you there, buddy? Hang on, we're

going to get you out.' Lucas was talking constantly as he frantically tore at the snow.

Jess's vision was blurring as the blood pumped through her muscles. Her breaths were coming in short bursts and her heart was pounding but she wasn't about to stop. She dug her hands into the pile of snow again and her fingers hit something hard. Something firmer than the recently fallen snow.

'Lucas! There's something here.'

Lucas helped her to scrape the snow away and Jess could see something dark in the snow pile. Clothing? A jacket?

'It's a boot,' he said. 'Keep clearing the snow,' he told her as he pulled the whistle from his pocket and blew into it hard. The shrill sound pierced the still night air and Jess knew it would be heard for miles. Lucas gave three, short, sharp blasts on the whistle before yelling, 'Some help over here.'

Jess's movements intensified. She had to hurry. She had to clear this snow.

'What is it?'

'Have you found him?'

They were bombarded with questions as other searchers arrived on the scene.

'He's here,' Lucas replied. 'We need to clear this snow.'

Jess had cleared the snow to expose Michael's foot and ankle and now that they could work out in which direction he was lying Lucas could direct others to start clearing the snow to expose Michael's head. There was a sense of urgency, though the snow muffled the sound so there was nothing loud about the panic but it was there, under the surface. Every minute was vital, every second precious.

In under a minute the snow had been cleared to reveal a child's body. A young boy, curled into a foetal position with one arm thrown up to cover his face. He wasn't moving.

'Call the ambos,' Lucas said to the crowd that had gathered around them. He whipped off one of his gloves and placed his fingers on the boy's neck to feel for a pulse. 'Pulse is slow but present.'

Jess bent her head and put her cheek against Michael's nose. 'He's not breathing.'

'We need to roll him,' Lucas said. 'Clear some snow from behind him.'

'I can't let this happen again, Lucas. We have to save him.'

'We're doing everything we can, JJ.'

'We have to hurry.'

The snow had been cleared now and Jess held the boy's head gently between her palms as Lucas rolled him. Stuffing her gloves into her pocket, she started mouth-to-mouth resuscitation as they waited for the ambulance. She had to do something. She had to try to save his life.

Clearing Michael's airway, she tipped his head back slightly and breathed into his mouth, watching for the rise and fall of his chest. She was aware of his parents arriving on the scene as she continued to breathe air into their son's lungs. She heard them but she couldn't stop to look up. Everything else had to be blocked out. She could feel tears on her cheeks but she couldn't stop to wipe them away, she had to keep going.

'JJ, the ambos are here.' Lucas rested his hand on her shoulder and finally she could stop and hand over to someone who was better qualified than her.

She was shaking as Lucas helped her to her feet. She knew the tip of her nose was red and cold and she could feel the tightness of the skin on her cheeks where the tears had dried and left salt stains. Her toes were numb and her fingers were freezing.

Lucas put his arm around her. 'Come on, let's get you warmed up.'

She knew Lucas wanted to get her out of the cold and she knew she should probably listen to him but she couldn't do it. 'I can't leave yet,' she told him, as she pulled her gloves back onto her hands. She had to stay. She had to know how this ended.

Lucas didn't argue. He kept his arm around her as they stood together while the ambulance officers inserted an artificial airway and attached an ambu bag and Jess was grateful for his additional warmth. She could hear that the ambos were worried about head and thoracic injuries but they weren't giving much away. They ran a drip of warm saline and loaded Michael onto a stretcher as they continued to bag him. At least they hadn't given up.

Jess and Lucas waited until the ambulance drove away, heading for the hospital, and then, somehow, Lucas wangled a lift for them back to Crystal Lodge.

Jess was exhausted and Lucas practically carried her inside when they reached the lodge. 'Do you want me to run you home?' he asked.

'Not yet.' She could barely keep her eyes open but she wanted to stay in Lucas's embrace for just a little longer.

'Come to my suite, then, and I'll organise something warm to drink.'

Jess didn't have the energy to argue, even if she'd wanted to. He led her into an office behind the reception desk and unlocked a door in the back wall. The door opened into the living room of his suite. The room was cosy and, even better, it was warm.

Lucas steered her towards the leather couch that was positioned in front of a fireplace. A wood fire burned in the grate. It was probably only for decoration—Jess assumed there would be central heating—but there was something comforting about a proper wood fire.

He undid her boots and pulled them from her feet. He rubbed the soles of her feet, encouraging the blood back into her extremities, and Jess almost groaned aloud with pleasure.

There was a knock on the door as Lucas propped her feet on the ottoman and one of the housekeeping staff wheeled in a small trolley. 'Dessert, Mr White.'

Lucas lifted the lid to reveal a chocolate pudding, apple pie and a mug of eggnog.

He took the eggnog and added some brandy and rum to it from bottles that stood on a small sideboard. 'That'll warm you up,' he said, as he passed it to Jess before pouring himself a shot of rum. He dropped a soft blanket over Jess's lap and sat down beside her. She lay next to him with her feet stretched out to the fire and his arm wrapped around her shoulders. Lying in front of the fire in Lucas's embrace with a warm drink and warm apple pie, she thought this might be heaven.

'Do you think Michael will be all right?' she asked.

'He has a good chance. His pulse was slow but the cold temperature means his systems had shut down and that may save him.'

'But we have no idea how long he wasn't breathing.'

'Maybe he'd only just stopped breathing. If there was an air pocket in front of his face he could have survived for thirty minutes or maybe a little longer in those conditions, provided the snow wasn't heavy enough to crush him. We'll just have to hope that we found him in time.'

'How did you know where to look for him?'

'I saw a similar scenario once before in Australia when a child was in the wrong place at the wrong time and was buried by a pile of snow that slid off a roof. No one picked up on it at the time so people were searching in the wrong places. It's stuck with me. I'll never forget the possibility that that can happen.'

'What happened that time?'

Lucas shook his head. 'We weren't so fortunate back then. By the time we found him it was too late. We were lucky tonight.' He took a sip of his rum. 'You said you couldn't let this happen again. You know what it's like, don't you? To lose someone. You've been in that situation before too, haven't you?'

Jess nodded.

'Do you want to talk about it?'

'It was my brother.'

'Your brother?' She could hear the frown in his voice and his arm around her shoulders squeezed her against him a little more firmly.

She let her head drop onto his shoulder. 'He died when he was six.'

'In an accident?'

'Yes, one that had a lot of similarities to tonight.'

'Was it here?'

'No. We spent most of our winter holidays here but Mum used to take my brother and me to spend our summer holidays in California with her family. Dad would join us for a week or two but it was usually just Mum and her sisters and our cousins and we'd spend the summer at my grandparents' beach house. We loved it. We were pretty much allowed to do as we pleased for six weeks. That summer we were digging a big hole with tunnels under the sand. We'd done this before but not with tunnels and one of the tunnels collapsed, trapping Stephen and one of my cousins in it. We managed to get my cousin out but not Stephen. The weight of the sand crushed him and he suffocated. His body was recovered but it was too late.'

'JJ, that's awful. I'm so sorry.' Lucas dropped a kiss on her forehead, just above her temple. It felt like a reflex response but it lifted her spirits. 'How old were you when it happened?'

'Eight.' Jess sipped her eggnog. She could feel the warmth flow through her and the kick of the added brandy gave her the courage to continue. 'My mother has never gotten over it. I think she feels a lot of guilt for not watching us more closely but we'd done similar things plenty of times before without any disasters. I think the combination of stress and guilt and trauma was all too much. We've never been back to California. Stephen's death cast a shadow over our family, a shadow I've grown up under, and it's shaped my life. I didn't want another family to go through what we've been through.'

'What did it do to you?'

'After he died my mother changed. She couldn't be around people. She couldn't bear the thought that they would ask about Stephen or ask how she was coping. She wasn't coping. With anything. She shut herself off from everyone, including me. Dad said she couldn't cope with the idea that something might happen to me too so her way of coping was to ignore the outside world and me.

'Dad, however, was determined that nothing was going to happen to me. One tragedy was enough. So I was protected, very closely and very deliberately. I wasn't allowed any freedom. Mum and Dad had to know where I was and what I was doing every minute of the day, which is why Dad flipped out when he caught us together. His whole mission in life had become to protect me from harm and there I was, in bed with a stranger. His reaction was completely out of proportion with what we'd been doing but it was a case of his mind jumping to the worst possible conclusions of not knowing what else I'd been up to without his knowledge. My whole life has been influenced by Stephen's death. In a way it's still influencing me.'

'How?'

'It had a lot to do with why I came back here with Lily.'

'Lily? That's your daughter?'

Jess nodded. She hadn't realised she hadn't told him her name. She wondered if he liked it.

'Before Stephen died I was allowed to walk to school with my friends and go on sleepovers and school camps. After he died that all changed. I didn't want Lily to grow up like that. But because I'd spent most of my childhood being taught to be fearful I found it hard to relax. When she was a baby I was very uptight, I was worried about what she ate and panicked every time she got a cold.

'I was nervous about leaving her with childminders while I studied and worked and when she started school I realised that I was bringing her up the same way my parents had brought me up. I was wrapping her in cotton wool and I didn't want that. I wanted her to have the childhood that I'd missed out on. I wanted her to be able to walk to school and to her friends' houses without me worrying that something would happen to her. I wanted her to grow up somewhere safe.'

'And what about Lily's father? What does he think about you moving here?'

'Lily doesn't know her father.'

'Really? What happened to him?'

Was now the right time to tell him? No, she decided, she needed to have a fresh mind.

'Sorry,' he apologised, when she didn't answer straight away. 'It's probably none of my business.'

If only he knew how much of his business it actually was.

She had to tell him something. 'Nothing happened to him. I was young. We both were.' She tipped her head up and looked at Lucas, met his forget-me-not-blue eyes and willed him to understand what she was saying. 'I loved him very much but our timing was wrong. It was no one's fault but Lily and I have been on our own for as long as she can remember.'

She knew she had to tell him about Lily but where did she start? *How* should she start?

She stifled a yawn. It was too late to have this conversation tonight; they were both exhausted. A little voice in her head was telling her that she was making excuses but she didn't have the emotional energy to have the discussion now.

She pushed herself into a sitting position. 'It's getting late,' she said, making yet another excuse. 'I'd better get home.'

'Are you sure? I hate to think of you going out in the cold just when you've thawed out.' She could hear the smile in his voice and knew she couldn't afford to look at him. If she saw him smiling at her she'd find it hard to refuse. Although he might not be intending to cause trouble he'd done it once before and she suspected it could easily happen again.

Mischief and mayhem. That's how she'd first thought of him and it still seemed to fit. Mischief, mayhem and trouble.

She was tempted to stay right where she was, on the couch in front of the fire wrapped in Lucas's arms. It felt safe. Lily was having a sleepover with Kristie so she could do it but she knew that it would just complicate the situation. Seven years ago she'd fallen for the charms of a good-looking boy and she knew she could easily fall again. She couldn't let herself get involved.

She reached for her boots, busying herself with putting them back on. 'I have to go. I have Lily, remember?'

'I'll walk you home, then.' Lucas stood and took her hand to pull her to her feet. He helped her into her coat and then took her hand again as they walked through the village. She kept her hand in his. There was no harm in that, right?

'This is where you're living?' He sounded surprised to find she was in the old accommodation block. 'We're back where it all began.'

He pushed open the door and Jess knocked the snow from her boots before stepping into the foyer. She hesitated inside, not wanting Lucas to walk her to her door, afraid of too much temptation.

'Thanks for getting me home safely and thank you for an interesting evening.' She sounded so formal but that was good. She was keeping her distance.

'My pleasure. We should do it again.' Lucas's voice was far from formal. It was full of promise and suggestion and Jess could feel her body respond. If he could do that to her with his voice she hated to think what he could do with a touch.

'Without the drama,' she said, as she fought for control. She was still conflicted and confused. She could feel the attraction but she knew she couldn't pursue it. Not yet. She couldn't let her hormones dictate to her.

'Definitely.' Lucas's voice was a whisper. He bent his head and his lips were beside her ear. Then beside her mouth.

Her hormones took over again as confusion gave way to desire. She wasn't strong enough to resist him. She never had been.

She turned her head and then his lips were covering hers. He wrapped his arms around her waist and pulled her close. Her hands went behind his head and kept him there. She parted her lips and tasted him. He tasted of rum and chocolate. He tasted like a grown-up version of the Lucas she'd fallen in love with.

His kiss was still so familiar and it made her heart ache with longing. She had seven years of hopes and dreams stored inside her and Lucas's lips were the key that released them. They flooded through her and her body sang as it remembered him. Remembered how he tasted and felt.

His body was still firm and hard. His hair was thick. He smelt like winter and tasted like summer. He felt like home.

She clung to him, even though she knew she shouldn't be kissing him. She knew she was only complicating matters further but she had no resistance when it came to Lucas. Absolutely none. She knew she'd have to find some.

She pulled back.

'We should definitely do *that* again,' he said as he grinned at her, and she was tempted to take him up on his suggestion there and then.

No. Find some resistance. Find some resolve, she told herself, and find it right now. 'I'm not sure that's wise.'

'Don't blame me.' He pointed up and she saw a sprig of mistletoe hanging from the ceiling. 'Someone has gone to all that effort, I thought it would be a shame to let it go to waste.'

A shame indeed. She smiled but she'd have to let it go for now. She wanted the fantasy but she was worried that the reality might be very different.

CHAPTER SEVEN

'LUCAS, WE HAVE a situation.'

Lucas looked up from his computer screen. His PA was standing in his doorway, smiling. She didn't look too perturbed by the 'situation'.

'What is it?'

'I think you'd better come and see,' Sofia replied.

Lucas followed her out of his office. He glanced around as he crossed the lobby. Everything looked to be in order. Sofia continued across the floor and exited the lodge out onto the plaza. It was late in the afternoon, the ski runs had closed and streams of people were coming and going through the village. Sofia gestured with an open palm towards the bay where the lodge sleigh was parked. Three young girls, one with her platinum blonde hair tied in two short pigtails, stood beside it.

Lily. Even if he hadn't seen her at the tube park last weekend he would have recognised her. She was just a down-sized version of her mother.

Lucas frowned. What possible reason could Lily have for being here? It had been almost a week since he'd seen Jess and he'd never met her daughter.

Since the kiss, he'd been snowed under with work, the hotel was at full capacity and he'd had some staffing and maintenance issues that had taken up a lot of his time, and although he had invited Jess and Lily to dinner during the week Jess had graciously refused. He wasn't sure if she was avoiding him or not but he'd been too busy to push the invitation. Nevertheless, his curiosity was now piqued.

'What do they want?' he asked Sofia.

'A sleigh ride.'

'I've got this,' he told her.

He'd been kicking himself since last weekend when he'd discovered that Jess had a child. He couldn't believe he'd been such an idiot. He should have come back to Moose River sooner. He'd thought he'd had time, he'd thought he could afford to wait until he'd achieved his goals. They were both young and he hadn't considered for one moment that Jess would have moved on. Not to this extent.

But a child wasn't a deal-breaker. Not in any way. If Jess had been married, that would be a different ball game but he could work with her being a mother. If she'd let him. And he was intrigued to find out more about Lily. This might be the perfect opportunity.

He approached the girls. One looked to be Lily's age, maybe a year older, and the other he guessed to be twelve or thirteen.

'Lily?' he asked. 'I'm Lucas. This is my hotel. Is there something I can do for you?'

Lily looked up at him and he was struck again by the resemblance to Jess. She was frowning and she got the same little crease between her eyebrows that her mother got when she was unsure of something. 'How did you know my name?' she asked.

Lucas smiled to himself. He'd been imagining that

Jess had mentioned him to Lily. He'd been flattered and encouraged to think she might have but obviously that wasn't the case.

'I know your mum. You look just like her. What can I do for you?'

'Is this your sleigh?' Lily asked, as she pointed at the brightly painted red sleigh that had 'Crystal Lodge' stencilled across the back of it in ornate gold lettering.

Lucas nodded. 'It is.'

'We wanted a sleigh ride. We have money but this man...' Lily looked up at François, the sleigh driver with an accusatory expression '...says he can't take us.'

'François isn't allowed to take you unless you have an adult with you,' Lucas explained.

Lily folded her arms across her chest and frowned. Lucas expected her to stamp her tiny feet next and he almost laughed before realising that would probably not be appreciated. Not if she was anything like her mother. Lily looked up at him with big green eyes that were nearly too big for her face. She was a *lot* like her mother. 'You could come with us,' she said.

'Me?'

Lily nodded. 'You said you know my mum. You could take us. We have money.'

'Where did you get the money from?'

'Annabel's mum,' Lily said.

Lucas turned to the other two girls. 'Is one of you Annabel?' he asked.

The older girl pointed to the younger one. 'She is,' she said. 'I'm Claire, her sister.'

'Is the money supposed to be for a sleigh ride?' Lucas asked.

Claire shook her head. 'No. We were going ice skating but Lily and Annabel ran off here.'

'Where is your mum?'

'She's at work,' Claire told him. 'She owns the bakery.'

'The patisserie?' he asked.

Lily giggled and her laughter set her pigtails swinging. 'You don't say it right,' she told him.

'Don't I? That's probably because I'm Australian. I don't speak French.'

'That's why you sound funny,' she said, as if everything made perfect sense now. 'I know all about Australia.'

'How much can you know? You're only five.'

'I am not. I'm six.'

Lucas was curious. He was sure Jess had told him Lily was five. 'How do you know about Australia?'

'My mum told me.'

Now he was even more curious. He'd been wondering about Jess's circumstances, he'd spent too much time in the past week thinking about her if he was honest, but there was a lot to consider. Why wasn't she living in her family's apartment? Why had she taken basic accommodation? And what had happened to Lily's father? Why wasn't he in the picture? And why would she talk to Lily about Australia? He couldn't ask Lily directly but he had another solution.

'I need to call your mum,' he told Claire. 'Would you girls like to meet Banjo while I do that?' he asked.

'Who's Banjo?'

'He's the horse.'

Lily and Annabel jumped up and down and clapped their hands.

'You've met François,' Lucas introduced the sleigh driver, 'and this is Banjo.' He was a handsome draught horse. He was dark brown but had distinctive white lower legs with heavy feathering and white markings on his face. Lucas rubbed his neck and the big horse nuzzled into his shoulder. 'Would you like to feed him? He loves apples.'

'Yes, please.' The girls all answered as one.

'Hold your hand flat like this,' Lucas took Lily's hand and flattened her fingers out. François passed him an apple that had been cut in half and he placed it in the centre of her palm. 'Banjo will take it off your hand but keep your hand flat.' He guided Lily's hand to the horse and held her fingers out of the way. 'He won't be able to see the apple so he'll sniff for it.'

Lily giggled as the horse's warm breath tickled her hand. He took the apple and Lucas let Lily rub his neck as he crunched it. Banjo shook his head and Lily pulled her hand away.

'François will give you each an apple to feed Banjo while I ring the patisserie,' Lucas said, as he took his cell phone from his pocket. He got the number and spoke to Fleur. He explained the situation and also explained he was an old friend of Jess's and offered to drop the girls off to her.

As he finished the call Sofia reappeared, carrying a small cardboard cake box, a flask and some takeaway coffee cups. 'What are those for?' Lucas asked.

'I thought the girls might like some hot chocolate and something to eat on their sleigh ride.'

Lucas raised an eyebrow. 'How did you know?'

Sofia smiled and shrugged. 'You're a soft touch.'

'All right,' he asked the girls, 'who would like a lift home in the sleigh?'

'Really?'

'Yep.'

His offer was met with a chorus of squeals and as Banjo had finished all the apples that were on offer to him Lucas helped the girls into the sleigh before climbing up to sit on the driver's seat beside François.

The sleigh had been decorated with pine wreaths, bells and ribbons, and François had also decorated Banjo's harness with bells and tinsel. The shake of his head as he started to pull the sleigh set the bells ringing. Lucas asked François to take them for a turn around the plaza before heading to the patisserie. He'd acquiesced on the ride as he wanted a chance to chat to Lily, wanted to find out what she knew about Australia, but sitting up next to François while Lily sat in the back wasn't going to get him the answers he wanted.

He delivered Annabel and Claire to their mother and told Fleur that he would take Lily to collect Jess.

'Banjo can take you to your mum's work, Lily. Would you like to sit up front next to François?' Lucas asked, and when Lily nodded he lifted her onto the driver's seat. This seat was higher than the passenger seat to allow François to see over Banjo, and the position afforded Lily an uninterrupted view of the Village. The sun had set and the streets and the plaza were glowing under the Christmas lights. Lucas grabbed a fur blanket from the back of the sleigh and tucked it over Lily's lap.

On the seat next to them was the cardboard box Sofia had given him. Lucas peeked inside. Sofia had packed some pieces of cake and Lucas's favourite chocolate biscuits. The girls had finished their hot drinks but hadn't had time to eat anything. He showed the contents of the box to Lily as Banjo set off again, pulling the sleigh through the snow. 'Would you like a piece of cake?'

'No, thank you, I don't really like cake.'

'How about chocolate biscuits, then? I know you like chocolate.'

'How do you know that?'

'Who doesn't like chocolate? And these are the best chocolate biscuits ever. I get them sent over to me from Australia,' he told her.

'Really?' she asked, as she picked one up and bit into it.

'Do you like it?'

Lily nodded.

'So that's something you know about Australia—we make good chocolate biscuits. Tell me what else you know.'

'I know about the animals.'

'Do you have a favourite?'

Lily nodded again. 'Mum says I remind her of a platypus but I like the koala best,' she said with a mouthful of chocolate biscuit, 'because it's so cute. I know what the flag looks like too but I like our flag better. Did you know you've got the same queen as us?'

'I did know that.' Lucas smiled. She really was adorable.

'I can sing "Kookaburra sits in the old gum tree".'

'Did your mum teach you?'

'No, I learnt it in school. Mum taught me "Waltzing Matilda".'

Lucas remembered teaching that song to Jess and explaining what all the words meant. Why had Jess told Lily so much about Australia? 'Did you know that in

Australia it's summertime now? It's so hot at Christmastime we all go to the beach for a swim.'

'That's silly. Who would want to go to the beach on Christmas?'

'Yeah, you're right.' Lucas had come to love a white Christmas but that might be because it reminded him of Jess. It was far more romantic to think of cuddling by a warm fire with snow falling outside than sweating under a blazing sun, battling flies and sand. He loved summer but he didn't have to have it at Christmastime.

Lucas checked his watch. It was almost five. 'We'd better get you to the medical centre,' he told Lily. 'Your mum will be finishing work soon and I promised Fleur I would have you there on time.'

'Oh.' Lily pouted. 'Is that the end of my sleigh ride?'

'I have an idea. Does your mum like surprises?'

Lily nodded. 'She likes good surprises. She says I was a good surprise.'

'Excellent. Why don't we go and pick her up from work in the sleigh? Do you think she'd like that?'

Lily nodded, her green eyes wide.

'That's healed up nicely, Oscar,' Jess said as she removed the stitches in the chin of a teenage boy. He had come off second best in a tussle between the snowboarding half-pipe and his board and Jess had assisted Cameron when he'd fixed him up a week earlier. She snipped the last stitch and pulled it from the skin. 'See if you can stay out of trouble now, won't you?' Oscar was a regular visitor to the clinic and Jess suspected his skills on his snowboard didn't quite match up to his enthusiasm.

'I'll try,' he said, as he hopped up from the examination bed. 'But maybe I should make a time for next week just in case I need it.'

'I don't want to see you again for at least two weeks.' She laughed. 'Off you go.'

Oscar was her last patient for the evening and she checked her watch as she typed his notes into the computer. She was finishing on time and was looking forward to collecting Lily from Fleur's and getting home. Sliding her arms into her coat, she switched off the computer and pulled the door closed as she prepared to leave for the day. Heading into the reception area to say goodnight to Donna, she was surprised to find Lily there.

'Hi, Lil, what are you doing here?' She frowned as she bent down to give her daughter a kiss.

'We have a surprise for you.'

'We?'

Lily took her hand and led her outside. Lucas was standing on the porch.

He looked gorgeous. He was wearing a grey cashmere coat that contrasted nicely with his forget-me-not-blue eyes. His coat looked smart and expensive. Her own coat was several years old and Jess was well aware of the contrast in their wardrobes.

'Lucas,' she greeted him.

'Hello, JJ.' He smiled at her and her heart beat a tattoo in her chest.

She hadn't seen him for a week and the sight of him took her breath away all over again. How was it possible that she could forget the effect his smile had on her? It was like seeing the sun coming out when she hadn't noticed it was missing. She'd never thought her day needed brightening until Lucas had popped into it.

But that didn't explain what he was doing there. In front of her work. With her daughter. Lily didn't know Lucas. He didn't know Lily. She had deliberately kept them apart. She didn't want him getting to know Lily. Not until she'd decided what to do. So what on earth were they doing together? What was going on?

'Why are you here?' she asked. 'Why are you *both* here?'

'Lily went walkabout.'

'What's walkabout?' Lily wanted to know.

Lucas looked at Lily as he explained. 'It's something we say in Australia. It means you went wandering.'

'What? Where?' Jess was worried. She had wanted Lily to be able to roam around the village safely, she'd felt confident that it would be possible, but she realised now that she'd assumed Lily would be wandering with her permission. Not taking off on a whim whenever the mood struck her. 'Did you find her?'

'No.' Lucas was shaking his head. 'She came to the lodge.'

'Why? What for?' Why would Lily go to Lucas? Jess turned to her daughter. 'Lily, what's going on?' She could hear the note of panic in her voice but there was nothing she could do to stop it.

'Jess, it's all right.'

Lucas's voice was calm, his words measured. He was always very calm, very matter-of-fact and practical. A whole lot of personality traits that Jess was sure she could use but it wasn't his place to placate her.

'Don't tell me it's all right!' she hissed at him.

'Lily, Banjo looks hungry.' Lucas turned to Lily, ignoring Jess's outburst. 'Why don't you go and ask François if he has another apple that you can give him?'

Jess watched as Lily went down the steps at the front of the clinic to where the Crystal Lodge sleigh was waiting in the snow. She hadn't even noticed it she'd been so distracted by Lucas and Lily arriving on her doorstep. She assumed Banjo was the horse, a very large but fortunately placid-looking horse.

Once Lily was out of earshot Lucas turned back to Jess. 'Lily was quite safe. I thought this was what you wanted—for her to be able to feel safe in the village?'

'Within reason,' Jess snapped. 'I didn't expect her to roam the streets alone or take off without notice.' Who knew what might happen? All Jess's insecurities, deeply embedded into her psyche by her parents, came to the fore.

'Is this about Stephen?' Lucas asked. He was watching her carefully with his gorgeous eyes. Was he waiting to see if she was going to explode with anger or dissolve into tears?

Jess had to admit that in a way it did all relate back to her brother. She nodded. 'I wanted Lily to have the freedom I never had but I expected to know where she was. She's too young to be getting about on her own. She'd supposed to have someone with her.'

'She wasn't alone. Annabel and Claire were with her. Claire was supposed to be taking them ice skating.'

'So what happened? How did Lily end up with you?'

Lucas shrugged. 'She wanted a sleigh ride so I gather she convinced Annabel to take off with her and they came to the lodge to see if they could use their ice-skating money for a ride instead.' he said, as if that was a perfectly natural request to make of a complete stranger.

'And you said yes, I see.' Jess was annoyed. Not only had Lily gone and found Lucas, she'd also managed to wangle a sleigh ride out of him. She'd been planning that as a holiday surprise and Lucas had taken that gift away from her. She knew it wasn't his fault—he hadn't done it deliberately—but it still irked her.

'I did clear it with Fleur first,' he told her. 'You should be proud of Lily. She wanted something badly enough to go after it. That shows initiative, determination and commitment, and I thought she deserved to be rewarded.'

He would think that, Jess thought, even though she knew her bitchy attitude was unfair.

'And I didn't think you'd mind, especially if you got to share it with her.'

'What do you mean?'

'We've come to give you a lift home in the sleigh. We thought we'd take the long way around. What do you say? Am I forgiven?' He held his hands out, palms open, beseeching her, and she couldn't stay mad. She knew she shouldn't be cross with him anyway, he had only been trying to do something nice for Lily and for her.

And he was right. Did it matter that she hadn't organised it? She should be happy. Lily was safe and she was getting her treat. And it wasn't costing her anything. Well, not money at least. It was costing her some pride and now she would owe Lucas a favour.

He smiled at her. His dimples flashed and his blue eyes twinkled. She would owe him a favour, but when he smiled at her she figured she could live with that.

She sighed. 'I'm sorry I snapped at you. And, yes, you're forgiven.'

'Good. Shall we?' He bent his elbow and Jess tucked her hand into the crook of his arm as he led her down the steps to the sleigh. She put one foot onto the running board and felt Lucas's hands on her hips as he helped her up. She sank into the soft leather seat as Lucas lifted Lily up beside her. He climbed in on the other side of Lily and tucked rugs around them all.

François clicked his tongue at Banjo and the big horse moved off slowly, bells jingling.

'Mummy, I can't see,' Lily complained.

She was tucked between Jess and Lucas and was too small to see past them or over the front of the sleigh.

'Hold up, please, François, while we do some reshuffling,' Lucas said.

Lily and Jess swapped seats so Lily could see out of the side of the sleigh but this meant that Jess was now sitting beside Lucas. Their knees were touching under the blanket and Jess was very aware of the heat of his body radiating across to her. He took up a lot of space and she could have shifted closer to Lily to give them both some room but she didn't want to. It felt good to sit this close to him.

'How has your week been?' he asked, as Banjo set off again.

'It was busy. Apparently the resort is almost at full capacity, I suppose you know that, but we also really notice the influx of the tourists as we get an increase in patient load.'

'Do you still think you've made the right choice taking this job?'

'Definitely. It's so much better than my old job in so many ways. No shift work, no weekends. Three minutes from home. It's heaven.'

'What are your plans for the weekend?'

'I'm not sure. Nothing much. We'll probably do a bit of skiing. Lily has been having lessons after school so I like to see how she's progressing. She's been pestering me for a sleigh ride since we arrived in Moose River but I won't need to do that now.' She smiled at him, all traces of her earlier irritation having vanished. The sleigh ride was relaxing and romantic, even with Lily in tow. It was a lovely end to the working week and sitting beside Lucas was the icing on the cake. 'Thank you.'

'My pleasure.'

She could see his forget-me-not-blue eyes shining in the light of the streetlamps. He looked very pleased with himself. As he had every right to be.

He was humming carols—something about it being lovely weather for a sleigh ride together—as François took them on a circuit around the village. Lucas's hand found hers under the blanket. He squeezed it gently and didn't let go.

Jess rested her head on his shoulder. She didn't stop to think about what she was doing. It just felt natural. It felt good. Banjo headed up the hill where François stopped to let them take in the view of the village, which was spread out before them. The lights sparkled and danced and the sounds of happiness drifted up to them on the breeze. Jess sighed. Sitting in the sleigh, listening to Lucas humming, and seeing Lily's smile, she imagined this could be what her life would be like if they were a real family. Cocooned in their own little bubble of contentment.

She suspected that anyone looking at them now would assume that's what they were. A blond family, bundled up in their furs, being pulled through the snow on a sleigh. They could be the perfect image on a festive season card.

Only it wasn't the truth.

Lucas wasn't her reality. He wasn't her Prince Charming.

She still didn't know if he even wanted a family.

Telling him everything might ruin it all.

Banjo had begun picking his way back down the hill and within minutes François had guided him to a stop in front of her apartment block. It was late now. It was time for dinner.

Lucas helped them down from the sleigh and walked them to the door.

'I know you have other priorities and I don't want you to feel as though I'm intruding on your life, but I would really like to spend some time with you. With you and Lily,' he said, as he held the door open. 'Tomorrow evening is the first Christmas market for the season and we're switching on the lights on the Christmas tree out the front of the lodge. I'd like the two of you to be my guests for the tree lighting. What do you think?'

Jess thought she should refuse politely but she couldn't. She wanted to see him too and Lily would love it.

If Lily and Lucas wanted something badly enough, they would both go after it. That was definitely a trait of nature, not nurture, but why shouldn't she do the same? She and Lily could spend time with Lucas, it would give her another chance to see how he interacted with Lily, another chance to watch him. Was it her fault if having Lily there meant she had to hold onto her secret for one more day?

'We'd love to,' she said. 'Thank you.'

CHAPTER EIGHT

THE THIRTY-FOOT FIR tree stood sentinel over the plaza. Lily craned her head to see to the very top where the star was perched, and even Jess looked up in awe. She'd noticed the framework being erected—that had been difficult to miss too—but the tree itself, with its spreading limbs, was simply enormous. Its dark green foliage had been decorated with myriad silver balls and shining stars and bells that rang when the breeze stirred the branches. A light, shaped like a candle, was attached to the end of each branch. It must have taken hours to decorate but the effort was well worth it. It was beautiful.

Lucas came to them as they stood under the tree. He had his grey cashmere overcoat on again with a black scarf wrapped around his throat. Jess had made more of an attempt to dress up tonight. She'd chosen her smartest woollen coat in a winter white and had taken time with her make-up.

'Ladies, your timing is perfect.' Lucas greeted them with a smile and Jess was pleased she'd made the extra effort.

Lucas had reserved a table for them on the outdoor dining terrace in front of the lodge. They had an uninterrupted view across to the tree as well as down to the plaza, where the colourful tented market stalls had been set up. Carol singers were performing at the edge of the terrace and Lucas ordered eggnog for everyone as they sat down.

As the eggnog was served Lily handed Lucas a box wrapped in Christmas ribbon.

'What's this for?'

'For you,' Lily told him. 'To say thank you for the sleigh ride.'

Lucas undid the ribbon and lifted the lid to reveal cookies in various Christmas shapes—stars, angels, reindeer, bells and sleighs. Each cookie had been decorated with icing and had a small hole in the top through which red ribbon had been threaded.

'Mum and I made gingerbread for the school Christmas cookie swap and I thought you might like some.'

'Thank you, Lily, they look delicious,' he said, as he lifted out a star.

'You can't eat them yet!' Lily admonished him. 'You're supposed to hang them on the tree. That's why they've got ribbons in them.'

'I see that now. Have you hung some on your tree?'

'We don't have a tree.'

'You don't?'

'I haven't got around to it,' Jess told him. She wasn't actually planning on having a tree, mainly because she didn't have any decorations for it. She hadn't brought decorations with them to Moose River—that hadn't seemed a necessity when she'd been choosing which belongings needed to fit into their luggage—but now that she was immersed in the festive spirit of the village she regretted her decision. It wasn't likely to change, though. She could get a tree but she still didn't have the money to splash out on new decorations. Of course, she wasn't about to tell Lucas that. Fortunately Lily piped up and redirected the conversation.

'Do you have a Christmas tree inside?' she asked.

'I do,' Lucas replied.

'I think you should hang them inside, then, so they don't get snowed on.'

'I think that's a very good idea.'

The carol singers were singing 'O Christmas Tree' and as they neared the end of the song Lucas stood up.

'That's my cue,' he said. 'Would you like to come with me, Lily? We need to start the countdown for the lights.'

He took Lily's hand and a lump formed in Jess's throat as she watched the two of them make their way to the tree. He was being so sweet with her. She didn't know what she was worried about. He would love Lily.

Actually, she did know what she was worried about. She was worried he'd think less of her for keeping the secret. She didn't want that but there was no way around it. She knew she had to tell him the truth. She just hadn't decided when.

Lucas took a cordless microphone from his pocket and switched it on. He looked confident and relaxed and very sexy.

'Welcome everyone to the inaugural lighting of the Crystal Lodge Christmas tree. I'd like to invite you all to help count us down from ten to one before we flick the switch. Lily, would you like to start us off?'

Lily looked up at Lucas and beamed. Jess thought her smile was so wide it was going to split her face in two. She was looking at Lucas as if he was the best thing that had ever happened to her, and Jess knew Lily would only benefit from having Lucas as a father. There would be no downside for Lily. Jess had to do the right thing.

Lucas handed Lily the microphone. 'Ready? From ten.'

'Ten!' Lily's voice rang out across the plaza and then the crowd joined in.

'Nine, eight, seven, six, five, four, three, two, one!'

As they reached 'one', the lights were switched on, accompanied by a massive cheer. The tips of the candle lights were illuminated and now glowed brightly against the night sky. The tree had a light dusting of snow and looked magical.

As the carol singers launched into another set of carols Lucas and Lily returned to their table.

'Did you see that, Mum?'

Jess had tears in her eyes as she got out of her chair and hugged her very excited daughter. 'I did, darling, you were fabulous.' Over the top of Lily's head she mouthed 'Thank you' to Lucas.

'Can we go to the market now?' Lily asked, and Jess knew she wasn't going to be able to sit still.

'Would you like to come with us or are you busy?' she invited Lucas.

'No, my duties are all done for the evening. I'd love to walk with you.'

They strolled through the market, stopping at any stall that caught their attention. There was a good variety selling food and gifts, everything from scarves, knitted hats and delicate glassware to souvenirs, Christmas decorations, hot food and candies.

Lucas stopped at a stall selling decorations. 'Lily, I think I need a few more decorations for my inside trees, to go with your cookies. Would you like to choose some for me?'

Lily agonised over her choices but eventually had filled a bag with a varied assortment of ornaments. Jess wasn't sure how they would match in with the smartly decorated trees in the lodge's lobby but seeing the pleasure on Lily's face she knew that wasn't the point. Lucas was doing all sorts of wonderful things for Lily that Jess couldn't afford to do but she couldn't begrudge him. Not when she could see how much pleasure Lily was getting from it.

Jess stopped at the next stall, which was selling barley candy. This was a Canadian Christmas tradition and one she could afford. It was also one she'd shared with Lucas years ago. She chose three sticks of the sugary sweets, one shaped like Santa, one a Christmas tree and the third a reindeer, and let Lily and Lucas choose one each.

They sucked on the candy as they wandered through the market. Lily skipped in front of them, in a hurry to see what lay in the stalls ahead. She stopped at one that displayed some intricate doll's houses, complete with delicate furniture and real glass windows, and spent ages admiring the display as Lucas and Jess talked.

'What are your plans for Christmas?' Lucas asked. 'Are your parents coming up to the resort?'

Jess shook her head. 'I don't think so.'

'Really? I thought that was a family tradition for you?'

Jess had no idea what her parents' plans were. They could be spending Christmas here but even if they were their celebration wouldn't include her and she wasn't going to explain why that tradition had come to an end.

She stopped to buy a bag of hot cinnamon doughnut holes, hoping that would distract him from any further questions.

'What about you?' she asked, as Lily traded her barley sugar for the bag of doughnuts.

'I'll be hosting the Christmas lunch at the lodge. A buffet extravaganza.'

'A bit different from your traditional Christmas,' she said.

'I've grown to prefer a white Christmas.' Lucas smiled. 'It feels more like a celebration to me.'

They had reached the ice-skating rink at the end of the first row of market stalls and they sat on a bench to eat doughnut holes and watch the ice skaters. Lily leant on the railing, leaving Jess and Lucas free to talk. Jess sat at one end of the bench, which was a long bench with plenty of room, but Lucas chose to sit right next to her.

'What has Lily asked Santa for?'

'It's the same thing every year, a baby sister.'

'I take it from your tone you have no plans to give her what she wants.' He was smiling.

Jess shook her head. 'I'm not doing that again. Not on my own.'

Lily came back to Jess and handed her the empty doughnut bag. 'Can we go ice skating?' she asked.

'I guess so.' Jess knew it was only a few dollars to hire the skates.

'I might have to sit this one out. I'm a terrible ice skater. I'm Australian, remember, there's not much ice where I come from.'

Disappointment flowed through Jess. She hadn't stopped to think that this might be something Lucas wouldn't enjoy. But, taking a leaf out of his book, she decided persistence might pay off. 'Lily and I will help you,' she suggested. 'We can hold your hands.'

Lucas flashed his dimples at her as he grinned and said, 'There's an offer too good to refuse. Let's do it.'

He scooped Lily up and she squealed with delight as he carried her over to the hire kiosk to choose skates. It seemed his charm worked equally as well on Lily as it did on her.

Jess tied Lily's skates and then she and Lily each took one of Lucas's hands and stepped onto the ice. Lucas struggled to get the idea of gliding on the slippery surface but his innate sense of balance meant she and Lily had no trouble keeping him upright as they skated around the rink.

They'd managed to negotiate their way twice around the rink before Lily saw one of her friends from school and skated off, leaving Jess alone with Lucas.

'Did you want to keep skating?' she asked him.

'Definitely,' he replied. 'I'm not going to pass up an opportunity to have you all to myself.' He pulled his gloves off his hands and put them into his pocket. He held out his hand and Jess slipped her gloves off too and gave them to him before putting her hand in his outstretched palm. His skin was warm but Jess knew she wouldn't care how cold it got, she wasn't going to put her gloves back on.

They did a couple more laps of the rink hand in hand and then Lucas let her go.

'Are you going to try by yourself?' she asked.

'No,' he said, as he put his arm around her waist and pulled her in closer. 'I still need to lean on you.'

Jess knew that was a bad idea—he wasn't steady enough on his skates yet—but before she could protest he'd pushed off and within a few feet their skates had tangled. Lucas stumbled and grabbed the railing that ran around the edge of the rink and just managed to keep his feet, but his momentum as he tried to regain his balance spun Jess around so that she was now facing him. They leant together on the railing as Lucas straightened up.

He was laughing. 'Sorry about that,' he said. 'Actually, I'm not sorry, it's put you right where I want you.'

She was almost nose to nose with Lucas and she could feel her cheeks burning but it wasn't from the cold. It was from being so close to him. Jess lifted her chin and looked into his forget-me-not-blue eyes. She could feel his breath on her cheek. Warm and sweet, it smelt of cinnamon doughnuts. She was close enough to kiss him.

Lucas dipped his head. She knew what he was going to do. But she couldn't let him kiss her. Not here. Not yet. But she couldn't move away. She was transfixed by his eyes. She held her breath as she watched his eyes darken from blue to purple as he closed the distance.

Jess felt something tugging on her coat.

'Mummy, I feel sick.'

Jess looked down. Lily was beside her. 'Lily? What's the matter?'

'I feel sick,' she repeated.

Was she dizzy from skating? Jess wondered. She did look a bit pale. Jess let go of Lucas to put her hand on Lily's forehead. She felt warm but Jess found it hard to tell if that was just because of all the layers she was bundled up in.

'Too much sugar, probably,' Jess said. 'We'd better get you home.'

'I can't walk,' Lily grumbled.

'I'll give you a piggyback,' Lucas offered, and Jess looked at him gratefully.

Lily didn't need to be asked twice. She whipped her skates off, pulled her boots back on and wasted no time hopping onto Lucas's back, where she held on tight and buried her face in his neck as he carried her home.

'You're making a habit of getting us home safely,' Jess said, as Lucas put Lily onto the couch.

'I'm happy to be of service,' he said with a smile. 'Are you going to be all right?'

'We'll be fine. Thank you.' It wasn't quite the ending she'd pictured to the night but there wasn't anything she could do about that.

Jess was browning onions to add to the meatballs she was planning to make when there was a knock on the apartment door. 'Can you answer that, please, Lily?'

'Who is it?' she called out to Lily as she heard the door open.

'It's a Christmas tree!'

Jess wiped her hands on a tea towel and stepped out of the kitchen. A pine tree filled the doorway. 'What on earth…?'

Lucas's face appeared around the side of the tree. He was grinning at Lily. 'G'day.'

'Lucas!' Lily jumped up and down and clapped her hands as she shouted. All trace of yesterday's illness had well and truly disappeared. 'Who's the tree for?'

'You. I thought it might cheer you up if you were sick but you look like you're feeling much better.'

'I am better but, please, can I still have it? I *love* Christmas trees, they're so pretty.'

'It's not pretty yet but it will be once we decorate it.'

'That's very sweet of you,' Jess interrupted before the excitement took over completely, 'but I haven't got time to be fiddling around with a tree.'

'What's the problem?' Lucas asked, as he leant the tree against the door frame and stepped into the apartment.

He looked as disappointed as Jess knew Lily would be but as much as she would have loved to have a Christmas tree she hadn't the budget for one. She'd thought about decorating the room with a small pine bough and maybe spending an afternoon making kissing balls with Lily as a compromise, but that was as far as she'd got. 'It's always so difficult to get it secure and then in a couple of weeks I'll just have to work out how to get rid of a dead tree.'

'That's why I'm here. I will make sure it won't topple over and I promise I will dispose of it when you're ready. All you need to do is tell me where you'd like it.'

'Lucas, have a look.' Jess waved an arm around at the cramped living space. 'There's nowhere for it to go.'

'Why don't I put it in front of the balcony doors? How much time do you spend out there in this weather anyway?'

He smiled at her and Jess remembered how it had been when she'd been seventeen. She would have given him the world when he'd smiled at her. She had. And she thought she still might.

But she wasn't ready to give in just yet. 'I like to look at the village lights,' she protested.

'How about, for the next three weeks, you look at the lights on the tree instead?'

He made a fair point but she didn't have any decorations and that included lights. 'I don't—'

'Have lights,' Lucas interrupted. 'No dramas. I do. I have everything you need. Just say yes.'

Did he have everything she needed? Should she say yes? It was a tempting offer.

'Please, Mum?'

Why was she refusing? She'd dreamt of giving Lily a perfect Christmas and Lucas was here, offering to help make that happen. She'd offer him one last chance to excuse himself. 'I'm sure you've got better things to do too,' she said to Lucas.

'Nope. It's Sunday. I'm taking the day off. This'll be relaxing.'

Jess laughed. 'You think? Why don't you go out snowboarding? Wouldn't that be more fun?'

'It'll be snowing for the next four months, there's plenty of time for that. Christmas is in three weeks, which makes this a priority.'

She couldn't resist a combined assault. 'All right, if you're sure.' She gave in. 'But you and Lily will have to manage without me. I've got a mountain of mincemeat waiting to be turned into dinner.'

'No worries. We'll be right, won't we, Lily?'

Lily nodded her head eagerly.

Jess would actually have loved to help but she'd already said she didn't have time. But Lucas didn't argue—he didn't seem to mind at all, leaving Jess feeling mildly disappointed. Had he only come to see Lily?

Lucas tossed his coat onto the sofa and then Lily helped him to carry all the paraphernalia into the apartment. He'd brought everything they would need, including all the decorations Lily had bought at the market the day before plus candy canes and some of the gingerbread. The tree was only small, maybe a touch over five feet tall, and Jess had to admit it was perfect for the compact apartment.

Jess watched out of the corner of her eye, unable to resist an opportunity to watch Lucas. She forgot all about the onions on the stove as she watched his arms flex and his T-shirt strain across his shoulders as he hefted the tree inside and fitted it into the stand.

The smell of burning onions eventually returned her focus to the kitchen and she pitched the singed batch and chopped a second lot as Lucas and Lily trimmed the tree. He had even brought Christmas music—Jess could hear it playing on his phone while they worked.

'What are you listening to?' she asked.

He named a well-known Australian children's group. 'This is their Christmas album.'

'Why do you have their music?'

'I downloaded it for Lily. I thought she'd enjoy it,' he explained. 'Surely you recognise the songs, even if you're not familiar with the artists?'

'I will by the end of the afternoon,' Jess quipped. 'You seem to have it stuck on repeat.'

Lucas laughed and the sound filled the space. It was a lovely sound, better than the music, and Jess wished she could hear that whenever she liked.

'We like it, don't we, Lily?'

'Yes, it's fun.'

Jess felt even more left out as she listened to them laugh and sing along to Lucas's music. But she'd had six years of having Lily to herself. It was time Lily got to know Lucas.

But was she ready to share? What implications would

it have? He said he'd come back for her but what if he changed his mind? What if he only wanted Lily? What if he wanted to take her away? What was best for Lily? Should she turn her world upside down? Could Lucas give her things that she couldn't?

She knew he could.

He already had.

The tree was finished and Lily had switched the lights on. It looked very pretty and lifted Jess's spirits. 'Would you like to stay for dinner?' she invited Lucas. 'We're having spaghetti with meatballs.'

'I don't want to be rude but I don't eat pasta.'

'Oh.' Her heart dropped. It seemed he didn't want to spend time with her.

'Would it be all right if I just had the meatballs?'

'I don't want spaghetti either,' Lily said, but Jess wasn't all that surprised. Lucas was Lily's new idol so, of course, she'd want to imitate him. She hadn't stopped talking about him all day and it had almost been a relief when he'd arrived at their door. At least then Jess hadn't had to listen to Lily's running commentary any more, but having Lucas there in the flesh had added other frustrations. She could see him and smell his winter-fresh pine scent but she couldn't touch him.

Lucas and Lily sat opposite Jess with their bowls of meatballs sprinkled with cheese. Jess could see some similarities. Lily may look just like her but her green eyes were more changeable. Tonight, sitting next to Lucas, Jess could see that flash of forget-me-not blue in them. It was odd that she'd never noticed that before.

Looking at them sitting opposite her, Jess had an-other glimpse of what it would be like to be a family, and she wondered what Lucas would say if she told him the truth tonight.

But she couldn't tell him in front of Lily. Despite how he'd treated Lily over the past couple of days, she couldn't assume that his reaction would be positive. Being nice to an old friend's daughter was one thing, finding out he was a father might be another thing entirely. Jess couldn't risk upsetting Lily if Lucas's reaction wasn't what she hoped. This wasn't a conversation she could launch into on the spur of the moment. They needed time alone, without interruption. She needed a plan.

Perhaps she should ask Fleur if Lily could have a sleepover with Annabel. She didn't like to ask for favours but given the circumstances it was probably her best option. Either that or get Kristie to come up to the resort to babysit. Kristie had been right. Lucas deserved to know the truth.

Christmas was fast approaching and Lily's calendar was chock-full of activities, far more so than Jess's was. In the past week alone she'd had the Christmas cookie swap, a Christmas lunch, yesterday had been Annabel's birthday party and tonight she was supposed to be going back to Annabel's for a sleepover, but right now it didn't look as though that was going to happen.

Lily had started vomiting after the party and fifteen hours later she hadn't stopped and Jess was beginning to worry. She called the clinic for advice as she spooned ice chips into Lily's mouth. She tried to think what she would advise a stressed parent in this situation if she was the nurse who took the call, but sleep deprivation and worry made it difficult to think clearly.

Donna answered the clinic phone and put her straight through to Cameron.

Jess explained the situation and Lily's symptoms. 'She's been vomiting since four o'clock yesterday, she's complaining of abdominal pain—that's not unusual but she's extremely lethargic.'

'Do you think it could be her appendix?'

Jess had thought about that but Lily's symptoms didn't fit and she'd just assumed it was a usual childhood stomach ache, which Lily seemed to get plenty of, but what if it was more serious than that?

'I've checked but what if I've missed something?'

'I'll come over as soon as I can.'

Jess sat with Lily and fretted while she waited for Cameron. This was one of the things she hated about being a single parent. There was no one to share the worry with.

'Has she had a temperature overnight?' Cameron asked when he arrived.

'No.'

'No, not now or, no, not at any stage?' Cameron clarified.

'Not at any point.'

'Any urine output in the last four to six hours?'

'No.'

'When was her last bowel movement?'

'Yesterday?' Jess wasn't one hundred per cent sure.

Cameron examined Lily and checked for signs of appendicitis. 'I agree with you. I don't think it's her appendix. How quickly did she get sick after the party?'

'Pretty quick. A couple of hours.'

'Too soon for it to be food poisoning. And no one else has had any gastro?'

Jess shook her head. She'd spoken to Fleur and between the two of them they'd rung and checked with the other parents.

Cameron motioned for Jess to follow him out of the bedroom. 'I think it would be best to take her down to the hospital. They should run some tests. She could have a bowel obstruction but she'll need an X-ray to check that out.'

'A bowel obstruction!' That was not good news.

'It's one possibility and I think it should be investigated. The hospital will be able to run blood tests and get the results faster than I can up here on the mountain. I can treat her for dehydration but that's treating the symptoms, not the cause. Would you like Ellen to drive you? She's not working today.'

'Thanks, but I'll call a friend.' Jess didn't want to impose on Cameron or his wife any more than necessary. She had made plans to have dinner with Lucas tonight and it looked like she was going to have to call him to cancel but she hoped he would offer to drive them down the mountain. 'If he can't take us, I'll call Ellen.'

'All right, I'll let the hospital know to expect you.'

Just as she'd hoped, Lucas offered to drive them. She'd rather he was with her than Ellen. They were both busy and probably neither had the time to spend being her taxi service but Lucas had more invested in Lily—he just didn't know it yet.

Lily didn't vomit at all on the hour-long trip to the hospital, which Jess was grateful for. Lucas dropped them at the entrance to the emergency department and went to park the car. The hospital was small. At the bottom of the mountain it was still more than an hour out of Vancouver, but it did have modern facilities. Jess carried Lily inside and walked straight up to the desk.

'This is Lily Johnson. Dr Cameron Baker was calling ahead for us.'

The nurse on duty took them straight into a partitioned cubicle. There wasn't a lot of privacy but Jess knew most patients in an emergency department had bigger priorities than to be fussing about privacy. Jess ran through all Lily's symptoms with the nurse while she took Lily's obs and then listened as the nurse repeated them to the doctor, who had introduced himself as Peter Davis.

'This is Lily. Age six, weight sixteen kilograms. She has been vomiting since yesterday afternoon but nothing for the past two hours. Complaining of stomach pains. Afebrile. BP normal. No diarrhoea.'

'Current temperature?'

'Thirty-seven point two.'

'No allergies?' He looked at Jess.

'No,' she replied.

'What has she eaten?'

'Nothing since yesterday afternoon.'

'What did she eat yesterday?'

'I don't really know. She went to a party but none of the other children are sick, I checked.' Jess knew the doctor was thinking about food poisoning as one option.

'Has there been any gastro at the school?'

'No. Nothing.'

'No major illnesses? No surgeries?'

Jess shook her head again.

'Any episodes of rumbling appendix?' Peter continued to question her.

'No, and her GP didn't seem to think it was her ap-

pendix. He thought she could have a bowel obstruction.'
Jess was getting distressed. She didn't want to tell the
doctor what to look for—she knew there was a routine,
she knew he would want to eliminate more common
possibilities first, and there was no need to run unnecessary tests if Lily's problem was something simple, but
she wanted to make sure he didn't miss anything or ignore something more significant. A bowel obstruction
could be nasty and Jess really hoped it wasn't the case
but nothing else seemed to fit.

'No diarrhoea, you said?' he asked as he conducted
the rebound test, checking for appendicitis.

'No.'

'Can you cough for me, Lily?'

Lily coughed obediently and didn't show any signs
of discomfort.

'Is there any past history of recurrent diarrhoea or
blood in her stools?'

'No.'

'I'll run a drip to counteract her dehydration and
organise an abdominal X-ray. See if that can shed any
light on the situation.'

Jess held Lily's hand as the nurse inserted a canula
and connected a drip. Lily was very flat but that might
have been related to lack of sleep. Jess wasn't feeling
so bright herself.

The nurse fixed a drip stand to a wheelchair and
helped Lily into the seat, explaining she would take her
over to the radiology department. Jess walked beside the
wheelchair and tried to keep a positive frame of mind,
but it was difficult when she could see Lily so pale and
quiet, with needles and tubes sticking out of her.

Jess waited as the X-ray was taken. Then she waited for the result.

'The X-ray was inconclusive,' Dr Davis told her. 'We'll do a CT scan next but I'm not sure we're looking in the right place.'

'What do you mean?' Jess was confused.

'Her pain has eased considerably and she's stopped vomiting. I don't think it's all as a result of the medication. I think she may have purged her system of whatever was upsetting her. Has she *ever* had any allergy testing done?'

Jess shook her head.

'Is there any family history of allergies or gastrointestinal problems?'

'She's a fussy eater with the usual childhood stomach aches but no allergies that I know of.'

'Any auto-immune deficiencies?'

'Not on my side, but I'm not sure about her father's side.' It was obvious that the tests weren't giving the doctor the answers he was expecting but Jess didn't have any other answers for him. She would have to talk to Lucas. She had to know what was wrong with Lily and Lucas could hold the key. 'I'll see what I can find out,' she said.

Knowing Lily wouldn't be able to see her while she was in the CT scanner, Jess returned to the waiting room to see if Lucas had appeared. She needed to find him. She needed answers. The time had come. She had secrets that needed to be told.

He was in the waiting room when she returned. He stood up when she walked in and came towards her with his arms open. She stepped into his embrace.

'How're you doing?' he asked. 'How's Lily? Do they know what's wrong?'

'They're still not sure. The doctor was thinking appendicitis or a small bowel obstruction but the X-ray was inconclusive. They're doing a CT scan now but the doctor seems to be leaning towards an allergy of some sort. He was asking about her family history but, of course, I only know half of the answers.'

'Well, there's not much you can do about that,' Lucas said, 'unless you can track down Lily's father.'

Jess took a deep breath. The time had come. 'I have,' she told him.

'What? Have you spoken to him?'

'Yes and no. Will you come outside with me? I need some fresh air.' She knew she had some explaining to do but she wasn't about to go into the details in the middle of the emergency department. Jess stepped out through the automatic sliding door. There was a bench just outside. She sat and waited until Lucas was sitting beside her.

It was time.

'I know where Lily's father is,' she said. She took another deep breath. 'It's you. You're her father.'

CHAPTER NINE

'WHAT?' LUCAS SHOT straight back up off the bench as if it was electrified. 'What the hell are you saying?'

'Lily is your daughter.'

'What? No. She can't be.'

Jess nodded. 'You're her father.'

'She's mine?' He shook his head in disbelief. 'I have a daughter?'

Lucas paced backwards and forwards in front of the bench while Jess waited nervously. What was going through his head?

He stopped and looked at her, a puzzled expression in his forget-me-not-blue eyes. 'You're sure about this?'

'Of course I'm sure.'

'But why haven't you told me?' Lucas stood in front of her, rooted to the spot. He ran his hands through his hair and stared at her with a fixed, unseeing expression. 'How could you keep this from me? *Why* would you keep this from me?'

'I'm sorry.'

'What for?' He was looking at her now, his blue eyes boring into her as if he was searching for any more secrets she had yet to divulge. 'For telling me? For not telling me? For keeping her a secret? Which one of those things are you apologising for?'

Jess felt ill. She swallowed nervously and she could taste bile in her throat. 'I'm sorry for telling you the way I did. I didn't mean to blurt it out like that.'

'How could you have kept this a secret?'

'I didn't mean to. I tried to find you.'

'When?'

'When I found out I was pregnant. Kristie and I hired a private investigator but after a month the PI told us we were wasting our time. Do you know how many Lucas Whites there are in Australia? And not one of them was you.'

'When was this?'

'It was April. The ski season was over, the resort had closed for the summer and you would have been home in Australia.'

Lucas's legs folded and he sat back down on the bench. His face was pale. He looked ill. 'I…'

'What is it? Are you okay?' Jess asked.

He looked up at her and she could see dismay in his blue eyes. 'April?'

Jess nodded.

'I wasn't in Australia then,' he said.

'What? I thought you were going back to university?'

Lucas was shaking his head. 'That was my plan. But my plans changed. I went home but I couldn't settle into uni. The father of one of my mates offered me a job in his new hotel and I jumped at the chance. It was a fantastic opportunity, I was going to get to do everything from housekeeping to bartending to running the activities desk and administration, so I took a year off uni. That April, I was in Indonesia.'

'I was looking in the wrong place.' Jess sat on the bench beside him. She was close to tears. All that time spent searching for Lucas, only to find now that she'd been looking in the wrong haystack.

'I'm sorry, JJ. I should have written like I'd planned to, but I thought I had time. I hadn't expected consequences.'

'Neither of us did, I guess,' she sighed. 'But I had to deal with the consequences and I've done the best I could.'

'But what about more recently? Did you look for me again?'

'Of course. I was eighteen, pregnant and alone—do you think I wanted to do this by myself? I searched again when Lily was born but I was still concentrating on Australia and the harder I looked without success the more I believed you didn't want to be found. My father told me you wouldn't want a baby, that you wouldn't want to become a father with a girl you barely knew, and I didn't want to believe him but in the end I didn't have a choice. I couldn't find you.'

'Lily is my daughter.' Lucas stood up and Jess could see him physically and mentally settling himself. He straightened his back and squared his shoulders and focused his forget-me-not-blue eyes on her. 'I need to speak to the doctor.'

'What for?'

'You said he was asking about allergies and family history. We need to tell him to test Lily for celiac disease.'

'What? Why?'

'I'm a celiac and if I really *am* her father then there's a good possibility she has it too.'

'Lucas...' Jess was about to say 'Trust me' but she decided that was a poor choice of phrase. 'Believe me, you're her father.'

'You said Lily had a lot of parties last week. If she has celiac disease and she's overloaded on gluten, that could explain the vomiting. We need to let the doctor know. He needs to run tests.'

'What sort of tests?' Jess felt she should know the answers but it was strange how everything she'd ever learnt seemed to have vanished from her head. Right now she was a patient's mother, not a nurse, and her head was filled with thoughts of Lily and Lucas. There was no room in it for facts about a disease she'd never had to deal with. A disease that quite possibly her daughter had inherited from her father.

Jess needed to focus. Lily was the priority here; she'd have to sort through all the other issues later, when her head had cleared and the dust had settled.

'I think it's just a blood test initially,' Lucas was saying. 'It's been fifteen years since I was diagnosed. We'll have to speak to the doctor.'

He headed back into the hospital with Jess at his heels. Dr Davis was standing beside the triage desk.

'Do you have the CT results?' Jess asked.

He nodded. 'There was no sign of a blockage on the CT scan either.'

'We'd like you to test Lily for celiac disease,' Lucas said.

'Why?' he asked Jess. It was his turn to be puzzled now.

'Apparently her father has celiac disease,' Jess replied.

Dr Davis frowned. 'And you didn't think to tell me?'

'I didn't know.'

'Lily is my daughter,' Lucas interrupted, 'and I have celiac disease.'

'She's never been tested?' Dr Davis asked.

'We were estranged,' Jess said.

At the same time Lucas said, 'I didn't know I had a daughter.'

Neither of the answers made things any clearer for the doctor.

'Look, that's all irrelevant,' Lucas continued. 'The bottom line is I have celiac disease, Lily is my daughter and her symptoms sound consistent with celiac disease. Even if she was asymptomatic, there's a high possibility she has it too. We'd like her tested.'

Dr Davis was nodding now. They'd managed to get his attention but if Jess thought she was going to be the one in control she was mistaken. Lucas was used to being in charge; she'd forgotten how much he relished it and he didn't mince his words with the doctor. He'd become like a wild animal protecting his offspring and nothing was going to stop him from getting what he wanted for Lily. Not this doctor and certainly not her.

If Lucas thought there was a strong chance that Lily had celiac disease they needed to find out for sure, but listening to him now and looking at his body language she knew that if she thought he would bow out of their lives, out of Lily's life, without a whimper, she was mistaken. She knew he would want to be involved, she knew he would fight for Lily, but where would that leave her?

'A blood test isn't conclusive. There are other digestive diseases with similar presentations,' the doctor explained.

'I know that but it's a start,' Lucas replied.

'What do you test for?' Jess asked.

'The best test is the tTG-IgA test. It's the most sensitive and is positive in about ninety-eight per cent of patients with celiac disease.'

'Positive for what?'

'Tissue transglutaminase antibodies. They'll be present if the celiac patient has a diet that contains gluten. But if they've already been avoiding gluten you may get a false negative. Does Lily eat food that contains gluten?'

Jess nodded.

'The result might still depend on whether or not she eats *enough* gluten.'

'It's our best chance,' Lucas insisted. 'Can you run the test?'

'I can order it but I'm also going to admit her overnight. I want to keep her here while we run the tests. If it turns out to be appendicitis or a bowel blockage, she's better off here. I'll go and make the arrangements.'

'Now what?' Jess asked Lucas, as they watched the departing figure of the doctor.

'We wait. The important thing is finding out what's wrong with Lily. Celiac disease isn't life-threatening but if left untreated or undiagnosed it can cause irreversible damage to her small intestine. You know that—you're a nurse. If that's all it is it can be controlled by diet. Just cut out gluten. It's much easier to manage now than it was years ago. The important thing is to get it diagnosed.' He ran his hands through his hair, making it more tousled than it normally was. He sighed and shook his head. 'I'm going to wait outside. Come and get me if there's any news.'

That didn't sound like he wanted company.

He headed for the exit and Jess waited inside. Alone. And wondered if she'd done the right thing. But she'd done what she'd had to for Lily's sake.

Lily was brought back from the radiology department and Jess sat with her as the nursing staff got her settled into a ward bed. Her blood was taken and a sedative was added to her drip and Jess stayed with her until she fell asleep.

Lily hadn't vomited since they'd arrived at the hospital and Jess would have been happy to take her home. She would have gladly put all this behind them but the doctor's reasons for admitting Lily were valid ones. She would stay at the hospital for as long as it took to diagnose Lily's problem. But what about Lucas? Had he waited? Was he still in the hospital or had he got out while he still could? She couldn't have blamed him, her announcement must have come as quite a shock. She should have broken the news differently.

She owed him an apology.

She found him sitting on a bench outside the emergency department with his head in his hands. He lifted his head as she sat beside him but he didn't look at her. He ran his hands through his hair as he stretched his legs out, before tipping his head back and resting it against the wall. He was casually dressed in jeans and lace-up workman's boots with a T-shirt under his coat. His hair was tousled but his infectious grin was missing. What had she done?

He sighed and finally looked at her. His forget-me-not-blue eyes were dark purple. He looked exhausted. 'You should have told me.'

'I know.'

'I understand you couldn't find me but for the past two weeks I've been right here. You've had plenty of opportunity to say something and you still chose not to. Why? Why would you continue to keep this a secret? Did you not think I deserved to know I had a child?'

'I was waiting for the right time. I didn't know what you'd think. I needed to find out what kind of person you had become. I didn't know if you wanted to be a father. If you didn't want Lily then she would be better off never knowing about you. Better that than for her to know that her father didn't want her.'

'Of course I would want her. How could you think otherwise?'

'You don't miss what you've never had. She might not matter to you.'

'How can you say that? Of course she matters, and think of all the things I've missed. I missed her being born, I missed her starting school, losing her first tooth, taking her first step, saying her first word. My God, JJ, I don't even know when her birthday is.' He listed all the milestones that Jess had witnessed. She hadn't taken them for granted but she had revelled in them.

'Her birthday is September thirteenth.'

He ignored her olive branch. 'And what about Lily?' he continued, as if she hadn't spoken. 'You thought I wouldn't miss her but what about her? Do you think she doesn't miss having a father?'

Jess had felt the absence on Lily's behalf and Lily herself commented when she saw her friends' families. But did she really know what she was missing? Jess suspected she did—Lily knew what other people's fathers were like. She just didn't know her own.

He had made a good point.

'Yes, she misses it,' she admitted. 'She would love to have a father. She would love you.' Jess could feel tears of regret welling in her eyes but she tried to fight them back. She didn't want to turn on the waterworks, she didn't want Lucas to think she was looking for sympathy—she didn't deserve sympathy. But she did hope to make him understand. She was scared that if he didn't understand he was going to hate her, and how would she live with that?

'And when she asked about her father? What were you planning on telling her?'

'I hadn't worked that out yet. I didn't think we'd ever see you again.' Jess's voice was quiet. There were so many things she'd refused to think about. So many things she'd just tried to ignore. It looked like those days were over now.

'Did you think you were the only one who could love her?'

Jess shook her head. 'No.' *But I was worried you wouldn't love me.*

'I thought I knew you, JJ. I came back here to prove myself to you but I wasn't prepared for this.'

'What are you going to do?'

'I don't know but I want to see Lily.'

'What are you going to say?' Jess was worried. Was she about to lose everything?

'Nothing yet,' he said as he stood up. 'I'm not an idiot. This is a shock for me, it's going to be a shock for her too. I just want to see my daughter. Is that too much to ask?'

Jess shook her head and walked with him to the ward. She hesitated outside the door to Lily's room.

'Aren't you coming in?' Lucas asked.

'I wasn't sure whether you wanted me to.'

'Lily might think it's odd if she wakes up to find me by her bed. You're the one she'll be looking for.'

Lily was still asleep. Lucas stood by her bed. He didn't speak, just stood and watched her. Jess knew that feeling. She used to spend hours just watching Lily sleep when she'd been a baby. She looked like a little angel.

She stirred and murmured. She opened her eyes and recognised Jess but didn't wake fully. 'I need Ozzie,' she said.

Jess pulled the little grey koala with white-tipped ears and a shiny black nose out of her handbag and tucked it under Lily's arm. Lily never liked sleeping without Ozzie. She hugged the soft toy into her chest and closed her eyes again.

'Is that…?' Lucas spoke.

Jess nodded. It was the koala he'd given her for her eighteenth birthday seven years ago.

'You've kept it?'

'It was all I had of you.' Jess could hear the catch in her throat. The little koala had been the cutest thing she'd ever seen, aside from Lucas, and it had become her most treasured possession throughout her pregnancy, and now it was Lily's.

'Does Lily know where you got it?'

'No.' Jess shook her head and turned as she heard the door open.

Dr Davis stepped into the room and he held a piece of paper in his hand. 'I have the blood-test results,' he told them. 'Lily has tested positive for TTG antibodies and the test also showed elevated antigliadin antibodies.

'What does that mean?'

'It means Lily *could* have celiac disease.'

'Could?'

'The blood test isn't definitive,' he reminded her.

'So what do we do now?'

'You can take her home once this drip has run through, provided she has something to eat and keeps it down.'

'She doesn't need to stay overnight?'

'No. With her history and the blood test and scan results I think a bowel obstruction is unlikely so provided she eats, doesn't vomit and can urinate, you can take her home. But she will need an endoscopy and biopsy of her small intestine in order to confirm the diagnosis.'

'A biopsy? What for?'

'To look for inflammation of the intestinal lining and changes to the villi. That's a more definitive indication of celiac disease. Lily will need to see a specialist for the endoscopy. It will be done under a GA. I'll organise a referral. Has she seen a gastroenterologist in the past?'

Jess shook her head. 'No.'

'Who would you recommend?' Lucas asked. 'Who is the best paediatric gastroenterologist in Vancouver?'

'Stuart Johnson.'

Jess had known that would be the answer. 'Is there anyone else?' she asked.

'Of course,' Dr Davis replied, 'but you asked who the best is and in my opinion Dr Johnson is. But I can give you some other names if you prefer.'

Lucas jumped in before Jess could protest any further. 'He will be fine. We'll take that referral.'

'Okay. Do you have any other questions? I'm not an expert but at this stage I wouldn't panic. It looks like celiac disease may be the problem and if that's the case it's one of the easier gastrointestinal problems to control. Just make sure you keep Lily eating some gluten. If you stop before she sees the specialist they may not be able to make an accurate diagnosis. If she has a diet that is already low in gluten we could see a false negative. The recommendation is that she should continue to eat two slices of bread, or the equivalent amount of gluten, per day.'

Lucas waited until the doctor had left the room before he turned to Jess. She knew what he was about to say.

'What is the matter with Stuart Johnson?' he asked. 'Do you know him? Is he a relative? What's wrong with him?'

'He's my father.'

'Your father! Your father is a gastroenterologist?'

'Yes.'

'And he's the top dog?'

'What's going on, JJ? If your father is the best in his field, why did you ask for a different referral? Why don't you want to take Lily to him?'

Jess had managed to delay the discussion until Lily had been discharged and they were in Lucas's car on the way home. Lily seemed to have fully recovered from whatever it was that had upset her. There was no trace of the vomiting, she'd had a good sleep and appeared to have no lingering ill-effects. Jess, on the other hand, was exhausted, physically and emotionally, but she knew Lucas wasn't going to let matters lie.

Lily was cuddling Ozzie while she listened to Lucas's Christmas music through the headphones on his cell phone when he raised the subject again, and Jess figured she might as well get the conversation over with while Lily was out of earshot and otherwise occupied. Maybe it would be easier if Lucas was concentrating on driving and couldn't interrogate her or pin her down with eye contact. 'What do you remember about my father?' she asked.

'That's a loaded question. The only time I came across him was on your birthday when he called me all sorts of colourful names and threw me out. You probably don't want to know my impressions of him as a person.'

'And you're asking why I don't want him to be Lily's specialist?'

'If he's the best in the business then I assume his behaviour that night isn't a reflection on his skills as a doctor. I'm prepared to separate the two. If he's the best I want him to see Lily.'

'My father and I aren't in contact any more.'

'What?' Lucas slowed the car as he took his eyes off the road and looked at her. 'At all?'

Jess shook her head.

'Since when?'

'Since Lily was born. I haven't seen him for six years. He's never met Lily.'

Lucas flicked his gaze back to her a second time. 'If we are going to have any chance of working things out between us, for Lily's sake, we need to operate on a policy of full disclosure. No more secrets. I think it's time you told me everything.' His hands were tight on the steering-wheel and Jess could hear in his voice the effort he was making to stay calm.

She took a deep breath and said, 'Remember I told you how Stephen's death shaped us into the family we became? How I was protected, supervised, guarded almost, from that day on? I went to school, I spent time with Kristie and we came up here as a family. I went to parties but only if Dad had thoroughly researched the event. I understood his reasons—he was determined to do everything he could to keep me safe—and it didn't really bother me until I met you.

'That was when I finally understood Kristie's point of view when it came to boys. For the first time I was prepared to disregard my parents' wishes. For the first time I was prepared to take risks, to ignore their rules, to lie to them or to my aunt and uncle. I couldn't resist you and I couldn't forgive my father for dragging me away from you, for separating us. You were my first love. I couldn't resist you and I gave you everything. My heart and my soul.'

'You gave me everything except for our child,' Lucas said, as he glanced in the rear-vision mirror.

Jess clenched her hands in her lap as she willed herself not to cry. Lucas's words were like a sledgehammer against her already brittle heart and she could feel how close it was to shattering. She had done her best but it didn't seem as though he was prepared to believe that. Maybe, given time, he would trust her again. She'd never deliberately kept Lily from him and maybe one day he would realise that.

She checked back over her shoulder to where Lily lay with her eyes closed. She was either sleeping or listening to music but either way she wasn't paying them any attention. Jess needed Lucas to understand what had happened. She needed to try to explain.

'That's not fair. I told you I tried to find you. If my father had had his way you wouldn't have Lily now either. She is the reason I haven't seen him for six years.'

'Lily is?'

Jess nodded. 'My relationship with Dad had been strained ever since we left Moose River. He was still furious that I'd lied to my aunt and uncle and that I hadn't followed the rules, and finding out I was pregnant was the icing on the cake. I thought that maybe it would be good news, maybe it would help to ease the pain of Stephen's loss, but Dad was convinced it was going to ruin my life. He didn't want me to keep the baby and, as I've explained, he convinced me that you wouldn't want to be a father. He used the argument that you'd never tried to contact me. He was quite persuasive and I even started to question whether you'd given me your real name.'

'Of course I had.'

'I know that now but you have to understand that I was only eighteen and not a very mature eighteen. I was naive and uncertain and scared, and Dad's argument was quite convincing.'

'What did he want you to do? Did he want you to terminate the pregnancy?'

'No! He would never have asked me to do that. We may have had our differences of opinion on lots of things but that wasn't one of them. After losing a child of his own, he wouldn't have wanted me to terminate a pregnancy. He wanted me to give the baby up for adoption.'

'But why?

'He was worried that I was too young. That having a baby at the age of eighteen would ruin my life, my plans for the future. He tried to convince me that there were other options, that I didn't have to be a single mother. Obviously, I refused to give her up. I hadn't planned on getting pregnant but I had a baby growing inside me and it was my job to protect her. Plus she was yours— I couldn't give her up.

'So I decided to keep the baby and prove to my father that I could manage on my own, that I didn't need his help. I was going to prove I could handle the consequences. It was stupid really. I had no idea about anything but I resented my father for taking me away from you and I wasn't going to let him take my baby as well. So I sacrificed the bond I had with my father for the love I felt for Lily. I told my father I was keeping the baby and if he thought I was making a mistake then I would do it on my own and he need have nothing to do with me or his grandchild.'

'Was it a mistake?'

'I certainly hadn't planned on getting pregnant but being with you wasn't a mistake. And Lily isn't a mistake.' Jess glanced back again at her sleeping daughter. Their daughter. Lily was perfect and Jess had never regretted her decision. 'I was a naive teenager with no clue but a massive stubborn streak. It hasn't been easy but I don't regret it.'

'I'm sorry, JJ. It's been tough on you and I'm sorry to have to ask you this, but don't you think it's time you swallowed your pride and moderated your stubborn streak? Don't you think you should try to sort things out with your father? For Lily's sake?'

Jess shook her head. 'No. Too much has happened. I'm not sure I can go back.' Her entire life had changed and all the decisions she'd made, for the right or wrong reasons, had brought her to where she was now. She didn't think her decisions could be reversed that easily. She didn't know if she could do it. 'Couldn't we just ask for a couple of other names? It would be a lot easier.'

'But your father is the best. You're telling me you don't want your daughter, our daughter, to have the best medical attention we can give her? Because I sure as hell do.'

'Let me make some calls,' Jess begged, as Lucas indicated and turned the car onto Moose River Road.

'Let me see what other specialists I can come up with. Please? Just give me twenty-four hours.'

'I'll do you a deal. I'd like to spend some time with Lily so assuming she's feeling okay tomorrow I will pick her up in the morning and she and I can do something together while you sort out a specialist. We both have some decisions to make.'

Jess was worried. Was this going to be the beginning of deals and bargaining? Was Lily's time now up for negotiation? But she couldn't refuse his request. Not if she wanted to win the argument over the specialist.

Lucas parked his SUV in front of the Moose River Apartments. He carried a drowsy Lily inside for Jess but he didn't stay. He didn't stop under the mistletoe and he didn't speak to Jess again. It was as if he didn't even notice she was there.

Whatever Jess had dreamt of having was surely gone. She wasn't going to get the fairy-tale ending. They weren't going to be the perfect family on a Christmas card. She'd be lucky if she was left with anything at all.

But was that just what she deserved?

CHAPTER TEN

'HOW DID YOU GET ON?'

Lucas spoke to Jess as she walked into the stables behind the lodge but there was no 'Good morning'. No 'How are you?' There were obviously more important things on his mind.

Lily had spent the morning with Lucas while Jess was supposed to be organising a specialist appointment. Lily had chosen to groom Banjo and she barely looked up when Jess arrived. It was obvious that Lily had enjoyed the morning far more than Jess had. She seemed quite content with Lucas's company and Jess knew Lily was smitten with him. Why wouldn't she be? He had that same effect on her. Did neither of them need her? Would they be just as happy with each other? Without her?

Everything was changing and Jess was worried.

Jess shook her head in response to Lucas's question as she tried to stem the rising fear in her belly.

'Lily, why don't you finish up with Banjo and then François can bring you to the restaurant for a hot chocolate when you're all done? Your mum and I have some things we need to talk about.'

'Okay,' Lily said. She barely looked up, content just to be with Banjo.

'Have you made a specialist appointment?' Lucas asked as they left the stable to return to the lodge.

Jess had spoken to Cameron but she'd got nowhere with alternative options. She shook her head. 'I couldn't get anything until well into the New Year,' she admitted. 'The doctors Cameron could call in favours from are both on holidays and Lily's condition isn't considered serious so no one else would squeeze her in.'

'I'm sure your father would see her earlier,' Lucas argued. 'I understand your history with your father—you were eighteen and on your own—but I'm here now and if you think I'm not going to be an active part of Lily's life you're mistaken. One way or another I will make sure she gets a diagnosis and the treatment she needs. If she is a celiac then staying on a gluten diet could be doing her more damage. If she is a celiac she'll feel a whole lot better once gluten is eliminated from her diet and we can't do that until she's had the biopsy. We already have a referral to your father,' he continued. 'If you prefer I'll take Lily. You don't need to come. You owe me this much.'

Jess shook her head. She'd already come to the same conclusion. She didn't want Lily to suffer any more than necessary. She knew what she had to do. 'I know she needs the appointment. I'll make the call but I'll take her. Lily is my daughter. She'll need me there.'

'She is also my daughter and that is something else I wanted to speak to you about. When are we going to tell her the truth?'

'Can it wait until the holidays? There's a lot for her

to digest and I think it will be better if she has time to think about it.' Jess honestly felt it would be better to wait a little longer but she also didn't want to deal with the repercussions.

'I'll wait,' Lucas agreed. 'But only until the end of the school term. She finishes on Friday, right?'

Jess nodded.

'I'll take you both to dinner on Friday night, then,' he said, as he held the door for her to step into the lobby. 'We can speak to her together. I'd like to be able to tell my parents about her before Christmas. I was planning on going back to Australia at the end of the ski season and I would like to take Lily too.'

Jess stopped dead in her tracks. He wanted to take Lily!

Black spots danced in front of her eyes and she thought she might either faint or throw up but if she couldn't stand the idea of giving her baby up at birth there was no way she was going to give her up now after six years of being her mother. She might not be able to deny him but she wasn't going to give up without a fight. She stood up as tall as possible and willed her vision to clear. She clenched her fists and tightened her thigh muscles as she tried to stop her knees from shaking. 'No.'

Lucas was frowning. 'What do you mean, "No"?'

'I left Moose River seven years ago, heartbroken and pregnant. Lily was all I had left.' Her voice was quiet but firm. 'I'm sorry I couldn't find you. I'm sorry I didn't try again. I'm sorry that you never posted me those letters and I'm sorry that you've missed six years of her life. I was foolish and I'm sorry but I'm not going to let you take her away from me. I've lost my brother and my mother and my father. Lily is all I have left. I won't let you take her from me.'

'I don't think you were foolish.'

'You don't?' After everything she'd admitted to he wasn't going to crucify her?

'No.' He shook his head. 'I've never said that.' He put his hand on her elbow and guided her to one of the soft leather couches in the lobby. He sat beside her and put his hand on her knee and only then did Jess stop shaking.

'You've made it this far on your own and from what I can see you've done a great job with Lily. She's a great kid and she's lucky enough to have a mother who loves her. I admit I wish I'd known about her before now but I know I have to take some of the blame for that. And I don't intend to take Lily away from you. I'd like to take her to Australia—she's got a whole family over there who would love to meet her—but I'm only talking about going for a holiday. My life is here now. My business is here and my daughter is here. I'm not going to abandon her and I would never take her from you. I assumed you would come with us.'

'Really?' Relief flooded through Jess and she thought she might burst into tears. Her emotions had been running high for days and being close to tears was almost becoming a permanent state for her. 'Even after everything I've done?'

'What's done is done, JJ,' he replied. 'We can't undo the past. We need to move on and Lily has to be our priority. She's the important one. We need to do what's best for her. We need to make sure she feels loved and secure and we need to sort out her health. So will you make an appointment to take Lily to see your father?'

'Yes.' She had no choice. She owed it to Lily and to Lucas. She would have to mend the relationship with her father. After seven years of making all her own decisions it seemed as though her time was up. Fate, or maybe Lucas, was taking over.

Jess was sweating as she picked up the phone and dialled her father's office number. She had never forgotten it, even after all these years. She just hoped he still had the same secretary. How would she explain her request if her father's admin staff had changed?

She'd delayed phoning her father's office until this morning. She'd spent last night trying to work out how to word her request. It seemed strange to be calling to ask for a favour from her father when she hadn't spoken to him in over six years. But it looked like it was time for Jess to be the bigger person and put her stubborn streak to one side, as Lucas had suggested.

She sighed with relief when Gabrielle answered. Jess launched into the speech she'd rehearsed before she could chicken out and she had just hung up the phone when there was a knock on her door. It opened and Cameron stepped in to her clinic room.

'Jess, has Lily gone on the school excursion to go dog sledding?'

What a strange question. Jess frowned and nodded.

'I don't want you to panic, everyone is okay at this stage, but there's been an accident.'

You couldn't tell someone not to panic right before delivering that sort of news. Jess shot out of her seat. 'What is it? What's happened?'

'There's been an accident on one of the chairlifts.'

Jess's hand flew to her mouth as her heart plummeted in her chest. *'Lily.'*

'The children are all okay at this stage but the lift has stopped working and there are people trapped in the cars. I thought you might want to go up the mountain. I'm sure the authorities will contact everyone but I wanted you to know.'

Jess changed her shoes and grabbed her coat. She didn't need to be asked twice.

She raced out of the building and collided with Lucas.

'What are you doing here?' She looked up at him as his arms went around her to steady her. One look at his face told her that he'd heard about the accident too. Of course, he was part of the search and rescue unit.

'What have you heard?' she asked.

'Not a lot at this stage except that no one seems to be injured yet and that a group of six- and seven-year-olds are involved. I thought that might mean Lily. But no one will notify me because I'm not her next of kin. I didn't know if you would call me so I came to you.'

'Have you been called in to the rescue?'

He shook his head and let her go. 'No, this is a mission for the trained team. I came to find out if Lily was in the gondola and to take you up the mountain.' He gestured to his left where a snowmobile was parked at the bottom of the steps. 'It'll be faster than taking the chair lift to the basin and then walking.'

She didn't waste time arguing. She pulled a knitted cap from her pocket and tugged it onto her head as Lucas handed her a pair of snow goggles. She followed him down the steps and climbed onto the snowmobile behind him. She tucked herself against his back and wrapped her arms around his waist. He was solid and muscular. He felt safe. Maybe he really was her knight in shining armour after all.

There was no denying he was a good man. Maybe they would be okay. She and Lucas would work things out. She'd make sure of it. For Lily's sake.

After several minutes Jess felt the snowmobile slow and knew they'd reached the basin. She peered around Lucas's shoulder and saw a group of people, parents of children in Lily's class, gathered around the base of one of the gondola pylons.

Lucas switched off the engine. The lift was motionless and the silence was eerie. Jess had expected noise and activity but everyone seemed to be standing around. Immobile. Uncertain.

They dismounted and Jess removed her goggles. She needed a clearer picture.

They were close to the edge of a gully. The gondola cable stretched across the ravine and Jess's eye was drawn to where it dipped lower. She could see what looked like two cars close together. Weren't they normally further apart than that? Or was she just looking at it from a funny angle?

'What's going on? Why isn't anything happening?' she asked Lucas.

'I'm not sure. I'll go and find out.'

He was back within minutes, bringing Fleur and her husband, Nathan, with him. Fleur's eyes were puffy and her nose was red but she wasn't crying at the moment. Jess hugged her tightly. 'Where are the girls?' she asked.

Fleur pointed down into the ravine to where it looked as though two cars had collided. 'They're in one of those cars.'

'Oh, no!'

'The girls are okay, JJ,' Lucas told her. 'There's a teacher in the gondola with them and she is in contact via her cell phone. No one is badly injured. The second car hasn't come loose but access is difficult.'

Jess released Fleur and turned to Lucas. 'When will they get them out?'

'It's going to take time. It's complicated. No one is getting out of any of the cars until the rescue team are certain that it is safe to do so. They're worried that emptying or moving the cars that haven't been involved in the derailment may cause the unstable cars to fall.'

'They could fall?' Jess clutched Lucas's arm.

'At the moment they think the cars are stable.'

'At the moment! I don't understand how this could happen. How is something like this even possible?'

'Apparently the emergency brake was accidentally activated, which caused one car to derail. The grip holding that car to the cable must have been faulty and when the cable jolted the car bounced and the grip released, but when it slid back into the other car they locked together and so far that has prevented it from falling. But because of where the cars are, getting to them will be tricky. They're talking about rigging up a second cable from tower to tower so that the mountain rescue team can access the gondolas from above. They'll have to secure the cars and then use harnesses and stretchers to lower everyone to safety. It's going to take time,' he repeated.

Jess wrapped her arms around herself. Despite the chill in the air she could feel herself breaking into a sweat. Fear gripped her heart and squeezed it tight. She couldn't bear to think of all the things that could go wrong. She couldn't bear to think of Lily up there, scared and in danger.

Lucas pulled her against his chest. She didn't want to imagine going through this on her own. Whatever happened, she knew she could rely on him. He would be there for Lily and she knew he'd be there for her too. He had promised her that much. She needed to give him something in return.

'If Lily is okay I promise I will give you whatever you want,' she said as she looked up at him. 'We'll tell her the truth tonight.'

Lucas hated feeling useless. He hated not being needed. He'd organised the lodge to send up hot refreshments but that had been the sum total of his assistance, and he wished there was more he could do. Standing around waiting while other people were being constructive didn't sit well with him. His child was trapped in one of the cars and he could do nothing.

He knew this rescue required the expertise of trained personnel and he didn't want to put anyone at risk by having people who were not fully qualified sticking their oar in, and that included him, but it didn't stop him from feeling inadequate.

Fleur and Nathan had gone to get something to eat, leaving him alone with Jess. She hadn't wanted to join the larger group of parents who waited anxiously to hug their children. She said she didn't want to talk to anyone. She sat on the snowmobile and chewed her lip while he paced around in the snow.

The whole process was slow going. Lucas and Jess had been on site for two hours and the gondolas had only just been secured. It was bitterly cold and unpleasant but no one was going anywhere. Hot drinks, soup and blankets were being passed around to the parents and some shelters had been brought up the mountain in an attempt to provide some protection from the biting wind. The wind was blowing straight up the gully, rocking the cars. The wind was strengthening and in Lucas's opinion the rescue team had managed to secure the cars just in time. Any longer and the wind would have made the project even more difficult, treacherous even, but at least the sky was clear. No snow was forecast and that was something to be grateful for. That was one less thing for the mountain rescue team to have to contend with.

'Do you want to sit down for a while?' Jess asked him.

He shook his head. 'I can't sit still. I'm finding it hard enough knowing that other people are being useful while I'm hanging around, twiddling my thumbs.'

Jess had promised him that if they got through this they would tell Lily the truth and he had to believe that everything would be okay. But it was proving difficult. He'd only just discovered the truth and he wasn't prepared to have Lily taken away from him now. 'I wish there was more I could do.'

'You're helping me.' Jess smiled up at him and reached out one hand.

'How?' he asked as he took her hand in his.

'It's nice to know I'm not alone. I'm glad you're here.'

He let her pull him down to sit beside her on the snowmobile. He wrapped his arm around her shoulders and tried to be content with the moment while avoiding thinking about all the things that could go wrong. He could sit still if Jess needed him to. She could anchor him. Sitting with her tucked against his side would settle him.

'Talk to me about Lily,' he said. Talking might keep his mind occupied. It might keep him too busy to worry and there was so much he didn't know about his daughter. He was still coming to terms with the idea that he was a father. He felt the weight of responsibility, to both Lily and Jess, but he was looking forward to the changes this development would bring. He didn't expect it to be easy.

There was a lot he and Jess needed to sort out but he was determined they would manage. He wished he hadn't missed six years of his daughter's life but that was as much his fault as Jess's and all he could do now was make certain he got to share the rest with them both. He refused to think that he wasn't going to get that chance and, in the meantime, he needed to learn as much about Lily as he could. He needed to get to know his daughter.

'She was born at half past six in the morning, six twenty-eight, to be exact, and she weighed seven pounds, five ounces.' Jess's voice lifted as she spoke about their daughter. This conversation wasn't just helping him. It was keeping her mind occupied too. 'She was in a hurry and she didn't come quietly. She hasn't been afraid to let me know what she's thinking ever since. She can be quite stubborn.'

Lucas smiled. 'Sounds like someone else I know.'

Jess nudged him in the side and said, 'She's got plenty of you in her as well.'

'Really?' He was surprised at how pleased he was to hear that. 'Good traits, I hope?'

'Mostly,' Jess teased. 'She's becoming quite a confident skier. I suspect she got her sense of balance from you, and her fearlessness—those things definitely didn't come from me. She has a very strong sense of self and have you noticed she has your ears?'

'I'm glad she got a little bit of me. There's no doubting she's your daughter, but it's nice to know I had something to do with it.'

'Don't worry, there's plenty of you in her. Her eyes aren't always green, they change colour depending on what she wears and if she wears blue they can look like yours. She started walking when she was thirteen months old and lost her first tooth at the beginning of this year. She loves roast chicken and carrots and Disney princesses and her koala and your horse, Banjo. Her favourite colour is pink and she loves to sing.'

Jess paused as around them noise started building. Low murmurs became a buzz of anticipation and people were on the move. The rescue crews in their bright yellow jackets were going past, carrying harnesses, and the ski patrol and ambos carried stretchers and first-aid kits. Lucas knew what that meant.

He stood and reached for her hand. 'They're starting to evacuate the cars.'

They hurried closer and stood waiting. The derailed car was the first to be evacuated but eventually it was Lily's turn.

Jess burst into tears when she spied Lily being lowered from the gondola in a harness. She ran through the snow and scooped her into her arms.

'My precious girl, are you all right?'

'I'm fine, Mum.' She was beaming. 'That was the best excursion *ever*.'

'She sounds okay to me.' Lucas grinned but relief washed over him too.

Jess laughed and wiped the tears from her cheeks. 'You've only been on one other excursion, Lil.' She brushed Lily's hair from her forehead and dropped a kiss there. Her fingers ran gently over the spot she'd just kissed. 'You've got a nasty bump on your head here— are you sure you're okay?'

'I was leaning on the window when the other gondola car crashed into us and I bumped my head. You should have heard the big bang it made.'

'Your head or the car?' Lucas asked.

Lily giggled. 'The car. It sounded like thunder and we all fell on the floor.'

Snow cats had been sent up the mountain to ferry the children back to the medical centre, where they would be checked for any injuries, frostnip or concussion. Jess climbed into the vehicle with Lily, she wasn't prepared to let her out of her sight, and Lucas took the snowmobile back down the mountain and met them at the clinic.

'Is she *still* talking?' he said, as he watched Lily gossiping with a group of friends as they drank hot chocolate and waited to be given the all-clear after their ordeal.

'The whole adventure has given her plenty to say. This is the most excitement she's ever had. She definitely takes after her father.' Jess spoke quietly but her words were accompanied by a smile. 'I always avoided drama.'

'Nature versus nurture?' he asked.

'It looks that way.'

Lucas took Jess's arm and gently pulled her to one side of the bustling waiting room. The noise level was high and he was fairly sure they could talk without being overheard but he made sure he kept Lily within sight. For Jess's sake and his own. 'Will you bring her over to the lodge when you're finished here? I'd like to talk to her tonight.'

Jess frowned and a little crease appeared between her eyebrows, making her look exactly like her daughter. Their daughter. 'I don't know. Don't you think she's had enough for one day?'

'I was as worried as you were up on the mountain, JJ. I want to be part of Lily's life and I want that to start today. I don't want any more missed moments. She's resilient. Look at how she coped with the events of today. She'll cope with this. Besides, it's good news.'

Jess paused and Lucas held his breath. He didn't want to wait. He wanted to be acknowledged as Lily's father.

Finally she nodded. 'All right. I'll take her home for a warm bath and then we'll come over.'

'Lily, your mum and I have something to tell you.'

Lily paused momentarily with one hand on Banjo's neck. It had been Jess's suggestion that they go to the stable and he had agreed without reservation. Grooming Banjo was a soothing, familiar activity for Lily and it meant they didn't have to sit awkwardly in the hotel to have this conversation. 'Is it a surprise?' she asked. 'I love surprises.'

'It was a surprise for me,' Lucas told her. 'But it's something I'm very excited about. Something I've wished for for a long time.'

'Lil, you know how I've always said you were made up of bits and pieces?' Jess asked her.

Lily nodded and tilted her head as she replied, 'Like a platypus.'

'That's right. Well, the outside bits of you are just like me,' Jess said, 'but some of the inside bits of you are different. Parts of your insides are funny and other parts are curious and other parts are brave, much braver than me, and you get those parts from your dad.'

Lily frowned and Lucas was reminded of how Jess had looked earlier in the day. 'I don't have a dad.'

'Everyone has a dad somewhere, sweetheart. I just lost your dad for a while and it took me a long time to find him again.'

'Is he nice?'

'He's very nice.'

Jess smiled at Lucas as she spoke to their daughter, and Lucas finally had what he'd wished for. He remembered the expression on Jess's face the night she'd told him about her relationship with Lily's father. How she'd looked when she'd told him that she'd loved Lily's dad. He'd seen the love in her eyes that night and he'd wished she'd been talking about him. He hadn't known then that he was Lily's father but she had that same expression in her eyes tonight. She'd said she loved him then. Did she love him still?

'Will he like me?' Lily wanted to know.

'He will *love* you. Very much. But I think he might want to tell you that himself.'

'When can I see him?'

'He's right here, Lily.'

'Where?'

'It's me, Lily,' Lucas told her 'I'm your dad.'

'Really?'

'Really.' He nodded. 'And I think I'm the luckiest dad in the world.'

'This is the best day ever,' Lily said, as she threw her arms around his neck and burrowed in against his chest.

He'd been worried about her reaction to their news. Holding his child in his arms was the most incredible feeling and he would have been devastated if Lily hadn't wanted him. He didn't think he would be able to give her up after this. What would he have done if she hadn't been as thrilled about the news as Jess had assured him she would be? What if she hadn't been as excited as he'd hoped she would be?

He wondered how Jess was feeling. He looked over the top of Lily's head. Jess was smiling but he could see a glimmer of tears in her eyes. How did she feel about having to share Lily?

Lily had fallen asleep on his couch after polishing off her dinner. Lucas looked at his sleeping daughter. Her blonde head was resting on Jess's lap and she had Ozzie, the koala, tucked under her arm. She was beautiful. She was perfect.

'What is it?' Jess asked him.

'I think it's incredible that we made her.' He'd never felt that anything was missing in his life but now that Jess was back in it, and Lily too, he wondered how he could not have known that there should be more. 'And that she accepted me so easily.'

'She thinks you're fabulous.'

'She does?'

'Why wouldn't she? You own a horse and sleigh.' Jess was smiling at him and his heart swelled with love for her and their daughter. His family.

He needed to make that his reality.

Thinking of family made him think of hers. 'Have you spoken to your father yet?'

Jess shook her head. 'Not exactly. But I did speak to his secretary this morning. Luckily she's been working for him for ever and she has booked Lily in for the biopsy on the Wednesday before Christmas. I meant to tell you but with all the drama today I forgot,' she said as she stifled a yawn.

'But you didn't speak to your father.'

'No. I couldn't do it. Talking to him on the phone didn't seem right but I don't know what to do. I don't want to have our first conversation in six years just before Lily goes into the operating theatre—that won't be any good for any of us—but I'm running out of time.'

'Sleep on it,' he said, as she stifled another yawn. 'A solution will present itself.' He had an idea that might just work. 'And why don't you take my bed for the night?' he offered. 'There's no point in waking Lily to take her home.'

Jess shook her head. 'Thanks, but if you bring me a blanket I'll be perfectly happy to sleep in front of the fire. I need to stay close to her, I don't want her to wake up in unfamiliar surroundings without me. Not after the day she's had.'

'I'll move her to my bed, then, and I'll take the couch.'

He picked Lily up. She was feather-light in his arms and snuggled in against his chest, still fast asleep. Jess followed him into his bedroom and pulled the comforter back. He tucked Lily under it before dropping a kiss on her forehead.

They stood together and watched Lily sleep. 'I still can't quite believe I have a daughter. It's incredible.

Thank you, JJ. For giving me this gift. For being strong enough to make what must have been a tough decision. Do you mind sharing Lily with me?'

Jess shook her head. 'Of course not. I never wanted to do this on my own and having you in Lily's life will be a good thing for her—provided we can figure out how it's all going to work.'

'We will,' he agreed, 'but not tonight. There have been enough decisions made today.' He turned Jess to face him. 'But I do have one more question for you. I want to be a part of your life too.'

'You will be. We'll always be connected through our daughter.'

'I want more than that. I want a chance to have a re-lationship with you that goes beyond us as parents. I want more. I want you.'

'You want me? After everything I've done?'

'Look around you, JJ. Everything I've done has been with you in mind. I know I said I wanted to prove a point to your father but I wouldn't have bothered with that if it wasn't for you. You were the reason I've done this. You were the reason I came back. I admit I've got more than I bargained for but I'm thrilled about that. The past is the past. I meant it when I said there's no point dwelling on it. It can't be changed. We all had a hand to play in the mess we made—me, you and your father—but what's done is done. It doesn't change how I feel about you or Lily. All we can do is look to the future. We have the rest of our lives to make up for lost time.'

'Really?'

'That was my plan.' He was smiling, grinning like a lovestruck fool. He loved her and he wanted to be 'the one' for her. He wanted them to be a family. 'Do you have other plans that I should know about?'

Jess shook her head. 'No.'

'Good.' He took Jess's face in his hands, cupping her cheeks gently between his palms, and tipped her head up. Her green eyes were wide, her lips plump and pink. He wanted her to be his. He wanted to claim her for his own.

He bent his head and covered her lips with his, pouring his love into her and sealing it with a kiss. She tasted like vanilla ice cream, innocent and sweet, and he made a promise to himself that he would take care of her, of her and Lily, if she would let him. He would convince her, he would persuade her, he would charm her and love her until she agreed to give herself to him. And then he would be content.

CHAPTER ELEVEN

JESS'S HEART POUNDED in her chest and her arm felt as if it weighed a tonne as she reached for the door handle of the lodge suite. Her hand was shaking and her palms were clammy. 'I don't think I can do this,' she said to Lucas.

He'd told her he would take care of things but she hadn't expected him to do it so quickly and she also hadn't expected her father to agree to Lucas's suggestion, but it seemed as though she had been wrong on both counts because her father was here, in Moose River, and he was waiting for her.

'It'll be okay, JJ, and I'll be just outside if you need me. Remember, this time I've got your back.' Lucas's voice gave her the courage to turn the handle. 'You can do this.'

She pushed the door open. 'Daddy?'

He was halfway across the room, coming to meet her. He was tall and still trim, although his dark hair was greyer than she remembered. He was sixty now. She'd missed his sixtieth birthday and he'd missed her twenty-first. For what? Why?

Because she was stubborn.

But his arms were open, forgiving, inviting. She

burst into tears and stepped into his embrace. 'I'm sorry, Dad,' she said, as his arms tightened around her. He'd only ever wanted to protect her and she'd repaid him by cutting him out of her life.

She closed her eyes and sobbed and let him hug her as he'd done when she'd been a child. She could feel the tension in her shoulders ease. She could feel the forgiveness in his embrace and all the anxiety that had been building up, all her nervousness over this meeting slipped away as he held her.

'I'm sorry too, Jessie.' He stepped back to look at her, pulling a clean handkerchief out of his pocket and handing it to her.

She smiled through her tears. 'You still carry a handkerchief.' It was one of the many things she remembered about him. Her father wore cufflinks and always had a clean hankie in his pocket.

'Always,' he replied. 'Some things never change. It's good to see you, sweetheart.'

'You too, Dad.' Jess looked around the room. She could smell coffee. There was a pot and two mugs on the sideboard. Only two cups. 'Is Mum here?' she asked.

'No. I wasn't sure how receptive you were going to be. She wouldn't be able to handle any confrontation.'

Jess was disappointed and she felt her shoulders drop. 'I wasn't planning on being confrontational,' she told him. She hadn't been planning anything. This had all been Lucas's idea. But it was silly to feel disappointed about her mother's absence when she hadn't even been sure if she herself wanted to come to the meeting. Why should her mother feel any differently?

Her father must have heard the disappointment in her voice. 'I'm sorry, Jessie. But we'll work it out. This is the first step. I promise I'll do everything I can to make sure we will be a family again.' He reached into his pocket and pulled out his wallet. 'I have something I want to show you.' He flipped his wallet open and handed it to her.

He'd always had a photo of her and Stephen as children in the plastic sleeve but that was gone now. Jess stared at the replacement. Her own eyes stared back at her. The photo was one of her and Lily. It was a photo Kristie had taken on Lily's sixth birthday.

She sat on the sofa and slipped the photo out of the sleeve. Behind it was the old photo of her and Stephen. She held the picture of Lily in her hands and looked up at her father. 'Where did you get this?'

'Kristie gave it to Aunt Carol. She gave it to me.'

'Why?'

'I asked for it.' Her father dragged an armchair across the floor, positioning it at an angle to the sofa, so that he was nearby without crowding Jess. 'I know I wasn't very supportive when you told me you were pregnant and were planning on keeping the baby. I didn't understand how you could make that decision at the age of eighteen but when you cut me out of your life I felt like I'd lost both of my children, first Stephen and then you. Kristie was my link to you, to you and to Lily. I tried to keep in touch with you but when you returned all my letters I had to rely on your aunt and uncle to give me news over the years. I couldn't stand the thought of you being lost to me for ever.'

Her father had sent her a letter, along with a birthday card and a sizeable cheque for Lily, every year. Kristie had always delivered it for them but Jess hadn't realised things had been going back in the other direction. Jess had kept the cards—she had boxed them up and put them away for Lily—but she had returned the letters and the cheques, still determined to prove she could manage on her own. Determined to prove she didn't need anything from her father.

But all this time he'd been hearing about Lily. She didn't know why she was surprised. If she'd ever given it any thought she would have figured out that Aunt Carol would have passed on any information her parents asked for. All this time he'd been following Lily's progress. Despite Jess's actions he had never stopped being her father or Lily's grandfather. He had never given up hope.

'I'm sorry I was stubborn. I'm sorry I've kept you out of our lives,' she apologised. 'I returned your letters but I've kept your cards for Lily. I was going to give them to her one day.' She wanted him to know that. It was important.

'Thank you, Jessie.' Her father reached for her hand and Jess gave it to him. 'I've missed you. Do you think we might have a chance to start fresh?'

'I wasn't sure if I could forgive you for separating me from Lucas. I loved him then, I love him still.' Jess felt her father tense and she hurried to continue, to put his mind at ease. 'But he says we need to leave the past behind if we want to move forward and I think he's right. I would like a chance to start again.' She stood up. 'Would you like to meet Lily?'

'Now?'

Jess nodded.

'She's here?'

'She's in the lodge. Lucas is waiting outside. He'll fetch her.'

'I'd love to, Jessie, and if it's all right I'd like to meet Lucas too. After all, I have him to thank for bringing you back into my life.'

Jess nodded. 'Okay. Give me a minute.' She was smiling as she left the suite. Lucas was waiting for her, just as he'd promised.

'You look happy.'

She walked over to him and threw her arms around him, hugging him tightly.

He picked her up and held her close. 'What was that for?' he asked, as he set her back down on her feet.

'It's a thank-you. I think it's going to be okay. Dad wants to meet Lily.'

'That's good. I've already asked Sofia to bring her up and I've ordered some champagne and afternoon tea for you too.'

'You knew it would go well?'

'I could tell when I spoke to him on the phone that he was keen to reconcile. I was pretty sure this would all turn out okay and I'm glad it has so far.'

'He wants to meet you too.'

'Now?'

Jess nodded and Lucas followed her back into the room.

'Dad, this is Lucas White. Lucas, my father, Stuart Johnson.'

Jess's heart was in her throat. *Please, be nice, Dad.*

Stuart was looking at Lucas closely but he stayed silent. He extended his hand and Jess exhaled as they shook hands. They seemed far more relaxed than she was. Perhaps this would turn out all right after all.

'Good to meet you properly at last, sir. I apologise for not taking responsibility before now—'

Stuart cut him off and Jess held her breath again. 'That's all right. I think I owe you an apology. I was hasty in my judgement of you and it cost me my daughter and my granddaughter. Thank you for bringing them back to me.'

'I want you to know that I intend to make it up to Lily,' Lucas said. 'And to Jess. I have the means and the desire to make it up to both of them and I'm not one to shy away from my responsibilities.'

Lucas stood next to her and she took his hand and squeezed it. He circled her waist with his arm and pulled her close, and Jess could almost feel her life turning around. With Lucas beside her, perhaps things would be okay. With him beside her, anything seemed possible. She'd felt lost, adrift and alone with no one except Lily and Kristie. She never would have admitted it, she was too stubborn, but now perhaps she could. With Lucas back in her life and her father and maybe even her mother, she and Lily wouldn't be alone any more.

Maybe she had a chance of finding happiness after all.

Jess was wearing scrubs and was sitting in the operating theatre at the foot of the bed while her father prepared for Lily's biopsy. The anaesthetist gave Lily a very light general anaesthetic and when she gave Stuart the all-clear he slid a flexible tube, complete with a tiny camera, down Lily's oesophagus, through her stomach and into the small intestine. Jess could watch the images on the monitor above their heads. Stuart examined the intestinal lining and took half a dozen samples at various points.

'What are you looking for?' Jess asked. She'd researched the procedure and the disease and she knew she was asking just to hear her father's voice. It was hard to believe he was back in her life.

'Atrophy of the villi and inflammation of the mucosal tissue,' he explained. 'There's a pathologist waiting for the samples as we speak so the results should be back almost immediately.'

The whole process took less than fifteen minutes and the light anaesthetic Lily had been given was reversed quickly. Then it was just a matter of more waiting.

Lucas and Jess were sitting with a drowsy Lily in the day surgery recovery area when Stuart ducked in between surgeries.

He kept his mask on as he spoke to them.

'The results are back. The villi are shrunk and flattened, indicating partial atrophy, and there is an increased presence of lymphocytes and some other changes consistent with inflammation. The Marsh classification is given as Marsh III.'

'What does that mean?'

'It means Lily has celiac disease.'

'Should I have done something about this earlier?' Guilt swamped Jess again.

Her father shook his head. 'From what I've read in her history from the emergency department, any symptoms she did have were so mild they could have been attributed to any number of things. Because it is commonly an inherited condition, finding out Lucas's history was the red flag. I know it's called a disease but you should think of it more as a condition. It's easily controlled as long as you are prepared to be vigilant with Lily's diet. I'm sure Lucas will agree with me, it's not difficult to manage. Once Lily has a gluten-free diet the villi and her intestine will recover.'

'How long does that take?'

'Usually around three to six months, but provided she sticks to a gluten-free diet there won't be any long-term effects. If she doesn't adhere to a strict gluten-free diet there can be other complications but there'll be time to discuss those later. I'll tee up an appointment with a dietician and a counsellor. It'll be okay, Jessie, we'll get through this.' He squeezed her hand. 'I have to get back into Theatre. Will you be all right?'

Jess reached for Lucas's hand and smiled at her father. 'We'll be fine.'

Lily was up bright and early on Christmas morning. She'd had no ill effects following the biopsy and had taken the news about her celiac disease in her stride, just like everything else. In all honesty, Jess suspected Lily was pleased to know that she and Lucas had something tangible in common.

That had been one problem solved. Jess had been busy ticking boxes over the past few days and things were going well. With Lucas's help she was mending her relationship with her parents, both her mother and her father. Lucas had invited them to the lodge for Christmas lunch and they were coming, along with Kristie and her parents. It would be the first family Christmas in many years and Jess and Lily were both excited. Lucas was helping to repair all the damage Jess had done but fortunately everyone seemed prepared to forgive her.

The only other thing still to be finessed was her relationship with Lucas and how they would parent Lily. But Jess knew they would get there. One thing at a time.

Lily was bouncing up and down on Lucas's bed, where she and Jess had spent another night while Lucas had slept on the couch. Jess felt bad about kicking him out of his own bed yet again but he had insisted. He wanted to be there when Lily woke up, he said. He'd missed all of her Christmases to date and he didn't want to miss another one. It was a good argument and Jess had happily agreed.

'Is it time for presents yet?' Lily was asking.

'We'll go and see if your dad is awake.' It was going to take some time to get used to saying that but Jess liked how it sounded.

'Merry Christmas to my girls,' he said, as he kissed them both and handed Jess a coffee.

'Did Santa come?' Lily asked.

'There seems to be a very big present by the fireplace that wasn't there last night,' Lucas was grinning. 'Shall we take a look?'

An enormous gift sat in front of the fireplace and Lily wasted no time in tearing the paper off it to reveal a magnificent doll's house. It was one she had admired at the Christmas market and had working lights and delicate furniture. A curved staircase led from the first to the second floor and a hollow chimney ended in a small fireplace in the lounge that was complete with tiny logs that lit up with fake flames at the flick of a switch. It was elaborate and beautiful.

'I think Santa might have stolen your thunder,' Jess said with a smile as Lily flicked the lights on and off before picking up a tiny music box that was inside the doll's house. She turned the handle on its side and squealed with delight as it played 'Waltzing Matilda'. 'You might not be her favourite today,' Jess added.

'Santa had six years to make up for but I've still got a few tricks up my sleeve.'

He handed Lily a small box. Nestled in tissue paper was a carved wooden sleigh. It had been painted red, just like the Crystal Lodge sleigh. Lily lifted it carefully from the box. Attached to it was a perfect replica of Banjo. 'I love it, Daddy, it looks just like Banjo.'

'Okay, Dad's turn, Lil,' Jess told her, once they'd all finished admiring the tiny horse.

Lily handed Lucas a flat, heavy parcel and then went to play with her doll's house as he unwrapped his gift, revealing a photo album.

He turned the pages of the album. It was filled with photographs of Lily, beginning on the day she'd been born and continuing to her sixth birthday. As Jess described each picture, telling Lucas something about each occasion, Lily's curiosity got the better of her. Fascinated as always by photographs of herself when she'd been younger, she abandoned the doll's house temporarily and climbed onto Lucas's lap. She snuggled against his chest and added to the commentary as he turned the pages. 'That's me when I lost my first tooth,' she said, 'and that's me when I was in the nativity play last year. I was a shepherd. And that's me on the day I started school in Moose River.'

'It's brilliant, JJ,' Lucas said, as he reached the end of the album and closed the book. He leant behind Lily and kissed Jess lightly on the lips. 'Thank you.'

'I have something else for you too,' she said, as she handed him a large, thin envelope. Inside was one sheet of paper.

Lucas slid it out. 'It's Lily's birth certificate.'

Jess nodded. 'I've had it amended,' she said. She

pointed to the word 'Father'. In the box underneath it said 'Lucas White'.

'This is the most perfect gift.'

'It's going to be a perfect Christmas,' Jess replied.

'I hope so. But there's one more thing to do before we reach perfection.'

'What's that?'

'Your present.' Lucas turned to Lily, who had returned to play, and Jess had to smile when she saw that Lily was busy showing mini-Banjo through the house. 'Lil, it's time for Mum's surprise.'

Lily put Banjo down and dived under the Christmas tree to retrieve a gift bag.

Lucas picked up Jess's hand and looked into her eyes. 'JJ, I loved you seven years ago and I love you still. You are beautiful and smart and I never forgot you. I love you and I love Lily. I want us to be a family.' Without letting go of her hand, he got down on one knee beside the couch. Lily was bouncing up and down on the cushion beside Jess, clutching the gift bag. 'Jess Johnson, will you do me the honour of becoming my wife? Will you marry me?'

Jess's eyes filled with tears.

'No! Don't cry, Mum.'

'It's all right, Lil, these are happy tears,' Jess said as she choked back a sob. 'You are my first and only love,' she said to Lucas. 'I have loved you and only you since the moment you first kissed me and, yes, I will marry you.'

Lily threw her arms around them both. 'Hooray,' she shouted.

'Okay, Lily, you can hand over the bag now,' Lucas said, when Lily finally released them.

Inside the bag was a tiny jewellery box. Jess pulled it out and lifted the lid. A princess-cut diamond ring glistened in dark blue velvet. Lucas pulled it from the cushion.

'Just as you have rescued me I promise to always protect you for as long as you need me. I promise to love you and Lily and to keep you safe. Always,' he said, as he slid the ring onto her finger before kissing her.

'I think she likes it,' Lily said, as Jess held her hand out so they could all admire it.

'You knew about this?' Jess asked her.

'Lily helped me choose the ring,' Lucas replied. 'She's nearly as good at keeping secrets as you are.'

'No more secrets. I promise.'

Lily was tugging Jess's arm. 'Now do you think I can have a baby sister?'

Jess smiled and looked into Lucas's forget-me-not-blue eyes. 'We'll see what we can do.'

EPILOGUE

Jess lay on a beach towel and let the autumn sun warm her pale skin as she watched Lucas and Lily playing in the famous Bondi surf. Lucas had swapped his snowboard for a surfboard and he was giving Lily her first surfing lesson. She was proving to be a natural, showing Jess once again that nature was just as strong as nurture.

Lucas came out of the water, leaving Lily to practise her surf moves with his youngest brother. He jogged up the beach to Jess and she didn't bother to pretend she wasn't checking him out. They'd been in Australia for a month and Lucas was tanned and fit and gorgeous. And all hers. He stood over her, blocking the sun and giving her a very nice view of his sculpted chest and strong thighs. His board shorts dripped water on the sand as he towelled his hair dry, leaving it even more tousled than normal.

She smiled up at him. 'Lily's having a great time. She's picked it up really fast. She must take after her dad.'

'Your husband,' he said, as he flopped down onto the sand beside her and kissed her.

They had married in Moose River in February and had just celebrated their three-month anniversary with a second ceremony with Lucas's family. It had been a whirlwind few months and Jess was exhausted but elated. She wouldn't change a thing.

'Happy?' he asked.

'Extremely,' she replied, as she rolled onto her side to look at Lucas. Some days she still couldn't believe her good fortune. Lucas was back in her life, he'd given her back her family and he'd given her himself too. She was happy and she had everything she needed. She reached out and picked up her husband's hand. 'But, in the interest of full disclosure, because I promised no more secrets, there is something I need to tell you.'

'Is it that you love me?'

'I do. But that's not a secret.'

'I know, I just like to hear you say "I do".' Lucas laughed and kissed her fingers. 'Sorry, go on.'

'You know how Lily always asks for a baby sister for Christmas? I've been thinking...'

'You think we should make a baby?' Lucas's forget-me-not-blue eyes lit up.

Jess shook her head. 'That wasn't what I was going to say.' She smiled as Lucas's face fell. She knew he was going to love her news. 'It's too late for that. We've already done it.'

'What?'

'I'm pregnant.'

'You are?'

Jess nodded. 'The baby is due the week before Christmas. So it looks as though Lily will get her Christmas wish this year. She's going to have a sibling,' she said, as she brought Lucas's hand to her belly.

'That is fantastic news, JJ. The best.'

'All those things you missed out on with Lily, I

SAFE IN THE
SURGEON'S ARMS

BY
MOLLY EVANS

Published in Great Britain 2015
by Mills & Boon, an imprint of Harlequin (UK) Limited,
Eton House, 18-24 Paradise Road, Richmond, Surrey, TW9 1SR

© 2015 Brenda Schetnan

ISBN: 978-0-263-24739-8

Printed and bound in Spain
by CPI, Barcelona

Dear Reader,

Thank you for picking up my new book! It is set in one of my favourite towns—Williamsburg, Virginia, USA—where history and fantastic foods are just steps away, no matter where you are in town.

This story is important to me as I'm a sucker for a tortured hero and I adore the strong women who love them.

We never know what we are capable of until we are put in a position to rise to challenges we never expected in life. These two are stronger together than either of them are alone.

I hope you enjoy the emotional journey these two characters take as they find love in each other's arms again.

Please visit me at mollyevansromance.wordpress.com.

Regards

Molly Evans

This book is dedicated to my friend,
fellow Hurricane Hugo survivor
and Williamsburg, VA, explorer: Jesse Bustos Nelson.
You've been there with friendship and support
since the beginning. Thanks, my friend!

Books by Molly Evans

Mills & Boon® Medical Romance™

The Surgeon's Marriage Proposal
The Nurse's Little Miracle
The Emergency Doctor's Chosen Wife
The Greek Doctor's Proposal
One Summer in Santa Fe
Children's Doctor, Shy Nurse
Socialite...or Nurse in a Million?
Her Family for Keeps

**Visit the author profile page
at millsandboon.co.uk for more titles**

CHAPTER ONE

EMERGENCY NURSE Emily Hoover pointed the way to the trauma room as an air-ambulance crew surged through the department. She'd heard the radio announcing the arrival of the rescue chopper as it had landed on the roof and had even smelled the diesel exhaust through the HIPPA air-filtration system that was supposed to remove it.

Those were all expected, anticipated and not uncommon events in a hospital close to a major highway. Where there was trauma there was a busy ER and one of the reasons she'd come back here to her hometown. Reclaiming her life was the first reason. Working great trauma was the second. At least that was what she told herself as the crew swept past her.

What she hadn't expected to see was an emergency surgeon riding atop the gurney, straddling the patient, both of them covered in blood. Her limbs began to tremble and sweat popped out on her back. *Oh, man.* The heartbeat she usually kept calm with meditation now raced uncontrollably in her chest as she recognized the man behind the dirty scrubs. He'd aged little in three years and was as handsome as ever. A tightness in her abdomen surged to join the erratic heartbeat. Fierce intensity showed on his face and confidence she'd never seen in him before. His hair, dark brown with a tendency to curl, was a mess. Those intense blue eyes blazed with a fire she'd never forgotten despite three years of separation.

"Get three units of whole blood going now. I need a central line placed and get OR on alert." Trauma surgeon and emergency doctor Chase Montgomery gave orders as the entourage rolled through the door. Staff scrambled to the first trauma room that had been set up for the arrival of this patient.

Emily choked down her anxiety, shoving it aside in the face of a true emergency, and grabbed the cardiac leads, placed them on the patient so his heart could be monitored and placed the blood-pressure cuff on the only arm he had left. The trembling in her hands was likely not noticeable to the others, but to her it was. This wasn't who she was, a nervous nurse on the first day of work. Like there weren't ten years under her belt already. But *this* place. *This* man. Those were the things that made her tremble now. Thoughts of how they'd been together in the past made her quake.

"Get anesthesia in here. He has to be intubated now."

"There was just an overhead page, Chase. They've been called to a code on the floor." Liz, the charge nurse, supplied the answer, but picked up the phone on the wall. "I'll see if there's someone else who can help out."

"Page any surgeon overhead. I'll intubate, and someone else can do the IV placement. We need a central line right away."

"Got it." Liz made the call.

"IV set-up tray is ready, Doctor, but if you'd prefer to intubate first, I'll get that one ready." Though keep-

promise you'll be there for every one of them this time around. Do you think that sounds okay?'

'I do.'

Jess closed her eyes and smiled as his lips covered hers.

This was the perfect start to the first day of the rest of their lives.

* * * * *

ing her focus on the patient, Emily spoke in the direction of the doctor leading the situation. He stood with his back to her and was in the process of removing his lab coat when he froze.

Then spun.

Clearly astonished at her presence, he stared at her with his mouth open for a few seconds as he tried to force his mind to accept what his eyes were seeing.

Emily's stomach tightened again; her heart beat as erratically as the patient's. Chase had never looked better, and her heart was out of control. A look of stunned shock crossed his face for a second or two. His eyes opened wide, his jaw dropped and he jumped as if he'd been pinched. Only a few seconds of lapsed control, but she saw it, felt it in her chest. The depth of pain mixed with his surprise at seeing her would be etched in her mind forever. She'd done that to him. She'd caused the hurt he'd momentarily betrayed. Except for the shock on his face, he hadn't changed in the three years since they'd broken up. Since she'd walked away from him.

"Emily?" He took a halting step toward her then stopped. "What are you *doing* here?" His blue gaze raked her from top to toe as if his brain still couldn't comprehend what his eyes were telling him. "What happened to your hair?"

Before she could answer, what seemed like an army of people burst into the room and the focus returned to the critical patient in front of them. This was apparently the *entire* team of surgeons, from the senior fellow down to the first-year resident. At a teaching hospital staff seemed to move in large herds.

"Who called for a surgeon? We're here."

As the physician in charge, Chase forced his focus

from Emily to the surgeon. "We need better IV access immediately. Can one of you put in a central line? Anesthesia's tied up, and I'll have to intubate." Chase whipped off the bloody lab coat he'd worn to the crash site and threw it into a corner of the room.

The most senior member of the group emerged and nodded to Chase. "Sure thing." He removed his lab coat and handed it to a student to hold.

"I'll assist, Doctor." Emily made the offer so she would be away from Chase's penetrating glare and the waves of hostile energy flowing off him to flood the room. There was enough tension in the room already without adding more fuel to the fire she'd not been prepared for. Even though she'd known it would come, she wasn't prepared for it on the first day. "I've got the tray ready."

"Okay. Great. I thought this was going to be something difficult," he said with a grin, and winked at Emily. Emily never knew whether to be relieved at the confidence of surgeons or shocked at their outrageous arrogance. "Hey, don't I know you? Didn't you work here a while back?" He, too, frowned, trying to make sense of his memory in the present situation.

"Yes, I did. Came back for more. Over here, Dr. Blaze." Emily motioned him to the opposite side of the patient, and he moved around to where she stood. Relief overwhelmed her that he only remembered her from being an employee, not the rest. Or, if he did, he had the good graces not to say anything.

"Dr. Blaze. Ha! I haven't been called that in years."

"I remember with you everything was an emergency, wasn't it? You flashed through rounds like your tail was on fire." Emily smiled and her peripheral vision caught the glare Chase threw her way.

"Oh, those were the days." He shook his head at the memory. "So what happened? He's missing an arm." He looked to Chase for answers.

"Trauma. Pinned under his truck. Had to amputate in the field." Chase supplied the information, reinforcing one of the highest rules in trauma care: a limb for a life. Focus. That was what he needed right now—focus. Nothing mattered right now except saving this man's life. That was why he was there.

It didn't matter that he'd just had a bomb go off in the form of his ex-girlfriend appearing right in front of him in the middle of a trauma. He had to focus right now and ignore the kick in his pulse and the pain in his heart. He continued speaking to the surgeon, though he focused on aligning the patient's head in the correct position for putting in the airway tube.

"Once he's stable you can take him to OR and clean the arm up. It was pretty quick and dirty out there." As an emergency surgeon, he was called on to perform such procedures as well as his normal shifts in the ER.

Though he would sound like he was in control to the others, Emily heard the tension in his voice, noticed the hardness in his eyes and the twitch of a muscle in his jaw. Always had been giveaways to his mood. He was brittle, and her shoulders tensed, waiting for him to snap. At her. She deserved it for not warning him she was going to be working with him again. But she'd been too chicken to call him and hear the intimacy of his voice in her ear and remember how that had used to feel. Now she could see it would have been better for her to have had someone let him know.

"Gotcha." The chief surgeon turned to face Emily and accepted her assistance to don sterile garb.

"Liz, let's get him intubated. Has next of kin been notified?" As the leading doctor in this case, Chase directed the care and the flow of procedures. This was *his* patient and *his* case until he turned it over to another physician.

"Family's on the way in." Liz expertly opened the tray and prepared it for Chase.

"Let's get a line in this fellow, and you can get that blood into him, shall we?"

Though Emily had assisted in this procedure many times in her career as a nurse and had been a travel nurse in all manner of hospitals from small community centers to large teaching hospitals, she'd never had the added pressure of having her ex-boyfriend breathing down her neck. After a deep breath in, she let it out slowly, trying to calm her nerves, which had shot out of control. Why had she thought this was a good idea again? Facing fears and all that? What rot that was. Right now, on the edge of panic, she'd be happy to spend the rest of the shift hiding in a dark closet somewhere.

The procedure went as planned and as soon as the surgeon had secured the line with a few stitches she connected two pints of blood and opened the tubes full blast. The sooner she restored the depleted amount of blood the man had lost, the better his chances of survival.

The hum around her was comforting and familiar, even though some of the staff were strangers. As they moved past the trauma room she recognized people with whom she'd previously worked. Some excitedly waved to her; others waved, then a memory surfaced in their eyes and their smiles stiffened. Coming back here, she'd known it would be a risk to her privacy. Some people would only remember working with her; some would only remember what had happened to her.

Regardless, staff had jobs to do, and everyone seemed to be able to do it while talking about mundane issues like the weather or the upcoming sailboat races in the Chesapeake Bay. Now that the most emergent procedures had been carried out, they could take a breath and relax a bit.

Except for Emily. She could never relax. That word was no longer part of her vocabulary, and she didn't anticipate it ever being again. Some days it was all she could do to focus on her work and not let the demons hiding behind every curtain or closet door terrorize her. Though three years had passed since the incident that had changed her life, there were times it felt just like yesterday.

"Liz, do you want me to call OR again?" She made the offer, hoping she could leave the room and make the call at the desk, give herself a bit of physical distance between her and Chase and draw a deep breath. Since the trauma she'd suffered three years ago, she had difficulty facing crowded rooms and tight spaces. Add stairwells and dark hallways to the list. Anxiety had been her dark shadow, and she hadn't managed to kick it. Yet. Now, with Chase in close proximity, that dark demon had a choke hold on her and wasn't letting go. She swallowed, trying to force down the memory of hands closing around her throat, assaulting her body. She coughed once, forcing her throat open, and clenched her hands into fists.

"No, you stay here and monitor the patient. I'm going to call them back. Their transport team should have been here by now." She reached for the phone just as the corner of a gurney poked through the entrance to the room.

"We're here. No worries." One of the large men in scrubs held up his hands in surrender. He looked around the room. "Looks like you're still at it. We'll wait outside."

"No, take him now. I'll go along and give you a report on the way." Chase spoke to the surgeon. "He was involved in a rollover crash that threw him from the wreckage, pinned his left arm beneath the vehicle." He shrugged into his crumpled lab coat as the crew prepared the patient for transport.

"You must have gotten *there* pretty quick to get him *here* in time." The surgeon also donned his lab coat and straightened his collar as if he were preparing to go to his office rather than about to perform a complicated emergency surgery. The man must have nerves of steel.

"I went in the chopper. That helped." Chase took a deep breath, as if some of that memory bothered him, but she knew better. Nothing really bothered him. Not back then and probably not ever. He must be part duck, because everything just seemed to roll right off him. Not that he was cold or unfeeling; he just compartmentalized things. And she'd been shoved into a compartment that hadn't fit her after the incident, and it was one she couldn't remain in and survive. She'd broken out and run until she couldn't run any longer.

Running never solved anything, but she'd had to figure that out on her own.

"Good times. Did you bring the limb with you? We might be able to reattach it. Vascular team is stellar." Chase nodded to the heavy-duty cooler on a counter behind him and one of the transport team picked it up, put it beneath the gurney. Both men grabbed opposing ends of the stretcher and moved with the patient toward the elevators, with the entire surgical team streaming down the hall behind them. Their voices faded into the distance as Chase and the surgeon continued their dialogue.

"Emily? You okay?" Liz asked, as she began to clean the room, preparing it for the next patient. "Hey, there. You okay?"

"What?" She blinked, took a breath and realized she was staring after Chase. "Oh, yes. I'm good." To hide her discomfiture, she shoved a handful of used gauze dressings into the hazardous waste can. Good thing it was a big one. "I can clean the room if you have other things to do." She'd appreciate a moment alone after the shocking experience she'd just had, and she didn't mean the patient.

"Let's work together. That's how we do things around here." Liz carefully picked up the needles from the tray and disposed of them in the puncture-proof container hanging on the wall. "You might be used to getting all the crappy jobs as a traveler, but here we treat travel nurses the same as permanent staff." She smiled at Emily. "Right off the bat you caught a tough case, so I'll try to give you some lighter patients for the rest of the day. Not a guarantee, but I'll try."

"Thanks." It gave Emily a surge of warmth in her chest to hear the unit philosophy hadn't changed since she'd last worked there. She smiled and felt a little bit lighter as she talked, a little more at home.

Together they finished tidying the room and preparing it for the next patient. There would always be a next patient, a next trauma, a next disaster, and they had to be prepared for every kind that rolled through their doors.

"So, the next question is that you seem to have recognized Dr. Montgomery. Am I right?" Liz had the skills of a trained ER nurse and no denial was going to get past her. She'd see right through it. "And some other staff seemed to know you."

"Yes. I used to work here with him. Three years ago." She looked down and tried to control the beating of her heart. At one time Chase had been her heart, her life and her future, but that had all changed when she'd walked away from him. Though she hadn't wanted to, she'd had to. "And there are other staff I know, too." Some had saved her life in this very ER.

"There seemed to be more than just a recognition of a former coworker, though." Compassion and curiosity hung in her words, as if she suspected what Emily was going to tell her.

"There was." How much to tell without giving away her life story? "We dated at one time. But it was a while ago." What seemed a lifetime ago. No need to tell Liz they had been a serious couple before she'd been brutally attacked by a serial rapist and had been forced to radically change her life. Without Chase.

That stopped Liz. "Is it going to be an issue between you? I mean, are you going to be able to work with him? He's one of our finest doctors and if you can't get along with him, we'll have to reconsider your contract, maybe place you in another unit or something."

"Oh, no. I'll be fine. I'll be nothing except professional with him. I'm certain he'll be cordial, as well." Work had always come first with him. His career, his work, saving lives had always come before her.

"If you're certain." Liz jerked the curtain back as the

last gesture of room readiness. "I will trust you to let me know if that changes."

"I will. I appreciate it." She shoved her hands into the pockets of her scrubs. She was an adult, and she would behave like one. Chase would probably just ignore her, anyway. Her brother had told her he'd been dating other women, *many* other women, so she was probably nothing but a blip on his radar at this point. "Now, what else do we have to do? I need to keep busy." Keeping her hands busy kept her mind busy and prevented her thoughts from taking her down the rough road of her past and the never-ending trail of what-ifs and if-onlys.

"There'll be plenty to keep you occupied here. This isn't a big hospital, but it sure is a busy one. As you know, we're right off the interstate, so we have trauma on a daily basis." Liz led the way to the nurses' station and Emily followed, eager to get on with her orientation. "If trauma's not your bag now, by the end of your assignment it certainly will be.

CHAPTER TWO

CHASE RETURNED TO the ER, kept his pace slow, his thoughts on his work and tried to remain calm, despite the churning in his gut. But the second he saw Emily take a seat at the nurses' station, his nerves shot into overdrive. What the *hell* was she doing here? In *his* ER? Not that it was really his ER, but it was his by default, since she'd left it to pursue a travel-nursing stint.

She'd packed up her apartment, stuffed everything in a storage unit and driven away, not caring that he'd suffered in a way she couldn't imagine. Had she blamed him? He didn't know because she'd never said, but he damned sure blamed himself for not protecting her and for not being what she'd needed. Whatever that was. Seeing her now brought up so many feelings he'd buried, having been unable to work through them at the time. He didn't need this now. He didn't need it ever.

She was the last thing he'd expected to see after coming in on the trauma chopper today. When she spoke, the tone of her voice, the soft, dewy vibrations cut him to the core, as if only yesterday she'd meant something to him. He hadn't been expecting her and hadn't prepared himself to see her there. Surely *someone* could have told him she was coming. He could have prepared, could have hardened his heart and his emotions against the first meeting, put up boundaries, not been broadsided, unprepared. He'd never imagined she'd come back here where it had all begun for them.

That was probably the biggest shock. She'd come back to where he was when there were other hospitals in the area. So why here? And why *now*? That was a puzzle he intended to solve and then get on with his life. There was an answer for everything, and he was going to find this one.

When she'd left for her travel assignment he hadn't expected to ever see her again. Their breakup had been bitter, doubly so due to the assault and rape he hadn't been able to protect her from. That was the sorest spot, which had never healed.

He blamed himself.

She'd been unprotected because of him and had nearly died as a result, sustaining permanent scars inside and out. He hadn't known how to help her afterward, had been unable to help her, and when he'd been unable to face his own failure he'd backed away from her. He'd meant to give her some time and space, but not for all eternity. Her brother was a good friend, but Danny hadn't mentioned she was coming back. Maybe Danny hadn't wanted to upset him or had thought perhaps he'd moved on, and she no longer mattered to him.

He *had* moved on when she'd burned him back then. He'd been hurt and angry and hadn't been able to cope with his failure and the loss of her. Guilt had nearly eaten him alive. He'd dated women left and right. Sometimes for fun, sometimes for sex and sometimes for spite. Some had been gorgeous, some had been entertaining and some for no reason at all, other than convenience.

Unfortunately, none of them had been Emily. No woman had ever measured up to what he and Emily had had before the event that had fractured their lives. Neither of them would be the same again. Obviously. The incident hadn't just happened to her, it had nearly destroyed him, as well. It had taken him years to crawl back to where he felt human again and now, in an instant, everything had imploded.

The moment he'd heard her voice in the trauma room his soul had reacted with utter joy and then utter sorrow. Her voice and those big, expressive eyes of hers hadn't changed and his body had reacted to her with vigor. Embarrassing in a room full of people in an emergency, but he'd never been able to control himself around her before, so why should it be different now?

He closed the door to the charting room with disgust and sat down at the computer terminal to write up his notes from the morning's trauma. The coffee sat untouched beside him, and the words blurred together on the screen. Nothing made sense at the moment, and he pressed his fingertips to his eyes, wanting to rip out the image of her standing there with all that spiky hair, looking so different yet much the same and so very beautiful.

Why had Emily come back?

Seeing Chase right off the bat this morning had shaken her, torn up the defenses she'd worked so hard to build. She'd hidden it well, or so she thought, from the others, but now the shakes had set in. She hadn't expected to see him first thing, first trauma of the day, but that was life.

What had she thought when she'd returned to this hospital? Had she just come here to test herself for some stupid reason? She had just thought she was going to waltz in there and never see him, never have him recognize her despite the changes to her hair, her body, her life? She snorted in self-disgust. Apparently, that was what she'd hoped, whether it had been conscious or unconscious in its creation. Reclaiming her life wasn't going to be as easy as it sounded.

If she were being honest with herself, she wanted to see him, wanted to see if there was any spark left between them. She'd healed so many parts of her life, but this one had been the biggest wound to her heart and her soul and it had been left cracked, bleeding and raw. So she'd come home to make amends with Chase and get over him for good. One way or another, it had to be decided or she couldn't get on with her life. She was stuck. Stuck on Chase.

Denial was a wonderful thing, which helped people cope with tragic situations. It also helped them be stupid a little too long sometimes. Like her. She'd needed it in the beginning, when things had been very bad. Over the years she'd thought she'd kicked her dependence on it, had been able to stand up on her own. She'd changed her life and had thought she'd changed who she was on the inside, too.

Chase had seen right through her little masquerade to the heart of her the second he'd leveled those surprised laser blue eyes of his on her. That had rattled her as nothing had in three years. Over that time she'd thought she'd forget about them, about him, and move on, the way she knew he'd done. She'd thought she'd been prepared to see him, to be coworkers again. But her plan had backfired the moment she'd seen him. *Kapow!*

The guilt and somehow the bitter relief of their breakup had hurt and rocked her world, but she'd been able to crawl out of the hole finally.

Nothing had rocked her world the way it had when his eyes had met hers this morning.

Nothing.

And now she had to reconsider this assignment, this idea of hers to return to her home and make a new life, to make a place for herself again. Her family was here. Her friends were here. And her memories were here. Maybe Liz was right. Maybe she needed to be assigned to a different unit so she didn't have to work with Chase every day. Was the answer just to avoid him and enjoy the rest of her assignment? She could still catch up with friends, with family, visit old haunts like the James River, the Chesapeake Bay and enjoy socializing again. That sounded like a fine plan.

For someone else.

Although she'd left the area after her assault, she didn't consider herself a coward to run away from things or run away from people. This return to her home was the last part of her healing, of coming full circle to where things had begun, and to come face-to-face with her fears, her anxiety, and spit in the eyes of the demons that had haunted her for three years.

It was time. She was ready. It was the last step to recovery. Today, she'd stepped into the pond, and she'd see if she could swim again.

A month ago, when she'd been talking to her nurse

recruiter, the idea had sounded like the right idea at the time. Go home to the Tidewater area of eastern Virginia, reconnect with her roots, be near her family for the fall and spend the holidays together. Her parents had been thrilled, and it had all seemed a good idea. Her brother, Danny, a firefighter, seemed to think it was a good idea, too. Time to come home and reclaim her life. Full circle.

That was the trouble with brilliant ideas. They always seem good at the time you cooked them up, but then, when the bacon hit the pan, you needed to expect some sizzle and smoke.

There was definitely sizzle when it came to Chase Montgomery. Lots of sizzle. That hadn't changed, but now she wasn't certain she was prepared to face it, to face him knowing she had been responsible for their breakup.

"You ready?" Liz asked, interrupting her train of thought.

"Sure. What are we doing now?"

"Computer training. That's probably new since you were here. Half the staff still don't know how to use it. Training has been a real pain."

"I've used a couple of different kinds of software, so maybe this one will be something I already know."

"Wouldn't that be great? Save us both some headaches."

Emily reacquainted herself with the computer system, and how the charting requirements had changed since she'd previously worked there. Then the moment she'd dreaded happened.

She came face-to-face with Chase in the hallway by the staff lounge. Alone.

"Oh. Hi there." Flustered, she tucked a strand of hair

behind her ear. Or she tried to. It was an old habit she hadn't dropped when she'd cut her hair short. The last time she'd seen Chase her hair had been halfway down her back. Now it didn't even cover her ears.

"Hi." Chase looked as if he was surprised to see her as well. He cleared his throat, and his gaze skittered away from hers. "Uh…you cut your hair."

"Yes. Yes, I did." How awkward was this? *Very!*

"It looked better long." He looked at her as if remembering or trying to remember how it had looked on her before.

"Yes, well. Suits my lifestyle now." She tried to walk around him at the same time he tried to walk around her, and they ended up bouncing off each other.

"Sorry."

"Sorry." She stomped a foot. "This is so annoying."

"What is? Running into your old lover or being told you look better with long hair?" Chase took a step back and paused, interested in hearing the answer. He crossed his arms and waited for her, knowing he wasn't going to like any reason she had. Why should he? She was the one interrupting the status quo of his life. That didn't come without risk or consequences. Did she think he was just going to accept her unexpected presence with open arms and forget how she'd destroyed his life? She was the one who'd walked away, not him. If he admitted his part, that he'd let her go, that he hadn't chased her down and made her stay, he'd have to look too closely at things best left in the past. At least, that was what he felt right now.

"Well, both, but mostly running into you when I hadn't expected it." Okay. There it was, out in the air between them. The honesty he could appreciate.

"Imagine my surprise when I saw you in the trauma room." He raised his brows and looked down at her. In the past he'd considered her height cute. She was short, but she'd hit him at just the right place when they'd been wrapped up in each other. He blew out a breath at the unexpected memory.

"There was no way to avoid it."

"Seriously? I had no advanced warning. You could have called me." Dammit. Someone should have called him and let him know she was coming.

"And what? Warned you I was going to be working in the ER and *might* run into you? For all I knew, you weren't even here, or were married with six kids." Big. Fat. Lie. She still had friends in the hospital, and they'd let her know he was still there. Still single. Still hot. *Very hot.*

"I see." He stiffened, and his eyes went icy. "Danny could have told me."

"Why? We're old news, right? Now we're just two professionals working together, and the rest doesn't matter, does it?" What mattered was that her heart was palpitating, her breath was tight in her throat, and her legs didn't want to move. Old news. *Right.* Denial was her BFF.

"Yes. Well. I can be professional, and I'm certain you will be, too." The ice hadn't left his veins, but at least he was being civil. That was more than she should expect from him. And there was nothing he could do about her presence. She was a good nurse, so he'd have to keep his personal reasons to himself. They had no bearing here.

"Of course. I expected nothing less. I'm sorry. I should have gotten word to you."

"Yes, you should have. It would have been simple courtesy."

At least she'd apologized and some of his irritation dissolved. Maybe he could overlook it, maybe not, but it was a situation he was going to have to deal with.

"Again. Sorry." She glanced away. "I was going to grab some coffee then head back out there."

"Pot's on the right. Creamer and sugar in cupboard above." Dammit. Why had he said that? He didn't care how she took her coffee any longer. Why had he told her that when he hadn't meant to?

"You remember how I take my coffee?" Surprise showed in her eyes. Blinking those big blue eyes of hers, she held his gaze for the first time since he'd seen her again. What was she looking for? Hell, what was *he* looking for? The past revealed in each other's eyes? Hardly.

"I never forgot." He paused for another second and took a long slow look over her. "Anything." With that declaration he pushed away before he said something truly stupid and headed into the main part of the ER. How in the world was he going to get through three months with her underfoot, under his skin? Had he just lied to her *and* himself by telling her he could be a professional? The way he felt now was nothing close to it. What he felt was…ripped open. Raw in a way he hadn't allowed himself to feel in the years since she'd broken him and left town.

He was a physician, an ER doctor and an emergency surgeon, and proud of what he'd accomplished in his career. He was a professional, and he saved the lives of trauma victims every day. That was why he was here in this hospital. But if he were being honest with himself, so was Emily. She was a damned good trauma nurse with excellent skills. The hospital had had a turnover of staff in the last few months, and they needed quality staff, hence the number of travel nurses presently in the hospital. Experience didn't come easily or without cost. He knew that, and he was forced to admit she'd worked damned hard for hers.

She also had the unfortunate, firsthand experience of being on the receiving end of a terrible trauma, which made her uniquely qualified to be doing the kind of work she did.

Not wanting to travel down that bumpy road again right now, he moved forward, moved toward the next patient, the next chart, the next issue in front of him, despite his memories wanting to drag him back into the past.

The day progressed more slowly in the afternoon. Staff came to him with more mundane issues that kept him busy, but he still felt as if he were walking through water up to his chest. Slowly, trudging along. The oppression of the past weighed heavily on his mind and his spirit.

"Dr. Montgomery? Chase?" The words eventually penetrated his brain that someone was calling to him.

"Yes?" He frowned as Liz and Emily stood beside him.

"I was going to introduce you to our new travel nurse, but I think you've met before, right?"

"Correct." That was the simplest, most unemotional way to present it. Dry.

"Okay. One less thing on the checklist to do." She gave an awkward smile. "I see. Sorry to bug you."

"No problem." Keeping all expression and emotion from his face was getting harder to do, and he felt himself gritting his teeth. Thankfully he had a good dental plan, because he would probably be doing that for the next three months.

"Actually, I had a question for Dr. Montgomery about a new patient." Emily spoke to Liz, but looked at Chase. Professional. Cool. Fine.

"Sure. What's up?" He could do it, too. Really. He leaned back in the desk chair and raised his hands over his head, waiting for her to speak.

"I'll catch you later," Liz said, and moved away.

Emily filled him in on the background of the patient in question. "This is a twenty-five-year-old male who is accustomed to being in the outdoors, hunting, fishing and camping. He's complaining of joint pain, fatigue, and general malaise. I'm going to put in a lab request for the usual workup, but I was wondering if we should test for Lyme disease as well."

Chase frowned as he thought about the details of the case and processed the facts. Concise, important symptoms, and a little detective work to boot. Smart, beautiful and still sexy as hell. Dammit. "Is he running a fever?"

"On and off for a few weeks, since his last camping trip in western Maryland." She didn't face him but stood beside him, facing the computer. "He also noticed a classic bull's-eye rash on his leg and got worried when it didn't resolve right away."

"That's ground zero for Lyme exposure." He nodded. "Go ahead and add the panel, but explain to him it's a two-part test and it will be a week before we get results."

"I will. Thank you, Doctor." She nodded, keeping her eyes downcast as she walked away.

So it was going to be the cool doctor-nurse relationship between them. He could do that, too. He watched as she walked away. Her body had changed since back then. There was something different about the way she walked, more confident, more sure of herself, and her posture was definitely more upright. She actually appeared to be a little taller than her five-foot-five, petite frame, which had fit him perfectly. Now he'd have to reconsider that. Not that there was going to be an opportunity for her to fit to his body anymore. *Ever.*

An hour later she approached again. He was still in the same position at the computer console, having gotten no further in his documentation. "Can you see this patient now? The possible Lyme guy?"

"Sure. Are labs back?"

"Yes. Chest X-ray, too."

"Let me have a look at them first." He clicked a few times, certain he was following the right pathway to the test results, but there was no X-ray. "It's not here. Are you sure you ordered the right tests on this patient?" Irritation crept into his voice, despite his desire to not react to her at all. "Being timely is important around here, Emily. We don't sit around—"

"Yes. I'm sure. I printed them up if you'd like to look at them the old-fashioned way." She gave a tight smile. "Might be easier for you."

"No." Focusing on the screen, he gave an irritated sigh, then clicked and clicked again, with no better results. "Dammit."

With a sigh, Emily leaned over his shoulder and took the mouse from his right hand. "Let me see. Oh, you've got the wrong patient up, that's all." She masterfully clicked here and there and in seconds had the proper patient with the labs and X-ray reports side by side on the screen. "There you go. Easy."

He cast a baleful eye at her and really wanted to feel irritated, but the fact was he hated this computer system and had refused to spend the time to learn it properly. As soon as he did that, it would be changed to something else, so why bother?

"Show-off." The second he turned to glare at her he knew it was a mistake, making him grit his teeth again. The fragrance he'd never been able to get out of his mind filled his senses and images of her in his arms hit him like a ton of bricks. The memories came over him hard and fast. The body wash she loved to use in the shower, her long hair slicked back from her pretty face, the water sluicing down her body, over the curves of her breasts and hips. Jeez, his thoughts were inappropriate. So much for being a professional.

His gaze dropped to her mouth, as lush and full as he remembered it. The smile on her face froze as she met his gaze full on. Her pupils dilated, and he knew she was thinking the same thing. Would there be anything, any spark between them again? Could there be? Then she straightened and took a step back.

"Yes. Well. There they are, Doctor. I've used this system a few times at other hospitals. Pretty simple once you get to know it." She dropped her gaze and blew out a quick breath.

"I see." Clearly, she was not unaffected by his presence and not as cool as she pretended to be. But that was not his problem.

Nothing Emily Hoover did was his problem. Ever again.

CHAPTER THREE

THE SOUND OF raised voices generally got some attention, even in an ER full of chaos. This one was in relation to Emily's last patient of the day, who had come in thirty minutes ago. A woman, in her midforties, had said she'd tripped over her cat and hit her cheek on a doorknob. Emily had seen plenty of trips and falls and doorknob injuries, but this was not one of them. The woman had warned Emily her husband was going to be making an intoxicated appearance. He stumbled his way through the automatic doors right on cue.

"I don't care who you are—I'm going in there to see my wife." The man was a belligerent one, not used to a woman who had her own power and didn't care one whit about his. He was used to getting his way by bullying and it wasn't working, which only made his color go from pink to a florid red.

"Sir, your wife doesn't want to see you right now. You're drunk and—"

"The hell you say." Unable to stand up without swaying only added proof to her statement. Emily kept him in full view of the security camera so there would be plenty of evidence if needed later.

"I don't say. *She* says, and what she says goes. Got it?"

Emily stood her ground, facing the large man dressed
in hunting camo. This wasn't the first time she'd had
to handle an upset family member, so she called on her
years of ER experience to remain calm and keep the
upper hand. She cast a glance at one of the staff members and nodded. It was a silent signal to notify Security
they were needed in the ER immediately. Her job was
to keep him distracted until they arrived.

"Get out of my way, bitch." The man reached out to
grab Emily by the shoulder, obviously intending to shove
her out of the way.

Emily had good reflexes and jumped back so he
couldn't touch her, but Chase hurried over to her, putting himself between her and the drunk. The man was
huge, and towered over Chase by a foot.

"Don't touch her." He spoke forcefully to the man
and tried to calm his nerves at the sight of him reaching for Emily. "Don't touch any of our staff, or you'll
be looking at assault charges." Chase didn't know if
the words were penetrating the man's whiskey-soaked
brain cells but he had to try.

"Like I care." He glared at Chase, but didn't move
to touch him.

"Sir, I said your wife doesn't want to see you right
now, and if you continue to resist, you'll be hauled out
of here by Security." Emily spoke from beside Chase.
She'd moved forward to stand beside him, providing
a unified front with him. Other staff members eased
closer. If the man lunged for Emily again, they could
jump him without anyone getting hurt.

"You got no reason to keep me from my wife." The
man was sweating, his face was red and he stunk to
high heaven.

"Actually, we can. You can't be in here drunk. Security's on the way, and they're going to call the police to haul you off to jail." Chase experienced significant satisfaction that the situation was going to end without incident. Having Emily assaulted in front of him would not have been good. Just thinking about it brought back all sorts of horrid images he'd buried. Or so he'd thought.

"What? You can't have me arrested." The man started toward Emily again and tried to kick her, but she avoided his inaccurate jabs. Chase held his hands out to the sides and jumped to block him from getting any closer.

"Dr. Montgomery, he can't get to me. Don't worry," Emily said. She gave a quick grin in his direction, and his heart reacted against his will. That impish grin had never left his mind and, combined with the short, spiky hair, she looked like a little fairy with a bad attitude.

Two muscled security team members, dressed in black, arrived and joined Chase. "We'll take it from here."

"He's all yours. I have patients to wrap up before the end of shift," Emily said, and stepped around the man, but he took a swipe at her and missed. Again. Nerves calming, Chase watched as Emily easily avoided the man's giant hand and wondered what she'd been doing to gain such reflexes.

"You little bitch. I'm gonna get you for this."

"Is that a threat? Are you threatening her?" Chase stepped forward, all amusement gone. "I think you've just threatened a staff member here. In front of witnesses and on security cameras. We'll add that to the trespassing charges already on the list."

"Oh, man." He began to whine and snivel. "I just wanna see my wife." Stomping his foot, he looked like a petulant toddler held between the security guards.

Chase approached and put his face as close to the drunk as was tolerable given the fumes emanating off him. Fortunately, it was a no-smoking hospital or they could have gone up in flames. "I believe *you're* the reason she's in the ER in the first place, are you not?"

Pause. "Yes."

"Did you drive here?" Chase asked.

"If it's any of your business, yes." He tried to spit at Chase, who moved deftly out of range.

"Fellows, let the police know to add impaired driving to the list."

"Got it." They hauled the man out of the ER to await the police.

"Are you okay? Really?" Despite himself, Chase moved toward Emily, concerned that the threat might trigger memories of her assault again, the way they were starting to in him. No matter what he felt for her now, he didn't want to see her hurt by anyone. This time he'd been able to help out, even though it had been a small effort.

"Nah, I'm good. I have new ninja reflexes. He didn't even get close." Demonstrating her technique, she jumped around in front of him looking quite like a ninja in scrubs.

She gave that grin again and his heart now seemed to have no immunity against it. "I see." He cleared his throat and clamped down his anxiety for her safety.

That reflex hadn't gone away just because they weren't a couple anymore. Of course, he probably would have reacted the same no matter what staff member had been involved in the kerfuffle. At least, that was what he told himself.

Turning away from the scene, Emily rolled her shoulders a few times then picked up her clipboard. "Okay. Dr. Montgomery, can you see this patient now?"

"Uh, sure." He stepped closer, more comfortable with the doctor-nurse role. "Is this the wife?"

"Yes. Superficially, she looks roughed up a bit, nothing serious, other than needing to get away from her husband." Emily shook her head. "Can't say I blame her."

"You think he beat her up?" Anger flashed hot and fast inside him. Women and children were precious, and were to be protected, not used as punching bags by drunken men who couldn't control their tempers.

"She won't cop to it, says she tripped, fell into a door. It's mostly the face. Black eye on the right, swollen shut, cheek bruised and swollen. Not sure if it's fractured, but it won't hurt to have an X-ray of it."

He followed her without comment to the patient room and when Emily held the curtain back, Chase's stomach clenched. The image of the woman before him sickened him. She was in her midforties. Her face was so swollen she looked as if she had been in a car accident and it instantly reminded him of the night he'd seen Emily in a similar condition. Trying to remain in that professional space, he took a quick breath and stepped close to the gurney. Emily was right. He didn't even need the X-rays to know she'd been beaten up. In their line of work they'd become unfortunate experts on the topic.

"Mrs. Billings? I'm Dr. Montgomery. Nurse Hoover has made some recommendations for your treatment, and I'm inclined to agree with her." He trusted her nursing experience, if nothing else.

"Like what?" She turned a defeated gaze to him. The sound of her voice was slow and thick. She'd probably bitten her tongue during the assault.

"Facial X-rays, possibly a CAT scan of your head to look for fractures in the sinuses and the left side of your face." He moved closer, and she jumped. "Sorry, didn't mean to startle you." More carefully, he approached her and focused on keeping everything slow, his voice soft. She'd obviously been conditioned to watch out for any sudden movements her husband made.

"Go ahead." She closed her eyes, as if trying to shut out the world. "I don't care."

"Are you in pain?"

She nodded and tears began to overflow. "Don't be nice to me, Doc. I can't take it." She sniffed. "I don't know what it's like."

"Then I'll try harder to be mean," he said, and received a crooked smile.

"Thanks."

He looked at Emily, who looked pale and a little wide-eyed. "I'll get right on those orders, Doctor." Then she turned back to the patient and the moment was gone, if it had been there at all. Maybe he'd only imagined the haunted look on her face as she'd watched her patient.

Avoiding Chase and the look on his face was her goal. Seeing this woman had brought back memories for both of them that neither of them cared to have. Caring for this woman was her job, and she would do it well, but making eye contact with Chase would be her undoing. She had to avoid it. Like her patient, she couldn't deal with his compassion for her pain. What she needed to do was keep busy and focused on her work. The rest would eventually go away. It always did. Situations like this brought everything back to slam her right in the gut when she wasn't looking.

Trying to stop the trembling in her hands, she prepared the lab tubes and labeled them appropriately, but her mind was elsewhere.

Night, being alone in the dark, was the toughest. Night was when the shadows darkened in her mind and the whispers of her attacker infiltrated her barriers. *Bitch. I'm gonna get you, bitch.* Sometimes all it took was hearing that word *bitch* to send her all the way back to that dark awful night.

She applied the tourniquet to Mrs. Billings's arm and inserted the needle into the vein. Emily swallowed hard against the sudden dryness in her mouth. She filled each tube the way she was supposed to and applied a small dressing to the tiny puncture site of the left arm. Focused. Clinical.

Emily placed the tubes filled with blood for testing into a zippered lab bag for transport. After setting them in the lab pick-up rack, she realized her heart hadn't settled down and the tightness in her chest hadn't eased. Was it Chase? Was it the husband? Was it this patient? Maybe all of it combined in such a short time worked together to rob her of her strength.

Making her way to the supply room, she checked to make sure she was alone then removed her lab coat, placed a towel on the floor, sat cross-legged on it and closed her eyes.

There was a place she liked to go mentally when stressed and it was a place from her past where she'd been happy, walking alone on the sand at Virginia Beach, feeling the warmth of the sun on her skin, the salt on the breeze and the coarse sand on her feet.

This was the place where she let go of stress, released it to the ocean waves and found some peace.

Until Chase walked into the supply room.

"What are you doing?" He stopped short just inside the doorway.

Startled, she opened her eyes. The serenity that had been on her face vanished and it was his fault. Dammit. She'd looked so peaceful for a second, and he'd ruined it.

"I *was* meditating." She blinked a few times, as if coming back to herself from wherever she had been.

"Now? In the middle of the shift?"

"Yes. I'm entitled to breaks. Several, in fact, over the course of twelve hours. What I do with them is my business." Closing her eyes again, she tried to ignore him, but it was impossible.

"Yes, that's true." He squatted down beside her, too close for her senses. "You never used to meditate." Obvious irritation showed in the frown between her delicate eyebrows and the downward turn of her mouth. Not that he blamed her.

"I never used to do a lot of things." She looked up at him, held his gaze, almost challenging him. "I've acquired some new skills."

"Like your new ninja reflexes? Are you taking karate or something?" He'd never seen her move so fast. That had impressed him.

"Not karate. If I had used karate I'd have taken out his knee first, but you got in front of me."

"Judo?" He really didn't know about martial arts and had just exhausted his knowledge.

"Hardly. In judo, I would have—"

"Whatever. Clearly, you're an expert now." And he'd had no clue.

"No. Just determined." There was an aura of steel

about her now. And, yes, determination showed in her eyes. That was the difference he'd been sensing in her.

"To what?" He really wanted to know the answer to that. Genuine curiosity had been roused in him and for the first time today he could set aside the pain.

Without answering the question, she unfolded her legs and stood. "Did you come in here for something or just to annoy me?"

"I saw you come in here and after the day's events I thought you looked a little off." That was okay. Looking after a coworker?

"Off? No. I'm fine." Turning away from him, she began to scan the shelves as if looking for something. "Gauze, suture materials, IV supplies over here. Good to know." She took a step to the next shelving unit. "GI supplies over here—oh, look, enemas. Never know when you need to get rid of some—"

"Stop it. You're not fine. If you're meditating in the middle of a shift, that must mean you're upset about something. Possibly nearly getting assaulted not long ago?" He let the question hang in the air between them.

She gave him a glare then kept scanning. "Maybe we need to order extra-large enemas for special cases." The glare she leveled on him left no doubt as to who she would use them on.

"Emily." Chase intended to make her face him, make her turn around, and placed a hand on her shoulder. Then squealed like a girl and nearly dropped to his knees in pain. "Augh!"

"Don't touch me, Chase." Again, her speed defied logic. He had been unprepared for her ability to take his wrist in her hand, apply pressure and leverage to the point of pain, yet she hadn't batted an eyelid. In fact, she looked calmer than she had since he'd entered the room. The control in her eyes impressed him and maybe scared him a little.

"Okay, okay, okay. Let go. *Let go.* Ow. *Ow.* I have to do surgery with that hand." She released him and the relief was great.

"Unless you want to have both hands in casts, don't ever try to touch me again." The calm, serious look on her face was something he never wanted to see aimed at him again, as if she were contemplating squishing an insect.

He shook his hand, grateful she hadn't really wanted to hurt him or it could have gotten ugly. Baffled, he looked at her as if seeing her for the first time, and maybe he was. Giving her a little space, he took a step back. "Where'd you learn all that stuff?" That was the change in her body he hadn't been able to identify before. She was muscular and toned in a way that wasn't from a weekly aerobics class. Yowza, she was strong.

Now she faced him fully, the brunt of her anger unleashed on him. "'Stuff'? Seriously?" Though half a foot shorter than he, the power of her was unbelievable and gloriously arousing. "That 'stuff' saved my life more than once. That 'stuff', as you call it—" she tossed her head "—has kept me sane for the last three years, and that '*stuff*' allows me sleep at night."

She nearly trembled with rage, and he could see it unfold within her. Her blue eyes sparkled, her face was flushed and pink, her chest rose and fell quickly. She was beautiful, and he did not want to see it, to feel anything for her, to be the recipient of her rage. But he couldn't help himself. He stood there in awe for a few seconds before he could speak.

"*Are* you okay?" His voice was a hoarse whisper that he barely recognized as his own. "Seriously?"

Then Emily blinked a few times, shook herself and let out a long, slow breath. "I'm fine. The meditation helped and now I'm ready to go out there and see if my lab results are back yet."

She tried to move past him, but he placed his hand on her arm. She stopped, looked at his hand then up at his face, calm and cool. Hastily, Chase extricated his hand.

"If you wish to continue to do surgery without having it yourself, I suggest you don't lay a hand on me again. *Ever.*"

"Sorry." Point made.

"I'll let you know about the labs as soon as they're back."

"O…*kay.*" Reaching out, he opened the door and watched Emily walk away.

CHAPTER FOUR

TREMBLING SUBSIDING, Emily returned to the nurses' station and logged onto the computer, pulled up the lab results, reviewed them and clicked the print key. She would have to return to Chase, Dr. Montgomery, as she needed to remember to notify him of these results. The woman had obvious issues with her husband, but she had deeper problems, too, and it showed clearly in her lab results.

"Dammit, I don't want to talk to him anymore today," she grumbled aloud.

"And who would that be?" Liz asked, and plopped down in a chair beside her.

"Oh!" She whirled. "I thought I was by myself."

"In this place? Never." She patted Emily on the arm. "Now, tell me how you are and who you don't want to talk to. I came to check on you after the incident, but you disappeared for a while."

"Yeah. I was taking a few deep breaths in the supply room." No harm in admitting that, regardless of what Chase thought. "A little decompression."

"I see. Good." Liz nodded. "And the rest?"

With a sigh and a downward turn of her mouth Emily leaned back in the chair. "I've got labs to review with Dr. Montgomery, but I don't want to talk to him right now."

"Why not?" Liz held out her hand, and Emily gave the lab reports to her. She took a few seconds to scan the numbers, automatically interpreting. "Everything looks good."

"Next page. Hematology."

"Oh, I see. Anemia and indications of infection. You're wondering if she has an underlying pathology you'll have to discuss with him."

"Yes." Thankfully, Liz understood. Maybe she would talk to Chase.

"I don't understand, though. Did he say or do something to you that upset you? He seemed impressed with how you handled the drunk husband."

"Really?" Now, that surprised her. He'd never been impressed about anything she'd ever done. Or at least he'd never admitted it.

"Yes. If I didn't know any better, I'd say he was concerned for you. But then he turned around and was the same old Chase."

"Same old Chase? What do you mean?" Despite her resolve, she was curious. After all, three years had passed since they'd seen one another and although her brother was good friends with him, he'd respected her boundaries and not mentioned Chase. Maybe she could surreptitiously get some information on Chase and it would satisfy the curiosity that had been plaguing her for the last year. Was he the same as she'd remembered?

"He's a regular guy—fun, friendly—but when it's time to be serious, he is."

Emily gaped. "Chase? *Fun?* Since when? He was never fun." She clamped her mouth shut and a knowing light entered Liz's eyes. "He was serious most of the time. Work came before everything else."

"I thought there was something serious between you two. You didn't just date a few times, did you?"

Keeping secrets was apparently not her forté, and she shouldn't look forward to a career in the international espionage field. Damn. Maybe Liz could keep a secret.

"It was a long time ago." But was it really?

"Not that it's any business of mine, but it doesn't seem like business is over between you two. If the air needs to be cleared for you to work together, then I'd suggest having a chat with him." She sighed. "I'd suggest it to anyone who was having a difficult working relationship. If needed, there's always mediation."

"Mediation? No. We were done three years ago. And it was a bitter breakup."

"I'm sorry, Emily. It's none of my business, like I said, but if you ever need to talk, I can listen and it won't go anywhere." She had the calm eyes and demeanor of a true leader.

"Thanks, but I just need to pull myself together and be an adult about it." She'd put her big-girl panties on a long time ago. They just needed a little straightening now and then.

"Okay. The offer stands." She handed the papers back to Emily. "And I think Chase should see those right away." She nodded over Emily's shoulder.

"I should see what?" Face serious, he moved closer. The cologne he wore hadn't changed and it caught her by surprise. She'd loved that on him. Then.

"Labs here indicate some infection and something going on with her hematology." She shrugged, looked away and placed the printout on the counter in front of him so there was no accidental touching of skin to skin.

Without touching the papers, he leaned over and read them, nodding and focusing on the numbers in front of him, then turned his attention to her. "So what do you think we should do?"

"Me? You're the doctor. You should examine her and then decide, but it appears she's losing blood somewhere." She stiffened at being put on the spot. "Although she didn't complain of any abdominal pain, and we were more concerned about her head trauma, it's possible she took a few hits to the abdomen and either her spleen or liver is leaking."

Just then the alarms in Mrs. Billings's room began to chime in earnest. Emily looked at the monitor beside her at the station displaying the vital signs in bold green numbers.

"What?"

"BP taking a nosedive and pulse shot up." She looked with concern at Chase and met his gaze full on. "She's in trouble."

They all raced into the room just in time to see the patient's eyes roll back in her head, and she lost consciousness. "Dammit," Chase cursed, and he rarely did that in front of a patient, no matter what the circumstance. "Call a code."

Emily hit the specially designed button on the wall behind the patient's head while Liz ran for the crash cart, the large tool chest on wheels housing lifesaving equipment.

People began arriving in droves to assist with the code. Thankfully, in a code situation no one was ever alone. Chase was in charge and ran the operation, but

Emily was next in command and delegated tasks to other staff members if she wasn't able to perform them herself.

"Let's give her some fluids, wide open," Chase instructed, "then epinephrine IV push." He kept his gaze on the monitor, watching everything the heart did.

Emily didn't have to call for it as Liz had it prepared in a few seconds and handed it to her. Pulling the cap off, she connected the needleless system and pushed the medicine in as quickly as possible. The patient's heart rate suddenly paused, then dropped dramatically.

Chase whipped off the stethoscope from around his neck and listened to the patient's abdomen, and then used his hands to palpate it.

"How's her belly?"

"Rigid. Think you're right, Nurse Hoover. She's got a cracked liver and is bleeding into her abdomen. Call OR and tell them we're on the way up now. No time to wait. I'll have to operate, but call the surgical team for backup."

"Now I wish I'd hit him," she muttered beneath her breath, and jerked the receiver off the wall.

"What?"

"Nothing. Got it." She dialed and informed the OR of the situation of an emergency patient coming their way.

Staff scrambled to get her to the OR. Emily trotted along next to the stretcher as the crew moved down the hall to the OR, which was on the same floor but through a maze of hallways and double doors.

"There's something wrong in your abdomen, Jenny, so Dr. Montgomery is going to operate on you." She stroked the woman's hair. Sweat had popped out on her face and neck. Emily knew it was from shock and the compensating mechanisms her body was engaging in. The heart raced to make up for in rate what it lacked in output, due to low blood volume.

And then Mrs. Billings was gone. Emily handed her over to the pre-op nurses. Watching through the slight opening in the doors, she watched Chase approach the stainless-steel sinks, pull on a hair cover, mask, and begin to scrub. He wore the green, sterile scrubs required in the OR and was ready to roll.

Back in the day she'd used to love watching him scrub, knowing he was entering a world all his own in surgery, knowing he was going to drag a patient back from the edge of death.

Back then he'd been her superhero. Saving everyone and everything.

Only he'd failed her when she'd needed him the most. Nothing in life had ever disappointed her more. Time had helped her realize he was just a man and no cape could turn him into what she'd needed. But right now that man was going to bust his butt trying to save this woman. If nothing else, she had to respect him for that.

The remainder of the day passed with much less fuss than the first part of it. A few coughs, colds and possible flu filtered in, but her mind was never far from thoughts of Chase and the work he was doing on their patient.

At the end of shift Emily gave in to mental and physical exhaustion, allowing it to wash over her as she exited the building out into the staff parking lot. Fortunately, it wasn't a long walk.

This was the kind of situation that could lead to an assault on a woman who was not prepared the way Emily was now. Women left their jobs after long hours, eager to get home, their senses and muscles weakened by their work, not paying attention to the immediate surroundings. And alone. That was a sure setup for an attack.

Now Emily was different and more prepared than she'd ever been. Though exhausted, her senses, her self-protective instincts she'd honed over the years surged within her, brewing just under the surface, reaching out into the night, as if sentient. Sounds came to her from the twilight. The abrasive whirring of a cicada attracted her attention to the tops of the trees. Crickets trilled from the grass along the edge of the parking lot. A flock of pigeons overhead swooped past in search of a roosting place for the night. A lone seagull hung on an updraft long enough to decide whether she was edible or not.

All familiar, comforting sounds.

Then footsteps crunched on the gravel behind her. Staff left the building at intervals, heading to their vehicles. *These* steps were deliberate and rapidly approaching her.

Without thinking, she dropped her bag and took a defensive posture, arms at the ready, prepared to defend herself. When she recognized the person approaching her she relaxed her stance, but her insides remained tense and jiggling for another reason.

Chase approached, still in the green scrubs, mask dangling from his neck and a grim look on his face. He must have news of their patient or he wouldn't be there.

"What are you doing out here?"

"I wanted to catch you before you left."

"How is she?" She didn't even have to ask. She knew why he was there.

"She's going to make it, but it was touchy for a while. Had to give her six units of blood. Livers are messy, as you know." And then he grinned. He was exhilarated by the success of the surgery and it showed.

That smile had always been infectious, and she returned it. For the first time since she'd arrived she thought they could have a good working relationship.

"Yes, they are, and you love it, don't you?" It was good to see, this glimpse of him at ease and in his element.

"Have to say I do." He placed his hands on his hips and looked overhead. "Looks like a nice night."

Emily nodded. "It is. I was thinking about going to the river to sit for a while." The James River gave peace to her soul. There were places she could go where she would be safe. No one would find her or accidentally run across her while on a walk, and she could let go.

"Really? You would still go down to the river even though it was our place?" Though he shouldn't have been surprised, some part of him was. The river used to be their spot, where they'd gone together to unwind, to splash in the shallows and toss off the stresses of the day. She still went there, and he hadn't been in three years. For some reason that surprised him. She'd been able to move ahead in areas he hadn't.

"Yeah. I still go. Not to our spot exactly, but nearby." She shrugged and looked away, watched her foot as she kicked a few pebbles off the sidewalk. "The water comforts me."

"I remember." The changing light reflected on her hair. What he'd known as a silky blond, down past her shoulders, was now a spiky mix of brown and red with platinum tips.

Unexpectedly, a lump settled in his gut at what she'd been through and how he'd been unable to help her, how he'd failed her. How she'd rejected him, and how he'd let her. She was an amazingly resilient woman and it was something that was very attractive in her. "You look good."

Startled blue eyes met his. In them he saw the woman that he'd once loved, but now the innocence had vanished, replaced by a strength and determination he'd never imagined she was capable of.

"You don't have to say stuff like that just because we're working together."

"I mean it. You look very good." That was probably something he shouldn't have admitted out loud, but she was a beautiful woman, short hair or long. "Different, but very good."

"Thank you." She took a step backward, away from him, almost shy again. "But I think I should go. Thanks for letting me know about the patient. I'm glad it was you working on her." She nodded, then turned.

"What are you driving these days? I can walk you to your car." He stepped up beside her, uncertain why he wasn't willing to let her walk away from him just yet. But he wanted to linger with her a few more minutes. Now that he'd gotten over the shock of her presence, he was more intrigued about why she was there.

"Small SUV, good for traveling but bad on fuel." She made that movement again, like she was tucking her hair behind an ear, but the hair wasn't there. That was what she used to do when she'd been nervous. "But I'm good. You don't have to walk me anywhere."

"I'd like to."

That made her stop and a smile lifted one corner of her mouth. "I take hapkido two nights a week, I can run a half-marathon and I have a big-ass can of pepper spray in my hand."

"Are you trying to tell me you can take care of your-self?" That thought lifted the corner of his mouth and eased some of the tightness in his chest.

"I am. I appreciate the offer, though." With the illumination from the streetlight he could see amusement sparkling in her eyes.

"Hapkido, eh? I don't even know what that is." That made him smile all the way. The thought of her in a martial-arts class, breaking boards with her forehead, just didn't jibe with what he knew of her. "No wonder you weren't afraid of that drunk."

"No need to be. I could have taken him down had there been a need." She leaned forward. "I would have protected you, too."

Now, that made him laugh full out. It was a good feeling. And having experienced the way she'd dropped him to his knees in the utility room, he believed her. "I have no doubt."

"Good night, Chase."

"Good night." He didn't say her name out loud. He'd vowed back then never to say her name again and watched as she disappeared into the night.

CHAPTER FIVE

BASKETBALL MADE HIM SWEAT. Handball made him sweat. Racquetball made him sweat, too, but nothing made him sweat the way last night's thoughts and erotic dreams of Emily had.

Dammit.

He didn't want to think of her, didn't want to remember, didn't want to want or hold or need or ache for her the way he used to. He'd moved on. He'd moved *on*. So had she. But last night it had all come back to him. All the pain, the pleasure and the bitterness. For just a moment there in the parking lot he'd been okay, been able to talk to her, but then he'd remembered. Really remembered. Against his will, against everything he'd vowed not to do, he'd remembered. And he'd ached for her.

Everything that had happened to her had been *his* fault. *His* responsibility. The changes, the tears, the rape, the attack, the sorrow. Everything. And there wasn't a damned thing he could do about it.

He couldn't change it, couldn't take it back, couldn't make it better, and it would never, *ever* go away. And he could never, ever forgive himself. Occasionally he could forget about it, but it never went away.

Rolling over on the bed, he looked out the window

at the rising sun. At this time of the year life was in suspended animation. Fall and its crisp air hadn't hit yet, and the heat of the summer lingered on for a few more weeks, giving a false sense of pleasure that summer tranquility was going to last forever. Trees to the east glowed gold with the light behind them, the leaves taking on a gilt edge with each second that passed.

Unable to rest any longer, he dressed in running shorts, a T-shirt and trainers, then plugged in some music on his phone loud enough to quiet the voices in his head and took off out the front door.

At this time of the day morning joggers were a fair-weather lot. Some people he'd see on a regular basis, others only when the mood struck them and others sporadically. Today he didn't care. Foul in mood and in mind, he took off at a moderate pace, not wanting to injure himself but fast enough to challenge himself.

And he began to sweat. Again.

Someone slapped him on the arm, and he nearly stumbled. Slowing, he yanked the headset out, prepared to give someone a piece of his mind.

"What are you doing?" the man beside him asked.

"Dammit, what are *you* doing?" He'd forgotten. After the events of yesterday he was lucky he remembered his own name.

"You were supposed to wait for me." He took off, and Chase fell into place beside him.

"I forgot." Dammit.

"Forgot, hell. You never forget anything." Danny Hoover, firefighter, running and racquetball partner, and Emily's brother, jogged with him in the early-morning sun.You could have told me." He glared at Danny, unleashing the full brunt of his anger.

"Told you what?" Danny took the inner part of the path around a corner, and Chase moved into the outside position. Danny looked a little like Emily at times, but not so much that Chase felt he was looking at her when he saw Danny. Over the years he'd been able to compartmentalize things and just forget they were siblings.

"You know exactly what I mean. That she was coming back. You could have told me." Like he hadn't known.

Danny grinned and narrowly dodged a tree. "What, and take away the element of surprise? Besides, you said you were over her. It shouldn't have mattered, right?"

"I was. I am. It doesn't. But some warning would have helped." He *was* over her, wasn't he?

"Helped what?"

The man was a pea brain. Maybe he'd inhaled too many toxic fumes during house fires and they had begun to affect his brain. "The first time I saw her. It would have helped me prepare."

"Why would you need to be prepared? You said you were over her." Another turn on the path, a flock of ducks down by the pond looking for an early morning hand out.

"Because I..." Why had he wanted to know? Good question he really didn't want to answer.

"You want to be in control?" Danny provided the suggestion.

"No, I don't."

"Really? Isn't that why you're a surgeon? Couldn't be God and that was the next best thing?" He grinned.

Chase gave Danny a shove and nearly knocked him off the trail. "Where'd you hear that? That's not me, and you know it."

"Around the station. One of the guys is married to an OR nurse. Her opinion of surgeons in general, I think."

"I see. Which one?"

"No way! I'm not ratting her out. You'll just have to be on your best behavior in the OR from now on."

"Like that's gonna happen." He knew what most surgeons were like in the OR: giant toddlers with scalpels. He'd had his moments, for sure, but now that he was a little older, a little more experienced, his confidence in his skills had grown, and he didn't need to yell at the people around him in order to work with them. Others hadn't evolved as much.

"So, a leopard can't change its spots, right?"

"Don't change the subject. You're not off the hook for not telling me she was coming back." Hardly. Danny would be paying for that one for a long time.

"I know. But I couldn't decide which was worse, telling or not telling you, so I let the universe decide. If you two ran into each other then it was fate, meant to be. You're both grown-ups. You can deal, right?"

"Right." Chase jogged along in silence through the beauty of the low country, what was called the Tidewater, an area strongly influenced by the ocean tides. The area was filled with marshes and estuaries for waterfowl and major fishing grounds for the commercial industry. A place he'd called home his entire life. A place where something had been missing until yesterday.

"So how is she? I haven't seen her yet."

"Fine." He paused. "But she cut her hair." It had once been a source of pride to her, and he'd loved the way it had looked on her. Now she looked like a completely different person. Still beautiful, but very different.

"Oh, yeah, she did that a couple of years ago. Right after. Then." He cleared his throat. "What color is it now?"

"Brown and red and blonde."

"Ha. Used to be platinum, then orange for a while. Even dyed it black and gold for her favorite football team once." He shook his head and laughed. "She's a kick in the pants."

"Literally," he said, thinking of her new martial-arts skills. "First day on the job yesterday and she took on some drunk without breaking a sweat."

"That's my sister. Doesn't take crap from anybody anymore."

"The guy was the husband of a patient. Beat his wife up pretty bad. Had to take her to emergency surgery, and then this drunk comes in, trying to give her a hard time."

"Emily wouldn't have taken too kindly to that."

"No. Especially not when the guy put his hand on her, or at least tried to." Chase still couldn't believe how deftly she'd handled that particular issue when he'd touched her in the utility room. His pride still stung that she'd gotten the drop on him.

Danny whistled as they rounded another turn. "I'd have paid money to see that."

"She was so fast." Chase barked out a quick laugh. "She was just cool as could be."

"Only on the outside."

"Huh?"

"She was cool on the outside, appeared to be calm. Inside, I'm sure there was a storm of rage boiling." They arrived to their usual turnaround spot and headed back the way they had come. "Been a problem for a couple of years, the rage, but she's learning to channel it."

"That's what she said later. She was meditating in the supply room. She never used to meditate. What's up with that?"

"She's learning new skills. Goes along with the martial arts. Calm mind, strong body. Nobody messes with you then."

"I see." Chase paused a moment, letting that sink in. He'd loved her once and wanted her to be whole again. "She did give me quite a warning when I touched her."

"Ouch! You still have a hand left? She could have killed you without breaking a nail." He laughed. "I'm surprised she didn't."

"Still have both hands, but...I don't know why I touched her. Or tried to offer her some comfort." It had been stupid, even he knew that. They were over, history, and he'd had no business speaking to her in more than a professional way.

"Comfort? From you?" Danny gave a whistle. "Wow."

"Yeah, even from me. She didn't need it and didn't want it, so I left it at that."

"She's tougher than she used to be, that's for sure, but it saved her soul, know what I mean?" Danny gave a quick glance at Chase.

"I know what you mean. And I'm glad she's doing well. I hope she finds a place where she can be comfortable again, even if it's here."

"Really?" Danny stopped to laugh. Chase stopped, but didn't get the humor.

"What's so funny?"

"You are! You believe that crap you just told me? You hope she finds where she belongs, blah, blah, blah. *Really?* You're so full of it you can't see it for yourself."

"What are you talking about?" Chase tried to ignore

the squiggle of something in his gut and it wasn't his breakfast. Maybe it was his intuition, or guilt, or maybe his conscience. In any case, it bothered him.

"You're not over her, never have been and never will be. So get over yourself, over your lies, and be a man. Go talk to her."

"I've talked to her. At work. Just yesterday." That was the absolute truth. He ignored the irritation rocking up his spine at the suggestion he was lying to himself.

"That's not what I mean, and you know it." Danny stopped laughing, his eyes now serious. "You owe it to her and yourself to see if there's anything left before you either of you can move on. It doesn't matter how much time has passed, it's not been over for either of you. It's time you settled it once and for all."

"Ha!" Pause. "Ha!" Pause. Emily faced herself in the mirror at her early-morning class at the martial-arts studio. This was the first place she'd taken a self-defense class and returning here felt like the homecoming she'd been waiting for. The people here had understood her needs at the time, after her attack, and had given her the skills she'd needed to defend herself and the privacy to work out her grief. She'd surrounded herself with women of courage and strength, and some little bit of those elements had seeped into her psyche every day. Every day she'd grown a little stronger, until she could stand on her own.

Then, it had been all she could do to live in the moment, let alone plan for an uncertain future. So she hadn't planned anything, other than going to the first class, then the second class, and the next after that.

"Hey, Emily, looking good." Approaching her was the

dojo owner, Rose. Asian, small and petite, she looked as fragile as her name on the outside, but Emily had seen the woman take down men three times her size with hardly any effort. This was not a woman to mess with.

"Thanks." She rolled her shoulders and stayed focused on her stance. Focus was the key. If she let her brain loose, it just went wild.

"I wanted to ask you about teaching some classes for us."

Surprised, Emily lost her focus. "What? *Me?*"

"Yes, you." Rose took a stance beside Emily and mirrored her movements. "You're perfect, and uniquely qualified to teach self-defense classes for women." Rose referenced Emily's attack that had led to her quest in martial arts without bringing up the pain of it.

"I see." She moved into another position, held it, focused on her breathing.

"Do you? You're ready now." Reposition. Breathe.

"But I don't think that is my path." Reposition. Breathe. "I am a student of hapkido but not a master by any stretch of the imagination and certainly not qualified to teach."

Rose kept her gaze soft, looking at the floor far in front of them. "Are you going to make me say it?"

"Say what?" Had she missed something? Rose rarely spoke in metaphors or in the vague ways some masters did. She was just a regular woman with an interesting job where she got to hit people without being arrested.

"Seriously?" Rose broke her focus with a laugh, her eyes crinkling up at the edges, and she actually snorted. "You must be tired if you're missing this one."

"Oh, quit and just tell me." What? What had she missed? Was she seriously brain dead today?

"When the teacher is ready..." Rose rolled her hand in a circle, indicating Emily should finish the sentence.

"Oh, God...and the teacher will appear." She closed her eyes. "You have students already, don't you?"

"The first class is full, and we have a waiting list." Rose grinned at Emily in the mirror, and then returned to her pose. "Keep breathing. It will be okay. Remember, it's okay if all you do sometimes is breathe."

"I think I saw that one on social media somewhere." She narrowed her eyes at her friend in the mirror. She would have to reconsider the wiliness of her friend.

"It's been revamped for the current culture, but it's based on an old saying that doesn't translate the same way."

"So, when's the first class scheduled?" Emily gave a mental sigh, knowing she couldn't let Rose or the students down. Just as her patients needed her nursing skills, these students might need her personal protection skills. If even one of them could protect themselves from an assault, it would be worth it.

"After we're through here we can look at the calendar and work it with your schedule. Just once a week."

"Oh, good." She relaxed a little. Maybe she could handle this. Maybe she could learn to be a teacher if it was just once a week.

"For now." Rose gave a Cheshire-cat smile.

"What?" Anxiety started to leak out her pores.

"No pressure."

"Really?" Emily raised one brow at that.

"Really. But with a waiting list..."

"You're *such* a bad liar. You have a plan already, don't you?" Why she was surprised, Emily didn't know, but she was.

"Of course. I'd love to have you become the key trainer for women's self-defense here." Rose clasped her hands together. "That would be just fabulous."

"You are out of your mind if you think I can do that." Really. "I have a career as a nurse."

"Yes. One that has served you well, and I'm not suggesting you give it up. I'm only suggesting you consider expanding your horizons, for lack of a better term, to help other women defend themselves in a way you could not."

Emily stood stone-faced. Her friend knew the whole story, the details of her assault as well as the aftermath and the agony she'd gone through. For her to make a suggestion was a serious thing, and one Emily was certain she hadn't considered lightly.

"You're really serious, not just yanking my chain?"

"I'm very serious. Women are determined to take care of themselves, and they need someone to teach them how." Rose also concealed her emotions from her expression. "They need you, and I would be honored to help facilitate their quest to find the right teacher."

Emily wiped the sweat from her forehead and faced Rose directly. "I will have to meditate on this, but I am honored and humbled you think I'm capable of this mission." It was a mission. She'd embarked on it when she'd begun to heal and had never stopped. Maybe it was a quest, as Rose had just said. Either way, she needed to consider it from all angles before coming to an answer.

Placing her palms together, she bowed to Rose, who returned the gesture.

"Meditate on it and let me know. You're ready." Rose laid those dark, dark eyes, filled with knowledge of the ancient ways, on Emily.

"I will let you know as soon as I can." She left the studio with her heart a bit lighter and decided to stop by the hospital to check on her patient from yesterday. That should be a nice, short distraction, then she could go home, shower, finish unpacking her stuff and make plans for the next few days.

She knew how to work the system of being a travel nurse. She'd been at it for years. Get moved into the apartment provided by the agency she worked for, unpack the necessaries, get through orientation, work hard for three months, and then move on to the next assignment. After three years she had it down to a system that worked for her.

Right now she was going to violate her own policy by going to the hospital in her practice clothes, her *gi*, which would give others too much information about her but maybe it was time to expand her boundaries a little, let her guard down just a bit.

She pulled into the parking lot of the hospital and parked in the employee lot, hoping she wouldn't run into Chase, that he'd be somewhere else, but as she put the car into Park she looked up and there he was, like he'd been waiting for her.

Was it her fate now to run into him at every moment?

CHAPTER SIX

Too late to back the SUV out, he'd seen her and nodded. He stood at the edge of the lot near the green space where there were trees and a little brook where patients, staff and family members could sit at the picnic tables and visit or smoke.

Although the area was the designated distance from the entrance for smoking, she could smell the ash a mile away. Unable to leave gracefully and maintain her dignity, she resigned herself to having to at least acknowledge Chase as she went by him. Denying the kick in her pulse at the sight of him just wasn't honest.

She clipped her badge to her *gi* and got out of the car.

"What are you doing out here?" she asked as she approached him.

"Taking a smoke break."

She scoffed. "You don't smoke."

"No, but I'm entitled to the breaks, so I might as well take them, right?"

What? Humor from the very serious Chase? "Uh… right." She kept moving. "See you later."

"Not going to work in that getup, are you?"

That made her stop and face him. "Obviously not, and I'd appreciate you not insulting me." Boundaries.

Boundaries. Boundaries. Boundaries were everything now. In the past she'd have let it slide, but not now, and not with him.

"I didn't mean—"

"Yes, you did. You don't understand it, so you make fun of it. I get it." She'd dealt with that attitude since she'd started martial-arts training.

"I just didn't know what to call it." He moved closer and they fell into step together toward the hospital.

"There are any number of things you could have called it, aside from 'getup,' such as uniform, or outfit even, but you didn't."

"Sorry. Really. Sometimes I just don't know what to say to you." He huffed out an exasperated sigh. "I'm sorry."

"I understand, but you don't have to say something insulting or sarcastic just because you're uncomfortable around me. In fact, we don't have to see each other at all. Ever."

"How's that gonna happen? We'll be working together."

"We can be professional. Outside of that, I don't want to see you, Chase." Boundaries. Remember the boundaries. Very wide, very tall and very strong.

"Now, just wait a damned minute." He stopped, and moved as if he were going to grab her by the arm, then recalled her previous warning. "I work here. This place is my home. You're the outsider here, not me. I'm not going to walk around on eggshells just because you decided to come back here on a whim."

"A whim? This is my home, too, and I have a right to be here just as much as you do." She faced him, ire warming her blood. It felt good to let it out. To hold that anger in her hand and unleash it on him. "It was no whim that I needed to finally close out the chapter of you in my life."

"Then I suggest we be cordial, polite and professional."

She gave a slight toss of her head. "Fine."

"Good." *Uh-oh.* When women used to use the word *fine* things were anything but.

"I'm going to ask the charge nurse to assign me to patients who aren't yours."

"You can't do that."

"Watch me."

"You know it doesn't matter what the assignments are—when it hits the fan, you work with whoever is there. The patient is the important part of the scenario, not us."

"Then I'll ask to switch to nights."

"No. Don't do that, either. You can't work nights." In fact, she never could. Messed up her system and biorhythms too much.

"I'll deal with it." Pride lifted her chin and made her say things she didn't mean.

Chase sighed and some of the fizz went out of him. "No. Now, look. Don't do that." He ran a hand through his hair, frustrated beyond belief. "I don't want you to do that. It messes you up too much." He paused until she looked at him. "How about this? I just be professional, and you just be professional, and things will be just fine. You'll leave in three months, and we'll both move on with our lives."

She glanced away and crossed her arms over her chest. "I was thinking of staying here. Moving back home, I mean. Permanently." She shrugged. "It's my home, too."

"Really?" That surprised him. When she'd left it had been like she'd been shot out of a cannon. He'd never expected to see her again, let alone be working with her again. Now he knew the definition of the word *gob-smacked*. "Wow."

"Yes, wow." She took a breath and let it out slowly. "I'm taking the place for a test drive. See if the memories are too much for me. See if I can handle it again." After a sigh, she looked into his eyes. "I need to be home again. I miss it. I miss the people here. I need to put us to rest for good."

He paused a second, observing her expression, trying not to let any memories of her find their place inside him. "How's it going? Are the memories bad?"

"Not so far." She looked away. "Look, I just came to have a visit with Mrs. Billings, to see how she was doing."

"Well, as the surgeon, I can give you an update. I was going to see her again after my break, so now's good."

"Let's go." This reminded her of the old days, when they would round together on their mutual patients. It had given their work a structure that she'd liked and respected. Now this familiar pattern warmed her a little, and she sighed, feeling the irritation of a moment ago dissipate. It just wasn't important.

"Nice, eh?"

"What?" Had he read her mind?

"This getting back to our common ground, the things we knew, the way we used to do it?" He shrugged. "It's nice, right?"

"It is. Thank you."

They moved through the ER and to the elevators

designated for staff. The elevator doors closed and the energy pouring off Emily was almost palpable in that confined space. "So, what kind of martial arts do you do, aside from hap…hap…?"

"Hapkido. Do you really want to know?" She turned curious eyes on him. Could this man be a genuine friend again? Could they put their past behind and be friendly? Only time would tell.

"Yes, I do." And he did. She was somewhat of a puzzle to him now. Not what he'd expected. And that intrigued him. Most people he could figure out in an instant, but this was a new Emily, and one who was puzzling him from all directions.

"I practice several. Started in hapkido, but moved on to try judo, karate and kung fu. There are benefits to each one, but the best for me right now is the hapkido."

"I hadn't heard of it, not until you mentioned it the other night."

"It's the best self-defense for women. It's Korean, but came to the States around 1980." She shrugged. "Probably why you've never heard of it. Relatively new."

"I'll have to look it up."

"You use some weapons, knives and swords, but the use of your body as a weapon is the most important. You might not always have a weapon but, no matter where you go, your body is always with you."

"True." He smiled at that.

The elevator stopped at the fifth floor, which housed all the critical-care units, including Trauma, Cardiac, Medical-Surgical and Pediatrics. Together they entered the medical-surgical ICU.

Emily paused when Chase stopped beside a patient room. She could see the patient inside whose bruised face from yesterday looked worse today. Pretty typical with the way hematomas evolved, they looked worse before they looked better. "Have you seen her this morning?"

"Yes. On early rounds."

Emily nodded for him to give report to her as a colleague.

"As you know, she's a forty-four-year-old female, entered the ER yesterday after being assaulted about the face and abdomen by her drunken husband."

"Yes."

"We opened her up and discovered, after your accurate assessment, that she indeed had a tear in her liver. By the time we got her to surgery she'd bled quite a lot. Once inside, we discovered that she appears to have some alcohol history of her own, but we managed to save her and the liver." He indicated the IV fluids hanging around the bed. "We have her on the DT protocol. Don't need her going into withdrawal while she's so critical."

"Certainly. I'd like—"

The cardiac alarm emitted its obnoxious call from Mrs. Billing's monitor. "She's crashing."

One look at the monitor and Emily saw the evidence of Chase's assessment. Lethal rhythm. They rushed into the room. There was no need to hit the code button as she was already in the ICU. Staff rushed to their side, alerted by the alarms.

"I'm sorry, ma'am. You'll have to leave." One of the nurses spoke to Emily. "No visitors now. I don't know how you got in here in the first place."

"I'm her—"

"Doesn't matter who you are, you need to leave." The older woman pointed to the door. "Now."

"Kim, she's with me. Emily was the ER nurse yesterday. She stays." Chase got all highbrow surgeon on the woman, leveling a stare at her. *O-o-o-h*... It seemed like he practiced that look, probably on the poor medical students, too. If things weren't so serious right now, she'd laugh.

"Oh."

"Get the crash cart," Emily said, also taking charge. "Open up the fluids till she gets here with the cart."

Emily did as instructed, programming the IV pump to infuse at a higher rate. As long as the kidneys were working, they could always get the extra fluid off the patient later.

Kim rolled the massive tool cart on wheels into the room and opened the top drawer. "Ready."

"Get the defibrillator charged and give her one hundred milligrams of Lidocaine." Emily took the medication Kim handed her and plugged it into the IV, pushed hard until all of the medication had been infused.

"Lido in."

"Charging. Two hundred." The whine of the machine signaled its readiness. Though she usually cringed at that sound, having Chase present decreased her anxiety.

Chase pulled the paddles from their cradle and pressed them against the patient's chest, one midsternum, one left side of the ribs. "Clear!" He squeezed the paddles, releasing the electricity into the patient's chest through the heart and hopefully disrupted the whacked-out electrical signal causing the chaos.

The monitor paused for a second, then beat, paused, beat again, then settled into a rhythm that was no longer deadly. "Check her pulse, make sure she has one," Emily said, and placed her fingers on the patient's swollen wrist, Chase listened with his stethoscope to her chest for a moment, then nodded.

"Good." He nodded and swung the stethoscope around his neck. "What's her Metoprolol dose going at now?"

Kim supplied the answer.

"Double it for the next four hours, get some blood gases, hematology and 'lights. Call me when they're back."

"Well, I had hoped she was going to be more stable than that." Emily spoke as they moved out of the patient room to the ICU doors.

"With the kind of injury she sustained, then surgery, then possible withdrawal, she'll probably be having more episodes, but I'm hopeful she'll survive."

"Yes, well, thanks, Doctor." Without meeting his gaze, she looked away.

Chase let out an irritated sigh. "I hate it when you call me that. It sounds so formal, so...old."

"Oh." She paused, uncertain how to proceed. "Then what should I call you?" *Your Royal Ass-wipe* just didn't have the right ring to it. But she'd come to make peace and continuing to annoy him wasn't in keeping with her quest. With a sigh, she let go of that, too.

"Chase, please. Just Chase."

"It's hard not to call you by your given name, but it adds familiarity I'm not sure I'm comfortable with right now." Not at all. But what had she expected? Obviously, she hadn't thought this plan through all the way.

"*Doctor* sounds a bit formal for us, don't you think?"

"Yes." Maybe she could get used to it. To saying his

name without the emotional attachment to it she used to have. "I'll try."

"Are you going to head home now?"

"Yes. I have other things to get done today, then I work the next three days. Off for the weekend, though." Why had she told him about her schedule? Old habits, she supposed, the way they used to do. Easy enough to fall right back into them. She'd also fallen into step beside him, too close, so she moved further away from him as they returned to the elevators.

His eyes were serious as he looked down at her. It was always his eyes she could read and know what he'd been thinking. But now there was confusion and concern and something she didn't recognize, couldn't figure out, in his eyes. Curiosity?

"You don't have to be afraid of me, you know."

"I'm not afraid of you." Without meaning to, she raised her chin in defiance and felt the muscles in her arms tensing.

"You said that very quickly." There was that unknown thing again in his eyes. Was it compassion or pain or grief? Or did he just feel sorry for her? She could tolerate a lot of things, but not that. Never that.

"What I'm doing is keeping an emotional distance from you—that's not the same thing." Really. She was not afraid of any man. Not any more. She could take care of herself very well now. She didn't need a man to protect her.

They remained silent as they left the way they had come, back through the ER to the parking lot. "You didn't have to walk out with me. I'm perfectly capable of taking care of myself."

"What, are you a lethal weapon now or something?"

He indicated her uniform. "I don't know anyone in the martial arts, so I know nothing about it."

"And you're interested?" Seriously? Admitting that to her was a revelation. She didn't think he was really serious, so she wasn't going to waste any time with lengthy explanations. She owed no one an explanation about how she lived her life now. No one.

"Marginally." He shrugged. "More curious than interested."

"I see." Then it wasn't worth the explanation. "Then, yes, I'm a lethal weapon, if that makes it easier." Actually, she was. Now that she'd been asked to teach a women's self-defense class, she would be like Rose, the one students looked to for guidance. How could she be an expert when she didn't feel like one?

Her attacker—she refused to use his name or hear it in her brain—had been convicted and had received life in prison. He was gone, but there were others out there. There would always be situations where women would be vulnerable and needing to defend themselves. How could she turn down women who were looking for answers the same way she was?

"What were you thinking about just now?" He peered at her, shading his eyes with his hand. "You were seriously gone."

"What? Oh, nothing." She waved it away with her hand.

"Didn't look like nothing." His voice was calm and reminded her for a moment of days gone by, when they'd had good times, when they'd cared about each other's lives.

"Well, I've been asked to do something I'm not sure

I am capable of doing or even if I want to." Didn't hurt to admit that, did it?

"What is it? Wait." He held up a hand to stop her from explaining. "You don't have to tell me, but the way I decide stuff like that is by asking myself whether it's helpful or harmful." He held up one finger and waited for her answer.

"Helpful." Definitely.

"Do you like doing it?"

"Yes." Absolutely.

"And would you learn anything from it?"

She sighed and let her shoulders drop, but her mind remained sharp and aware of her surroundings. That awareness never changed, would never change. "Yes." Undoubtedly.

"Then I'd say your decision is already made." He dropped his hand. "Well, gotta go save the world." He saluted her, turned away and returned through the ER doors.

She got into her car, started it up and drove away. Sticking to her training schedule kept her sane. Three times weekly she walked or ran five miles, twice weekly she practiced tai chi, hapkido was twice weekly, and she meditated every evening without fail. If work was stressful, she added an extra meditation.

Instead of taking medications for anxiety and stress, she worked it out at the dojo on the mat. Her mind and body were in sync and it had taken commitment and practice to accomplish what she had.

Her phone rang, and she knew by the siren ringtone it was Danny. "What do you want, brother?" She smiled when she said it. She figured it was her job as the older sibling to give him a hard time.

"Hey, big sister. Whatcha doing today?"

"The usual workout schedule. Why? You need something?"

"The station is hosting a spaghetti-dinner fundraiser tonight and I thought you'd like to come by with an appetite and your donation to a worthy cause."

"Which is?"

"The Wishes And Hope Foundation for kids with cancer."

She knew the charity and it helped kids who were dying from cancer achieve one fantastic wish. "Okay, I'll come but I have a similar request for you." Turnaround was fair, right?

"Should I be afraid?"

"Only if you're allergic to a tux." He was, and she knew it.

"Uh-oh, what do you have in mind?" Hesitation sounded clearly in his voice.

"Fundraiser for the Rape Recovery Center." They had saved her ass after her assault and there was no way she could give them back what she had received, so this was a little help, something she could do for them.

"I see. Still helping out there?" The topic made him feel uncomfortable, but she wasn't bothered by his distress. Most men were uncomfortable with talk of rape, especially with the women in their lives. Good guys had a hard time imagining such violence against the women they loved.

"Yes, on occasion. This is a black-tie event, get dressed up for an evening of dinner, dancing and coughing up some money for a worthy cause. I'll cover the tickets, just say you'll go with me so I don't have to go by myself." She held her breath. He was notoriously difficult to pin down due to his work schedule as a firefighter, his need to test his manliness in adrenaline-surging sports, and general lack of organizational skills.

"Okay, what's the date?"

She gave it to him. It was three weeks away, and even he could get his life arranged to accommodate one night with his sister. "I fully expect you to pick me up and dance to every song I like."

He laughed into the phone, and her heart warmed. He was a nut, but he was her brother. "So you want the whole Cinderella package?"

"Yeah, but I don't want to turn into a pumpkin at midnight, though. Orange is not my color." Not with her hair.

"Gotcha. I will see to it that you have a lovely evening."

"And, for God's sake, clean out your car. If it was a building it would have been condemned."

"I will. See you tonight." The phone went dead, and she clicked off her hands-free device, suddenly looking forward to tonight at the fire station, saying hello to his work buddies. That meant she had to get her act together and get her workout done.

A good, hard run would help dislodge the images of Chase lingering in her mind and images from the past that began to surface. Some part of her wished she could just let those images of him hang out in her brain so she could visit with them a while. But there was no good purpose in hanging onto the past she'd worked so hard to forget.

There were times when images of Chase came to her, like the middle of the night, and she'd remember how good they'd been together. Those nights she'd wake up with tears on her face and an ache between her legs only he had been able to assuage.

CHAPTER SEVEN

CHASE ARRIVED AT the fire station just in time to see Emily enter the building. He loved helping out his community by attending fundraisers, especially when there was food involved that he didn't have to cook, but, damn. He should have thought she'd be there. Danny was her brother first, before he was Chase's friend. The giant fire trucks were out front, all shined up for the public event. Cars filled the lot, lined the streets, and Chase had to walk a few blocks from where he'd parked the car.

Evening was approaching. Though still early October, the evenings were beginning to chill. Not enough for a jacket, but the damp air from the ocean so close by added a depth to the cold not found in dryer climates. He loved living this close to the water, surrounded by it, really, but there were times when the humidity complicated life.

The station was a madhouse. Kids ran around, screaming and carrying on, a continuous line from the hall itself to the large, inflatable castle jumpie-thing out front. Who knew what they were called, anyway? Kids didn't care. They just wanted to bounce around till they barfed. Good thing it had been set up *before* the spaghetti dinner.

Balloons, streamers, even a disco ball hung from the center of the room. No wonder they'd moved the trucks out. Needed room for all the chaos inside. The place sounded like a nightclub.

"Chase! There you are. Thought you might be held up at work or something." Danny approached, gave him a fist bump, then a one-armed bro hug. Several other firefighters shook his hand and offered him a hearty welcome.

"Made it." *Just in time to see your sister come in.*

"Grab a plate, eat all you want. Step up onto the scale now and after. We charge you per pound you eat."

"What?" He laughed. "Are you serious?"

"Kidding. It's a donation by the plate."

"Almost had me on that one." Danny was such a kidder, it was hard to know when to take him seriously.

Danny snorted and slapped his thigh. "You should see the women when I tell 'em that. They'd rather starve than get on the scale in front of a bunch of men."

Chase narrowed his eyes at Danny. "There's a reason you're not married, you know that, right?"

"You're right about that!" He pointed to his temple and nodded. "Too smart."

"That wasn't what I was going to say." Chase shook his head and got into line behind a family. There was the mom, dad and three girls who looked like they were all between the ages of eighteen months and six years old.

"Hi!" The middle girl waved at him, her bright blue eyes sparkling with an overabundance of personality. "I have two dogs." She held up three fingers on one hand.

"That's very nice." He grinned. Kids always spoke their minds and didn't have that pesky social filter ingrained in them yet.

"One is black, and one is brown." After that statement she nodded, as if mentally checking her colors.

"Is that right?" He couldn't help but smile at her enthusiasm.

"Yes." She bobbed her head and rose up and down on the balls of her feet. "One's a boy, and one's a girl."

"That's good."

"I know one's a boy because he has—"

"Sara!" The mother interrupted, a horrified expression on her pale face. "I think this man doesn't need the whole explanation."

"But—"

"No. He knows about boys and girls already." The mother gave Chase such a pleading look that he had to laugh. She mouthed "I'm so sorry" to him and crossed her eyes. Chase could see where Sara got her personality from.

The little fireball looked up at him, blue eyes questioning and curious, trying to determine the truth. "Do you?"

"Yes, I do." He nodded.

"Oh." She stuck out her lower lip and got back in line, obviously disappointed she couldn't share her vast knowledge with him.

"Sorry about that." Sara's father spoke to him and adjusted the toddler in his arms. "They say boys are a handful. Try three girls."

Chase laughed. "I completely agree." He looked at the little imp again. That was what Emily must have looked like as a child, all the wonder in her blue eyes, and gilt in her long hair that curled up at the ends. Then he sobered, realizing the youthful innocence that had attracted him to Emily in the first place was absent in her now. Curls had been replaced by short spiky locks, the gilt tarnished to a red-gold, and the innocence replaced by determination, anger and, somehow, courage of unfathomable depth. That saddened him to a degree he hadn't thought he was capable of feeling for her now.

After going through the line and dishing up a plateful of pasta, choosing a white sauce with clams from the Chesapeake Bay, Chase nabbed a cup of some sort of red juice and a slice of fresh garlic bread. He sat down at a table a family was just vacating. It was the only one left in the house and, don't you know, the only one left behind was Emily.

"Don't say anything, just sit down and eat." She waved to the seat across from her. "We stragglers have to sit wherever there's a seat."

Soon they were surrounded by others and the chatter of children and families drowned out any pretense they could have made at small talk. Sara took a place beside Chase and sat with her feet folded beneath her in order to reach the table. The little chatterbox kept up more small talk than Chase had ever heard at one time.

"And that's how plants grow." She reached for her glass, but it slipped out of her little fingers.

The milk spilled, immediately followed by an ear-piercing scream, the pitch of which was enough to deafen people three counties over. Several people sprang back from the table, already accustomed to such mishaps at mealtimes with children. Unfortunately, Chase wasn't fast enough, and ended up with most of the cold milk in his lap.

Sara leaned closer and gave him an innocent look. "You got milk all over you, mister."

"I see that." He accepted the pile of napkins Emily handed to him. With her ninja reflexes, she'd managed to spring back from the table in time to miss the white flood.

"Looks like you're gonna need some clothes." Emily provided the succinct statement and smirked at the sight of his wet lap.

"I've got extra scrubs in the car." Trying to pluck the wet fabric away from his skin would only draw more attention to an area he'd rather avoid.

Just then the most obnoxious alarm rang out, lights began to flash on the trucks outside and firefighters raced for their equipment.

"What's going on?" someone asked.

"They must have had a call." Although her brother loved his chosen profession, she still worried when he geared up to go out. She never knew if he would be coming home, but that was another area of control she'd had to give up. If Danny died in the performance of his duties as a firefighter, then he would die happy in service to his community.

Danny jogged over to them. "You guys should probably head to the hospital. There's been a ten-car pile-up on the freeway and, from the initial sound of it, it's bad."

Emily stood. "Right away. I'll go now."

"Come on. You can ride with me." Chase tossed down the wad of napkins. "It'll save time."

"Okay. Okay." She turned to Danny and hugged him. In his protective gear, he felt huge. "Be careful, please."

He grinned and winked at her, confident as usual. "Always, big sister, always."

Emily and Chase followed Danny out the door and quickly walked to Chase's car around the corner.

Fire trucks raced away in one direction, and they raced away in the opposite one.

"I wonder what happened." Emily chewed on her lower lip, a frown of concern marring the beauty of her face.

"It's always the same. Someone did something stupid, then someone else pays for it." Chase supplied the answer with disgust. He'd been at it too long to believe otherwise. It was the stupidity of humanity that people suffered from.

"I see."

Chase shot a quick glance at her. "I didn't mean anything by that." He clutched the steering-wheel tightly, feeling like he'd just stepped in it big time. He hadn't meant the remark to be in relation to what had happened to her in the past. He'd said he didn't want to walk on eggshells and apparently he wasn't. He couldn't monitor everything that came out of his mouth, could he? "Dammit."

"It's true." She turned to face the window, not really seeing the scenery. "It's the innocents who usually pay for the indiscretions of others, even something as simple as a lane change without looking."

Grim-faced, Chase focused on driving, getting them to the hospital without incident. There was nothing he could say, because it was all true.

They entered the ER together. "I'll go find some scrubs to change into." She looked down at her casual workout attire. "I want to at least look semiprofessional. I'll see you in a few."

"I'll have to change, too."

She disappeared down the hall. Chase headed toward the staff lounge, but was stopped by the charge nurse.

"Chase? What's going on? What are you guys doing here?" Liz asked, a puzzled expression on her face. "No one's hurt, are you?"

"No, we're fine. We were at the fire station when they got a call with a ten-car pileup, so we're anticipating you'll need us."

"Oh, wow. Absolutely right." Liz nodded, her expression changing to one of disbelief. "We don't have enough people on duty to cover that plus the usual mayhem." She grabbed the phone. "I'll start the disaster protocol. If I forget to tell you later, thanks for coming in."

"Sure. Gotta change, though." Chase entered the locker room and stepped inside.

Emily was there in a state of undress he'd not seen in three years.

"Get out." Emily grabbed her scrub shirt and covered what she could of her body, but he'd seen her many times without clothing.

"No." Hell, no. Not when there was an imminent emergency breathing down their necks.

"Then turn your back." She stood still, staring at him until he nodded.

"Fine." He turned his back, then backed up toward the benches between the rows of lockers and began to undress.

"What are you doing?" She struggled to get the scrub top over her head. Punched her hand through the neck instead of the sleeve, reoriented it, and tried again.

"I'm changing for an emergency, the same as you." He whipped the milk-sodden shirt off and dropped his pants. Right there, in front of her, like he'd been doing it all the time!

"Well, stop it!" God. She didn't need to see him and all that muscle, those runner's legs. Not now. Not just when she'd thought she'd gotten them out of her mind.

"No. We're in a hurry. There's no time for modesty now. Besides, we've seen each other naked a million times."

"I don't care—it's not appropriate anymore." Seriously, not appropriate. Because it was making her mouth water and diverting her attention from the issue looming in front of them.

"Fine. I'll just pretend I didn't see anything." Like that was going to happen anytime soon. He'd certainly gotten an eyeful of her figure the second he'd entered the locker room. A man accustomed to making snap decisions based on quick assessments, he'd made one then. Beneath the loose scrubs and bulky martial arts uniform, Emily was a knockout, and he wasn't over her.

She'd toned her body to the point of very little body fat. The muscles in her calves and thighs were well defined, arms looked strong and toned and her abdomen looked like he could have bounced a quarter off it.

So that was why he turned his back, to hide the immediate and surging arousal his body had experienced when he'd seen her in just her bra and panties. Boxers weren't very helpful at hiding anything.

Pushing her feet into the loose scrubs, Emily tucked the shirt into the waistband and tied it tightly against her waist. She'd grabbed medium-sized scrubs and the legs were too long, so she put a foot up on the bench, rolled up the cuffs and secured each of them with a twist, then put her shoes back on. Her heart thrummed in her chest, and she was certain it wasn't just from the anticipation of the arriving traumas. Seeing Chase that way made her think of the many ways she'd seen his skin in the past, and she just didn't want to remember. She'd spent too many years trying to forget.

"I'll see you out there." Chase stuffed his clothing into a locker and went into the ER without looking back.

Having not been assigned a locker yet, Emily stowed her clothing in Chase's locker and closed the door, trying to ignore the whiff of male fragrance emanating from the unit, of the memories it evoked from deep in her mind. But it was the deodorant or aftershave that she'd always loved on him that locked into her mind and followed her out into the ER, suffocating her with memories of him.

CHAPTER EIGHT

"WHAT DO YOU need me to do?" Emily asked. Anticipation hummed through her as if she were going into an arena to spar with an opponent.

"Emily, you're with Chase in trauma room one. It should be set up, but double-check. You'll have the first patient through the doors so everyone else can wind up their patients and get them to the floors or discharged." Liz checked something off the paper on her clipboard and gave a brisk nod.

"Got it." Liz continued to act as unit commander, per the hospital protocol, giving out assignments and orders to those in her department. The usual assignments were on hold in this situation until they were certain of the toll of the disaster. Patients with minor issues were asked to go home, or seek care elsewhere. Most of them left, grumbling but understanding the serious nature of the request.

"Everyone get something to drink and a snack now. There's no telling when you'll have a break." Liz made an overhead page to all staff.

Emily entered the largest trauma room of the ER. There was enough equipment and space in there to handle just about any emergency, including the time they'd had to extricate a local farmer from a piece of equipment, a corn picker that had nearly taken the man's leg off. She opened up three bottles of IV fluids, spiked the tubings into them and hung them on poles suspended from the ceiling, ready to go.

Chase entered, his movements hurried and tense. "Suit me up."

Emily held out the blue paper gown for him, and he punched his arms through like a surgeon in an operating room. She moved behind him, tied the string behind his back and then held out the gloves for him.

"Have you heard what the first one is yet?"

"Yes. Gonna be ugly. Delivery truck with a load of fencing materials hit the brakes, the load shifted, and we're getting the passenger from the car behind it."

"Driver okay, then?" She gave him a hopeful look, but he shook his head and the look in his eyes said it all.

"No. Impaled through the windshield. Didn't have a chance."

"Oh. Do you know what kind of injury the passenger has?"

"We'll know in a few seconds but, guessing head, neck and chest injuries."

The doors burst open and the first patient arrived. The ambulance crew was high from the excitement of the rescue and pulling the person back from the edge of death.

"What do we have?" Chase asked, settling into his role.

"Fifty-year-old female passenger, sustained loss of consciousness. Bruising on forehead indicates she hit the dash. Lacerations widespread from glass, but none serious."

"Let's move her over." Emily directed the crew and six people prepared to shift the patient to the gurney. "One. Two. Three."

Smoothly and gently, the patient was moved onto the hospital gurney and the crew pulled their cart out of the way.

"Vital signs are all over the place. Intubated in the field as a precaution because her oxygen level kept dropping. Not sure if she has a lung injury or not."

"Let's find out." Chase moved to the left side of the patient.

"Sorry, but we have to head back out there. It was worse than first reported. Lots of other crashes, trying to avoid the big one."

"Go. We've got it." Chase took his stethoscope and listened to the patient's lungs.

Emily hooked up the monitoring equipment then patted the patient's face. "Can you wake up? Cecilia? Can you open your eyes for me?"

The woman didn't move, her eyelids didn't flutter, and she didn't try to pull away when Emily pinched her earlobe, a minor test for response to painful stimuli. "Chase, she's not responding. At all." Emily pinched a fingernail, but the results were the same. Not good.

"Get Radiology on the phone. We need a scan of her head right away." He proceeded round the patient, continuing his examination, then stopped at the head of the bed and pried open her swollen eyelids.

Emily alerted the department of their need. "They'll be ready in ten minutes."

"Good. Lungs are good, belly's soft. I think the majority of what's going on is in her head," he muttered, almost to himself, as he listed her injuries.

"She's probably got a fractured femur, as well. The left is swelling up like a balloon."

"Dammit. If it's that fast, we've got trouble. Cut the clothing." Emily deftly sliced the patient's jeans from hem to hip with her trauma shears, scissors that could cut through sheet metal, then exposed the patient's leg for Chase to see.

"There." Emily gasped. A large shard of wood protruded from the woman's thigh. "Whoa. Didn't see that through the jeans." Emily whistled at the magnitude of the giant splinter.

"Being there is one thing—if it's punctured the femoral artery, that's another thing." He palpated the top of the thigh, trying to find the end of the irregularly shaped projectile. "I can feel it. We need to open it up before we do anything else."

"The head won't matter if she bleeds to death before we get to X-ray." Emily made the point and raised her brows at Chase.

"Right."

"What do you want to do first?"

"Get a cut-down tray. I can use that."

Heading to the cupboard, Emily pulled out the sterile tray and placed it on a bedside table. In seconds she had opened the wrappings, keeping everything sterile, handed Chase a pair of sterile gloves and poured half a bottle of Betadine cleanser into a cup on the tray.

Chase lifted his brows in amazement. "You go, girl!" He scrubbed the thigh near the splinter with the Betadine. "You could work in surgery. You're very efficient."

"Thanks, but I'll stick to ER. I'm too antsy to stand for long hours." A bit of warmth surged in her chest at his words. Chase wasn't one to offer compliments without cause. At least, he hadn't been in the past; no reason to think that would have changed about him. A person's core personality didn't change in three years. But it made her feel good to hear the words, reminding her of how well they used to work together. If only things hadn't fallen apart.

When Chase pressed the tip of the scalpel into the flesh beside the splinter and what looked like a river of blood flowed from the opening. "There's a gusher. Dammit."

"What do you need?" Not being an OR nurse, she couldn't anticipate the way they could, but she would try her darnedest to help Chase save this woman. Now she had to admit she'd missed him, missed this, missed working together when they'd been at their best. Tears pricked her eyes as sorrow turned in her chest. Unable to give in to the emotions right now, she forced them back and concentrated on the patient, on Chase's instructions.

"Put on sterile gloves. Put both retractors in and pull them in opposite directions so I can see where the little bastard is." There was such determination in his face she couldn't respond in any other way. Some part of her heart melted at this. This was what they did. They did it together, and they saved people. How could she ever have let go of that no matter what had happened to her? She'd been so stupid. So broken.

Emily complied and was able to do what he needed. Unaccustomed to the strain, her arms tired quickly, but due to her physical training she was able to focus and not lose her grip. "Got it?" Deep breath in, out very slowly. The tremors of her arms were transmitted to the instruments, but she hung on.

"There it is." He glanced up at Emily's face. "Hang

on, baby, hang on." He continued to grumble and cuss at the bleeding artery as if it were a sentient organism bleeding just to annoy him. The click of clamps cut through the air as he identified the correct vessels and used the clamp to hold them in place. "Sutures." Without looking up, he held out his right hand.

Emily released one retractor and handed the materials to him with the needle clipped into another specialty clamp designed for sewing. "Sutures," she repeated.

"Suction."

"One second." She reached for the suction machine connected to the wall and pulled out the excess blood obscuring his vision.

"Perfect. You broke scrub with that hand." He said it without recrimination, just a fact to remind her.

"I know. Just the right, left is still sterile." She accepted his statement without rancor.

"Don't mix them up." He gave her a quick glance, then a nod of approval and a wink.

"I won't." Though they were in the midst of an intense situation, something inside her chest warmed at his gentle compliment of her skills when things could so easily have gone another direction. These were the kinds of moments that had bonded them, had knitted them together. Oh, how she had missed them! Now she began to tremble inside for an entirely different reason.

They worked together to finish tying off the artery. Moment by moment the chaos around them surged and crested as more and more patients were brought in, and the ER was filled to capacity and beyond. This patient was whisked away from the ER to Radiology, then brain surgery.

Chase and Emily washed their hands, changed gowns

and gloves, and took the next patient. Hours and hours passed as they repeated the scenario several times. Though some patients had been diverted to other hospitals nearby, the worst came to them because they were the best.

"I feel like I'm in the TV show *M*A*S*H*." Emily shook her head in wonder and widened her eyes.

"Feel like you're working in a war zone?" Chase asked, and he gave a tired sigh. "Me, too."

"Yes. Just no one shooting at us."

"Yet."

"Don't you remember that one episode we watched?" Emily stood very stiffly, mimicking the character. "The one surgeon, and his famous quote: *I do one thing. I do it very well, and then I move on.* You could be him."

Chase huffed out a laugh despite himself, despite the exhaustion of the day and the critical patient lying between them. "It's true. I do have a tendency to be overly focused at times."

Emily laughed naturally for the first time since they'd been working together and it felt wonderful! It may have been the first time in years she'd felt this good. "And then, after we watched the *M*A*S*H* marathon, we…" She paused and the laughter slid away and the joy faded from her eyes as the rush of memories hit her. "Yes. Well. That was back then, wasn't it?"

Chase paused and met her gaze fully. He took a step toward her, his gaze burning into hers, urgency and questions swimming there. "Yes. And this is now." He cleared his throat. "Emily—"

"How are you two doing in here?" Liz asked as she charged into the room, looking frazzled and exhausted herself.

"I think we're ready to finish up with this patient, right, Chase?" Emily asked, looking away. He noticed a tremor of her hand as she reached for the surgical instruments on the tray table, and two of them clattered to the floor. She'd just exceeded every possible expectation with the surgical instruments, and now she had butter fingers? Something else was going on, but it would have to wait.

"Yes." He heaved out a sigh and rolled his shoulders to ease the stiffness there. That short moment when he had connected with Emily vanished. "How many more are out there?"

"We've cleared the decks. Eight damned hours later." She raised her arms in the air and did a victory dance around the room like a mixed-martial-arts fighter. "Wahoo! We did it. God, I'm tired."

"Eight hours? Are you serious?" Emily removed her protective gear. "I had no idea." She tossed the wadded-up gown at the trash can, but missed by a mile.

"This one is good to go, just needs a room with a view." Chase removed his gear and wadded it up, preparing to give it a toss across the room like a basketball player, but noticed a change in Emily, and he dropped the gown to hurry over beside her.

"You need to sit down." He hesitated to touch her, but she looked like she needed it.

"I'm fine. Legs are wobbly from standing so long." She attempted to take a few steps. "I'll shoosh it off in a misnus." She took those few steps, then her eyes went wide, and she reached for his arms. "Ch... Shase?"

He quickly wrapped his arms around her as she went down.

Liz dropped her clipboard and rushed to them. "What's wrong with her?"

"My guess is low blood sugar." His gut tightened as his brain went wild with all the crazy possibilities, but he wrangled them back. Keep it simple. Things like this were usually simple.

"I told everyone to eat something." Exasperated, Liz clucked her tongue.

"About ten seconds before we got our first patient, Liz. Neither of us had time to get anything." He hated snapping at her, but he was as worn out as everyone else, and his concern for Emily overrode his good sense.

"Let's get her to the lounge, we'll check her blood sugar and you two can get something to eat." Liz made the suggestion and held out her arm for Chase to lead the way.

"I'm slirpy fio."

Chase lifted her into his arms, some protective instinct tugging at his chest, wanting him to shield her as he should have done years ago. "Yes, you are slirpy fio. Now shut up."

He shouldered his way through the lounge door and set her down on the couch. Liz appeared seconds later with the blood-sugar monitor. "Let me see your hand."

Chase rattled around in the refrigerator and pulled out a jar of orange juice, poured some into a glass and held it to Emily's mouth. "Here. Chug it."

"Wait! Check the expiration date!" Liz held up her hand to stop him. "Some of that stuff's been in there for months. It could be rancid."

Instead of doing as instructed, Chase took a large drink of it. "It's fine." He returned the glass to her mouth. "Drink."

Emily took a few sips, then jumped when Liz pricked her finger for a drop of blood to check her blood sugar. "Ow."

"Really? That made you jump? Aren't you some hotshot kung fu expert?" Chase kept asking questions, trying to make sure she stayed awake until her blood sugar rose out of the danger zone. It kept his nerves under control and his hands from shaking.

"Hap-hapkido, An' that hurt." She frowned, and her lower lip stuck out. Before he leaned over and kissed that luscious lip, he pressed the glass against it again.

"More."

"Okay. Your sugar is forty." Liz provided the information with a downward turn to her mouth. "Too low, my friend."

"Oh." She drank the rest of the juice.

"You guys got this? I've got the rest of the crew to check on."

"We're good now. Go." Chase pulled a chair alongside the couch, needing to be a little closer physically to Emily, though she wasn't very happy about being touched by him. The close proximity appeased his need and didn't breach her boundaries.

"Got any protein in the fridge? Cheese or something? I'm going to need some when the juice is gone." She was no longer slurring her words, and she was able to hold the glass without trembling.

"Let me check." He rummaged around and found hard cheese, a jar of peanut butter and some bread. At the table he cut a chunk of cheese and handed it to her, then proceeded to slather the bread with peanut butter. Two slices. One for him, one for her.

"Great midnight snack."

"Actually, it's the after two a.m. snack." He sat again, the effects of exhaustion now hitting him. "Whew. I'm beat, too."

Emily looked at her watch with surprise showing on her face. "Seriously? Two a.m.?"

"Yep. If I didn't have to take you back to the fire station to get your car, I'd just crash in one of the on-call rooms." One of the few benefits of on-call: a readily available bed, no driving involved.

"I can call a cab. No big deal." She started to swing her feet over the edge of the couch.

"That's not what I meant, Em. Just meant..." He held out a hand to her, but hesitated. Then he looked into her eyes, wanting so much to connect with this woman, but he didn't seem to know how. Every time he faced her he faced his guilt, and it stopped him.

After a second's hesitation her eyes met his and the anger, the pain in them softened. Instead of being angry, instead of yelling at him or breaking his hand, she slowly stretched out her hand and laced her fingers with his.

"I know. It would be easier without me." The tone of her voice dropped with emotion he could feel pulsing off her. It matched the emotions churning inside him, and he looked down at her, at this petite woman who had been through hell. He wanted to reach out to her, to make it all go away, to somehow take them back in time to the place they used to be, to the people they used to be, but it was impossible.

"That's not what I meant, either." He dragged his hand through his hair and blew out a long sigh as she extricated her hand from his. "I'm just tired, too."

"We have to be back at seven. We'll only get a few

hours of sleep." Now she was back to being professional and that moment of connection was gone. But she had reached out to him and that meant something, didn't it? She had let him touch her and had initiated the contact.

"Don't remind me. But there's more than one on-call room, there's a shower, we can eat here." He presented the option to her. It was what he would have done if left to his own devices. He didn't even have a house plant that required his attention so he didn't have to return to his place for days if necessary.

"I have a routine I do at night. I want my own things." She swung her feet to the floor and wobbled a bit when she stood. "Whoa."

"You're not fit to drive yet. Your blood sugar hasn't stabilized, so driving home isn't an option for you, either." There was going to be no argument about that.

"Well, I want to go home." She put one finger up. "Correction. I'm going home."

"Okay. You can go home, but only if I drive you."

"Then how will I get to work?" She took a few steps, testing out her muscles again, but grabbed on to the table. "Oh. Still dizzy. Dammit."

"I'll pick you up and take you to your car in the morning."

Liz burst through the door. "Okay. Schedule change for everyone. Since you can't realistically or legally show up here in five hours, we're sliding your shift back until eleven a.m."

"How are you covering the morning, then?" Emily asked, and folded her bread in half and took a bite, but leaned against the table for support.

"Nights will stay a little longer in the a.m., and then

will come in a little later tomorrow night, then we'll be back on track with everything the next day."

"Good plan." Chase picked up his sandwich, folded it in half. "Let's get out of here before she changes her mind."

"Okay. I'm ready." Defeated, Emily followed him, too tired to argue any longer. Without a word she reached for Chase's elbow and tried to look nonchalant as she held onto him. Falling on her face would definitely have no dignity, so this was the lesser of two evils.

Immediately, Chase looked down at her, reminded once again of how they used to leave the hospital together after a long shift. She would lean on him, and then they'd sleep for hours tangled up together, drawing strength from each other as they'd slept.

They emerged from the ER into the dark and chilly fall night. Stars shone brilliantly overhead and a light breeze moved inland, bringing the scent of the ocean with it.

"Nice night." Chase led the way to his car.

"This is the kind of night I want to curl up with a fuzzy blanket and a hot cup of cocoa and just melt away."

"You used to do that, as I remember." The brunt of a memory kicked him in the gut as he got into the car. He paused for a second to take a deep breath. So much had happened to them. So much time had passed. So much pain had been left unresolved and it still haunted him daily, even though he tried to deny it.

"I indulged too often back then. Now it's a luxury." She reached for the seat belt and buckled it.

He started the car and pulled out onto the empty roadway, easing onto the street. "Where do you live?"

"Fisherman's Point apartment complex."

"I drive by there on the way to work every day."

"Then you know how to find it." She pressed her head against the cool glass window and closed her eyes, trusting him to get her home. When she felt Chase's hand rest on top of hers she didn't protest. It was an old gesture and one she drew some comfort from now. Besides, she didn't even have the energy to muster a defense against him had she really wanted to. All of it had been used on their patients, and she'd been drained dry. Her boundaries were at their lowest right now, and she cupped her thumb around his pinky, reaching out to him in a small way to offer him some comfort in return.

Shadows from the past haunted him as he pulled into the area she indicated. Without thinking, he'd reached out and placed his hand over hers. When he'd felt her thumb close around his finger, he had nearly been lost at that small gesture of connection. It gave him a small amount of hope that the connection they'd once shared hadn't been completely lost. He unbuckled his seat belt and turned off the engine. There was only one way to find out. Maybe right now wasn't the time, but he wanted to know.

"What are you doing?" she asked, her voice sleepy.

"I'm seeing you home. Safely." He opened the door and put one foot on the pavement. "No argument." Never, ever again would he leave her in an unsafe position.

"It's okay. I don't need you to do that." She opened her door and got out as well. Her movements were slower than usual, an obvious expression of the depth of her exhaustion.

"Too bad. I'm doing it." He exited the car and closed his door.

"Let me rephrase. I don't *want* you to do that. I can

take care of myself." Though she stiffened, he didn't think she would be able to defend herself right now if she needed to. That protective instinct that had surfaced an hour ago kicked into overtime.

"I know, Emily. I'm satisfying my own needs right now, not yours." She couldn't even protect herself from herself right now, so he had to do it.

"Chase! Why are you doing this? I don't want you here."

"Because I need to." He made his way around the car to where she waited. "I *need* to, Em. Just let me."

"But—"

"You can't run away forever, Emily."

Brushing around him, she made her way to the door, and he hurried after her. He blocked her in the doorway as she was about to charge inside.

"I'm not running from anything, Chase Montgomery." He would not convince her otherwise right now, but he knew differently. She was running now just as surely as she had three years ago, but he wasn't about to let her run, not if he could help it. She'd come back here for a reason, and he was going to make her see the truth of it, of them, of what they might still recover, if it was even remotely possible. If it was, he wanted it. All of it.

"You've been running for three years, and you're still doing it."

"I've been building a new life. That's what I've been doing." She opened the door, and he shoved his way inside behind her, stiff-arming the door before she had a chance to slam it in his face.

"You've been building walls, not a life." Before she could shove him out the door he slammed it shut and followed her a few steps into the room, tempting fate as far as he could.

"I have not. Get out!" She spun, fire in her eyes like he'd never seen. His words had obviously triggered something in her, and he was going to see what it was right now. She snapped and crackled with electricity, and he was amazed as well as fascinated and aroused by the passion in her.

"Liar."

With a cry of outrage she pinned him against the wall before he knew what had happened. Though her height was much shorter than his, she had him. And he grinned. Then he laughed.

"What's so funny?" Her breathing came in short ragged gasps.

"You are. We are." Seriously. This was funny. Maybe he was exhausted, but this was damned funny to him. All of the tension from the day eased, though he was tied up like a pretzel.

"I am *not* funny." Her breath came in short gasps and she had apparently regained some of her strength. "Do I look funny to you?"

"I didn't mean it like that." He looked down at her mouth, breath coming quickly from between parted lips. Lips he'd been wanting to explore since yesterday, since forever.

"You're saying that a lot lately." Her eyes narrowed as she watched him.

"Everything comes out wrong lately. You have me in an uproar on the inside." Inching his head closer, he focused on her luscious mouth. "Come closer," he whispered to her, the way he used to do before he kissed her.

She would remember that.

He couldn't forget it.

For just a second she dropped her gaze to his mouth, then returned it to his eyes. "Don't look at me like that."

"Like what?" Inching a millimeter closer, he was almost where he wanted to be.

"Like you want to kiss me." Her voice softened, and her gaze dropped to his mouth. She licked her lips, but didn't pull away. Her focus on him intensified, as if she struggled with herself to pull away.

"But I do, Em. I do. I've wanted to kiss you since the day began." What the hell? Why not? His voice dropped to a whisper and curious desire he had never expected to feel for her again surged through him. Before he changed his mind or she beat him up, he pressed his mouth against hers. It was the only thing he could move, as she had the rest of him tangled up in her tight grip.

The feel of her lips was something he'd never thought he'd experience again. She was soft and her lips clung to his as if she didn't want to let him go. God, he was in so much trouble. He should *not* have done that. But the fact was, he had. If he could get out of the clinch she had him in, he'd show her he didn't have to let go of her ever again.

CHAPTER NINE

EMILY COULDN'T BELIEVE he'd got to her. In this hold he shouldn't have been able to move, but he had. He'd kissed her.

He'd *kissed* her! Dammit, Chase Montgomery had kissed her!

And now she didn't want him to stop. Memories overwhelmed her, and she trembled from the onslaught of emotions.

Physically and emotionally he'd gotten to her, she'd have to admit that. His close proximity, his energy, the desire in his eyes had all gotten to her, and she'd dropped her guard. Gone in an instant.

Pushing away, she relaxed her hands, released him to do what he would because she could no longer fight him, or was it herself she was fighting? What he did was put those arms around her and draw her into his embrace, the embrace she'd fought to forget about, and now it was gone in a flash of heat and fire.

She *was* a liar, and he knew it.

He cupped her face with his hands, those long-fingered surgeon's hands. And he plundered her mouth, exploring with his tongue, coaxing hers forward. She didn't want to give herself to him, she wanted to hold still, to hold herself from him, but her defenses were weak from so much exposure to him in the past hours. And she couldn't do it. She wanted this connection with him too much. Maybe she would hate herself for it later, but right now stopping herself was out of the question.

Two days ago she never would have let him into her apartment, breaching her boundaries. Now? Now it seemed she'd changed her mind about him somehow, that she wanted him there, wanted him in her life again, contrasting sharply to her previous position. But was it really? Wasn't this exactly the reason she'd come back to Williamsburg? She'd had to find out if there was anything left between them and there was.

"I've missed you, Em." He choked out the same words that had been lodged in her throat. He'd been her friend, her lover, her partner, and she'd missed so much about him! He pushed her hair back from her face the way he'd used to when it had been longer.

"I've missed you, too." Pulling back, she looked at the face she had once loved and tears formed in her eyes. There were new lines of fatigue, probably from the crazy night they'd had. But the rest was the same. That little scar he'd gotten on his chin as a kid from falling out of a tree, the same crow's feet that fanned out from his eyes when he smiled and the lips, the mouth she'd loved exploring her body.

"Seems like you haven't changed much." Had he? Did she really know?

"No. Not much. But you've done a lot." He ran his hand over her spiky hair and watched it spring back into place. "This is really new."

"Yes. It's a new me." She dropped her gaze and

retreated a little. "Not sure you'll like the new me. The old one is pretty much gone."

"So far, I'm admiring the new you a lot. You're stronger than you've ever been physically, and that doesn't come without internal strength." He let his gaze run over her face, as if trying to reconcile the difference between the old Emily and the new.

He curved his hand around her ear, the way he'd done when her hair had been longer. Unexpected tears pricked her eyes at the bittersweet gesture. It was one she'd loved and it took her by surprise now. "I just wish..." His voice cracked, heavy with emotions too numerous to name.

"Chase..." With reluctance, she started to pull back. This wasn't what she'd expected tonight at all, and she wasn't prepared for it. Despite her months of getting ready for this assignment and coming up against Chase, in the moment she wasn't prepared.

"Give me just one more minute before I have to say goodbye again." The pleading in his eyes nearly undid her. The want, the need, the pain were all there and no longer hidden, the way they had been.

Uncertain, she raised her gaze to his and gasped aloud with the emotion struggling to break free, the pain in his face, the want, the need, the joy and the sorrow that filled her. She hadn't known the depth of his pain, but it was there now, exposed, bleak and raw.

"Chase..." The right words wouldn't come, and she leaned closer. She wanted to be close to him again, but in truth she didn't know if she could, if she was too broken to ever be that close to anyone again.

With a groan he reached for her, and she gratefully went into his arms. This kiss, this embrace nearly destroyed her. He reversed their positions so she was held against the wall by his body. He kissed her, devoured her as if he'd never get enough of her. Her arms went around his shoulders, and she held on like he was her lifeline, the way he'd used to be, and for a few moments she forgot.

Arousal shot hotly and fiercely through her and then the fear sliced through the heart of her, pushing everything else away.

She stiffened and instead of holding his shoulders pushed at them until he released her. "Stop, stop, stop. *Stop*!" She took a few steps away from him in the small kitchen, trembling from need and remembered fear. Sweat broke out all over her body. Her breath came in short, chirpy gasps, and she clutched the counter for support, embarrassed that panic had hit her at such an inopportune moment. She'd never tried to make love with anyone except Chase since the attack, so her reaction shouldn't have surprised her. After all the counseling she'd had for PTSD, and all the martial-arts studies, she'd hoped she'd gotten further along in her recovery, but here she was. Not.

"I'm sorry. I should have let you go, but I didn't want to." He watched as she prowled back and forth from the counter to the wall and back again, her thoughts inward, and he didn't even know if she heard him. "Emily?"

"What?" She looked up at him, eyes wild, and he was certain she was having a panic attack. He'd seen her like this before and it had been right before their breakup. The first time, the only time they'd tried to make love after the assault it had ended badly, ended with a rift so wide they hadn't recovered from it. Neither of them had been prepared or able to cope.

"It's me. Look at me. Talk to me." The pain of watching her was like someone had taken an ice pick and stuck it in his gut.

"I can't. You need to go now." Her hands shook as she took hold of the counter again.

"I'm not going anywhere." Never again would he leave her in a fragile state, no matter what the reason. He was a better man than he'd been three years ago. He needed her to know that.

"Go." She pointed to the door, but her eyes were still wild, agitated, filled with demons from the past.

"No. I'm not leaving you the way I did before." The guilt of that had weighed on him for years. "I won't ever leave you again like that."

"I don't need you, Chase."

"But I need you, Emily." He took a few more steps away from her and moved into the living area, hoping she would follow. "Come sit down for a few minutes."

Numb, she followed him, trying to figure out how she was going to get him out of her apartment, to take back her peace. "I need to do my relaxation exercises before I can go to sleep."

"Then do them."

"Not with you here, watching me."

"I don't know how to do anything remotely relaxing, so why don't you give me a lesson? I need to learn something to help me sleep that doesn't consist of a medication or alcohol."

"Seriously?" Doubt covered her expression, and he deserved it. He hadn't been very supportive of her self-care practices.

"Seriously." He sat down on the floor and tried to cross his legs the way he'd seen her do, but he couldn't.

"You don't have to do this." She plunked down beside him and crossed her legs easily. Show-off. "It's completely unnecessary."

"I want to, but my legs won't go the right way." He shrugged. "Besides, it will be a distraction for you to have a terrible student. Can't get any worse than me, right?"

"Right. You need to stretch more, or you'll be a stiff old man who can't tie his shoelaces. For now, just straighten them out in front of you." She let out a slow sigh, then took in a breath.

He did as she said and there was an immediate release of the tension in his body. "That's better. Now what?"

She gave additional instructions for his positioning, knowing what he was doing, distracting her from the panic. Since it was helping a little, and there was some ease of tension between her shoulders, she continued. "Now, close your eyes and listen to the sound of my voice." She took a cleansing breath in and let it out slowly.

"Okay. I'm listening."

"Now, close your *mouth* and listen to the sound of my voice."

Amused, he cracked an eyelid at her, but she was concentrating, her eyes closed. He tried to mimic her as he took in deep breaths, held them for a count of three and then released to a count of five.

As she led him through the exercise, his body began to relax. The tension in his shoulders loosened and the humming in his groin began to ease. Amazing that just breathing could accomplish so much.

Moments later he began to nod off, his body relaxed, and he realized she'd stopped talking. Opening his eyes slowly, he wasn't sure what to expect. But seeing Emily's gorgeous eyes watching him made him freeze.

The moment, the connection, the electricity between them was nearly palpable. He wanted to reach out to her, to touch her, but he was afraid if he moved the moment would vanish and so would she.

"I'm going to bed now. There's a blanket on the back of the couch you can use." This time, her voice was calm, the wildness was gone from her eyes and the relaxation had obviously done its job.

Graceful and controlled in her movements, she rose from her position on the floor beside him. Before she disappeared and the moment was gone forever, he clasped her wrist gently in his hand. He wanted to drag her down onto the couch with him and tear their clothing off, make love with her until they were both spent and exhausted. But he didn't. It wasn't what she needed.

"Thank you," he whispered.

"For what?" She didn't pull away or move but stood there for a moment, seeming transfixed.

"For helping me learn something new, opening my eyes to things I never would have otherwise considered. I didn't expected anything like this when I got up this morning."

A small smile tilted up one corner of her mouth. "Neither did I." She eased away from him, and he released her wrist, but the warm, smooth feel of her skin sliding against his lingered. "I'll wake you when it's time to go in."

"Okay. Good night."

"Good night." Emily turned to go and wished for just a moment that she could invite him into her bed, that things were different between them and they could love again.

Dropping her clothing by the bathroom door, she

paused as a surge of unexpected energy pulsed within her. The kind she hadn't experienced in years, not since before the attack and subsequent rape that had drained her of feminine energy, feminine power, and her sexuality. This close proximity to Chase was having quite an effect on her nerves.

Stepping into the shower, she turned her face to the spray, wanting to drown out thoughts of Chase on her couch, Chase in her apartment, Chase in her arms. Chase in her bed.

"Emily." Chase spoke, his voice raw and husky from the doorway.

"What are you doing in here?" The shower curtain offered little protection, but she pulled it against her, anyway.

"I heard the shower." A deep bruised look haunted his face, as if he was remembering their past together, too. Dark circles deepened his eyes.

"And, what, you thought you'd join me?" Damn. She shouldn't have said the words out loud. Now they were out there to become real.

"I could use one." Chase approached. He still wore his scrubs, still had that bruised, exhausted look about him, and her heart broke. The casement that had protected her for three years fractured.

She'd never felt more vulnerable.

He'd never been more wanting.

With her gaze glued to him, she drew back the curtain, silently inviting him inside the cocoon of heat and water with her. This day was a time out of time, a little bubble of protection where they could forget about the past and just live together in the moment.

In seconds he'd stripped and entered the shower with

her, keeping his eyes on hers. Doing the dance to adjust positions in the narrow space, they pressed against each other, sliding slick bodies against each other until Chase had his back against the spray. Tilting his head back, he immersed himself fully under the water and rubbed his hands over his face and groaned. "Oh, God, this feels good."

When he leaned back, Emily used the moment to take a good look at his body, at what she'd been missing for three years. Swallowing became difficult and her heart thundered in her chest, roaring in her ears over the sound of the shower. Remembering to breathe also seemed a foreign concept at the moment.

He'd dropped some weight, was now made of lean muscle and sinew, and looked like the runner he was. Long and lanky, arms and legs were finely muscled. His chest sported a light sprinkling of hair across his pecs and a finely muscled abdomen tapering downward.

Without removing his gaze from hers, the only thing he moved was his hands, to reach for the body scrubber and body wash. He poured a generous amount onto the scrubber and squished it up so it made suds, the way she liked. He'd said he remembered everything and seemed that was so right now.

"Turn around," he said, and she complied. Maybe if she didn't see him, she'd be okay. Maybe if… The scrubber hit her back she closed her eyes at the stimulating touch. Chase applied it to her skin in circular strokes, beginning at her shoulders then moving downward.

She placed the palms of her hands on the wall in front of her, needing the support. He touched her nowhere else, just with the scrubber. Beginning at her wrists, he stroked her skin, stimulating, teasing and torturing her body and her mind.

She hadn't surrendered control like this in forever and it was overwhelming, standing still as the scrubber moved over her neck, and she tilted her head back to give him greater access. The heat from the water and his body created a steam that nearly choked her. Or was it the heat of attraction that had never left her?

He was tall enough to reach over her shoulder and apply the scrubber to her chest, her breasts, teasing around each nipple until they were tender, stimulated peaks, aching for more. Moving his hand beneath her arm, he moved the scrubber across her upper abdomen, then her lower abdomen, then between her legs.

"Lean back," he said. "Let me take your weight. You can trust me." He stroked the hair back from her face and with a little pressure on her forehead eased her head back against his left shoulder and stayed that way until she released the tension in her muscles and let her weight fall against him. "Trust me, Em. I won't drop you, ever again." The feel of his erection against her backside aroused her more than she thought possible. He was hard and sleek and ready for her.

It was so foreign at first, to lean back against him, to let him hold her against his body, to let him stroke her. Turning her head slightly, she leaned her face toward his and he kissed her.

It wasn't the out-of-control passion they'd had in the past. This was a kiss of deep reverence, of passion and honor, and of a man seeking forgiveness.

She parted her lips and allowed him in, allowed him to take her where she'd longed to go since the first time she'd seen him again. Had it really been just days ago?

Three years away from him and it seemed like just yesterday she'd been in his arms.

Groaning, she turned to face him, clutched his shoulders and plastered her body against his. His arms went around her waist and pressed her harder against him, his hips jutting forward into hers, his erection hard and demanding against her abdomen.

Kisses ranged everywhere, and he scooped up one of her nipples in his mouth, teasing it without mercy. The rasp of his light beard stimulated her sensitive tissue. She clutched his head to her chest, spreading her kisses wherever she could reach.

Then her hand moved between them, but he stopped her, his grip like a vice on her arm. "This isn't about me tonight, Em. I don't want you to…be uncomfortable."

"Then just hold me for a little while longer."

"I will." He pressed a kiss to her head and let the water wash over them, cleansing their bodies and maybe a little of their souls.

After long moments passed and she relaxed, the stress of the day faded away. "Are you getting cold?" Her head fitted snug and perfectly beneath his chin. He'd forgotten that.

He'd missed that.

"What?"

"The water's getting cold."

"I hadn't noticed." Seriously, hadn't noticed.

They got out of the shower, dried each other off in between kisses and sighs. Emily was wrapped in her bulky robe and she hesitated at the door.

"What's wrong?"

"I don't know." She looked like a sprite with her hair

all spiky and wet, her eyes huge and dark, her mouth swollen from his kisses.

He approached, wrapped only in the towel. "Why don't you tell me what you do know?"

"It's so hard to put into words." She stood there swallowed up by the robe, arms hugging her middle.

"It's wonderful and awful at the same time, isn't it?" He shared the thoughts swirling like mad inside him.

Tears flashed in her eyes, and her chin trembled. "Yes."

"Why don't we go to bed, and you can tell me.'

"It's probably five a.m. by now. I don't want to keep you up any later than necessary."

Indeed, his body was telling him things he didn't want to know about, like it was going on twenty-four hours since he'd been horizontal. "I don't care what time it is. If you want to talk, I'll listen."

CHAPTER TEN

"WILL YOU HOLD me awhile? Just hold me. I won't ask you for more."

"Yes." He didn't trust his voice to say any more than that. He was exhausted and choked with emotions he couldn't name.

She led him to the bedroom, dragged the covers back and they got in. She'd always liked to be on her left side with him cuddling her from behind. That was the position they gravitated into now, and Chase felt like the past three years had fallen away from him in an instant.

But now she was tense.

"Do you want to talk?" Although he whispered in the dark, it sounded very loud.

"I... I... The words won't come." Her voice was small and soft, evoking the protective side of him from the place it had hidden, licking its wounds, for three years.

"Relax. Sleep. Let me hold you. I'll keep you safe." The soft breathing and the gentle rise and fall of her chest soothed him. Again, she fitted him perfectly, fitted in a way no other woman ever had.

There was no reason for her to fear him, but she didn't know that. It was up to him to tell her, show her, prove to her that she could trust him again. She'd deny she was afraid of anything, but deep down he knew he was right.

Unable to keep his mind awake any longer, he pressed a kiss to the back of her head and allowed sleep to overtake him, more content than he'd felt in a very long time.

Hours later he awoke to the scent of coffee brewing and the sun bright in the window. Emily was gone, her place beside him cold. Easing from his place, he grabbed the towel from the floor and wrapped it around his waist.

He paused in the doorway when he noticed Emily performing a series of slow movements, a small rubber ball in her hands. She was graceful and elegant as she moved the ball around, then she stopped when she saw him.

And smiled.

"I'm sorry. I didn't want to interrupt you."

"No problem." She released the position she was in and placed the ball on the couch. "I was just about through, anyway."

"I smell coffee. What time is it?"

"Noon." She padded on bare feet to the kitchen.

"*Noon?* Aren't we supposed to be at work, like, an hour ago?"

She was obviously unconcerned, and that wasn't like her. She was never late for anything.

"I got a text that staffing had changed once again. Since we were the last to go home we get the day off. They found some staff to cover." She nodded to his phone, which lay on the counter. "Check your phone. You probably got the same text."

"Wow." He checked the phone. "I haven't had a day off in like a billion years." Seriously.

"Well, I've got coffee going, but don't have much besides a few essentials."

"Whatever you've got is fine, or I can just have coffee and go." But as he looked at her, he didn't want to go. He didn't know what he wanted, what he needed, or what she needed, either. "Or I can stay."

"Actually, I'll need you to either drive me to the studio or take me to my car."

"The studio?"

"The Rose Lee Martial Arts Studio. The dojo where I practice." She shrugged and reached for two mugs, filled them with coffee and opened the fridge for the milk. "Since I have the time today I thought I'd go over there and mess around."

"Since I've got no other plans, how about I go with you?" Watching her face, he looked for signs of tension but found none. Joy and happiness weren't there, either. More resignation.

"I'm not sure you'd like it there. Very martial-artsy."

"After seeing you in action a couple of times, I have a new admiration for the art and would like to watch you work."

She considered him a moment, her eyes narrowed, and she tilted her head to one side. For some reason, he felt much like a mouse being stalked by a cat. "Do you have scrubs in the car?"

"Yes. I always carry extra."

"Just so you know, at Rose's no one is an observer. If you're there, you're there to participate. If you're not intimidated by that, you can come—otherwise you can take me to my car, and I'll go by myself." She just left the words to hang in the air a moment for his consideration.

"That has the smell of a challenge in it." He was not

above a good challenge, but this one could have unfore-
seen consequences. Things could go either way. He had
to decide quickly if he could deal with it.

"Call it what you like, but those are the rules."

"I'm up for it." He sipped the brew, hot, strong and
bold, just the way he liked it. And a good description of
what Emily had become. He liked that, too.

Within the hour they arrived at the studio, Emily
in her *gi* and Chase in his scrubs. They removed their
shoes at the door and entered the practice room. During the day few people were there, but at night the place
was packed.

At the moment Emily was glad of the space. She'd
hardly had a chance to catch her breath in the last few
days, and now here she was, about to take Chase to the
mat, literally.

"Chase, this is Rose, owner of the studio and my
teacher, my *sensei*. You may address her as Rose or *sensei*." Emily gave a slight bow from the hips, as did Rose.
Chase followed their lead.

"He is a tall one," Rose said, her eyes scrunching up
at the corners. She was just over five feet tall, so Emily
had her by a few inches, and Chase towered over both
of them by quite a bit. "I'm not sure you can teach him.
He might need someone taller." She looked up at Chase
as if he were a tree.

"I am happy to have Emily teach me a few things.
She nearly took on a man larger than her at the hospital
the other day and height didn't seem to matter."

"I see." Rose gave Emily a look with raised brows
but a serious face. "So you have already defended Chase
at the hospital?"

"Yes, well, no, not really. The man was intoxicated

and upset. No one got injured and Security escorted him away." She explained the situation in dry terms, giving only the facts. "But I would have, had the need arisen. As it was, Chase defended me, or perhaps we defended each other." As she said the words she looked at Chase, and he nodded.

"Have you considered what we previously discussed?" Rose asked.

It was not a question without consequences, and Emily had considered it from all angles.

"Yes, *sensei*, I have. I will teach one class for you and see how that goes."

"What class is that?" Chase asked, suddenly very interested in their conversation.

"Self-defense for women. There is a need for good teachers at my studio. Emily has the soul of a warrior and the heart of a teacher. I believe she will be the best person to teach this class." There was no false flattery in her words, just simple facts.

Emily bowed, her face flushed and pink. "Thank you, *sensei* Rose." She clasped her hands together in front of her heart and gave a slight bow. "Thank you."

"Please, proceed with what you were going to do, and we'll talk schedules later." Rose returned to the office, leaving Emily and Chase alone.

"What were you going to do if you were by yourself?" Chase asked, curious about the little warrior in front of him that he was beginning to get to know.

"I was going to do some sword work, but I can do that another time."

"Sword work?" Now, that was impressive. She was very serious about this. He'd never have guessed.

"Yes, it utilizes different muscles than you would in

running or sparring. But now I think we'll start with basics." She looked him up and down, deciding on what to do.

"What would you teach in your class?"

"Basic self-defense."

"Show me something."

She thought for a second with her lips pursed. "Okay. Reach out to me like the guy did in the ER. Like you're going to grab my shoulder."

Hesitating a second, he reached out slowly, not wanting to hurt her.

"Come on. Do it like you mean it. Charge me if you have to."

"I don't want to hurt you." This was so weird. Even in play it felt uncomfortable.

She snorted. "You can't. Now do it!"

With a toss of his head he did what she'd asked. Before he knew what was going on he was on the floor, looking up at the ceiling.

"Oh, Chase! Are you okay?" Emily knelt beside him, serious concern in her eyes. "I'm sorry!"

"What happened?" He blinked a few times, but nothing seemed broken, and he still had his testicles, though they were cringing against his bottom. All good.

"Well, I think I went a little overboard." She bit her lower lip, hesitating but not afraid.

He struggled to a sitting position and let her help him up. "I reached out like you said…"

"I should have just pinned your arm behind you. But instinct kicked in, and I swept your feet out from under you, too. Jeez, I'm sorry." Trembling, she pressed a hand to her forehead.

Rose approached, her face the picture of serenity.

"Don't worry. Even teachers make mistakes. Better to make one now with him than later in your class."

"But what if I hurt someone? Unintentionally." That was her biggest fear about teaching women who had no skills. What if she made them worse?

"You could. You probably will at some point. But it will be a lesson they need." Rose looked up at Chase, considering, but kept her thoughts to herself. "Carry on. You'll be fine." She turned to Emily. "You're a good teacher."

"Thank you, *sensei*." Emily bowed slightly as Rose left the room again.

"Okay. Let's try it again. I'll grab your shoulder like this." With his left hand, he reached for her right shoulder.

"Then I push your arm away and wrap my hand all the way around your arm with my right, push your shoulder up to the point of pain and use my left hand to control your head movement away from me." She held him that way for a second. "Ha! That's it."

"You really do have me in a grip there." There was no wiggle room at all.

"Now try to get free."

He struggled to move and extricate himself, but he couldn't, not without causing himself pain. "You're hurting me. No matter which way I try to move, it's painful."

"I'm not hurting you. I'm simply holding you still. When you move *you* are causing yourself pain. Eventually an assailant will learn to hold still because he is causing himself pain. Even if it's a woman who is holding him." She released him, and he rolled his shoulder around, easing the joint, and the pain ceased.

"Wow. That's really impressive." Eyes wide, he looked

at her anew. "You're really amazing. Do you know that? I mean *really* know it? How powerful you are?" He was just beginning to understand it himself.

She stared at him, met his gaze straight on. "I wouldn't have had to become any of this if I hadn't been raped."

That statement punched him in the gut like he'd been assaulted himself. His chest tightened and it felt like a vise clamped around his throat. He swallowed, hard, emotions strangling him. "I'm sorry."

"It's not your fault a serial rapist broke into my apartment, beat me up, raped me and tried to kill me."

He swallowed. There it was. The statement of what had happened. What had nearly killed her, but had made her stronger, had broken them apart and nearly destroyed him. "I don't know what to say. In the past everything I said was wrong." Why should it be different now?

"There's not a lot to say." She sighed and the energy seemed to puddle out of her. "I think I'm done for today."

"Is it because of what I said?" Again.

"No." She dropped her gaze away from him and withdrew into herself. She began to walk toward the door, and he followed, his heart heavier than it had been in a long, long time. There was nothing he could say to change the past, nothing he could say to change the present either. Time healed some wounds, but others stayed raw forever.

They found their shoes and headed to the parking lot. "Do you want me to take you to get your car now?"

"Yes. I think that's best." She sat in the passenger seat, looking out the window, as Chase started the car. By now the sun had passed its zenith and was on the long, slow decline down to the horizon.

The radio played low in the background, but it was

the only thing that broke the silence in the vehicle. Emily had withdrawn, and Chase didn't know how to bring her out. He didn't know if she would ever recover from her assault. Was it reasonable to expect that she would? He just didn't know.

"He's gone for good now." She spoke to him but still looked out the window.

"Who?"

"Bernard Twist. The rapist." She'd come to think of him as Bernard Twisted. The things he'd done to women had been gut-wrenchingly awful.

Without answering, he negotiated a turn and then another. "I know. I followed the trial."

"He's such a sick bastard, but I have no sympathy for him. None whatsoever."

"I wanted to kill him." He pulled up near the side of the firehouse and parked, but kept his hands on the steering-wheel. The tremors inside him were visible, and he clutched the steering wheel harder. "If I'd found him before the police, I think I would have."

She turned, surprise on her face. "Really? You wouldn't just have let the police handle it?"

He shook his head in an anger, a hatred so deep even the memory of it scorched him. He blew out a breath. "I don't think I'd have been able to control myself."

Emily stared at him, seeming to come to a decision. A small smile lifted one corner of her mouth. She leaned toward him and placed her hand behind his neck, pulling him forward, and pressed her forehead against his.

"I'm glad you didn't, but thank you for thinking of it."

"You're welcome." That was kind of funny, being thanked for murderous thoughts.

"Sometimes I forget I wasn't the only one who was

raped. You were assaulted in a different way, and I'm sorry for that, Chase." She stayed that way, not moving, just breathing.

Then he realized she was saying goodbye to him without words. "Wait a minute."

"I'm going to go now, and I'll see you at work."

"I don't want that." He pulled back, but took her wrist in his hand and held her hand to his face. "I mean, I don't want to just see you at work."

"A relationship between us won't work. I thought perhaps there might be a chance for us, but I was wrong. I needed to come here to see it for myself. You've seen how messed up I still am, probably will be the rest of my life. I want to focus on my work at the hospital, at the studio, and with the new class I'm going to teach." She gave a watery smile, her lips pressed together for a moment, trying to control her emotions. "That's enough for me. It has to be. If I want too much, I'll be disappointed the rest of my life."

"No, it's not. It never was. And it's not enough for me." Anger began to boil inside him. Being ripped apart at the seams twice wasn't acceptable. Somehow he had to change this. Somehow he had to get through to her. Somehow he had to make her see.

"The old Emily is gone. I still have the same name, but the rest of me has changed. You need to face that, Chase, the way I did. I'm not the woman you once knew, you once loved." She pulled the handle on the door and eased out of the car.

Danny was trotting across the parking lot, waving. Any moment Chase would have had to talk to her about their situation now was gone, and he might never get another chance. The walls around her he'd breached for a little while were now as high and strong as ever. Maybe he was chasing the wrong Emily. Maybe he was chasing a ghost that no longer existed, and she was right. Maybe the Emily he'd loved was gone, and he needed to move on for good. Or maybe he needed to chase *this* Emily and see where she led him.

He wasn't giving up.

He watched through the window as Danny hugged his sister and met Chase's look over her head. The man, his best friend, her brother, waved at him, then placed his arm around her shoulders and guided her into the fire station.

This woman had known more pain than she ever should have and it was his fault, his responsibility, his burden for the rest of his life. The rapist was in jail for the rest of his life, and Chase was in a prison without bars for the remainder of his years.

CHAPTER ELEVEN

DAYS LATER, Chase warmed up in the racquetball court at the community center. He wasn't the kind of man to join a gym, no matter how convenient it seemed to be. With his schedule it wasn't worth it, and he liked supporting his local community. So he utilized the center whenever he could, like today.

Whap. He hit the ball again with a satisfying slam. This was the way men worked out their issues, by beating something up, even if it was something as insignificant as a hard rubber ball in an enclosed court.

The door opened, and Danny entered. "Starting without me?"

This was their usual date and time. Sometimes they jogged, sometimes they played racquetball, depending on their moods and the weather. Today it was pouring outside, the gloom moving in from the ocean like a living creature sweeping over the land. It matched his temperament.

"Yeah. Feeling stiff, so thought I'd warm up." Partially true.

"You know, stretching helps." *Whap.* Danny entered into the game when the ball came in his direction.

"So I hear." The words Emily had said echoed in his

mind. *You'll be a stiff old man unable to tie his own shoelaces.*

"Uh, so how's it going with you and Emily?" Danny whacked the ball.

"What do you mean?" Had she spoken to Danny about them?

"At work. How's work going?"

"She's a great nurse. New skills these days."

"The martial arts?"

"Yeah. She's a regular ol' ninja nurse." *Whack.* "Impressive."

"She is. For more than just that."

"You never did answer my question about why you didn't tell me she was coming back."

"Figured you'd find out soon enough. You hadn't asked about her for a while. Figured you'd moved on, and I didn't want to get in the middle of it."

Moved on. How do you move on from the love of your life?

"I thought I had." The thought cramped his gut. He'd tried. He'd tried entirely too hard, especially in the beginning, but now seeing Emily again made him want to take it all back and try harder, try to be the man she'd needed him to be back then and he hadn't been. But it was too late. She'd made that clear the other day.

"And now?"

"Don't know."

They finished their game sweaty and worn out, then dropped onto a bench and cooled off.

"Think I'm gonna hit the shower here. Amber doesn't like it when I come to her place after my workout. Says I smell like a goat," Danny said with a grin, and took a sniff at one of his armpits. "She's probably right." He cleared his throat. "So, uh, you didn't really answer my question, either."

"Which one?" He knew, but stalled.

"About you and Emily. What's going on?" Danny didn't look directly at Chase, but bounced the ball between his feet.

"Don't know. Spent some time with her at the studio the other day. She taught me a few moves."

That got a reaction out of him and a rise of his brows. "That's amazing. I thought she'd karate chop you to pieces."

"She probably should have." That made him smile. The thought of her as a trained martial artist was fascinating.

"So what do you think? Going to get back together?"

"No. I don't think so. After that she withdrew, wouldn't talk to me, and I haven't seen her since." The real question was did he want to? They were vastly different people now.

"She's changed, that's for sure. But she had to. You know that, right?"

"I know. It's almost painful to watch her now, though." He rubbed his face with a towel. "Like she's still struggling every minute with the past riding on her back."

"I think she is. The physical stuff healed, but it's the stuff on the inside that's still broken." Danny sighed, leaned forward and placed his elbows on his knees. "It's been a long couple of years for her, but sometimes when I look at her I wish the old Emily was still there, still in there."

"After something like this I don't know if she can be *that* Emily ever again. She's tried to tell me that, and I'm not sure I was listening." He'd thought about it. She'd alluded to it. He just had to accept it or move on. Again.

"The new Emily is pretty awesome, though. Tough as nails. She even took me at arm wrestling."

"Yeah. She is." Flashes of her in the ER, in the apartment, and in the shower hit him hard. "Well, I gotta roll." He stood. He didn't have anything else he needed to do but he couldn't sit there anymore, ruminating about the past and his poor performance, his contribution to Emily's attack, and his unforgivable absence during her recovery. That was what killed him most. He hadn't been there for her.

He shoved out the doors of the community center into the drizzle, which had turned into a downright downpour. He made it to his car and got in, turned on the engine and let the wipers do their work. The heat of his body and the rain misted up the windows. He reached out to wipe some of it away with his hand and froze.

It had been a day exactly like today, three years ago, that Emily had been attacked. His heart thundered in his ears as he listened to the blast from the defroster trying to keep up with the condensation on the windshield. Frozen in the driver's seat, he sat there as memories of the past washed over him. Guilt he'd thought had been long ago dealt with ripped through him with the precision of a surgical blade.

It had eviscerated him then and nearly gutted him now.

He'd raced off in the early morning hours to the hospital, just as always, and had forgotten to lock the door of Emily's apartment, his mind occupied on the day ahead. Her place had been closer to the hospital and when he'd been on call he'd sometimes stayed with her.

He'd run into surgery and saved the day the way he was supposed to. As soon as the case had finished he'd

been called to the ER for another emergency, but had
been cornered by the attending physician before he'd
been able to see the patient.

Unprepared for what he'd been told, he'd nearly
dropped to his knees in disbelief. He'd raced to the side
of a woman lying on a gurney in the ER, bloodied, battered, on the ventilator and disfigured beyond recognition.

"That's not Emily," he'd said, and had stormed out.
"How could you misidentify a patient like that?" The
force of his anger had sliced through him at such an
egregious error, but the look on the face of the man
he'd known and trusted had made him stop. The trembling inside him had escalated, and he'd looked back
at her. "Is it?"

The remembered fear, the remembered pain of seeing
her like that made him clench the steering-wheel now.
How could he have not recognized the woman he loved?

But he'd expected to see her the way he'd last seen
her, beautiful and lively. But she'd been near death from
the injuries sustained in the attack in her own home.

Both of her eyes had been swollen shut, bruises had
covered her face, and blood had trickled from her mouth
around the breathing tube. The ambulance crew had
placed a neck collar on her for transport and it had
been stained red. Her nose had been swollen, obviously
broken, and her lips had been cracked and bleeding in
several places.

Dumbfounded, he'd moved forward in a fog and
picked up one of her battered hands, seeing the broken
fingernails, the abrasions and cuts. The ring he'd given
her the previous Christmas had screamed out to him
from beneath dried blood. "Em?" His voice had cracked,

then he'd whipped around to the physician. "Is she going to live?"

"We don't know." It had been the bald truth.

Those words had just about killed him. She'd had to go to surgery to repair a broken jaw, multiple lacerations in her mouth, a broken nose and plastic surgery for the lacerations on her face. Her parents had been hysterical when they'd arrived. Seeing their beautiful daughter mauled in such a way had been something no parent should witness.

The windshield began to clear, and Chase looked out at the day of drizzle and gloom, trying to pull himself out of the memory, but unable to as the rain drilled his car, drowning out all other sound. He covered his face with his hands, allowing the guilt of his responsibility to wash over him. Guilt, guilt, guilt. It hung on him like a worn and tattered coat he could never remove.

He should have taken the time to lock the damned door, but he hadn't. It *was* his fault.

Days had passed with Chase and Emily's families standing watch by her side until she'd roused from the coma she'd been put in by heavy sedation. The swelling around her eyes had improved, but they'd still been purple.

Over the next few months her physical condition had improved while the rapist had continued to terrorize his way through the city. He'd violated nine women before being caught for a traffic violation. Stupid, but par for the course.

Getting close to Emily after that had been hard. They'd tried to have a normal life again, but both of them had realized there was no normal any longer.

And he'd been an idiot. He'd been angry and impatient and unable to be the man, the friend, the support she'd needed at the time, and she had been right to kick him out of her life. The first and only time they'd tried to make love had been a disaster.

Her body had finally healed physically and they'd wanted to be close again, each of them aching for it, needing it, but not understanding how long it might take to get there. She'd panicked. Even with the light on so she'd been able to see it had been Chase with her hadn't helped. She'd vomited when he'd touched her intimately.

All she'd felt had been pain and terror where once they'd experienced great joy together. All they'd had was great sorrow. The strangling sensation in her throat hadn't stopped and she'd screamed until she couldn't anymore.

He'd left then, left because he'd been afraid. Afraid of the demons inside her that might never go away. And he'd been selfish. Wanting her back to the same old Emily had been ridiculous. He'd had no concept of grief or recovery of this magnitude. Grief worked in strange ways and now, looking back, he could see it had been his grief that had overwhelmed him and made him act in ways that hadn't served him or Emily.

Weeks had passed, and she hadn't contacted him. He hadn't called her, wanting to give her some space, and then he'd heard she'd taken off on a travel assignment. Without saying goodbye. He'd been hurt beyond measure, but had covered it up with more anger and by convincing himself it had been her loss.

That was when he'd started on a womanizing spree, trying to bury himself in any woman so long as she hadn't reminded him of Emily.

Chase sighed, turned down the defroster and put the

car in gear. Once out of the parking lot he didn't know where he was going, where to go, but found himself driving past Emily's apartment, and discovered her car wasn't there. Minutes later he found it at the martial-arts studio where his car had mysteriously driven to. Puzzled at his need to see her again, he entered and sat on a bench outside the workout room.

Inside the glass-walled studio he found Emily. She hadn't seen him, didn't know he was there, and he could watch her without disturbing her.

"Today is a women-only day. No men allowed." Rose approached and sat on the bench beside him.

"What?"

"It's Wednesday. Women-Only Wednesdays. No testosterone allowed in the studio." Though she gave him the info, she didn't look like she was going to toss him out on her ear.

"I'm sorry. I didn't know."

"She's very strong, you know."

Chase turned back to watch Emily as she led a group of women through poses and exercises. "She is. More than she ever was."

"That's because she's done the work." Rose peered at him, looking like a bird contemplating a bug it was about to eat.

"Training, you mean? I can see that."

"She's done the physical training, yes, but she's done the emotional and spiritual part of it, as well. Still continues to do it daily."

"Therapy, you mean?" He'd suspected that.

"Yes, and meditation, and giving over to the universe that which no longer serves her. The anger and the fear. 'Whoever can see through all fear will always be safe.'

That's a quote from *Tao Te Ching*, by Lao Tzu, a very ancient, very wise man."

"I never thought of it that way."

"No. You would not have because you have not done the work she has."

"Excuse me?" Really? Had she just had the gall to say that to him? After all he'd been through, after all he'd lost?

"It's true, but you don't want to admit that, do you? You have not done the work she has, so she is further ahead in her recovery than you are in yours." Rose shrugged as if it were a simple thing.

"I see." Anger began to fill him.

"No, you don't see, which is why you need to come back on Manly Monday, a men-only day, and begin your own recovery."

"I don't have the time for that sort of thing." Frowning, he turned away from Rose. Some *sensei* she was.

"Then you will never recover, and you will remain stuck where you are in this life." She stood. "Until you deal with an issue, it will continue to show up in your life over and over again. Then you will be forced to deal with it at some point and it will be more painful for you than if you had dealt with it when you were supposed to."

"You're a pretty smart woman, too." He nodded, acknowledging some part of what she said rang true for him, and the anger fizzled away. Dammit. He hated being wrong and he hated being told he was wrong even more.

"Because I, too, have done the work."

Recovery. He'd not thought of it that way, that he needed to recover from the trauma that had affected

Emily, from the powerlessness of it, the helpless way it made him feel. Squirming a little on the bench from the discomfort of his thoughts, he stood, not wanting to violate the Wednesday rule.

The restlessness that had been invading him all morning eased. Now that he'd seen Emily, seen her in her element, he could go on with his day in peace.

With his heart somehow lighter, he walked out into the rain.

Chase got to work early the next morning, anticipating seeing Emily. The anticipation humming through him was a new yet familiar sensation but one he hadn't experienced in some time. He felt happy, and for the moment peaceful.

Patients seemed to whiz by him all day long until he felt a change in the atmosphere of the ER. It became heavy, serious, quiet. Uncomfortable.

"What's going on?" he asked Liz. As the charge nurse, she knew everything going on.

"Rape victim came in from the university. Apparently, she went to an event last night on campus, but when she woke up this morning she had empty spots in her memory. She feels like she engaged in sex, but has no memory of it, and may have been raped."

"Oh, jeez." Inside, Chase's guts churned. "Do we have any female docs on right now? Who's going to do the rape kit?"

"No, I was going to see if you could help out. Emily's in there with her now, doing the preliminaries."

"*Emily?* That's not right. Isn't there a way to find a woman to help out? I can do it, but she will probably be very uncomfortable with it." This was not a road he wanted to go down unless absolutely necessary. Perhaps this was what Rose had talked about yesterday.

Emily approached them, her face stoic, and she was a little pale. "I agree. There's a SANE hotline number we can call and find someone to come in and perform the exam."

"Sane? What's that?" Chase asked.

"Sexual Assault Nurse Examiner. I've taken my training, but haven't tested yet, so I can't officially do the exam, and not as a travel nurse. My company won't let me." She shifted her position from one foot to the other. "I can call the center. They always have someone on call who can come do the kit and collect evidence."

Chase nodded, and so did Liz. "Go ahead. Give them a call."

"We get this kind of patient so infrequently I don't know if we have an official policy about it."

"It happens more than you know, so there should be a policy and one nurse on every shift who is the designated nurse for rape victims." Emily offered the advice and it was good.

"There's no nice way to put that, is there?" Liz asked.

"No. Sexual assault and rape are not nice things to put a nice label on, anyway," Emily said, her face becoming pink and her eyes glittering with anger. "People need to be held accountable for their actions. Too often things like this are brushed aside as boys being boys, when it's really an act of violence."

"If this upsets you, Liz will assign you to another patient," Chase said, and kept his voice calm and clinical.

"It's not the patient that upsets me. It's the lack of knowledge and the act itself that anger me." She held onto the counter and took a few deep breaths. "I'm sorry. I shouldn't let my personal feelings affect my work."

"It's a terrible thing for her," Liz said. "Do you know if they will also do counseling? Can you set that up for her, as well?"

"Yes, the SANE nurse will do preliminary assessment and then get her set up for further support."

"Boy, you know all kinds of stuff!" Liz said. "Good thing she ended up being your patient, or we might not have gotten her the right attention."

"I'm glad I'm with her, too."

"Let me make that call so I learn the process." Liz stepped around the desk, and Emily faced Chase. The compassion in his eyes was almost her undoing, almost led to her falling apart when she couldn't afford to and almost made her want to reach out to him.

"Are you okay? This can't be easy." The energy coming off him was pulsating, almost as if it put its arms out to surround her with an energetic layer of protection.

"I'm okay." She nodded and took a deep breath. "I'm okay, but later I might need some down time."

"If you need to meditate, I'll watch her for you."

"Thank you." That spontaneous offer created a warm pulse in her chest and made her heart beat a little faster.

"I know it hasn't been easy on you these last few years, but you've come an amazingly long way." His gaze dropped from hers for a second and then he looked at her, fierce and intent. "I want you to know I'm so proud of your accomplishments."

Her jaw dropped for a second, and her eyes went wide. "What?"

"I want you to know I'm...proud of you, Em. You're doing so much to help other women, and you're so much stronger than you ever were." His voice cracked with emotion and tears sprang to her eyes unexpectedly.

"Thank you, Chase," she whispered, and took a step back from him. She needed the distance, the distraction, the space between them or she was going to come unglued. "Please let me know when the SANE nurse is here. I'll be sitting with the patient until then."

Turning, she hurried away from him and the emotions swirling around him or she was going to get sucked back into the vortex of the past.

By the end of the shift Emily felt like someone had beaten her with a hammer. Every possible body part hurt, even her hair felt like it was on fire. The energy of holding back her emotions, keeping her past memories at bay was exhausting work. She gathered her belongings and headed out the door.

"Can I talk to you?" Chase asked, hurrying to catch up to her in the parking lot.

"Did I forget something?" As tired as she was, it wouldn't have surprised her.

"No, I just wanted to see you before you left."

"About what?" Puzzled, she stopped in the light of a streetlamp. From habit, she always was aware of her surroundings, never putting herself in a potentially dangerous situation by standing in the shadow.

He fidgeted, ran his hand through his hair the way he did when something bothered him. "That patient today, the…the…"

"The rape victim? You can say the word to me, Chase. It's just a word."

"Okay, then, yes, the rape victim. I didn't know how sensitive you were going to be about that, and I didn't want to say anything if it was going to bother you."

"Bother me? What bothers me is people walking on eggshells around me, thinking I'm so fragile that one word will break me." She turned and kept walking to her car. "That's what bothers me."

Chase followed along. "I don't know what to say to you sometimes. All I can think of is, 'Will this bother you?' or 'Will that bother you?' I'm trying to be considerate about this, but I don't know what to do."

"I'm not fragile, and you just need to be yourself around me." She paused and pushed her hair behind her ear. "I mean, if you want to be around me."

Without speaking, he closed the gap between them and put his arms around her shoulders, drawing her closer, slowly but firmly until their energies mingled and his chest pressed against hers. "I do, Em. I do want to be around you. So much it hurts."

With her defenses so low, that was all it took to break her. She huffed out a breath and took in another one and another that were sharp and short, and tears filled her eyes, her chest burned, and she cried out when she wrapped her arms around his middle. "Oh!"

They stood that way, holding each other in the parking lot, while Emily cried. He felt the tremors in her body as her tears saturated his shirt, and he soothed her by stroking her shoulders and the back of her head, keeping his hands to the upper part of her body and offering her comfort the only way he knew how.

"I hate this, you know?" She pulled back, sniffing.

"What?" His voice was a whisper, and he tipped her face up to his.

"Crying. Serves no purpose. I'd rather hit something."

"It's a release, and one you apparently needed." He

pulled out his shirt to examine the wet splotches on the left shoulder area. "I'm happy to be your handkerchief."

"Oh, stop," she said, and frowned, then a laugh bubbled up inside her. "Just stop."

"Or, what, you'll laugh? How tragic is that?" Smiling, he gave her another nudge.

"Chase!" The giggles seemed to have a life of their own and took over her body as she wiped the heels of her hands against her eyes, smearing her mascara down her face. "Oh, my God, I can't stop." She turned away from him and kept moving to her car, but it didn't help. The laughter followed her.

The man kept following her and the grin on his face was something she thought she'd never be happy to see again, but she was and it was beautiful.

"Don't stop, Emily, don't ever stop."

"Stop...what?" She pressed a knuckle to her mouth and bit on it, hoping to stop the cascade of giggles with pain, but it wasn't working.

"Don't ever stop laughing, finding joy in the little things, the stupid things in life. They matter."

And that was what stopped her laughter. "I did. For a long time, I did." Taking another shaky breath, she began to get control of herself again.

"I know, and I'm sorry. I'm so sorry I wasn't there for you when you needed me to—"

"You okay, miss?" A security guard pulled up in a white van.

"Uh, yeah, I'm okay," Emily said, and took a step back from Chase. And then another.

"Okay. Parking areas can be dangerous, so I'd like to see you safely in your vehicle."

"Thanks, anyway. I think I've got it from here." She waved him away.

"If you say so," he said, and pulled away to patrol elsewhere.

"Emily, will you go out with me?" Chase asked, and his brows rose, like he hadn't meant to ask that question.

"Will I go out with you?" Was he *serious*?

"Yes."

"Like on a date?"

"Yes, like on a date." The smile that moved his mouth sideways had always been a heart-killer for her and it was no less forceful on her now. "Friday. I'm in surgery all day tomorrow, but Friday would work."

"That's like in two days." An eager trembling began in her stomach. Anticipation filled her even though she hadn't said yes yet.

"It is. I'll pick you up at five, we'll go have dinner in Virginia Beach, then take a walk by the ocean, watch the sunset."

"Chase..." she began, not sure how to handle this situation. She didn't want to hurt him, but she didn't want to hurt herself, either, then she remembered a previous engagement. "Actually, I have an event Friday night. There's a fundraiser for the rape crisis center. I go every year."

"I see." A mask covered his face. "I could go with you."

"I already have a date." *Squeal*. She did, but it wasn't what he thought it was.

"I see," he said again, looking closed and distant.

She couldn't mislead him on purpose. "Okay, so Danny is my date, all right? Maybe another time. Like Saturday night?"

"I will hold you to that," he said, and the expression

on his face changed, his eyes glittering with something she couldn't identify. It wasn't sneaky or sinister, but there was definitely something going on in that brilliant mind of his.

"Okay. Okay." She quickly unlocked her car, got in and locked it again. She had to get away from him before she did something stupid. Something out of character. Something wild and wanton. Her body began to hum as she drove home, still charged from the contact she'd had with his body. Although it had just been a hug, it hadn't been just a hug, and they both knew it.

It had been the beginning of something she wasn't sure she wanted, but wasn't sure she didn't want either. The next time they were together could be combustible, and she had to prepare herself for it before it swept her away.

CHAPTER TWELVE

FRIDAY ARRIVED AND Emily spent half the day congratulating herself on maintaining her dignity and the other half berating herself for not inviting Chase back to her place for the night. What had been there between them in the past had been good. Not perfect, they'd had their issues, but they'd liked and respected each other, and *that* had been the basis for their relationship.

She went to the studio to work out the angst and sexual hunger that had kept her awake for half the night. That worked, then she'd showered, eaten a light snack and now waited for Danny to pick her up in his hopefully clean car. Their parents would meet them at the hotel ballroom. They had been pillars of support for her in her recovery and had been staunch volunteers at the rape crisis center ever since. Although they'd never been involved in an organization like that, there was only one way they could see to give back to the people who had saved their daughter's life. With their time.

With a last look in the mirror, she declared herself fit to go to a black-tie event. Her hair had been spiked to perfection and sprayed a bit, the tips blonde, the base auburn, and it suited her but made her look a bit like a pixie. The makeup she had applied was subdued with just a dash of sparkle at the corners of her eyes and cheekbones.

The only really good piece of jewelry she'd indulged in was a large black pearl she'd found at an estate sale and it hung now on a delicate silver chain around her neck. The pearl itself lay perfectly between her breasts, which looked more voluptuous than they really were thanks to a lacy push-up bra. Once in a while she indulged in the feminine and enjoyed it thoroughly, when it was safe for her to do so. When she could just be herself, she enjoyed herself more.

The dress had been a find at a vintage store. It had been an indulgence, but she didn't care. She felt beautiful in it and that was enough reason to wear it. The black lace bustier hugged her torso and cupped her breasts as if it had been made for her. The skirt fell in flirtatious waves of satin past her knees to a respectable tea-length, mid-calf. When she spun around the dress moved with her, the skirt flaring out and making her feel like she'd been thrown back in time to when dancing had been an art form.

Danny knew she loved to dance and would be her partner until the band quit playing or they dropped dead from exhaustion.

Little black bag. *Check.*

Lipstick. *Check.*

Little black shawl. *Check.*

Keys, a little cash and her ID. *Check, check, check.*

She was ready, just waiting for Danny. When the doorbell rang promptly at six, she was surprised. For him to be ten minutes late was not usual. For him to be exactly on time was a miracle.

She grabbed the doorknob and opened the door. "You're really on time..."

Chase stood in her doorway.

In a *tux* and her jaw dropped.

She'd never seen him look more handsome. Ever. Ever. *Ever.*

"Good evening, Emily." Even his voice sounded husky and sexier than she'd ever known it.

The hair on her arms and the back of her neck stood straight up, a flash of desire shot straight to her groin and her mouth went dry. "What are you doing here?"

"We should get going, or we'll be late. Traffic can be a bear when there's a football game at the university, and we have to pass by there to get to the hotel."

"You didn't answer my question." That was true, but she still proceeded as if she were going somewhere with him.

"I know." He stepped forward and escorted her out the door, then took her keys, locked the door and placed the keys into her purse. "I'll tell you on the way."

Dumbfounded, Emily allowed him to lead her down the stairs to the parking lot and to a very shiny black limo. *Squee!* The driver stood beside the back door and held it open, an enigmatic smile on his face. "Evening, miss."

"Good evening." The only proper way she knew to get into a vehicle in formal attire was to sit, then swing her legs inside, *à la* Marilyn Monroe, Hollywood style. A ridiculous giggle erupted in her throat. She felt like a movie star!

Chase entered right behind her and settled so he could look at her.

"You look stunning, Emily. Absolutely stunning." His

gaze traveled over her body, and he gave an apprecia-
tive whistle.

"Yes, well, thank you." Nervous when the car moved
forward, she tried to tuck her hair behind her ear, but it
wasn't long enough to tuck. "You don't look half-bad
yourself." Indeed, the black tux against the crisp white
shirt was just devastating to her senses, as was the cologne he wore. It was her favorite, and he knew it. He'd
always worn it when he'd wanted to tempt and tease
her, torment her senses. It worked now as well. She was
definitely tempted.

"So, are you going to tell me what's going on?" Soft,
soothing music began to play in the vehicle. Chase handed
her a champagne glass and reached for the bottle she
hadn't seen until now.

"Yes. Your brother couldn't make it, so he asked me if
I would give you a ride."

"Some ride." Her eyes widened as suspicion mounted.

"Isn't it, though?" He poured champagne halfway
up the glass, then poured some in another for himself.
He clinked her glass with his. "Cheers."

"What happened? He arranged to have tonight off
weeks ago." She'd nagged him until he had, too, or he'd
have forgotten.

"Apparently, one of the guys was hurt, and he's covering an extra couple of shifts to help out. This happened to be one of them. Unfortunate, don't you think?"
Chase raised his glass and drank, but kept his sparkling
gaze on her.

"Terribly. Lucky for me you could fall on your sword
and sacrifice yourself for the good of others, right?"
Emily drank from the glass and let the tiny bubbles work
their magic on her anxiety at seeing Chase in such a sur-

prising manner. Her heart fluttered wildly in her chest and a flush seemed to overcome her body. Maybe it was the effects of the champagne, though she'd only had a sip, or maybe it was Chase, but either way it was exhilarating. Living in the moment had its benefits.

"Exactly. I do love to support my community when I can."

The driver negotiated his way around the stadium traffic and delivered them to the front doors of the Williamsburg Governor's Mansion, the fantastically elegant historic structure very close to the historic section of town that had been built over two hundred years ago. The evening had begun to chill, but with the fizz of the champagne and her dashing companion she really didn't notice it.

"Allow me." He held out an arm to escort her formally into the ballroom, where he handed over their tickets to the person at the front. She was a woman, mid-sixties, with sparkling blue eyes and a winning smile.

"Welcome! Have a wonderful evening, and thank you so much for supporting our event."

"What a nice woman."

"Her daughter was raped and murdered."

Chase did a double-take. "Are you sure? She looks so happy."

"Oh, she is, because of the assistance of the center. She's one of the board members and is a driving force to keep the place going."

"Looks can sure be deceiving."

"You aren't kidding. She put her anger to good use."

"Maybe we should send her to congress. She'd get some things accomplished."

She stopped, her face serious. "Chase, stop a minute."

"What?" Puzzled, he raised his brows at her. Nothing had changed, but she was dead serious.

"I just wanted to thank you for coming. You didn't have to, but it means a lot to me that you're here."

Touched at her words, he cupped his hand against her cheek, allowing himself the softest touch. "There's no place I'd rather be."

Before Emily could respond to the kink in her stomach they were overcome by a group of attendees in high spirits. Mostly ladies, but a few men rounded out the group, who were laughing and hugging and carrying on with each other as if they were old friends. Soon they were swept away by the tide of people and conversation became impossible as the volume in the ballroom grew to disturbing proportions.

Chase disappeared for a few moments but returned with two glasses of champagne and handed her one. "Trying to get me intoxicated, are you, Dr. Montgomery?" For some reason the vision of him handing her a fluted glass evoked the playful side of her that had been buried for some time.

"Just wanting you to relax and enjoy the night."

"Indeed."

"Are you?"

"I am." She accepted the glass from him and a thrill of sexual energy shot through her as his fingers lingered on hers. It was just a touch, just a whisper of his skin against hers, but it was enough to make her take a step closer to him. The energy humming off him came in waves of heat that literally made her want to be closer to him, to reach out and trace the lines on his face that hadn't been there three years ago, to push away the fatigue etched in his brow and trace her thumb over those lips of his.

Swallowing took great difficulty as Chase held her gaze. He didn't move, he didn't speak, nothing in him changed, yet everything in her did in that moment.

"Isn't the champagne to your liking?" With one finger he reached out and touched the bottom of the glass, raised it toward her lips. She parted them and let him tip the champagne into her mouth. She swallowed without taking her gaze from him. "It's perfect. Everything is just perfect."

Intense, Chase held her gaze and the energy between them nearly crackled. He leaned forward, but didn't touch her. His cologne swirled in her mind, evoking feelings from the past she'd thought had been cremated and set free in the wind.

"So are you."

Unable to think of anything clever to say, she guzzled the rest of the champagne and then took a few breaths. "Wow." The buzz in her head was nothing compared to the buzz in her groin.

"Hey, here they are!"

She turned at the sound of her brother's voice. Astonished, she suddenly wished for more champagne and clutched Chase's arm as he drew near. She waggled her glass at him. "I think I'm going to need more of this."

Approaching them were her brother in a tux, a sight she'd never seen before, his girlfriend, looking stunning in a red sheath, and, gulp, her *parents*. The hostility between her parents and Chase had been overpowering in the early days of her recovery. They had held him responsible for the attack, and she'd been caught in the middle of it.

Now, who knew what was going to happen? They'd realized it hadn't been his fault, but by then she and Chase had split up. She stiffened as they approached. Danny grabbed her into a big brotherly hug.

"What's going on?" She hugged him, then pulled away and slugged him in the shoulder the same way she had when they had been kids. "I thought you had to work, big fat liar."

"I was, but there were too many guys covering shifts, so I volunteered to take off." He held his arm out to his girlfriend. "You remember Amber. Let me introduce you to Emily's date, Dr. Chase Montgomery." Danny introduced them, and Chase shook her hand, said a few polite words, but remained in close proximity to Emily.

Then Chase did something that surprised her and made her very proud of him. He strode toward Emily's mother and father, held his head high and his shoulders firm. "Mr. and Mrs. Hoover, it's nice to see you again."

"Why, Chase! I didn't expect to see you here tonight." Her mother gave the exclamation, her eyes soft and her smile pleasant. Then she did something that shocked Emily. She hugged Chase and patted his back. An act of forgiveness and acceptance. The work of the center was clear in that gesture.

A waiter going by with a tray of champagne slowed down long enough for Emily to grab two more glasses of it. She was going to need them.

And then her father, the tough nut that he was, reached out to shake hands with Chase. Two of the men she'd loved most in this world faced each other as true gentlemen. Tears clouded her eyes, and her heart pounded mercilessly in her chest. If she hadn't had two hands full of champagne, she'd do something, at least wipe away the dribbles of tears running down her face and ruining her makeup.

Forced to abandon one of the glasses, she set it down on the table closest to her and dabbed at her eyes with one of the linen napkins. She swallowed and took a few deep breaths. She had to control herself, control her emotions, control all those feelings bubbling to the surface that she totally hadn't expected and totally wasn't prepared for.

"Hey, you okay?" Amber asked, and patted her shoulder.

"Yes, yes, thank you." She pulled away from Amber and blew her nose on the napkin. "I don't know what happened."

"Chase happened. That's what," Danny said, and took the second glass of champagne and gave it to Amber. "Caught you off guard, didn't it?"

"You could say that." She controlled herself and watched as Chase approached. "You could definitely say that."

CHAPTER THIRTEEN

CHASE WORE AN enigmatic expression as he left her parents. She opened her mouth to say something. She didn't know what it was going to be, but she was interrupted by someone speaking from the front of the room. "Attention, everyone, please take your seats. We've a lovely dinner for you, so please enjoy."

The usual mayhem ensued where people found seats and conversations changed topics while the servers set plates in front of everyone. The clatter of utensils on plates was a low undertone as people ate more and talked less.

"It's so nice to see our young folks together and dressed so nicely, isn't it, Bob?" her mother Lois observed. Though her mother had been a homemaker and had never experienced trauma the way Emily had, she had stood firm with her daughter through the entire court process and had been more of a rock than Emily had ever known her to be.

"It is. And looking pretty snazzy, too, I might add," her father said. "Haven't seen either of you dress up like this since your proms."

"Don't remind me," Danny said. "That tux was horrible."

"Have any pictures?" Amber asked, and waggled her eyebrows at Danny. "I'd love to see them some time."

"I kept some, just in case I needed to blackmail him later in life," Emily said. "I can email them to you, Amber." She winked.

"You. Did. Not." Danny stared at her, mouth open and eyes wide in shocked horror.

"What are big sisters for, anyway?" She laughed and it felt good to share this night with this company in this way.

After dinner the speakers began by thanking the patrons and attendees, as well as the volunteers and the other people who made the whole place run efficiently. While the band got organized, people shuffled together and broke into small groups.

"Anyone else need more champagne?" Chase made the offer and only Emily nodded. "I'll be right back."

Chase stood in line at the bar, listening to the conversations near him. He had to take a deep breath as he overheard a woman talking about the reason she was there.

"Yeah, I thought he was a good guy. Seemed nice enough, but when I said no, he went off on me."

"I'm just so glad you were able to find help at the center."

"I would have killed myself if I hadn't found them. I was on the verge of it when I had my first meeting." She gave a caustic laugh. "Going to the center was actually a last-ditch effort before doing something terrible to myself."

"I'm so glad." The women hugged.

"So am I. My life is different now for sure, but so much

better than I could have ever imagined. I'm even going
to take a self-defense class too. Can't wait."

Chase closed his eyes, not wanting to hear the pain of
the women expressed so openly, but it was unavoidable
as he stood in line right beside them. And it was more
humbling than he could ever have imagined. He'd been
such an ass back then. Such a complete and utter ass. No
wonder Emily had left him in the dust. He'd deserved it.

"What can I get for you?" the bartender asked. "More
champagne?"

"Yes. Two, please," Chase said absently, as conversations around him buzzed in his ears.

"Excuse me," a man said. He was tall, carried himself well and looked vaguely familiar. "Aren't you Dr.
Montgomery?"

"Yes," Chase said, nodding, wondering if he'd taken
care of the man as a patient in the ER at some point.

"I'm Mark Hampton, Detective Mark Hampton. I
worked your girlfriend's case. Emily Hoover, right?"

"Yes. That's her." Words had difficulty forming in
his throat as Chase was instantly transported back to
that time and the guilt that washed over him. Guilt that
had never resolved.

"She's one remarkably lucky woman."

"Really?" Chase couldn't fathom that.

"Really." Mark moved closer and the two men
stepped aside where they could talk without being overheard. "She was the first victim. As bad as her injuries were, she survived by her wits and her personal
strength. The longer he went without getting caught,
the more violent he became. You may or may not know,
but he killed the last two." Mark's face was stern, his

eyes cold as he talked of the man who had nearly ruined
Emily's life.

"I didn't... I didn't know." That took a minute to
sink in. Oh, God. If it hadn't been for his one careless
mistake that day, things would have been completely
different.

Mark huffed out a long sigh. "Take good care of that
woman. She's a fighter. That's what got her through the
whole thing." He shook hands with Chase and walked
away.

All of the people in this room had in some way been
affected by a sexual assault and the traumatic aftermath.
It was staggering, looking around at the number of people who were here, who were victims, friends or family
of victims and had come in support of something that
needed to be brought from the shadows into the light.

"Here you go."

Chase paid the man and took the drinks back to
Emily. She simply shone like a light tonight. Though
dressed all in black, it suited her and was a striking
contrast to the vibrant color of her hair, her eyes, the
ruby lips. The strength of heart and soul shone in her
tonight. He was dumbstruck by her.

She was anything but a victim, and he was so proud
of the accomplishments she'd made it nearly staggered
him. As he approached, she looked up. The expression
on her face froze, then molded into something else,
something he hadn't seen on her face in some time.

Female. Gloriously female. Confident in her body,
her mind and her heart, she stood there, silently declar-
ing she was whole once again.

"Thank you," she said, and accepted the glass, just
as the music started.

Danny grabbed the glass from her hand and set it down before she could take a sip. "Come on, big sister. This one is mine." He dragged her out onto the dance floor before anyone else got there and spun her around several times.

Chase watched as she grinned and the two of them fell into a routine they'd obviously done many times in the past to a song about shaking it up. Chase shook his head. Things were definitely shaking up in his life since Emily had returned and he didn't think he ever wanted to go back to the way it had been before.

Three songs into it, Chase had had enough and cut in on Danny. "You have your own girl to dance with. She's looking awfully lonely over there by herself."

"Oh, good point. Better go take care of my lady and you can take care of yours." With a gallant bow, Danny placed Emily's hand in Chase's. "Now, get to it."

Gladly, Chase eased into position with his right arm around Emily's waist and her right hand cupped in his left.

"You're gorgeous, and I've been a complete idiot."

"I like the first part, but not the second." She placed her left arm on his right shoulder and moved with him to the music. There was a light sheen of perspiration on her brow and the lighting picked up some sort of sparkle at the corners of her eyes. The pixie was emerging.

"It's true." They moved on the dance floor together, remembering how to move as one, and in seconds their bodies melded together in time with the music as if they'd never been apart. "I have to admit it, admit my part in our breakup."

"It's blaming, Chase. In the therapy I've taken, blaming doesn't work for healing. Forgiveness does."

"Don't tell me you've forgiven that bastard." Righteous indignation burned white hot in him.

"No. I will never forgive him for what he did to me...to us, and my family. Never. I'm still working on letting it go." She took a deep breath and pressed her right temple to his right cheek. "But I've forgiven *us* back then. The people we were couldn't cope with what happened, and I've let it go." She cupped his cheek. "I want you to let it go, too. For you and for me. It wasn't your fault, ever."

He pulled back slightly to look at her face. Nothing except serenity showed, and he returned to his position with her cheek against his, her arm around his shoulders and his hand splayed on the small of her back.

"Let go, Chase."

"I don't want to let you go." Not yet. Not when he had her in his arms. He couldn't.

"I mean the pain. It's the only way you'll heal. The memories will always be there, but will fade away if you lay down new memories on top of them. Kind of like paving a new road in your mind."

"I... I haven't done that." Thoughts of other women in his life the past few years were meager at best. Memories had power and emotion associated with them, and he hadn't built any new ones. Hadn't wanted to, had simply roiled in his pain.

"You need to."

"I will. Starting now." He closed his eyes, savoring the sensations of her in his arms, the way her body felt and moved in time with his. Right now. This was a memory he wanted to keep in his brain forever.

The night progressed, and they danced, drank champagne and danced some more. Tonight Emily felt freer than she had in the past three years. She laughed, her spirit was light, and she needed nothing else, aside from being in Chase's arms on the dance floor.

Her parents said their goodbyes after a few dances, but Danny and Amber still hung in there on the dance floor. As the night wore on, the tempo of each song seemed to get slower and more intimate. More attendees left, dwindling down to just a few couples hardy enough to stick it out until the very end.

Reluctant to leave just yet, Emily wanted to have just a little longer in Chase's arms. She didn't know where things were heading with him, if anywhere, but right now, living in the moment, in *this* moment, it was pure bliss.

"Hey, I think they're gonna kick us out now." Danny approached them with Amber clinging to his side, looking lush and in love. "We're gonna head out."

"Okay. Good night." Emily extracted herself from Chase's embrace to hug each of them. "Be safe."

She turned back to face Chase and had to catch her breath. The way he looked at her right then she almost felt like she was being devoured. "Guess we should call it a night, too."

"I'll call the limo and have it meet us out front." He led her to their table and collected her wrap, placed it around her shoulders, then frowned. "Hmm. That's too bad."

"What?" She looked down at the black velveteen shawl. "Did something get spilled on it?" She couldn't see anything.

"No." He gave a wistful sigh and brought his gaze to hers. "It just covers up too much of your skin."

"Oh." She held his gaze. "You liked that, did you?" Flirty and playful weren't her norm anymore, but tonight, right now, it was perfect.

"Very much." Casually, he appeared to be tying a knot in the middle of the wrap, but he traced a finger over the curve of her right breast and down into the dip of her cleavage, then up over the curve of her left breast.

Tingles flashed through her nipples and shot straight to her groin. Savoring the sensations, she leaned closer to him, wanting more, aching for his touch against her skin again. "Perhaps we should go."

"That's a fine plan." Casually, he placed one hand on her back and escorted her to the door. Once seated in the limo, her heart raced, her mouth went dry, and she pressed her lips together, eyes on Chase, who leaned against the seat in the corner. He took her hand in his and tugged a little, urged her closer until she leaned forward and placed her weight on her hands on the seat.

Teasing him was fun and made her feel sexier than she'd ever felt before, especially in recent memory. "What can I do for you, Dr. Montgomery?" She licked her lips and watched his gaze linger on them.

"Nothing. Absolutely, nothing." He untied the knot of the shawl at the front of her chest slowly, allowing his knuckles to rub against her dress. With talented fingers he eased the knot free and let it drift away, exposing her décolletage to his gaze. Turning his hands, he used his thumbs to stroke the rising curves of her breasts, pushed up by her bra and enhanced by her position.

She closed her eyes, allowing the sensations to flow over her, to bubble up within her, and became familiar with them again, as they had been strikingly absent for too long. When Chase bent his thumbs and used them to draw down the edge of the dress and the bra, he teased her nipples at the same time. Leaning forward, he stroked his tongue around her nipple on one side, then licked his way over the curve of silk lace to her left breast, stroking his tongue across the other nipple.

"Oh…oh, my." Trembling on her arms, she wasn't prepared for the onslaught of emotion and desire he unleashed in her with that simple action.

"Don't move."

"I don't think I can." He pulled down the front of her dress on the left and took her entire nipple into his mouth, teasing, stroking, suckling it, and desire shot white-hot through her body straight to the core of her. With her hands still holding her weight, she really couldn't move as he eased that side of her dress up and revealed the other side to his gaze and his mouth.

The hum of the car engine changed and the vehicle slowed. Chase eased her dress up and retied the knot of her shawl in the front.

"We're here." She sat up straight and gathered her purse in front of her, certain she looked like she'd been fornicating in the back of the car—which, really, she had been. "Will you come in for a while?"

"I'll take care of the driver, then I'll take care of you." He leaned forward and pressed a firm kiss to her lips, then pulled back.

They emerged from the car into the cool night air, which felt pleasant against her skin and a refreshing boost to her brain. He took her hand and tucked it into the crook of his arm as they approached her apartment.

Her hands fumbled with the keys and he took them from her, unlocked the door and escorted her inside. "Don't be afraid of me, Em. Ever."

She barked out a nervous laugh. "It's not you I'm afraid of."

"Then what?"

"Me."

CHAPTER FOURTEEN

CHASE LEANED BACK against the door. "You're going to have to explain that one. Communication needs to be very clear between us. I don't want anything to go wrong between us now, not when we're starting to find each other again."

Before answering, she put her purse and shawl on the counter and eased her feet out of the killer pumps, letting her feet return to their natural shape. Chase watched, his eyes glittering as she removed each piece of clothing.

"That's better." She wiggled her feet in the carpeting.

"Don't stop on my account."

She tossed a look his direction. "Nice try."

"So why don't you tell me what you mean?" He removed his jacket, hung it on the door behind him. He moved into the living room, pushed the coffee table away from the couch and settled onto the floor. He was relaxed and confident and reminded her of the other day when she'd taught him some relaxation techniques.

Hesitating, Emily followed him. She removed her watch and placed it on the coffee table, followed by her earrings and pearl necklace.

Although he looked calm, she was a mass of churning nerves inside. This man had been her lover, and her friend, and right now she wanted to reach out to him more than ever, but she held back, with three years of pressure churning inside her.

He'd also burned her more than anyone ever had. Though she'd forgiven him, taking that first step was a doozy. Trust was a huge deal. One minute she wanted him, the next second fear overwhelmed her.

"I don't think this is a good idea after all. Why don't I change my clothes, and I'll take you home, or you can call a cab. That would be best." Decision made. She headed to her bedroom, but Chase quickly caught up to her.

"Don't do that to me, Em. Don't do it again."

"Do what?" She backed up against the doorframe to support herself.

"Shut me out like that. Like you're doing right now."

He was angry. More angry than she'd ever seen him, and her instincts kicked in. She took a protective stance. "Back off."

"Emily…" He reached for her again.

"I said back off, Chase." She raised her arms and parted her feet.

"I said you shouldn't be afraid of me, and I meant it. I'm not going to hurt you." He took a step away from her, respecting her boundaries, but inside he shook, the power of the emotions coursing through him making him tremble. He clenched his hands into fists at his sides and wanted to punch something.

He flashed around and faced her. "Hit me."

"What?" Confusion covered her face, and she backed up a step, but still kept her stance. "No. I'm not going to hit you."

"I said hit me." He moved closer and closer until she was cornered.

"I'm not going to—"

"It's the only way you're getting out of this tonight. You're going to have to hit me." It would feel better if she did. It would be some relief if she would. "I'll feel better if you do."

"Chase, no!"

"Emily!" He grabbed her hand and placed it against his chest. "Please…" His voice cracked. "Hit me. I need you to."

"No, that's not why I'm here, not why I came back here. I didn't come to punish you."

"Then why did you come back here, Emily? Why?" Frustration oozed from every pore. He had to hear her say it.

"This is my home, too, you know." She relaxed a little, but her eyes were still wary and bruised with remembered pain and she curled one hand into a fist.

"There are several hospitals where you could have worked, yet you chose the one I'm at." She tried to move around him, but he countered her move.

"I wanted to be where I was comfortable, where I knew people." She tried to go around him again, but he blocked her movement. "I was tired of learning a new hospital with every assignment, so this was easier."

"Liar. After the last hurricane and reconstruction, it's totally new."

"But I didn't know that." Or had Danny already told her that, and she'd forgotten?

"Liar."

She jumped like he'd shocked her and stomped her foot. "I am *not* lying."

"Yes, you are. You came to where I was because you wanted to see one thing. *Me*." With that, he reached for her and dragged her against him, catching her off guard before she could react. "Tell me I'm wrong, Emily. Tell me you don't want me anymore and I'll go and never bother you again." His voice broke and his heart raced. His breathing was harsh in his chest, but so was hers. "Tell me you don't still love me," he whispered.

She clenched her teeth and tears filled her eyes as she stared at him. "I. Can't." Her breathing was ragged, making her breasts rise and fall enticingly.

"Then let me love you, Em, let me love you." He cleared his throat when his voice cracked again.

She licked her lips, and her gaze dropped to his mouth. "I just wish…" A caustic laugh escaped her throat, and she relaxed, leaning further against him, letting her body get to know his again. "I wish…"

"I know, baby, I know." His gaze dropped to her mouth, that luscious mouth he'd used to love exploring his body. With one hand, he cupped the left side of her face and neck. She pressed her face against his palm, closed her eyes, and his heart broke. "Emily." Bridging the slight gap between them, he drew her face forward, hesitated. "I really want to kiss you."

"Kiss me." The words were a breath that released him.

The first touch of his lips against hers felt somehow foreign, as if he'd never been there before. He hadn't, not in this way. The last time he'd kissed her she'd held back. Now he moved in, relaxed, opened himself up to her as he never had.

Soft and sweet, her lips parted, and he met her tongue with his, eased against hers, glided together, stirring his passion for her that he'd thought had died and now surged strongly within him. A moan stirred in her throat, and she pulled back from him, blue eyes startled and fiery.

"Oh, God, Chase, what have you done?" Her thumb stroked his lower lip.

"What do you mean?" His breath was tight in his throat, his heart catapulting in his chest and his body aroused beyond belief. Had he somehow misunderstood the words *kiss me*?

"You've freed me." This time she wrapped her arms around his shoulders and hauled him to her, her mouth searching for his.

Eagerly, he met her, one hand against the small of her back, the other cupping the back of her head. This was no small kiss but a barn-burner, setting them both ablaze. Passion unleashed between them had always been stimulating, but now there was a fire between them that wasn't going to be easily contained.

He backed her against the wall, needing the stability before his legs gave way. She was so sweet, so special, so beautiful.

Mouths searching, hearts aching, they found a way to the path of forgiveness they'd never imagined. Once the light had been shined onto the trail to lead the way, there was no turning back.

She pulled away and held him close. "Oh, God, Chase. I'm so scared, but so turned on, I don't know what to do."

"Why are you scared?" That puzzled him.

"I haven't been with anyone since our last time, since before…" She met his gaze full on. "You're the last man

I made love with, and I don't know what to do, how to do it anymore."

That stopped him a second. Compassion for her swelled within him. She wanted him, there was no doubt, but this moment was precious, and he didn't want to mess it up.

"Let's just go slow, and you be the guide."

She kissed him again then, soft, slow. Each touch, each sigh drew them closer together.

He struggled to keep his hands on her tiny waist, until she reached for one of his hands and guided it upward to cover her breast. Allowing her head to fall back, she took in a breath and let it out slowly. The angle of her head, of her neck, the light perspiration on her skin made him want to take a bite out of her.

Her nipple stirred beneath his thumb. He could feel the lace of her bra through the dress and his curiosity was roused beyond belief. Using the tip of his thumb, he hooked the front of her dress and drew it down, exposing the lace of a dangerously red bra. The cup seemed to only be half-there, pushing her breast upward, firm and ripe, toward him and his mouth actually watered.

"You're beautiful, Em."

She was ready, she wanted him, and he leaned down to satisfy himself. To take her nipple, barely hidden by the very edge of the lace, into his mouth.

The feel of Chase's tongue on her breast nearly made her climax at once. He teased a lazy path over the crest of her right breast, his tongue dipping beneath at last to tease and stimulate her nipple. Then with a very clever use of his thumb he tugged the cup downward slightly and sucked her nipple into his hot mouth.

She actually jumped, as if the last bits of her soul

had suddenly returned to her body. The feelings were so intense, so pure, so passionate. She'd never expected to feel this way again, this excited, turned on and wanting. Her body hadn't forgotten after all. Her body had waited for the right man to bring it to life again.

The dress was of no further use to her and it needed to go. Fortunately, the material had an abundance of stretch and forgiveness in it. Reaching up with her left hand, she clasped the neck and dragged it down, shrugged, and the garment lay in a heap at her feet.

"That's certainly convenient."

"Indeed." She almost didn't recognize her own voice, so deep and husky, filled with desire.

Chase, being a man to take advantage of opportunity, used the thumb of his right hand to trace the edge of the left cup of her bra, teasing that nipple, as well.

He didn't kiss her again, but watched her, and she kept her gaze on his face. "You're beautiful. You're luscious. And I want to make love with you."

Nodding was about all she could do, and she licked her lips as his head dipped downward again to her left nipple this time. Slowly, languidly, he traced and teased both of her nipples until she was certain they would never go down again.

This time, when he pulled back, he looked down over her body, over her abdomen that quivered slightly with her breathing, the curve of her hips, and lingered on the red thong she wore.

"I'm surprised. A thong?"

"Hate panty lines."

"Me, too." His gaze wandered further down her thighs and calves, all the way to her red toenails. "I

like this look, a lot. You're strong and capable and in-
dependent, beautiful and passionate."

Trembling, she reached out to his clothing to find
his skin beneath the tux shirt. She wanted to see him,
all of him, and wanted him against her. Soon his shirt
was gone and the button on his pants hung open. There
was little between them now and this was her opportunity to stop.

"Are you okay?" With one finger, he blazed a trail
between her breasts and headed south, downward over
her abdomen and belly button, then paused at the edge
of her thong.

"I'm good." She licked her lips. "Very good." She
closed her eyes and felt him move.

He was on his knees in front of her and his mouth
hit her abdomen, where he rubbed his face against her
skin, placed searing kisses there, tugging with his teeth
at the ring in her belly button.

His hands came up the backs of her thighs to cup her
buttocks. With his breath hot on her skin and his fingers doing their best to drive her crazy, Emily nearly
fainted with wanting him.

Each touch brought them closer, each kiss made her
want more. Slowly, he clasped the waistband of the
thong in his hands and eased it down until it joined her
dress on the floor at her feet.

"Turn into me," he whispered against her skin. She
knew what he wanted, and she wanted it, too. Turning her hips forward, she waited until his breath was
hot against her skin and heading downward, over her
mound. Trembling, her thighs parted, unable to contain
herself. "That's it. Easy, babe. Just let go, just enjoy. Let
me please you."

With one hand he cupped her bottom and pulled it forward, with the other hand he parted her feminine flesh and pressed his face toward her. The first touch of his tongue seared her and she sucked in a breath through clenched teeth. "Oh, God."

"Nice, huh?"

"Yes. Oh. Oh. Yes." She sank her hands into his hair, needing something to hold onto as she let go and let him have her body. For the first time she could let go.

Legs unable to hold her weight up any longer, she began to slide, easing her way down the wall. Going with her, he adjusted his position and somehow they made it to the couch nearby. Down on his knees in front of her, he scooted her hips to the edge of the cushion and resumed his quest.

"Relax. Enjoy." He kissed his way up her right thigh to the juncture, then returned to her left knee, repeating the same trail there, upward. She needed this so badly, and she needed him more than she wanted to admit. And then he was opening his mouth over her center again, hot and wet, tongue searching for her bud, circling it, teasing it and driving her wild.

The pressure, the electricity built within her, and when he eased a finger inside her sheath she gasped and nearly screamed with the power of her climax, the first one she'd had since back then. Passion overwhelmed her, and she cried out. Pulses of white light and pure energy formed in her core and pulsed outward. Chase held on to her as the orgasm released inside her.

Then he moved upward toward her. "Are you okay?"

"Yes. Very." She moved to lie back, and he stripped and adjusted position and placed his body over hers, moving until his erection lay against her thigh. Swollen and needy, he wanted her, but he didn't, couldn't, rush her.

"Come closer." He adjusted his position. "Closer." Again he moved upward until the tip of him brushed against her at her apex.

"I want you inside me, Chase. Now." She felt like she was losing her virginity all over again. Somehow he managed to dig a condom out of his pocket and put it on. She was glad he'd thought of it as she hadn't, hadn't even considered she was going to be making love tonight. Feeling Chase ease slowly inside her, carefully, made her want to cry. For the things they had lost, for the pain they'd experienced and the chasm that had developed between them.

"Keep your eyes on me. Focus on me, on us. I want to see you."

She did. The connection with him, the fullness he created inside her, the stretch of her body to accommodate him kept her focused on him and only him. On the sensations pulsing between them, drawing open that door that had been closed between them.

Something in his eyes changed as he eased fully inside her.

Sweat popped out on her skin at the weight of him and a choking sensation closed her throat. The room spun around her, and she couldn't breathe. Eyes wide, breath strangling in her throat, panic threatened her mind and she turned her face away and scrunched her eyes closed as images of her attacker flooded her mind.

"No. No!" Frantic, she pushed at his shoulders, tried to get him off her.

"Stay with me, love. Emily, stay with me."

"It's...your weight." Being pressed down into the

couch was what had done it, reminding her of the assault, taking her back to that awful night. Struggling to push it away, she battled to rise. "Get up, get up!"

He backed off and sat, his hands raised, waiting for her to make the next move. She straddled his thighs, taking control of the situation, her position facing him.

"Better?" His voice was soft, a mere whisper in her ears, encouraging her to proceed.

Chase kept his hands on her hips and pulled a nipple into his mouth again. "Oh, that's it, that's what I want, what I need."

Slowly, she rose up onto her knees and his erection sprang upward between them. She positioned herself to allow him to enter her, and she angled her hips back and forth, teasing him, teasing herself with him, becoming more comfortable with the feel of him inside her as she eased onto him.

He threw his head back against the couch, drawing his breath in through gritted teeth at the exquisite torture. His fingers dug into her hips with the effort to control his body, control his mind.

When she was ready, when the moment was right, she took him fully into her and waited until her body molded around him. "Oh, my, Chase."

"Emily." He pulled her forward to kiss her, to plunder her mouth with his, and she gave him back everything she had. Hips angled, he pulled her back and forth over him, stimulating her flesh, and she clutched his arms.

"Oh-God-oh-God-oh-God." She was going to climax again and she let her body go as she never had before. Chase clutched her hips and kept the pace up until she was nearly exhausted, and the trigger of her climax clicked. Pulses of heat, electricity and pure pleasure swept through her as she came. Her sheath clutched him over and over again until he stiffened and cried out with his pleasure.

Pulsing and electric, he released, letting her body work him over until he was just a mass of twitching nerve endings.

Hot and sweating, they clutched each other. Chase moved his arms upward to clasp her around the middle and began to rock her. Rocked back and forth, pushed her hair away from her face and pressed a kiss to her hand.

And she cried. For the first time since the rape she cried in his arms. His heart broke and tears filled his own eyes at the anguish and sorrow unleashed. The sound of her sobs would never leave his mind or his heart, and he knew he was responsible for them. Back then she'd wanted to forgive him, but he hadn't been able to let her. Now he didn't know. The pain was still so sharp.

"I'm so sorry, Emily. So, so sorry."

Some moments passed as he held her, rocked, listening to her tears and releasing his own that had been pent up.

"This was beautiful, Chase, and something I didn't know I needed. Thank you."

Pushing her damp hair back from her face, he used his thumbs and wiped away the tears making black trails down her face. "Seriously?"

"I never thought I'd make love again. I'd convinced myself I didn't need sex, or the physical contact with a man anymore, that I'd had enough in the years we were together."

"That's just sad." He raised his brows at her, trying to make her laugh. There was healing in laughter as well as tears.

"I know, right?" She laughed, then tried to take a breath but snorted instead. And that made her laugh again, and Chase watched the joy of her unleash in his arms.

He laughed too, like he hadn't done in years.

CHAPTER FIFTEEN

THEY STAYED UP for half the night, showered together, made breakfast and coffee at 3:00 a.m. and then finally slept, cuddled together naked.

Emily slept like the dead for the first time in three years. No dreams, no nightmares, no waking up trembling from some unfamiliar noise she'd heard in the dark.

Chase slept deeply contented, with no haunting feelings of loss, of pain, or emptiness surrounding his mind or heart.

They woke to bright sunshine streaming in the window. Gone was the gloom of the past few days, and the overcast atmosphere had given way to the bliss of an Indian summer. The morning was half-gone by the time they roused, and dressed with a side trip to Chase's townhouse for a change of clothing and his running shoes.

What was supposed to have been a leisurely walk around the park ended up as a competitive sprint, with Emily in the lead and Chase bringing up the rear, snagging her around the waist and dragging her to the grassy lawn. "Caught you!"

With a squeal she tumbled to the ground with him, gasping for breath.

People raced and ambled around them. On a Saturday there were all kinds of people out there in the park with them. Moms with babes in strollers, young people chasing Frisbees and throwing balls for dogs to retrieve.

The sound of thundering footsteps neared them as two young men chased around. One held up a beanie high in the air, like he was running across the finish line of a race. "I got it now, sucka!" Laughter followed him, and so did his companion.

"Come back here, you. Bitch!" The second young man raced after the friend with the hat. "You bitch, I'm going to get you!"

The smile on Emily's face froze and her eyes widened, her breathing came in short little gasps. A humming began in her ears and drowned out everything else. She rose from the grass and began walking. She didn't know where, didn't know why, but she had to move, had to leave, had to get out of there. The sensation of panic, choking, drowning saturated her and stole the breath from her lungs.

Someone grabbed her by the arm and stopped her. Panic and finely tuned instincts surged to the surface. She lashed out with her fists and knocked Chase on his ass. "I told you not to touch me!" She stood there, hands in fists, legs braced apart as if she were going into battle.

"Emily. Wait. It's me. It's Chase." He jumped to his feet, rubbing the center of his chest where she'd hit him.

"What?" The haze of panic began to lift, primal, protective instincts began to recede, and the world came back into focus. *"What?"* She blinked several times, looking at Chase as if she didn't know where she was.

"Focus on me." He panted, but kept a short distance from her.

"Why are you looking at me that way?" She took in a deep breath and blew it out, tried to get her heart to stop racing and quieten the buzz in her ears.

"Are you okay now?" Concern emanated from his face.

She looked around at the blue sky, the changing leaves on the trees swaying in a light breeze, the people moving around them. "I don't know what happened." She took a step closer to him and raised a hand to her forehead. "Chase?" Starting in her middle, the tremors began.

"Can I touch you now? Are you okay with that?" He held his arms out and let her move into his embrace when she was ready to.

Hesitating, deeply saddened, and shaking, she allowed her body to touch his and slowly raised her arms around his middle, and pressed her face against his chest. The thumping of his heart was strong in her ear, and she closed her eyes as he put his arms around her.

"What happened?"

"I...don't know."

"We were having a good time, then those two guys with the beanie ran by, and then you panicked." He rubbed her back.

It all came back to her in an instant, and she pulled away from Chase. "We need to go now. I need to go home now. Or take me to the studio." With quick strides, she began to walk away from him, but he kept up with her.

"Okay. I'll take you home. I'll take you to the studio, whatever you need—just tell me what happened." They arrived at the car and he unlocked it and opened her door, but she didn't get in.

The space was too confined, too narrow, too dark, even on such a bright day. "Maybe I'll just walk home."

"Nonsense. If you aren't ready to get into the car we'll wait. It's okay."

Anger flashed inside her like a lightning storm over the Chesapeake Bay. "It's *not* okay. It'll *never* be okay." She slammed the door shut and covered her face with her hands. Tears hit like a storm, and she screamed until she thought she couldn't scream anymore. Down on her knees, she couldn't press back the force of the emotions swirling like a deadly tornado inside her.

"Emily, Emily!" Chase knelt near her and called her name. "Emily. Honey. Stop crying. Please, stop crying."

Finally, his voice and his words penetrated her mind. *Breathe, just breathe.* The voice of her *sensei* entered her mind, emerged from the depths of the place she'd crawled into when she'd first entered her recovery. She took a breath, then another and another. Controlling the shaking in her limbs was quite another issue. "Okay. Okay." Tears still streamed down her face, but her breathing was better.

"That's it." His voice was soft and soothing to her, the same way Rose's had been, and she turned into him now, pressed her face into his shoulder and allowed him to help her up. "Can you stand?"

"Yes. I think so." She nodded and clutched his arm. Then he placed his other hand at her waist and helped her back to the car. He opened the door, but before helping her inside he opened both windows all the way.

"This might help." He assisted her into the passenger seat, reached in to buckle her, then hurried around to the other side of the vehicle, got in and pulled out of the parking lot. "Where do you want to go?"

"Take me home."

"Okay. Do you want to go to the studio?"

She took in a few breaths. "No." Her voice was flat and unemotional, reminding him of times past. "It's too crowded there today. Too many people. Just take me home."

Minutes later he unlocked the door to her apartment, pushed it wide, and they entered. "You can go now." Emily started for her bedroom.

"No. You stay put. I'm going to check out your apartment, make sure everything's okay. Then we'll talk."

Emily ignored him, her brain paralyzed by the event at the park. She needed her control, needed her armor on to protect her. Now. Shucking her clothing, she put on her *gi* and tightened the belt around her waist.

For the first time in an hour she could take a deep breath, felt the energy of who she was now flowing over her as if it poured over the top of her head, down her shoulders and all the way to her feet, encapsulating her in the protective shield she required for her personal safety. She'd momentarily forgotten it.

With her eyes closed, she stood by the bed and focused, turned inward. Raising her hands against her shoulders, palms facing out, she slowly moved her hands away from her body as if she were pushing out of a balloon, enlarging her energy to a larger bubble. Another deep breath, and she could feel the presence of her new self returning to her, having been temporarily displaced.

"How are you?" Chase spoke from the doorway.

She opened her eyes, blinked, having forgotten he was there. Then it all came back to her and her shield pulsed strongly, more protectively around her. "You can go."

"I'm not leaving you." He took a hesitant step forward. "What happened back there? One minute we were having a great time, and the next you weren't there."

"It doesn't matter." She brushed past him to the living room and spread out her meditation mat, sat down on the edge of it. Her feet were tucked beneath her, and she sat back on her heels, something Chase was certain would cause him considerable pain, but she moved into the position as if she'd been doing it for years. Maybe she had. Hell, there was so much about her he didn't know right now, but really, really wanted to. If she would let him.

He sat down on the other end of her mat with his feet extended.

"I said you can leave now." The only things that moved were her mouth and her eyelids opening. "I actually *need* you to leave." The tone of her voice was flat, unemotional, controlled.

"I'm not leaving." He kept his tone even, his eyes on hers, but inside he raged, at the universe, at the rapist, and the society that had made such a creature, but mostly at himself for not seeing her PTSD when he'd needed to. It all made sense.

"I left you before, and I'm not doing it again."

"You think you're helping me right now, but you're not."

"I don't know that I'm helping you, but I want to. Something set you off back there, and you need to talk about it. I'm here, and I don't have to be anywhere until Monday morning." He spread his hands out in front of him. "Tell me."

"No."

"Emily, holding stuff like this inside you only gives it more power."

"Like you'd know anything about it." Anger finally blazed in her face, seeming to shoot out the ends of her hair, the blond tips looked like they were on fire.

"Why don't you tell me?" Now he kept his voice modulated and calm, not reacting to the emotion in hers. He needed to be a rock for her now.

She closed her eyes, shutting him out. Okay. If she wouldn't talk, he would. "I wanted to kill him. I wished I had found him and killed him myself."

She took a deep breath and let it out slowly.

"No, you wouldn't have. It's not you, not who you are."

"I wanted to."

"So did I. For a while, then I had to let it go so it didn't rule my life." She opened her eyes, now calmer, and he could almost see the energy swirling around her, soothing her, and he wished he could do that for her. The powerlessness he felt at the moment overwhelmed him, emasculated him and nearly drove him to his knees.

She was withdrawing into herself right in front of him, and he couldn't do a damned thing about it. She was back to the distant figure he'd known before.

"Come back, Emily. Stay here."

"I can't, Chase. Not right now."

"I'll wait for you here."

"No. You need to go. I'm fine." Another deep breath. She rose elegantly from her position. "If you care about me the way you say you do, you'll leave now and never come back. I don't want you. I don't need you." Tears filled her eyes. "I thought I could come back here and pick up with you, could have a relationship with you, but I realize now I can't. It's too much for me."

"Emily…" The pain in his chest was almost unbearable. He couldn't do it, couldn't walk away from her. "I do care about you, more than ever." How could he tell her he'd never healed, never recovered from the trauma that had ripped apart both of their lives?

"Then go." She took a breath, and he heard the jagged edges of it catch in her throat. "Please." Her voice was just a whisper, but it cut through him as surely as a scalpel would have.

Hurt, pained beyond comprehension, he went to the door and paused. "I'll leave, but not because I want to. We'll talk again soon."

"It's what I need right now." She stayed in the living room, keeping as much distance between them as possible.

He paused with his hand on the knob, took one long look at her, opened the door and stepped outside, then closed it behind him. He would wait until she locked the door before he left, he'd make sure she was safe this time.

Then something overcame him, in that nanosecond of waiting for her to lock the door, it possessed him at a cellular level and urged him to action. He twisted the knob and burst back through the door.

CHAPTER SIXTEEN

"I WAS ABOUT to lock that." She stood in the kitchen, her eyes wary, her body stiff and tense, watching and waiting for him to make a move.

"The hell you were. I'm not leaving. I love you, and I'm not going anywhere."

"Chase…" she said, and her voice cracked. "Don't say that. You don't mean it, and I don't want to hear it." Not now. Not ever. Never again would she set herself up for being hurt that way.

"I do, and I know you still love me. I don't know how I've gotten through these last few years without you." He gave a caustic laugh and looked down. "Actually, I do know. I was arrogant as hell. I don't know why you stayed with me as long as you did. I was an idiot for not being more patient, having more insight, and I don't know how you can ever forgive me."

She paused, her eyes narrowed at him, her face flushed. "Are you asking me *now* to forgive you when you wouldn't let me do it before?"

"No." Another harsh laugh erupted from his throat. "There's no way I'm asking that. No way you should do it. I'm just hoping we can move past this."

"Then what do you want? You wouldn't let me

forgive you back then. If you won't now, there's nothing. Without forgiveness, there's no future for us, or anything." That was a lesson it had taken her a long time to understand. Letting go, forgiving. They were the same to her. But if he didn't allow her to forgive him and forgive himself, there was nothing for sure. Neither of them would have lives.

He raked both hands through his hair, then punched the air. "Hell, I don't know. I don't know, Emily, I just know I can't go on this way, pretending you don't mean anything to me because you do." He paced the kitchen several times, then clutched his hands to his head and yelled. "Argh!"

"Chase—"

"I can't take it anymore, Emily. I can't take it!"

"Then you have to let it go." Her voice was soft, certain and pure. He'd have felt better had she screamed and railed at him, validating his need to suffer.

"I can't. I don't know how." He paced again, wishing there was something he could do to get the demons out of his head and his heart.

Compassion overwhelmed her. This man had suffered nearly as much as she had, and she hadn't seen it. But there it was right in front of her, and she couldn't ignore it or him any longer.

"Tell me about it."

"I couldn't do anything. I couldn't help you. There was nothing. I couldn't operate on you, I couldn't put you back together. Other people had to do it for me. Other people helped you through rehab, your parents took care of your apartment. I was left out." He clutched the counter for support and dropped his head, panting as if he'd just run a marathon.

"I didn't need you to do anything, I needed you to listen and be present. Neither of us really knew how to do that then, but we're learning, Chase. We'll always have lessons to learn in life, and this is just one of them."

"I wanted to do something, and I couldn't." He took a breath. "That's not who I am, who I was."

"That's what I needed, who I needed you to be. Now I know you couldn't take on that role I was trying to force you into. I didn't know it, either."

"I *fix* things. I'm a surgeon. I cut things out or sew them up, make people better than they were before." He turned his head and pain-filled eyes looked at her. "I couldn't fix you."

"But I didn't need fixing, Chase. I needed to be listened to. I needed to be held, and loved, but mostly I just needed to *be*."

"You did, and it was because of me it all happened."

"Chase, it wasn't." Shock filled her at his admission. "You can't seriously believe that anymore."

"I'm the one who left the door unlocked. I was so focused on my work. The second I woke up I was gone mentally, I was out of there."

"That's not true." At least, not at the beginning of their relationship.

"It is! I have to admit it. Admit and accept my part in the terror that has become your life. I didn't listen to you, I didn't *hear* you. You would be talking to me, and I got so good at not listening I nodded in all the right places, and you never knew. When I got out of bed that morning it was no different. I was just gone, thinking of work, rounds, surgery, planning my day, and I left without making sure you were safe."

"Chase—"

"Don't! Don't say you forgive me because I can't bear the words." He hadn't forgiven himself. Would never forgive himself.

"It's not your fault. It was a simple oversight that you didn't lock the door. You were on an emergency call in the middle of the night, and there was a predator on the loose. You couldn't have known. No one did!"

"I should have protected you!" He grabbed her shoulders. "I should have kept him from hurting you, but I didn't, and I couldn't, and everything that's happened to you since that night has been my fault, my responsibility." He pounded his fist on his chest. "Mine."

"No, it wasn't then, and it isn't now. You couldn't have known. The serial rapist started with someone, and it happened to be me." She placed her hands on his arms, her touch gentle. There was no fear in her, no anger, just compassion for a man who was tortured by a burden that wasn't his to carry. The effects of the panic attack had worn off in her efforts to console Chase, and she was in control of herself again. "Look at me."

"No." He avoided making eye contact with her, but she put a hand beneath his chin and turned his face toward her.

"Chase, honey, please, *look* at me." Her voice dropped, emotion hung heavily in the air between them. "And *listen* to me."

After a few seconds he haltingly raised his eyes, damp with moisture, to hers. His breathing was harsh, his face was flushed, and he trembled.

"I'm listening."

"I forgive you, Chase. I forgave you a long time ago. When I tried to forgive you, you wouldn't let me and that's what drove us apart."

"Emily." He gripped her arms painfully, but she could take it.

"It was never your fault to begin with." Emotion tangled in her throat. "Never. I was angry at you at first. Really, *really* angry, but I came to understand it wasn't your fault or your responsibility. The blame lies in a man who is a predator."

Unable to handle the emotions churning in him, he clasped her against him, needing her strength, the amazing amount of strength she had to hold him upright. Tears leaked out of his eyes and the pressure of holding onto this responsibility for three years burst out of him in a powerful surge, leaving him breathless. He hadn't known he'd needed to hear her say those words.

His knees buckled and more of his weight went onto Emily, but she held on to him, she held him up and she used her strength to support him for a moment. Though she trembled, he could feel the strength in her muscles, and she stood firm. When his knees and legs were able to bear the burden of his weight again he pulled back from her.

Her face was a mess, and so was his. Hers had tears and red blotchy spots, and he was certain his face looked about the same. Pulling himself up to his full height, he cupped his hands around her face. "I'm sorry. I shouldn't have—"

"It's okay. I can take it. I'm stronger than I ever used to be, and for that I'm grateful. Very grateful." She smiled at him—it was soft and sad and bittersweet, but he could see the forgiveness in her eyes and knew it to be the truth.

"I am, too." He eased her closer. "I know I'm not supposed to touch you, but I have to do this." He pressed a very soft, very chaste, very heartfelt kiss to her forehead. For a moment neither of them moved, each caught in the power of that purity, that moment of grace between them.

When Chase pulled back, Emily wrapped her hands around his wrists and fresh tears fell from her eyes. "I am sorry. For everything." She took a breath. "This wasn't how our lives were supposed to have turned out. We were going to get married, have babies and live happily ever after, weren't we?"

"That was the plan." She moved away from him, needing a little space, a place to take a deep breath. "So what are you going to do now?"

"Go back to work on Monday, finish my assignment, maybe go on to another one after that." She shrugged. "I still haven't decided about where I want to put down roots again."

"This is your home, as you said, and you have as much of a right to settle here as anyone." He stepped forward. "Don't let that bastard run you away from your home again, Emily."

"I won't. I'm not." She cast a look over her shoulder at him. "Now I'm not sure working with you long term is a good idea, either."

"I see." He cleared his throat and took a step closer. "When we made love last night, it was beautiful."

"It was, and I thank you for that. For helping me get through that first time." She gave a small laugh. "Kinda felt like I was a virgin again."

"In some ways you were. You're a new you."

"True."

He clasped her hand and his fingers intertwined with hers. "Do you think...? Could you...?" He sighed. "I don't even know how to ask you this."

"What? It's usually better if you just ask things straight out."

"Emily Hoover, will you go out with me on a real date? Start over? Let me get to know the new you, get to know the new me?"

"I'm gonna have to think about that one." There was so much potential for pain.

"Really?" He pulled back, anger surfacing in his face. "I'm good enough to have sex with but you won't let me take you out?"

"That's not it. Not it at all."

"Then you'll have to explain it to me because I don't understand where you're coming from."

"I'm just trying to keep my life simple right now. Going out with you would complicate things. I know the other night I said I would go out with you, but now I'm not certain it's a good idea. For either of us."

"That's not a valid excuse." He stepped forward and cupped her face with his hand.

"I know, but I'm trying to come up with something." A sparkle returned to her eyes. Maybe there was hope for them after all. The power of the panic attack had been overwhelming and took time to recover from. Each time it would get better, but it would take time and patience.

"Then you'll go out with me? Let me try to make things up to you?"

"You can't make things up to me, because it's not your fault. Again. It's not your fault." She released his hand. "I don't want to go out with you if you can't accept that."

"It's hard." For both of them. They each had their own demons to slay, but maybe together they could do it.

"I know. It's very hard. I worked for a lot of months before I was even able to start to understand that." She blew out a breath. "I'm a whole person again. It's taken three years, but I'm whole. I'm not the woman I used to be. I'm different. I'm new. But I'm here. I want the same thing for you, too, Chase. But *you* have to want it."

"If you help me, I think I can do it. I can at least try."

"You thought you were my superhero, Chase, and you're not. You're just not."

"Well, thanks for *that* vote of confidence."

"Seriously. You're just a man, I'm just a woman, and that's all there is that needs to be there between us. You don't have to rescue me, and I don't have to be your salvation." She cupped his cheek and brought his face up to look at her. "We need to be who we are. Who we are *now*, not who other people *think* we are. And we can't be who we were back then."

"The question now is do you still love me? Can you love me again after all this?"

"We can't recapture what we used to have. We're different people now. You know that." As painful as that was, it had to be said out loud between them.

"Yes, but it doesn't answer my question." He faced her, cupped his hands around her face and drew her closer to him. "Look at me now and tell me you don't want me, don't need me, don't love me." It was a challenge for sure, but he needed it.

"I do love you, Chase." Tears rolled from her eyes down onto those beautiful cheeks, and he wiped them away with his thumbs. "I loved you then, and I love you now." She looked down then back up at him. "Thinking of you helped me get through the rough times. Thinking of the good times we had before it all came crashing down. In that way you were my strength."

"I should have been there for you." He gritted his teeth against the pain his actions had caused her.

"You couldn't. I was in survival mode. I couldn't take care of you and myself, so I took care of myself, and maybe I'm better for it."

"What do you mean?"

"I mean I needed more space than I knew at the time and if I'd been with you, maybe I wouldn't have found the strength to be who I am now, might not have found the courage to stand on my own, would have depended on you too much."

"We'll never know, will we?"

"No. And it's okay that we don't."

"We can't pick up where we left off, I know that." He took a deep breath. "I'm seeing it. I'm okay with it." He didn't want her to leave again at the end of her assignment. "Will you stay awhile and let's see if we can really find our way back to each other again? I know you're only a few weeks into your assignment, but I don't want you to take off and go somewhere else when it's over. I don't know what the future holds, Em, but I want you in mine." He cleared his throat against the emotion trying to choke him. "If you'll have me. I want to be the man you need. Now."

With a gasp she threw herself at him. Trembling, they clung to each other as another layer of the past fell away from them. "Me, too. Me, too. But I think we should do some couples therapy at the center."

"Is that necessary, do you think?" He didn't know.

"I do. For you, for us together."

"Then we will."

"Thank you, Chase. It'll be good, you'll see."

"I do have one question." Chase said.

She snorted out a laugh. "Seriously? Just one?"

"Do you still have the ring I gave you?" He rubbed the ring finger on her right hand. "The last time I saw it was the night you were...you were attacked." Demons from that night tried to surface, and he let out a long breath. Somehow now they had less power than they'd used to, and he could push them aside for the moment. They might never go away and might try to take a bite out of him at times, but he had the strength now to vanquish them.

She rubbed her lips together as emotion overwhelmed her. "I have it. I didn't... I couldn't...get rid of it." Slowly, she pulled the chain she always wore around her neck and the pendant emerged from beneath her *gi*.

"Do you remember when I gave this to you?" He turned it over in his hand and examined the ring of promise he'd given her.

"I do. We were walking down by the river and it was the first time you said you loved me."

"May I?"

She nodded, and he reached behind her neck to open the clasp then slid the ring off the chain. "I couldn't wear it for a while so I put it on a chain, and then I didn't want to wear it, but I couldn't let it go."

He held out the silver ring with a single fire opal gemstone in the center. With his left hand, he took her right and slid the ring part way onto her finger. "When I gave you this ring, I gave you a promise."

"You promised your love, your faith, your fidelity

and your honor." Tears that had been hiding beneath the surface surged over and trickled down her cheeks.

He huffed out a self-deprecating laugh. "I didn't do a very good job of keeping those promises." The trembling inside him bubbled up, but merged into a well of bounty and promise and hope for the future. It was still an unknown, the future, but with her by his side it no longer frightened him as much as it had.

He remembered the words from Lao Tzu that *sensei* Rose had spoken to him a few days ago, and though he hadn't understood them at the time they now began to make more sense. *Whoever can see through all fear will always be safe.* Now he could see the proof in Emily. She hadn't yet conquered all of her fear, but she had tackled the most dangerous of them all alone, and won.

"Circumstances weren't exactly conducive for either of us to keep any promises we made back then." She took in a shaking breath. The look in her eyes was soft and full of hope where just moments ago there had been none. Though he'd been partly responsible for it, he had to accept it was in the past and he couldn't change it, but he could change every day in the future by being present in it with her.

"I would like to make you a new promise, right now." The feelings in his heart swelled and his chest grew tight as the words emerged from someplace deep in his soul. There was no stopping them, and he'd never been more vulnerable than at this very moment.

"Chase, let's not make promises neither of us is prepared to make or keep. One thing I've had to learn is to live in the moment. Let's do that now."

"I'm prepared, and I will keep this promise." He cleared his throat and looked deeply into her eyes. "I promise to love you and respect you, to be your friend and your lover as long as you will have me in your life." He slid the ring the rest of the way onto her finger, then brought it up to his lips and kissed it.

"Chase Montgomery, you were the love of my life then and one I could never forget, no matter what happened to me or what happened to tear us apart." Tears lingered on the tips of her lashes, and she blinked to clear them away. "You hurt me more than anyone ever has, and you have the power to hurt me again."

Speechless, he opened his mouth to say something, but no words came out. Was she going to deny him now? Would she walk away from him again the way she had before? Anxiety stirred in his gut. *Please. Don't walk away from me again.*

"I can live my life alone, be without you, but I don't want to anymore." She placed her right hand on his chest and looked at the ring she hadn't worn in three years, then looked up at him. "I want you in my life, in my bed and in my heart."

"I don't know what the future will bring, but I want to be there for you, and you to be there for me." The anxiety lifted at her words, and he knew there would never be another moment like this one for them. Living in the moment. He had to learn to do that. With her new skills and her teacher's heart, maybe she could help him learn how.

She rose up on her toes and pressed her lips to his in a kiss of honor sealing their promise to each other. They didn't need a ceremony. They didn't need witnesses or a church for the vow they just made to be sacred. "I love you, Chase Montgomery, and I need you in my life."

"Emily." The joy that bubbled up in him was out of

control. "I don't know what to say, how you can say that, but I'm so glad you did." He shook his head in disbelief. "I don't know where we're going from here, and I don't care. As long as you're with me I know we'll be okay." This was living in the moment, and now he knew what it was.

Unable to contain himself any longer, he kissed her deep and hard, wanting to impress himself on her and imprint her on him, wanting to fill his mind and his heart with all of her.

He wrapped his arms around her, and she clung to him. "I know we'll be all right."

* * * * *

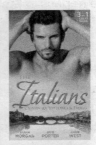

MILLS & BOON®

MEDICAL ROMANCE

THE ULTIMATE IN ROMANTIC MEDICAL DRAMA

A sneak peek at next month's titles...

In stores from 6th November 2015:

- **A Touch of Christmas Magic** – Scarlet Wilson *and* **Her Christmas Baby Bump** – Robin Gianna

- **Winter Wedding in Vegas** – Janice Lynn *and* **One Night Before Christmas** – Susan Carlisle

- **A December to Remember** – Sue MacKay

- **A Father This Christmas?** – Louisa Heaton

Available at WHSmith, Tesco, Asda, Eason, Amazon and Apple

Just can't wait?
Buy our books online a month before they hit the shops!
visit www.millsandboon.co.uk

These books are also available in eBook format!

1015/03